10/21

W9-BYV-046

CUL-DE-SAC

CUL-DE-SAC

A NOVEL

JOY FIELDING

THORNDIKE PRESS
A part of Gale, a Cengage Company

LIBRARY OF CONGRESS CIP DATA ON FILE.
CATALOGUING IN PUBLICATION FOR THIS BOOK
IS AVAILABLE FROM THE LIBRARY OF CONGRESS.

ISBN-13: 978-1-4328-9165-7 (hardcover alk. paper)

Published in 2021 by arrangement with Ballantine Books, an imprint of Random House, a division of Penguin Random House LLC.

Printed in Mexico
Print Number: 01   Print Year: 2022

For Hayden and Skylar

PROLOGUE

It's normally such a quiet street. Small, unassuming, solidly middle class. Not the sort of place one usually associates with the shocking events of that hot July night. Ask any of the residents and they will agree that none of their neighbors seemed capable of committing such a cold-blooded, heinous act.

How could this happen? they will ask when they gather together the next morning, shivering despite the intense heat, shaking their heads in collective wonder and dismay. *I'm stunned. I had no idea. I thought it was a car backfiring. Or maybe some leftover firecrackers.*

The street is what they call a cul-de-sac. From the French, the literal translation of which is "bottom of a sack," itself derived from the Latin *culus,* meaning "bottom." It was originally an anatomical term meaning "a vessel or tube with only one opening," but here in Palm Beach Gardens, Florida, as in the rest of North America, it has come to mean a short, dead-end street with a circle for turning around at the end.

Picture a horseshoe. Now picture five houses, virtual carbon copies of one another — modest, two-story, in delicate shades of pink, yellow, and peach, each with a double-car garage — placed at strategic intervals along that horseshoe, one at its rounded tip, two to each side. A variety of palm trees fill in the spaces between the houses, and the street has no sidewalks, only a raised curb separating the paved road from the small front lawns. The lawns, in turn, are dissected by short, flower-lined walkways ending with two steps before each front door.

The street is officially, and for no discernable reason, named Carlyle Terrace, and is situated just off Hood Road, a not overly busy thoroughfare that runs east and west between the Florida Turnpike and Military Trail, about a ten-minute drive to the ocean, and a stone's throw from any number of private, gated, golfing communities that populate the area.

On the surface, the people who live on this street seem average, even boring: a recently separated single mother and her two children; a doctor and his dentist wife

8

with their two sons; another married couple and their three offspring; a widowed grandmother; a young couple married barely a year. They have the usual array of problems — money concerns, difficult teenagers, petty jealousies, the everyday conflicts of married life. No one would claim it's all been candlelight and soft music. There has been the occasional raised voice, an argument spilling out of an open window, an unexpected altercation, even the odd slamming door.

Rumors abound — this one might be having an affair, that one might have a drinking problem, that one thinks she's too good for the rest of us. Neighbors talk, after all.

Especially when you give them something to talk about.

Who knows what evil lurks in the hearts of men? Sean Grant, one of the residents of Carlyle Terrace, is fond of quoting, referencing an ancient radio show that his parents used to listen to when they were children. *The Shadow knows,* he'll answer in the next breath, finishing the quote with an ominous lowering of his voice.

There are lots of shadows on this tree-filled cul-de-sac, this horseshoe-shaped dead end that leads exactly nowhere. And shadows make excellent places for secrets

9

— to hide, to grow, to flourish. Until some grow too big, too powerful to contain, and they explode, like a deadly grenade tossed from a careless hand, forever shattering the quiet façade so meticulously presented to the outside world, spraying bone and blood and illusions as far as the eye can see, beyond where the mind can grasp.

So indeed, one might be forgiven for initially assuming the shots that rang out in the middle of that hot July night came from leftover Independence Day firecrackers or a car backfiring somewhere along the main road, and not from a gun held mere inches from its target's head.

I can't believe it. How could this happen? the neighbors will mutter repeatedly. *This is normally such a peaceful neighborhood. Such a quiet street.*

CHAPTER ONE

It's early May, a couple of months before the fatal events of that sultry summer night, and the clock radio in Maggie McKay's bedroom wakes her up at six A.M., as it has every weekday morning since the school year began. She reaches across the empty half of the king-size bed to the nightstand and silences the cloying strains of "Oh, what a beautiful morning" with a decisive slap of her hand before the refrain can repeat.

Probably she should move the radio to the nightstand on *her* side of the bed so she won't have to stretch so far. At the very least, she should reprogram the alarm to play another tune. She's come to hate that stupid song. She doesn't need reminding that Florida is the land of beautiful mornings. She hates it anyway.

But she doesn't move the radio and she doesn't reprogram the tune. And she probably won't. Because there have been enough

11

changes in her life lately. Too many.

The music was Craig's idea. A gentler way to wake them up each morning than the shrill beeping jolting them into consciousness. Her nerves were frayed enough as it was, he reminded her unnecessarily. What she needed, he said, was less stress. What *he* needed, he *didn't* say — maybe wasn't even aware of at the time — was less Maggie.

Not that she blamed him for their marriage falling apart, at least not entirely. The move to Palm Beach Gardens had been her idea. A new beginning, she'd told him when she first championed the idea of uprooting their family, abandoning their home, leaving their friends and their careers behind in Los Angeles, and moving across the country. It would be a fresh start. A new beginning. Better for everyone.

Virtually the same words Craig used when he'd packed up his personal belongings and moved out three months ago. "I'm sorry, Maggie," he added, managing to look as if he meant it. "I just can't do it anymore."

"Fuck you," she mutters now, pretty much the first words out of her mouth every morning since he left. "Fucking coward." She rolls back to her side of the bed, the sheets cool beneath the flimsy cotton of her pajamas, and opens the top drawer of the mirrored nightstand beside the pillow. Her hand feels for the cold, smooth surface of the compact Glock 19, secreted beneath a chiffon swirl of multicolored scarves. The 9mm handgun is by far the most popular handgun in the United States, due to its size and reliability. Or so said the salesman who sold it to her the same afternoon that Craig moved out.

Craig had been adamant about not having a gun in the house, despite everything that had happened. Despite, God forbid, every-thing that *could* happen, and probably *would* happen the minute they became too com-placent, she'd argued to no avail. *If you'd really wanted to reduce my stress level,* she thinks as she lifts the relatively lightweight gun into her hands, *this little guy would have done a much better job of relaxing me than that stupid song from an old Broadway musi-cal.*

But it's a classic, she can hear him say.

"Fuck you," she says in return, refusing to be charmed and returning the gun to the drawer. She swivels out of bed, her bare feet padding across the mock-hardwood floor of the narrow hallway toward the bedrooms of her two children. "Erin," she calls out, knocking on her daughter's door before opening it, hearing the teenager moan

13

beneath her mountain of covers. "Time to get up, sweetie."

"Go away," comes the muffled response.

Maggie backs into the hall, understanding there's no point arguing. Erin will stay in bed until she can no longer tolerate the sound of her mother's exhortations and only then will she deign to get up and dressed. She will spend the next twenty to thirty minutes in the bathroom, fixing her hair and makeup. She will refuse to have anything for breakfast. She will decline to engage in anything resembling a conversation with either her mother or younger brother. She will check her phone, toss her hair, and roll her eyes more times than Maggie can count. And after finally climbing into the black SUV beside her mother, she will remember that she has forgotten something of vital importance — occasionally the homework she hasn't completed, usually the cellphone she left in the powder room while doing a final check of her appearance — thereby delaying them further. She may or may not remember to reset the house alarm, in which case Maggie will have to get out of the car to do it herself. Maggie will then chauffeur the kids to their respective schools, dropping Leo off first, then Erin, who will exit the car without a backward glance just as the bell is sounding.

"This could all be avoided, you know," she hears Erin say. *"All you have to do is —"*

"You're not getting your own car."

"Why not? Dad could probably get me a good deal. . . ."

"You're not getting your own car."

"What's the point of having my license if you won't let me drive? Besides, if I have my own car, you won't have to drive us back and forth to school every day. You could get a job, get a life. . . ."

"I have a life."

"You had *a life. You threw it away."*

"Okay, that's enough."

"I think you enjoy playing martyr. . . ."

"I said, enough!"

And enough of that, Maggie decides, banishing the unpleasant thoughts as she enters her son's room. She touches him gently on the shoulder. "Leo, honey. Time to wake up."

The shy eight-year-old flips onto his back and opens the deep blue eyes he inherited from his father. "What day is it?"

"It's Wednesday. Why?"

"So we're having dinner with Dad?"

"That's right."

"And he'll pick us up after school?"

Maggie nods. "If he's not there when you

15

get out, you call me immediately."

Leo tosses off his Star Wars blanket without further prompting and climbs out of bed, his favorite stuffed Super Mario toy in hand, heading for the bathroom he shares with his sister, experience having taught him that he'd better get in there while he has the chance.

Maggie returns to her bedroom. She takes a quick shower in the small en suite bathroom, then throws on a T-shirt and a pair of shorts before fluffing out her chin-length, mousy brown hair, hair that used to be lush and shoulder-length. *Used to be,* she thinks, mindful of all the things she once was: employed, confident, married. "Don't forget pretty," she says out loud, staring at the defeated-looking stranger in the full-length mirror on the inside of her closet door. "Who are you?" she whispers. "What have you done with Maggie McKay?"

"Erin!" she calls as she heads down the stairs, eyes on the alert for anything that looks even vaguely out of place. "Time to get up." She does a quick check of the downstairs rooms — the combined living-dining room to one side of the stairs, the kitchen, powder room, and den to the other — before turning off the burglar alarm to the right of the front door.

16

She knows she's being silly — Craig would use the word "paranoid," *had,* in fact, used it on more than one occasion — that there's no need to check every room in the house, as she's done every morning since they moved in eighteen months ago, that no one could circumvent the state-of-the-art alarm system she insisted they install despite its prohibitive cost, and that even if someone did, surely she would hear his footsteps on the stairs, stairs she's deliberately left uncarpeted for that very reason.

She opens the front door, her eyes doing a quick pan of the small cul-de-sac as she bends down to retrieve the morning paper. Hers is the house at the street's rounded tip, a location that gives her a clear view of the two houses on both sides. The yellow school bus is already parked in front of the house to her immediate right, waiting to transport Tyler and Ben Wilson to their tony private school in North Palm Beach. Maggie acknowledges the bus driver's nod with an uneasy wave of her fingers and a sigh of relief. It's the same man who's been picking them up for the last four months. No reason to panic, as she did after the last driver retired and this much younger one appeared. She'd even called The Benjamin School for confirmation they'd hired someone new, then questioned his references.

"I'm sorry. Who are *you*?" the school receptionist asked.

"You're being paranoid," Craig told her.

"Okay, so I'm paranoid," Maggie mutters to herself now, retreating into the house. Better paranoid than dead.

She would have loved to send her children to a private school like the Wilsons, but the price tag was way too high. The Wilsons are high-earning professionals — he, a well-regarded oncologist and she, a dentist — but Maggie no longer has a job, and even though Craig makes good money selling luxury cars, it isn't nearly enough to cover the cost of two tuitions, especially now that he has two residences to maintain. Whatever savings they once had went toward the move.

"There's absolutely nothing the matter with public schools," she reminds herself, needing the confirmation of hearing her words out loud. She used to teach in one after all.

Used to, she thinks, setting the kitchen table, a white plastic oval that occupies the center of the small space. She boils an egg for Leo and puts two pieces of raisin bread in the toaster, glancing at the day's depressing headlines before turning to the puzzle

18

page, the only reason she buys the paper anymore. "Erin!" she yells, and then again, "Erin! You better be up and out of bed."

"I'm up!" Erin yells back. "Chill, for God's sake!" Upstairs, the bathroom door slams shut.

I would if you'd let me, Maggie thinks, knowing she's being unfair. It's not the teenager's fault their lives have been turned upside down. "This is on me," she says.

"What's on you?" Leo says, entering the kitchen.

Maggie jumps at the sound of her son's voice. How did she not hear him come down? "Where are your shoes?"

Leo glances toward his bare feet. "Oh," he says, indicating the backpack on the floor beside him. "I think I packed them."

Maggie smiles. *My little space cadet,* she thinks, wondering if this is the reason he and Ben Wilson have never become more than casual acquaintances. She'd been so excited when she'd learned their new next-door neighbors had a son the same age as Leo, and hoped they'd soon become fast friends, but sadly, this has not proven to be the case. She suspects this has more to do with Dani Wilson than her son, the prevailing wisdom being that Dani Wilson considers herself too good for her surroundings,

19

that she would prefer to live in a more upscale development, one with a prestigious address more fitting a family headed by two doctors. Perhaps she also resents the professional deference regularly showered on her husband by the residents of Carlyle Terrace, a deference that, as a mere dentist, she rarely gets to experience.

Or maybe she's just a bitch.

"Is it a spider?" Leo asks.

"Is what a spider?"

"What's on you," he replies, turning the question he asked earlier into a statement, his eyes growing fearful.

I put that fear there, Maggie thinks. "Oh," she says. "No. There's no spider."

"Then what?"

"Just some crumbs, I guess," she improvises.

This seems to satisfy him. He sits down in one of the four white plastic chairs, removes his sneakers from his backpack, and pushes his feet into them, struggling with the laces.

"Here. Let me help you." Maggie is already kneeling in front of him, hands outstretched.

"No, it's okay. Dad says I need to start doing things by myself."

"Your father . . ." Maggie bites her tongue to keep from saying something she'll regret.

She has too many regrets as it is. She's running out of room. She hears the toaster pop out the two pieces of bread. "Do you want to butter your toast by yourself?" she asks. Surely he can't hurt himself with a butter knife.

"No," he says. "You can butter them."

"Okay." She fights the urge to thank him. "Erin!" she calls as Leo is taking his final few bites. "It's after seven. School starts in less than half an hour. We're going to be late." Why schools have to start so damn early is something she's never been able to figure out.

"I'm in the bathroom."

"I know you're in the bathroom. It's time to get *out* of the bathroom." She walks toward the stairs.

"God, could you be any more annoying?" Erin mutters, flinging open the bathroom door as Maggie reaches the upstairs landing, a blur of waist-length, light brown hair and long bare legs brushing past her down the hall.

"Probably," Maggie says as she enters her bedroom and opens the top drawer of the nightstand beside the bed. She reaches inside and extricates the Glock 19, turning it over in the palm of her hand and admiring it before dropping it inside her large canvas bag.

One of the reasons Maggie chose Florida is that it's considered "accommodating" regarding guns, the state policy being one of "shall issue" for a concealed carry license. This means it's legal to carry a concealed weapon and relatively easy to get a license to do so. Which Maggie did, filling out the necessary forms and submitting them, along with her fingerprints and a recent photograph, to Tallahassee for a background check, then waiting five days to receive her permit.

She completed the three-hour-long obligatory course in firearms training within a week of buying the gun. And she's been carrying it with her ever since.

Just in case, one day, it becomes necessary to use it.

CHAPTER TWO

Dani Wilson looks out her kitchen window to see the school bus idling on the street. "Boys," she calls toward the den at the back of the house. "The bus is here. Tyler! Ben! Let's go. Y'all know Manuel doesn't like to be kept waitin'." She counts silently to ten, taking several deep breaths to still her growing irritation at the lack of response, trying not to take it personally.

After all, it's nothing new. She deals with this every day at work, her patients rarely replying to her polite queries — about their day, their health, their lives — with more than one-word answers. "Fine," they'll grunt, or "Good." True, their mouths are open wide and often stuffed with cotton, but would it really be so hard to add, "And you?"

The hard truth is that no one gives a damn whether Dani Wilson is happy or not. No one is interested in the problems of an erstwhile Southern belle with a handsome doctor husband, a thriving practice, and a six-figure income. She is all too aware that the people with whom she spends the bulk of her time would rather be somewhere — *anywhere* — in the world other than with her.

Is it any wonder that the suicide rate among dentists is higher than in any other profession?

She looks toward the kitchen's center island with its four high-top chairs lined against one side. "How 'bout you guys? How you doin'?" she asks the two betta fish, one red, one blue, each as pretty as a peach, swimming aimlessly in separate bowls on the island's granite countertop. Two bowls are necessary because of a fierce territorial instinct that sees them fight to the death if put with other fish. Even surrounded by glass, they must be kept a suitable distance apart.

"I thought we agreed, no pets," Nick said when Dani brought them home one day after work, an impulse purchase she still can't explain.

"Well, they were so pretty and I just thought . . ."

"You thought what?"

"Well, it's not like a dog or a cat. . . ."

24

"That's not the point."

"I thought it'd be good for the boys," she said.

"Trust me," Nick said. *"They'll lose interest in a week."*

Of course, he was right. At least as far as their younger son, Ben, was concerned. After loudly insisting that the blue betta was his, he'd proceeded to largely ignore him. "He's boring," he proclaimed. Tyler, on the other hand, has spent hours with his forehead pressed against the smaller red betta's bowl, talking to it to the point that the fish, whom he named Neptune, now actually allows the boy to put his hand inside the bowl and stroke him.

Dani finds this amazing; Nick is unimpressed. "I'm worried about that kid," he'd say, with a shake of his head.

"He's sensitive."

Another headshake. "Who bonds with a fish?"

Dani sighs and heads for the back room. "Boys! Let's get goin'. The bus is fixin' to leave without you."

"No, it's not," her husband contradicts, his back to her. He is standing in front of the glass-fronted cabinet that houses his impressive firearm collection, ten-year-old Tyler to his left, eight-year-old Ben to his right. "He's early. He can wait a few minutes. And it's 'let's get go*ing*,' " he adds, stressing the final *g*. "Not 'goin'.' The *g* is not silent." He glances at his sons. "Proper pronunciation is important," he tells them. "People judge you by the way you speak. Remember that."

Dani nods. She knows he's right. He's right about most things. But she was born and raised in Alabama, and even though she's lived in Florida since they got married almost fifteen years ago, a Southern cadence isn't the easiest thing to lose.

To which Nick would undoubtedly counter that, last he heard, Florida was still considered part of the South, and that her habit of peppering her sentences with corny aphorisms makes her sound like a hillbilly, and dropping her *g*'s as well as using contractions like "y'all" has nothing to do with geography and everything to do with being grammatically lazy.

And he'd be right. Because he's always right. Although she remembers a time when he found such speech idiosyncrasies endearing. *Funny how the very things that once charmed us become the things that irritate us the most,* she thinks, remembering that she used to find his self-confidence — some might call it arrogance — appealing. Her

26

father, a successful internist, had been casually dismissive of her stay-at-home mother in much the same way. Wasn't that at least part of the reason she'd been so determined to have a career?

Of course, it hadn't hurt that both men are tall and handsome, saved from being a cliché by being fair-haired instead of dark. Dani has always assumed arrogance went with the territory. And Nick is pretty high on the medical hierarchy, being a well-respected, even revered, oncologist. There's no question that his patients adore him. His website overflows with tributes praising his diagnostic genius and warm bedside manner.

Of course, she's a doctor, too, she reminds herself. Although her father would argue that a dentist isn't *really* a doctor, not in the strict sense of the word.

And she doesn't need reminding that no one likes going to the dentist, regardless of competence.

Maybe if she were young and beautiful, instead of forty, on the short side, and still carrying around the ten extra pounds in baby weight she hasn't been able to shed since Ben's birth, it would be a different story.

"Maybe if you watched what you ate and

stuck to an exercise regime," Nick has said. *"I'm tryin'."*

"*Try*ing," he corrected.

He's right, of course. He always is. She can't keep blaming her extra weight on her younger son. Ben is eight years old, for God's sake. It's time to take responsibility and get proactive, cut back on those calories, get a membership at the gym, maybe even hire a personal trainer.

"What're y'all doin'?" she asks now, exhausted by the mere thought of a trainer.

"Dad's showing us his new rifle," Ben answers, swiveling around to face her, pointing a weapon almost as big as he is in the general direction of her heart. "And it's 'do*ing,*' not 'doin'.' "

Dani gasps and takes a step back, not sure if her reaction is due to the rifle aimed at her chest or her son's admonishment.

"Whoa there, partner," Nick says, quickly removing the weapon from his son's hands. "What have I told you about never pointing a gun at anyone?"

"It's not loaded," Ben protests.

"Doesn't matter." His father returns the rifle to its proper place, then locks the cabinet door. "Now, listen to your mother. Get moving."

The boys respond immediately, Tyler offering up a shy smile as he hurries by.

"You didn't tell me you bought a new gun," Dani says when her sons are out of earshot.

"Didn't think you were interested."

For an instant, she's tempted to chide her husband on his frequent habit of leaving out nouns, then decides she's being petty. Turnabout might be fair play, but she's learned it rarely works in her favor.

" 'Course I'm interested. How many does that make now?" Her eyes do a silent count of the many guns and rifles on display.

"Eighteen."

"Well, bless my heart." Dani has never shared her husband's passion for guns, and never accompanies him when he goes to the nearby shooting range for target practice.

"Thinking of taking the boys with me to the range one of these weekends," he says, as if reading her mind.

"What?" The unnerving image of eight-year-old Ben pointing the weapon at her chest flashes before her eyes.

"It's time they learned how to shoot." He looks around the room. "Where'd you put my iPad?"

"What?" she says again.

"Left it here last night."

"I haven't touched it."

"You're sure?"

" 'Course I'm sure. You probably left it in the bathroom."

"I didn't leave it in the goddamn bathroom."

Dani tenses at the unexpected irritation in his voice and is grateful for the sudden shouts — "Stop it!" "Leave them alone!" "Mom!" — coming from the kitchen. She runs toward the sound and sees her boys wrestling with the fishbowls, the two bettas being tossed carelessly from side to side as water sloshes from the tops of the bowls to the island countertop. "My goodness! What's goin' on here?"

"Ben keeps putting the bowls too close together," Tyler says, his voice quivering. "Neptune's getting all upset."

"It's fun," Ben says, laughing. "You should see them. They get all puffed up, start banging at the glass."

"They'll hurt themselves," Tyler argues.

"So what? They're just fish."

"Okay, that's enough." Dani returns the bowls to the counter, leaving plenty of space between them. "Time to go. Manuel's waitin'."

"Wait*ing*," her husband corrects, entering the room, iPad in hand. "You heard your mother. Go on. Off with you."

30

"Kisses?" Dani asks as they race for the front door. Only Tyler returns, offering up the side of his head to be kissed. Her lips brush against a lock of golden-brown hair. "Have a good day," she calls as the front door opens and shuts.

"So, what was all the yelling about?" Nick asks.

"Ben put the bowls too close together again."

Nick laughs.

"It's not funny. It upsets Tyler."

"Kid's too soft. He could use some toughening up."

Dani decides not to argue. "I see you found your iPad."

He nods.

"Where'd you find it?"

"Bathroom."

"So, I was right."

"I guess. Is that really so important to you?"

"I just don't like bein' accused. . . ."

"Nobody accused you of anything. I just asked if you'd seen it."

"No, you asked where I *put* it. There's a difference. And you shouldn't be correctin' — correct*ing* — my grammar in front of the kids."

Nick shakes his head. "Look. I don't have

the time or the energy to argue with you right now. I have a full day ahead of me and I didn't get a lot of sleep last night. . . ."

"Why didn't you sleep?"

Another shake of his head, causing several strands of the same golden-brown hair as Tyler's to fall across his eyes. "I don't know. Some stupid bird kept squawking. I was tempted to go outside and shoot the miserable thing. And . . ." He stops, pushing the hair back into place.

Don't ask, she thinks. "And?" she asks anyway.

"Well, I hesitate to say anything, because you seem to be in a mood. . . ."

"I'm not in a mood —"

"But you've got to do something about your snoring, babe," he interrupts. "I know you don't do it on purpose. . . ."

Dani sighs. They've been through this before. There's no point reminding him that he also snores, or that he could at least *try* the earplugs she bought him the last time he complained about her snoring.

"Anyway," he says, "let's drop it. I have a tough enough day ahead of me." A third shake of his head. "I have to tell a man his cancer has spread and we've run out of options."

"I'm so sorry." Dani feels immediately

guilty for giving him such a hard time. *At least your patients have the good grace to die,* she thinks, feeling even guiltier. When did she become so insensitive to the suffering of others? *What's the matter with me?*

"I'm sorry, too," Nick says, surrounding her with his arms, drawing her into a tight embrace. "I *did* imply you'd moved my iPad. You had every right to be pissed. And I had no business correcting your grammar in front of the boys," he adds without prompting. "That was wrong. I'll try not to do it again."

"Thank you," she whispers as he withdraws.

"I love you," he says.

"I love you, too."

He tweaks her nose. "But you really must do something about that snoring."

CHAPTER THREE

From his usual position at the living room window, Sean Grant watches the school bus pull away from the curb in front of the house next door, taking with it the privileged offspring of the eminent Doctors Wilson. He wonders, not for the first time, why two successful professionals would choose to live on this simple cul-de-sac when they could be living in one of the more upscale gated communities nearby. They had to have a combined yearly income of close to half a million dollars, if not more. Hell, as one of the top cancer specialists in the area, Nick Wilson probably earned that all by himself. Sean knows that if he were making that kind of money, he'd be living in Palm Beach proper, or maybe he'd buy a house at the Bear Club, Jack Nicklaus's exclusive golf and country club over on Donald Ross Road. He used to be a pretty good golfer. Of course, it's been a while since he golfed, golf being an expensive habit to maintain.

One he can no longer afford.

"Sean!" his wife calls, her high heels clicking against the beige ceramic tile that runs throughout the downstairs rooms. "Where are you?"

He reluctantly leaves the window, joining his wife in the small center hall at the foot of the stairs before she can ask again. He finds the layout of the house awkward — the combined living-dining room to the right of the stairs and virtually everything else to the left. Who designed these houses anyway? *Shouldn't the kitchen and dining rooms be closer together?* he thinks silently, although this sort of thing never bothered him before he became the family's chief cook and bottle washer.

All kinds of things bother him now, things that never used to annoy him, too many things to dwell on, not if he wants to start the day off on the right foot. One of those things is standing right in front of him, he realizes, trying to mask his irritation at his wife with a smile. She's dressed in a perfectly tailored suit that shows off her equally perfect figure, and grinning her big Cheshire-cat-that-swallowed-the-canary grin, her full lips emphasized by the bright coral lipstick she's taken to wearing since she returned to work. Her long dark hair is pulled into a neat bun — she refers to it as a chignon — at the nape of her neck. At thirty-nine, Olivia Grant looks even better than the twenty-three-year-old he married, back in the days when he was a successful marketing executive and she was a lowly account manager with a neighboring advertising firm he sometimes did business with. She considered it a job back then, not the career she calls it now, and she'd been only too happy to give it up after the birth of their twins, Zane and Quentin, now twelve, and then Katie, two years after that.

Sean didn't object to his wife choosing to be a stay-at-home mom. His career was thriving, and it was a source of great pride that he could support his growing family on his income alone. Over the years, he continued his steady climb up the corporate ladder, becoming one of five vice presidents of the mid-level firm that employed him and was confidently on track to becoming a full partner.

And then two years ago — ironically, just as they were considering a move to a larger house — he was handed his walking papers. Business was down, way down. The company could no longer afford the luxury of five vice presidents, something he'd suspected for months, but never thought would apply to him.

Once he got over the shock of losing his job — the idea that he was dispensable hurting even more than his abrupt dismissal — he relished the time off to relax and reassess what he wanted out of life. And what he wanted, he decided during those first few weeks, was more. More money, more power, more respect. He was certain that a man with his experience and credentials would have no trouble securing another job. Plus, he could afford to wait. His severance package was excellent and, combined with a small inheritance from his father, ensured that he wouldn't have to settle. He could hold out for the perfect position.

"We'll be fine," he assured Olivia.

"I'm not worried in the slightest," she said.

It took several months for his optimism to fade, a year for it to disappear altogether. It seemed that, even with an upturn in the economy, no business wanted to hire a man on the cusp of fifty, regardless of his experience or credentials. Not when they could employ someone half his age at half his salary. Sean reluctantly lowered his sights, tried for positions he'd initially refused to consider.

And was turned down for all of them.

"Too qualified," they said. Too old, they meant.

He grew increasingly depressed. He stopped wearing the neatly pressed shirts and silk ties he'd been known to wear even on weekends. He went days without shaving. He stopped exercising. He put on weight. What was the point in maintaining appearances when nobody gave a damn whether he appeared or not?

His wife — ever-supportive, relentlessly optimistic Olivia — urged him to see a therapist. When he argued that therapists were expensive, she offered to pay for his visits with the money she'd been saving to buy a new car, which, of course, only made him more depressed. He didn't want his wife sacrificing for him. It was a man's duty to support his family, to be the breadwinner, to "bring home the bacon," as his father used to say.

His father had been full of such sayings. "Bringing home the bacon" was one. "Never send a boy to do a man's job" was another.

Now it seemed that all employers *wanted* were boys.

Or women.

How else to explain the ease with which Olivia found a job? Eight months ago, his wife, who hadn't worked in over ten years, walked through their front door and proudly announced that, on a lark, she'd driven up to Jupiter to see her old boss, and he'd hired her on the spot. Why shouldn't she go back to work? she'd asked when he objected. Now that all three kids were in school, she was getting bored sitting at home, doing nothing but laundry and preparing meals. Besides, they'd almost eaten through both his inheritance and his severance, and his unemployment benefits would soon be discontinued. Simply put, they needed the money.

He couldn't argue with that.

But now he's the one sitting home all day, doing nothing but laundry and preparing meals, while she's out there, making money and having a grand old time. Dressing up. Wearing four-inch heels. Looking better than she has in years. Taking meetings. Batting those long eyelashes at her superiors. Hell, she was promoted to account supervisor after barely six months on the job. How does that happen without some serious flirting?

Not that Sean doesn't trust his wife. He does. Olivia has never been anything but loving, loyal, and supportive. "You'll find something else," she'd said when he told her he'd been let go. "You've got this one," she said whenever he went for an interview. "Remember what your father used to say — 'When one door closes, another one opens.' "

Except that when another door opened, she was the one who'd walked through.

She tries to hide it, but he knows he's become a thorn in her side. He can see the disappointment in her eyes. It makes it difficult to look at her.

"You smell so pretty," he tells her now, forcing himself to do just that. "Is that a new perfume?"

"Yes, and it's called So Pretty." She laughs. "Great nose," she says, kissing the tip of his. The high heels that have become part of her daily uniform add inches to her height, making her taller than he is. A daily reminder of how their situations have reversed. Why can't she wear flats like she used to?

Why can't anything be like it used to be?

"So, what's on tap for this morning?" She's stopped asking him if he has any interviews.

He shrugs, looks toward the back of the house, where his three children are getting their things ready for the day. In a few minutes, Olivia will drive them to school on her way to work. It will be his job to pick them up when school ends at two-thirty. How is he supposed to make plans when he has to be back by the middle of the afternoon?

Of course, old Mrs. Fisher, who lives catty-corner across the street, has offered to babysit, even to pick the kids up from school, should that be necessary, but the woman's eighty-four years old, for God's sake. He's not about to entrust the lives of his children to someone whose license probably should have been taken away years ago.

"I noticed we're running low on coffee and Cheerios," Olivia says.

Sean tenses. His wife never makes a direct request for him to go grocery shopping. She just "notices" they're running low on various items. Can she not just come out and say what she really means? "I'll pick some up this morning," he says.

"Oh, and Zane was requesting macaroni and cheese for supper. How does that strike you?"

Right between the eyes, Sean thinks, but doesn't say. "Sounds good."

"Great. I might be a little late getting home," she adds, almost as an afterthought. "We have this presentation in Fort Lauderdale this afternoon, and with the traffic . . . well, you know. So if I'm not home by six, just go ahead and start dinner without me."

"No problem."

"I'll call you when the meeting's over, so if you haven't heard from me by five-thirty . . ."

"I'll know to start without you."

"Okay. Thank you. Kids," she calls, "let's go!"

Immediately, their children are at the front door, laughing and wrestling with their backpacks. Sean struggles to find a trace of him in any of their faces, but finds only their mother. Dark-haired and hazel-eyed, all of them, while his eyes are the same sandy brown as his still-thick head of hair. *At least I have that going for me,* he thinks.

"Bye, sweetie," Olivia says now, kissing his cheek. "Wish me luck this afternoon."

"Good luck this afternoon," he replies dutifully.

"Love you," she says.

"Love you, too." He watches his family from his usual spot at the living room window as Olivia backs her Honda Accord out of the driveway and disappears down the main street.

In his mind's eye, he pictures a truck come flying out of nowhere to crash head on into the car, the old Honda collapsing like an accordion as his wife's head snaps

42

back, then forward, and the steering wheel disappears deep into her chest. He sees two uniformed police officers walking solemnly up the concrete path to his front door, mouths downturned, eyes downcast. "We're so sorry to inform you . . ."

God, what's the matter with me? he wonders, banishing the horrifying images. *I love my wife. Where are these thoughts coming from?*

Who knows what evil lurks in the hearts of men? his father whispers in his ear, another of the sayings he was so fond of.

Sean glances at his watch and is only vaguely alarmed to realize that almost an hour has passed. "Guess time really does fly when you're having fun," he says with a laugh, watching a silver Tesla turn onto the cul-de-sac and pull into old Mrs. Fisher's driveway. "Uh-oh," he says as both front doors lift into the air and a man and woman emerge simultaneously. The woman pulls at her short, tight skirt as the two march purposefully toward the front door. "Looks like trouble."

CHAPTER FOUR

Julia Fisher is finishing her second cup of coffee and trying to figure out an eight-letter word for "spend wastefully." It's the only word in today's so-called quick crossword puzzle that she hasn't been able to get, despite knowing the first letter is an *S* and the seventh letter an *E*. She's concentrating so hard that, at first, she doesn't realize that the knocking floating around the periphery of her conscious mind is intended for her. It is only when the knocking is joined by the persistent ringing of a bell that she understands someone is at her front door.

And who that someone is.

"Shit," she says, although she's been half expecting them. She takes a deep breath and slowly pushes herself out of her chair, taking a cursory glance up the stairs as she enters the tiny front hall. Arthritis-riddled fingers pat at the short, frosted blond curls she's been sporting since college, then stretch reluctantly toward the doorknob before falling back to her side. Maybe if she doesn't answer it, they'll go away.

No such luck.

"Mom!" a man's voice calls, accompanied by more knocking, more ringing.

Julia takes another deep breath and opens the door to Norman and his wife, Poppy. *Who names a child Poppy?* she thinks, staring into their anxious faces. "My goodness. What's all the fuss?"

"What do you mean, 'what's all the fuss'?" her son repeats. "Do you have any idea how long we've been standing out here?"

"It can't have been that long. . . ."

"Long enough. We thought you might have fallen and couldn't get up. Or something."

Julia recognizes the "or something" for the euphemism it is. What Norman means is *We thought you might be dead.* She stands back to let her son and his wife — his *fourth* wife, if anyone's keeping track anymore — enter. "I'm perfectly fine," she tells them. "And you don't have to worry about me falling. You bought me one of those necklace-alarm thingies I can push —"

"You have to wear it for it to actually work," Norman interrupts, glancing at her bare neck.

"Picky, picky," Julia says, hoping for a smile she doesn't get. Has her son always been so humorless?

"It's not funny," he says, as if to confirm her suspicion. His eyes follow his wife's high, round backside as she wiggles past Julia into the living room and plops down on the chintz sofa, a frown on her already turned-down mouth.

Julia lowers herself into one of two mismatched chairs opposite the sofa, waiting for her son to occupy the other. Instead he remains standing. How had she and Walter, her husband of more than half a century, managed to produce a son whose four marriages combined don't add up to half that? Not that she doesn't love her only child. She does. She just doesn't *like* him very much. "You're looking well," she tells him, as if to counteract such thoughts.

Besides, it's true. Norman and his young wife are indeed handsome specimens, both standing over six feet tall, and in wonderful shape, thanks to daily workouts and regular weekend golf games. She studies Norman's deeply tanned face, finding it hard to believe her son is fifty-one years old. It's even harder to believe *she* could have a son that age since, aside from the standard assortment of aches and pains, she doesn't feel much older than that herself.

Her glance shifts to Poppy — slim, blond, voluptuous, porcelain-skinned, undeniably beautiful Poppy, Norman's wife of almost three years, whom he met at the gym in the building that is home to the hedge fund company he helped found, and for whom he promptly discarded wife number three.

Julia sighs. Not that she was particularly saddened by the loss of wife number three, whose lovely face she can barely recall. The fact is that Norman has always liked his women as stupid as they are beautiful. *Unlined, uninformed, and unthreatening,* she thinks, and sighs again.

"What's the matter?" her son says now.

"Nothing's the matter."

"You sighed."

"I did?"

"Twice."

"Is your arthritis giving you problems?" Poppy asks, leaning forward on the sofa, her surgically enhanced breasts straining against the seams of her tight pink jersey.

"No more than usual." Julia holds up her two misshapen index fingers, the tips of which curve almost comically toward each other. "They look like parentheses," she says with a laugh. "Brackets," she explains before Poppy can ask. "To what do I owe the pleasure of this visit?"

"A couple of things," Norman says. He walks toward the window, stares out at the street. "Have you seen Mark?"

"Mark? No. Not since last week." Mark is Norman's twenty-year-old son, her only grandchild, courtesy of wife number two. She'd lasted almost a decade, the longest of any of Norman's wives, probably because she turned a blind eye to his constant philandering. But two years ago, she'd remarried and relocated to New York, and Mark had opted to stay in Florida and move in with his father, an unexpected development that hasn't exactly gone over big with the fourth Mrs. Fisher.

To be fair, Mark is quite the handful.

To hell with fairness, Julia decides. "Is something wrong?"

"We caught him smoking weed . . . marijuana," Norman explains.

"I know what weed is. I may be eighty-four, but I'm not senile." *Not to mention, I might have indulged a few times in my youth,* she thinks, but considers it wise not to say.

"And I'm pretty sure he's been taking money out of my purse," Poppy volunteers.

"You're *pretty sure?*" Julia repeats. "You're not positive?"

"I'm pretty positive," Poppy says, as if this

48

settles the matter. "I mean, there was about forty dollars missing from my wallet the other day, and he's the only one who could have taken it."

"Did you ask him about it?"

"I did. He denied it."

"Maybe he didn't take it."

"Anyway, we got into a whole big fight about it," Poppy says, brushing aside the question of Mark's possible innocence with a wave of her long, manicured fingernails, "and he called me the C-word. . . ."

"A cunt?" Julia asks with more relish than she'd intended.

"Mother, really . . ."

"How can you even say that word?" Poppy asks, squirming.

Julia shrugs. She's always rather liked the sound of it.

"Anyway, he stormed out of the house," Norman says. "We haven't seen him in two days."

"I mean, we're sure he's okay," Poppy says. "It's not like this is the first time he's pulled something like this."

"But it will be the last," Norman insists. "There are limits to what we'll tolerate. He dropped out of college; he can't keep a job for more than a couple of weeks. If he doesn't straighten up and fly right, we'll be forced to kick him out for good."

Julia is about to say something, but the fact that she has produced a son who says things like "straighten up and fly right" renders her temporarily speechless.

"Anyway, I know you two have a special relationship," Norman says, managing to make the word "special" sound vaguely distasteful. "So if he should happen to come by, I'd appreciate it if you'd call us immediately. And whatever you do, don't give him any money."

"Let him see what it's like out there without Norman paying all the bills," Poppy adds.

I'm sure you'll be able to tell him yourself in a few years, Julia thinks, and has to bite down on her tongue to keep from voicing it out loud. She looks toward her son. "What else? You said there were a couple of things. . . ."

"We've been through this before," Norman says. "It's this house."

"Oh, dear. Not again."

"Look," Norman says, speaking over her. "I understood your desire to hang on to the place after Dad died. I mean, all the experts agree that you shouldn't make any major changes for the first year after someone dies, but it's been almost two years now, and

50

you're not getting any younger. You shouldn't be going up and down all these stairs, you could fall and break a hip —"

"Actually," Julia interrupts, "they say your hip breaks first. . . ."

"What?"

"The hip breaks first," Julia repeats. "And that's why you fall. Not the other way around."

"Okay, fine. Whatever," Norman says dismissively. "The fact is that this house is getting harder and harder for you to look after. There are too many stairs, too many rooms to clean. Besides, it's dangerous, a woman your age, living alone. Someone could break in . . ."

"Nobody's going to break in."

". . . and here you'd be, all alone, at the mercy of some predator. . . ."

"Nonsense," Julia states firmly, seeking to put an end to the discussion. "Besides, I have a gun."

"What?! Since when do you have a gun?"

"It was your father's."

"Oh, for God's sake. That antique? Does it even work anymore?"

"Why wouldn't it?" In truth, she has no idea whether the old handgun works or not. "At any rate, I'm not selling this house, so . . ."

"The market is hot right now. We could get a good price. . . ."

"*We?*"

"You could move to an apartment, be surrounded by people your own age. . . ."

"I don't want to be surrounded by people my own age."

"I could invest the money for you. You could live very well. . . ."

"I already live very well."

"Will you at least agree to have a look at Manor Born?"

"Manor Born? *Manor Born?* You want to put me in a home?"

"It's not a home. It's a first-class assisted living community."

"You can call it whatever the hell you like. I'm not moving there."

"You're being unreasonable," Norman tells his mother.

"You're being an ass," Julia tells her son.

"He's just trying to look out for you," Poppy chimes in.

"How sweet." Julia pushes out of her chair and marches toward the front door with as much speed as she can muster. "Thanks for stopping by, darling. I know how busy you are." She opens the door just as the young couple who recently moved in next door are pulling their blue Hyundai out of their garage.

"Nice wheels!" the young man says, stopping in the driveway to admire the silver Tesla. "You just buy it?"

Julia laughs, flattered he could even think such a thing. "It's not mine," she says, as Norman and Poppy join her in the doorway.

"Nice wheels," the young man says again, this time to Norman.

Julia can't remember the man's name, but thinks it's one of those new, modern ones. He waves goodbye as he backs onto the street. His wife — Julia can't remember her name either, but thinks it's a surprisingly old-fashioned one — also waves.

"Will you at least consider what I've said?" Norman asks his mother.

"I will not," Julia says.

"He's just looking out for you," Poppy says, as she said earlier. She follows her husband to their car, stepping back as the doors lift into the air.

Like a giant insect about to take flight, Julia thinks. Way too intimidating. She much prefers the unfussy Chevrolet her husband bought the year before he was diagnosed with pancreatic cancer. She looks across the street to the home of Dr. Nick Wilson, grateful as she always is for the wonderful care he gave her husband in the months before his death. Can almost two years have passed since then? She swallows a deep breath of warm, humid air, then goes back inside the house, shutting the door before the Tesla is fully out of the driveway.

"They gone?" a voice asks from the top of the stairs.

"They are." Julia watches her grandson descend the steps, the long, skinny legs appearing first, followed by the long, skinny torso, then the long, thin face, framed by the long brown hair that falls to his bony shoulders in uncombed waves. "You're going to have to call them, you know."

"I know. I will. Thanks for not giving me away. And for defending my good name, even though . . ."

"You took the money?"

"I did," Mark admits, walking into the kitchen and grabbing a stale store-bought muffin from the counter. "I mean, she left her wallet just sitting there on the counter, like it was some kind of test."

"Which you failed."

"Or I passed, depending how you look at it."

Julia smiles. At least *someone* in her family has a sense of humor.

"Do you really have a gun?" he asks.

"An antique, apparently."

Her grandson's turn to smile. "Where is it?"

"I have no idea." Julia assumes it's in the garage, in one of the boxes full of Walter's belongings, but she keeps this to herself.

Mark pops a bite of the muffin into his mouth. "Nana . . ."

"Yes?"

"I've been thinking . . ."

Not too sure that's a good idea, Julia thinks, waiting for him to continue.

He surprises her by saying, "Maybe I could move in with you for a while. Then I wouldn't have to go back home and you wouldn't be alone. I'm even a pretty good cook."

"Really? When did you learn to cook?"

He shrugs. "None of Dad's wives, including my mother, were too great in the kitchen. I didn't really have much choice if I wanted to survive. Anyway, think about it. My moving in with you would solve everyone's problems."

Julia isn't sure that his moving in wouldn't create a whole bunch of new ones, but the fact is she adores her grandson, has from the minute he was born. It isn't his fault that his father is a humorless jackass and his various mothers have been a series of self-absorbed bimbos. She's reminded of the punch line to the old joke about why grandparents and their grandchildren get along so well: *They have a common enemy.*

Mark picks up the morning paper lying on the counter. "It's 'squander,' " he says, tapping the puzzle with his elegant fingers.

"What is?"

"The word you're missing. For 'spend wastefully.' It's 'squander.' "

"You're right." Julia fills in the word. "Thank you."

He laughs and grabs another muffin. "These are terrible," he says, eating it anyway. "Pretty sure I can do better."

"You're certainly welcome to try."

"We'll go grocery shopping this afternoon. You'll see," he says with a smile. "You're gonna like having me around."

CHAPTER FIVE

"That was quite the car," Aiden Young is saying as he turns the blue Hyundai onto Hood Road.

"A little plain," his wife says. "Except for the doors."

"Those doors are something else."

"I still like a Corvette," Heidi says. Before they got married, almost a year ago, Aiden had promised her a Corvette. But Aiden's mother, Lisa, was adamant that a sports car was both too expensive and too impractical, and since it was her money that was paying for the car's lease — to be fair, it was her money that was paying for almost everything, including the down payment and mortgage on their house — Aiden had gone along with her choice. Which wasn't unusual. To Heidi's great and continuing dismay, Aiden went along with almost all his mother's decisions.

She was the one exception.

Heidi smiles, lowering her visor and checking her reflection in the small mirror, pleased with what she sees: big brown eyes, model-high cheekbones, shoulder-length amber-colored curls that miraculously don't frizz up in the humidity, full, bow-shaped lips.

Everyone's always saying that she and Aiden make such a cute couple, a regular Ken and Barbie come to life. And the comparison is true — as far as it goes. Her husband is indeed tall and lean and muscular. But there's more to him than his blandly handsome exterior would suggest, something deep, even mysterious, going on behind those dark blue eyes.

A thirty-year-old former soldier who served two tours in Afghanistan, her husband has the swagger Heidi has always found appealing in a man. But he's surprisingly sweet, too, which is what she finds most attractive about him. That sweetness is the main reason she said yes to his proposal, despite the red flags she saw waving on the horizon.

At twenty-seven, Heidi had been dreaming of a home and family of her own ever since she was eight years old and her mother succumbed to the cancer that had left her bedridden for much of Heidi's childhood.

Her father had quickly remarried, to a woman with three children of her own and no desire to look after a fourth.

Heidi knew that Aiden's mother considered her "poor white trash," but she'd hoped — perhaps naïvely — that she could change her mind, that when Lisa had the chance to really get to know her, she would love her.

She was wrong.

Even after it became glaringly obvious that Lisa would never accept her, Heidi had been hopeful — again, perhaps naïvely — that when it came to a showdown between the woman who gave Aiden life and the woman who gave him blow jobs, she would emerge victorious.

Something else she'd been wrong about.

"What're you thinking about?" Aiden asks now.

Heidi shrugs and says nothing, glancing at the tiny sliver of a diamond in the center of her engagement ring. The stone is so small, she can't even be sure it's real. Could just be glass, for all she knows. The fact is that nothing is what she assumed it would be. "You had another one of those nightmares last night, didn't you?" she says as Aiden turns onto PGA Boulevard, heading east toward the Gardens Mall.

"Did I?"

"You were moaning and groaning and pulling at the covers."

"Really? Don't remember." His grip on the steering wheel tightens.

Heidi watches his knuckles turn white and knows he's lying. She reaches over to give his fingers a reassuring pat, wondering if his nightmares will ever disappear. He's been out of the army for five years, and seeing a psychiatrist for the last three, weekly sessions paid for by his mother.

Heidi can deal with her husband's PTSD. It's his mother she can't handle.

Aiden puts on his signal when they reach the second of the multiple exits leading into the huge, upscale mall and waits until the arrow indicates his turn to go. He proceeds slowly. *Very* slowly. *As if he's driving through a minefield,* Heidi thinks, pushing down on the invisible accelerator at her feet. The snail's pace continues into the parking lot that surrounds the two-story indoor plaza. Aiden parks where he always does, by the entrance to Saks, which is where he works.

At least for the time being.

Aiden has had several jobs since they got married. He has trouble concentrating and, combined with a general problem with authority, it's made holding down a job dif-

60

ficult. Currently, he's working in the jewelry department at Saks, and it seems to be going reasonably well. Heidi also works in the mall, at the nearby Lola's Lingerie, which is where they met.

He'd come in to buy a birthday gift.

"For your wife? Your girlfriend?" she asked, fishing.

"My mother," he replied, sheepishly.

I should have run right then and there, she thinks now. Instead, she'd found his honesty charming, his awkwardness even more so. "What did you have in mind?" she asked.

"I was thinking maybe a nightgown or a robe."

Heidi picked out ones she thought most suitable, and Aiden left with both a nightgown and a matching robe, then came back two days later. With his mother. To return them.

"Not exactly my taste," Lisa said, giving Heidi the once-over, her implication clear.

Heidi slipped Aiden her phone number as she was processing the return, and he called her that same night. Three months later, she and Aiden were engaged. At their wedding the following month, he vowed to love and cherish her, to put her above all others.

Well, that first part might be true, Heidi thinks as they enter the air-conditioned department store, but it didn't take her long to figure out who really came first.

"What time's your break?" he asks now.

"Not sure. I'll text you."

"Don't forget."

Heidi smiles. *He's like a big kid,* she thinks. Impulsive and sweet and needy. Hard to believe he served two tours in Afghanistan. Which means he probably *killed* people, although she can't be sure. It's something he never talks about.

She watches Aiden take up his position behind a glass counter filled with men's watches and checks her own fake Chanel. It's almost ten o'clock, when the mall opens to the public. She heads toward Lola's Lingerie, already looking forward to the day's end. What she'd really like to do is quit work to start a family, but she's afraid to raise the issue. Not because she thinks that Aiden might be against the idea, but because she *knows* Lisa would.

And what Lisa says goes.

"Damn it," Heidi mutters as she enters the large store.

"What's your mother-in-law done this time?" her co-worker Shawna asks, coming up beside her.

Heidi laughs. She's still chuckling when the store opens its doors and several customers appear, as if by magic.

One woman looks vaguely familiar, and Heidi follows her with her eyes as she wanders between the aisles, running desultory hands across the provocative push-up bras and bikini panties on display. She seems skittish, repeatedly glancing over her shoulder, as if afraid someone might be following her. Or maybe she's just waiting for a chance to slip some merchandise into the large canvas bag she's carrying.

"Can I help you?" Heidi says, approaching cautiously.

"Just looking," the woman says.

"We're having a special on bras. Buy two; get one free."

"Thank you."

Heidi is about to turn away, then stops. "I'm sorry, but you look so familiar. Do I know you?"

The woman barely glances in her direction. "I don't think so."

"I know!" Heidi proclaims. The woman jumps, the canvas bag she's holding dropping from her hands to the floor. "I'm so sorry. I didn't mean to scare you like that." Heidi kneels to pick up the bag. "You live over on Carlyle Terrace, right?"

The woman's eyes shoot toward hers. "How do you know that?"

"We're neighbors," Heidi tells her. "We moved into the house nearest Hood, number 1834, a few months ago. Next to the old lady. You live right in the middle, at the curve. Right?"

"That's right."

"I knew you looked familiar. I'm Heidi Young. Nice to finally meet you."

"Maggie McKay," the woman responds, taking another glance over her shoulder, as if someone might be listening.

"Pretty name. Sounds like that old Rod Stewart song," Heidi says. "Except that was Maggie May. Kind of a silly song." She stops when she realizes she's rambling. Her mother-in-law once accused her of having verbal diarrhea. "You have two kids, right?"

Maggie nods.

"Yeah. We're thinking of starting a family." Why had she told her that? If she were to say anything to Aiden, or God forbid, his mother . . . "Your daughter's really pretty," she says to mask her anxiety.

"Thank you." Maggie reaches for the straps of the canvas bag still in Heidi's hand. "I should get going."

"You're sure I can't help you with anything?"

"Another time. Thanks." She takes the bag from Heidi's hand, causing it to gape open.

Heidi feels her breath catch in her lungs and she takes an involuntary step back. "Oh my God. Is that a gun?"

Maggie pales. "Just a toy," she says, although her eyes say otherwise. "My son's. I took it out of his backpack this morning. The teachers get kind of bent out of shape when he takes it to school."

Heidi nods, even though she recognizes it's no toy. She knows what a real gun looks like. Aiden owns several.

"Well, I guess I'll see you around the neighborhood," Maggie says.

"Have a nice day," Heidi tells her, pulling her phone from her pocket as she watches her leave. She texts her husband: *You won't believe what just happened.*

CHAPTER SIX

Maggie spends the next hour driving aimlessly around Palm Beach Gardens, alternating between berating herself and trying to calm herself down. What on earth possessed her to go to the mall? She almost never goes to the mall, for God's sake. And Lola's Lingerie, of all places? What was she thinking?

Okay, calm down. Calm down. It's not the end of the world. No one followed you. You didn't see anyone suspicious.

Except, of course, that girl. That . . . what did she say her name was? Heather? Hilda? Something with an H . . . Heidi? Yes, Heidi. What difference does it make what her name is? What matters is that she knows where you live.

Of course she knows where you live. She's your neighbor.

Or so she says. How can you be sure?

Maggie has a sudden image of a large

moving van parked in the driveway of one of the two houses closest to Hood Road. She remembers watching from her window and carefully checking out the two men carrying boxes and furniture inside. She has a vague recollection of a woman, a woman several decades older than this Heidi person, directing the movers from the doorway. So how can she be sure the young woman she ran into in Lola's Lingerie is really who she says she is?

I should have paid more attention. It's one thing not to get too chummy with the neighbors. It's another thing to ignore them so completely that you don't recognize them.

"You're being paranoid," she hears Craig say, accompanied by the familiar sad shake of his head. *"I thought it would improve with the move, with time, but you're actually getting worse. I'm sorry, Maggie. I don't think I can live like this much longer."*

"Fuck you," Maggie says out loud, hearing her phone vibrate in her bag. She reaches inside it, the back of her hand brushing against the handle of the Glock 19. She recalls the stunned look on Heidi's face when she saw it and wonders if the young woman really believed it was a toy.

She glances at the phone and sees the call is from Craig. "Sorry, but you're the last person I want to talk to right now," she says, switching off the phone and steering the car toward the ocean. Her husband has been pestering her about his coming over to pick up a few things he inadvertently left behind when he moved out — an old camera and some cuff links he rarely wears. Maggie promptly threw the items into a box and hid them at the back of the closet in her son's room, claiming not to have seen them.

When did I become so petty? she wonders, pulling into a parking lot across from the public beach. "Petty and paranoid, that's me."

Of course, he could be calling because something has come up and he won't be able to pick up the kids at school or take them to dinner as planned. So she'll have to phone him at some point.

Just not now.

She gets out of her car and cuts across the already crowded lot toward A1A, the surprisingly calm ocean stretched out majestically before her.

She wonders if Craig is calling because he's lonely, because he still loves her, misses her, wants to come home.

It's possible. It's been three months since he left and neither one of them has been to see a lawyer, so maybe he's having second thoughts. Would she take him back?

Maggie breathes in the ocean's heady scent as she crosses the road and descends the wooden steps to the beach. She glances at the young women in bikinis sunning themselves and the young men tossing Frisbees back and forth as she takes off her sandals and walks barefoot in the sand. Surely no one would risk attacking her on a public beach, she thinks, casting repeated glances over her shoulder nevertheless, re-assured by the presence of the lifeguard sitting on his high perch and the sound of toddlers playing nearby.

She walks for maybe half an hour before plopping down on the warm sand and watching a group of teenagers trying to bodysurf the small, intermittent waves. She feels the sun on her legs, on her arms, in her hair, and she smiles, her body finally starting to relax, her insides to untwist. The ocean has always been a soothing influence in her life, regardless of what coast she's on. It calmed her after the death of her parents, her father from a stroke when she was thirty-three, her mother from cancer five years later.

At least they'd been spared the events of the last few years, Maggie thinks, noticing two burly-looking men walking toward her.

Instinctively, her hand reaches into her purse, searching for the gun's handle. But the men, both wearing the skimpiest of bathing suits, don't even look in her direction as they stroll past.

Maggie shakes her head as she pushes herself to her feet. Had she really thought there might be weapons secreted inside their Speedos?

Is that a gun in your pocket, or are you just happy to see me?

Okay, Maggie decides. When she starts quoting Mae West, it's time to go home.

The small cul-de-sac is quiet when she pulls her SUV into the driveway. No one is outside watering the lawn; no one is watching her from a window; no one is squatting behind a stubby palmetto palm. There's a luxury car she doesn't recognize parked in front of Mrs. Fisher's house, but it probably belongs to the old lady's son. Even so, she checks the license plate to make sure the car isn't a rental.

She knows something is wrong the second her key unlocks the door. Her hand is reflexively reaching out to silence the thirty-second warning beep that precedes the full-blown alarm when she feels the house's eerie quiet seep into her pores and realizes that the alarm isn't on.

70

How can that be? I watched Erin set it this morning. Didn't I?

She leaves the front door open as she pulls her gun and her cellphone out of her purse, holding one in each hand as the bag drops to the floor. *Don't be stupid,* she tells herself as she tiptoes toward the stairs. *You aren't some girl in a cheesy horror movie, going where common sense dictates you don't go.* Maggie stops, about to call 911 when the realization that she could be mistaken stills her fingers. Is it possible that in the morning rush to get out, Erin had tapped in an incorrect code? She has to be sure before she calls in the troops. She can't afford to be known as the girl who cried wolf.

Maggie proceeds slowly and cautiously up the stairs, gun in one hand, phone in the other, the first two emergency digits already pressed. But surely if someone has been waiting to ambush her, he would have heard her car pull into the driveway, and she'd be dead already.

Unless he wants to confront her directly. Unless he wants to see the look on her face when he follows through with his implied threats, to let her know he made good on his silent promise, that his will be the last eyes hers see before he closes them forever.

A sudden noise echoes down the hall.

Maggie swings around, her phone dropping to the floor as she aims the gun in the direction of the sound and prepares to pull the trigger. "I have a gun," she warns the intruder, as she was taught to do.

"Maggie?" her husband says, emerging from their bedroom. "Shit! What the hell? . . ." He drops to his knees. "Are you fucking crazy?!"

"Are you?" she shouts. "I almost shot you, for God's sake. What the hell are you doing here?"

"You have a fucking gun?! Holy shit!"

They continue screaming expletives at each other until they both run out of breath. Maggie bursts into tears as she collapses to the floor across from him. It is several minutes before either can speak with any coherence.

"I don't believe you," Craig says finally. "You bought a gun?!"

"You left. What was I supposed to do?"

"How about see a fucking psychiatrist?"

"I don't need a psychiatrist."

"Really? You almost shot me!"

"You broke into my house!"

"I didn't break in," Craig tells her. "I have a key. I know the code."

"Where's your car?"

"I borrowed one from the lot."

Maggie pictures the unfamiliar car parked on the street, trying to wrap her head around what just happened. She'd almost shot her husband, for God's sake. *That's what happened.* "What are you fucking doing here anyway?"

"I came to get my stuff. . . ."

"So . . . what? You don't call? You don't ask permission? You just show up?" Maggie demands.

"I tried calling. You didn't pick up. I left a message. . . ."

Maggie looks toward the phone on the floor beside her. *Shit. That's why he was calling.* "Then you should have waited till I returned your call. It's just a camera and some old cuff links. What's the big hurry?"

"I need the cuff links."

Maggie senses his reluctance to say more and raises an eyebrow, waiting for him to continue.

"I have a wedding this weekend," he explains. "Not that I have to justify wanting my personal belongings back."

"A wedding?" Maggie searches her brain for anyone they know who could be getting married. "Who's getting married? We don't know anyone."

"It's someone at work."

"Someone at work," Maggie repeats,

knowing she's not getting the full story. Craig was never very good at hiding things from her. And he's a lousy liar, always has been. "Who?"

"What difference does it make?"

"What aren't you telling me?" she counters. "Remember — you're talking to a woman with a loaded gun in her hands."

Craig sighs. "Okay. Fine. I'll tell you . . . on the condition that you put the damn thing away."

Maggie lays the gun on the floor beside her. "Shoot," she says, hoping for a laugh. "Sorry," she says, when one isn't forthcoming. "So, who's getting married?"

"Actually, I don't know the couple personally." Craig hesitates. "I'm kind of . . . the plus-one."

Maggie takes a second to let his words sink in. "Are you saying you're someone's date?"

"Not really." Another hesitation. "Well, I guess you could call it that."

"You have a date," Maggie repeats, trying to remain calm. "You don't think it's a little early to be seeing someone? Unless, of course, you started seeing her before we separated . . ."

"Don't be ridiculous. You know I would never do that."

"I never thought you'd leave," she says, which silences him. "Is it serious?"

"No. It's just someone at work."

"Someone at work." Maggie does a quick mental scan of her husband's co-workers. "Who?"

"What difference . . . ? One of the sales reps," he says, his face acknowledging the futility of prolonging the discussion. "You don't know her. She's new."

"Well, then," Maggie says when she can't think of anything else to say. *So, that's that.* Her husband isn't lonely. He doesn't still love her, miss her, want to come home. She pushes herself off the floor, pocketing her gun and pushing her shoulders back as she heads toward Leo's bedroom. Behind her, she hears Craig scrambling to his feet.

"Where are you going?"

Maggie doesn't answer as she walks into her son's room, opening his closet and retrieving the box with Craig's belongings, then returning to the hall and pushing it toward his chest. "You can leave now."

"Maggie . . ."

"Just take the fucking box and get out of my house."

He doesn't move. "It doesn't have to be this way."

"Really? What way would you like it?"

"You know I still care about you. . . ."

His words slam against the side of Maggie's brain. What do they mean? That he still loves her? That he wants to come home?

"Will you do me one favor?" he asks.

"What's that?"

"Will you get rid of the damn gun?"

"No way," she says. *Fuck you,* she thinks.

"For God's sake, Maggie. Think about the kids. . . ."

"I *am* thinking about the kids."

"What if it had been Leo and not me just now?"

"It wasn't."

"What if it *had* been?"

An uncomfortable silence follows. If she were still teaching English literature, she would tell her students that this is what would be considered a "pregnant pause." But then, she no longer teaches English literature. She no longer teaches anything. She is none of the things that once defined her — a confident California girl, a high school teacher, a loving wife. In her place stands this insecure imposter, a lonely woman with fear in her heart and a gun in her pocket.

"Don't be late picking up the kids," she says when she can find her voice.

"Maggie, please . . ."

"You know the way out." She walks into her bedroom. "Enjoy the wedding," she says, closing the door behind her.

CHAPTER SEVEN

Maggie sits on her bed for the better part of twenty minutes, unable to move. Gradually, she feels the numbness that had overtaken her body start to recede. The soft buzz of the central air-conditioning system gradually worms its way into her ears; sensation returns to her fingertips; she feels the weight of the gun in her pocket pressing against her hip.

I almost shot my husband, she realizes, extricating the gun and burying it beneath the myriad assortment of scarves inside the top drawer of the nightstand. *My husband doesn't love me,* she thinks with her next exhale.

He has a date.

He isn't coming back.

Dear God.

He's moving on. Without her.

How is that even possible?

Somehow, despite everything that's happened, the unbelievable strain the past few years have put on their marriage, she always assumed that theirs was an unbreakable bond. Even when Craig announced he was leaving, told her that she was "losing her spark," and that he couldn't take it anymore, she thought that they'd somehow find their way back to each other in time.

They'd met at a party during their last year at UCLA. It was the quintessential case of opposites attracting. Maggie loved Craig's laid-back manner and easygoing charm. Craig loved Maggie's spunk, her intensity and high ideals. They got married; Maggie got a job teaching high school English; Craig settled into a job selling luxury cars; they had two children.

They were happy.

Sure, they had their share of arguments. Craig sometimes complained that Maggie was *too* intense, her standards *too* high, *too* exacting, while Maggie occasionally accused her husband of being *too* tolerant, *too* laid-back.

"Sometimes you have to take a stand," she told him.

"Sometimes you have to back off," he countered.

Still, he was happy. She was happy.

She might have been losing her spark, but

she never thought she'd lose him.

She walks to the bedroom window overlooking the street, checking the small cul-de-sac for anything out of the ordinary. Anything to stop the memories that are now flooding into her brain.

Because Maggie knows exactly the day everything changed, the precise moment two years ago that altered their lives forever.

It was a Saturday. Craig had taken the kids to the beach and Maggie was enjoying the spa day he'd gifted her for her fortieth birthday. It started with a relaxing sauna, then an even more relaxing massage, followed by a glorious facial and a much-needed mani-pedi. She'd left the salon at the Beverly Wilshire Hotel feeling refreshed and ready to take on the world.

The world, in turn, was preparing to come crashing down on her head.

She was stopped at a red light when she heard a commotion beside her. A Lincoln Town Car had apparently cut off a motorcycle, and the two drivers — one a middle-aged, well-dressed businessman, the other a rough-looking, leather-vested biker — had leapt from their vehicles and were now flailing at each other in the middle of the road, the sun flashing like a strobe light across the tattoos covering the biker's bare arms.

And then another flash — my God, was that a knife? — as the weapon sliced through the smog-filled air to pierce the driver's jugular.

"No!" Maggie screamed as the biker calmly replaced the helmet he'd tossed to the ground only seconds before, instantly hiding his scraggly brown hair and angry black eyes. He shook his head in Maggie's direction, as if issuing a silent warning, then mounted his bike and sped away.

The police arrived minutes later.

"I saw the whole thing," Maggie told them, describing the altercation and giving as detailed a description as she could of the biker — the unkempt hair, the dark, menacing eyes, and the jungle of tattoos covering his arms.

"You told the police you could identify the killer?" Craig demanded when she recounted the events to him later.

"I saw a man murdered," Maggie argued. "And I saw the person who did it. You're telling me I should just keep quiet?"

"I'm sure you weren't the only witness."

"I'm the only one who saw his face."

"No, you're the only one foolish enough to admit it."

The argument extended into the night and continued over the next days and weeks. They intensified after a man fitting the description Maggie had given the police was arrested, and she identified him in a lineup.

It was then that the intimidation started. Hang-ups on the phone. Anonymous, vaguely threatening messages on social media, the *vroom-vroom* of motorcycles outside their bedroom windows at all hours of the night.

They called the police, who notified the U.S. Marshals, who visited them immediately, telling them they might qualify for Witness Protection.

"How does that work?" Maggie asked.

It was explained that Maggie, Craig, and their two children would be given new IDs and spirited to a secret location, where they would be provided with a monthly stipend and money to live temporarily, as well as new SSNs, fake birth certificates, and other necessary documents. But, while they would still be liable for any debts they'd previously incurred, they would not be able to buy a car or make any other major purchases because there would be no credit history on their new IDs.

It also meant leaving their relatives and friends and virtually their entire lives behind.

It meant they would have to lie to everyone about everything.

"It seems as if we're the ones being punished here," Maggie observed. "Not the killer."

The Marshals didn't disagree.

"We'll need some time to think this through," Maggie told them, increasingly torn between wanting to do the right thing and worries for her family's welfare. Could she really ask them to give up their home, their friends, their *names*? She assured herself that such drastic measures were unnecessary, that once her testimony put the killer behind bars, everything would be okay, their lives could return to normal.

Except the case never went to trial.

It was dropped because the man she'd identified produced an alibi, however suspect — half a dozen fellow bikers, all looking vaguely alike, all sporting the same tattoos, all swearing they'd been together at the time of the incident. The Assistant State's Attorney insisted that any half-decent lawyer would attack the validity of Maggie's identification. How could she be so sure his client was the man she saw when she'd been inside her car a lane away, her windows were closed, the sun was in her eyes, and she'd been scared, possibly even traumatized? Combined with the biker's alibi, that would likely be enough to create reasonable doubt in the jury's mind, making it impossible for the prosecution to obtain a conviction.

"Look on the bright side," said her obviously relieved husband. "It's over."

Except it wasn't.

The charges might have been dropped, but the harassment continued. Their house was pelted with eggs; wherever Maggie went, young men on motorcycles appeared; a dead bird was found in their mailbox.

They called the U.S. Marshals, who explained that, because there would no longer be a trial for Maggie to testify at, the family was no longer eligible for Witness Protection.

Six months later, they moved to Florida.

After a brief breaking-in period, everyone not only adjusted to the move, they flourished. Craig got a job at a local luxury car dealership, becoming their top salesman within a matter of months; Erin quickly became one of the more popular girls at school; even quiet Leo seemed happy.

Only Maggie failed to thrive. Only Maggie failed to move on.

She sought help from a therapist and religiously practiced the recommended breathing exercises and meditation meant to calm her, but stopped when the time it took to do them only made her more anxious.

She dyed her long, thick hair a mousier shade of brown, then cut it short. She chose not to work, ostensibly so she could be home for the kids "till they get used to everything." She interacted only fleetingly with the neighbors, became increasingly antisocial and wary of strangers.

"There was this man," Maggie informed Craig one day. "I'm sure he was following me. . . ."

"There was no man," Craig said.

"There was a hang-up on the phone this morning. . . ." she said another time.

"Probably a wrong number."

"There was this guy at Leo's school, he looked at me kind of funny. . . ."

"Maggie . . ."

"We need to buy a gun."

"We're not buying a gun."

"You're being stubborn."

"You're being paranoid."

And so it went. Until the night of the concert. The night he went from "You're losing your spark" to "I'm sorry, Maggie. I just can't do it anymore."

The concert was in Miami and was billed as a country music extravaganza. The owner of the dealership where Craig worked had invited Craig and Maggie to join him and his wife for the sold-out event. Craig had been both flattered to be asked and excited at seeing some of his favorite artists perform. Even Maggie had been looking forward to the evening. But as their host was pulling his white Jaguar into the parking lot of the American Airlines Arena, Maggie saw a small army of bikers circling the grounds and felt a huge bubble of panic lodge in the pit of her stomach, a bubble that grew as they entered the arena and people began occupying their seats. It expanded even further as the lights dimmed and the show began, then threatened to burst when she saw two men with beards and tattoos laughing across the aisle.

"Those men . . ." she whispered to Craig, pointing with her chin.

"What about them?" he asked, although she knew he knew.

"We have to leave."

"We can't leave. Just calm down. Take deep breaths."

The deep breaths did no good. "I'm going to be sick," Maggie said.

"You're not going to be sick."

"Is there a problem?" Craig's boss asked.

"No. Everything's fine," Craig told him.

"I can't breathe," Maggie said, gulping at the air.

"You can't panic every time you see a man with a tattoo," Craig muttered between clenched teeth.

But Maggie was already on her feet. "I have to get out of here. We have to leave. Now!"

Craig grabbed her arm, forced her back into her seat. "We just drove an hour and a half to get here, and it's not our car."

"Then *you* stay. I'll take a taxi. . . ."

"Keep it down, will you? You're embarrassing me. . . ."

"Is everything okay?" Craig's boss asked.

In the end, they left the concert after the opening act, Craig's boss speeding up I-95, as if whatever madness had infected Maggie was contagious, his wife so angry at having her evening ruined that she barely said a word until Maggie was climbing out of the backseat. "I hope you're feeling better," she said, throwing the words over her shoulder like grains of salt.

"I hope you're happy," Craig said once he and Maggie were inside. "I'll be lucky if I still have a job come Monday."

Monday came and Craig still had a job. But Maggie no longer had Craig.

"I'm sorry, Maggie. I just can't do it anymore."

The landline on the nightstand beside the alarm clock rings and Maggie jumps. Leaving the window to answer it before it can ring again, she says, "Hello?" and braces herself for the menacing voice she's sure will follow.

Instead the voice she hears is soft and lyrical, a faint Southern drawl winding through each word. "Is this Maggie McKay?"

"Who's calling?"

"It's Dani Wilson. From next door?"

"Yes?" Maggie asks. Dani Wilson has barely spoken to her since they moved in. If anything, she's gone out of her way to be unfriendly. The one time Maggie phoned to ask if they could arrange a playdate for their sons, she'd been given the brush-off. So why was Dani Wilson calling now?

"Sorry to bother you, but I'm in a bit of a bind and I was hopin' you might be able to help me out. . . ."

"What can I do for you, Mrs. Wilson?"

"It's Dr. Wilson, actually."

"Sorry." *Bitch,* Maggie thinks. "What can I do for you, *Dr.* Wilson?"

"You have a daughter, right? Erin?"

"What's this about?"

"Well, we were wonderin' if maybe she might be free this Sunday to babysit for us. We've been invited to play golf and have

88

dinner with Mrs. Fisher's son and his wife. You know Julia Fisher? She lives across from us. My husband was her husband's doctor before the poor man died? That's how we know her son. . . . Anyway, they've asked us to play golf and have dinner with them on Sunday, and our regular sitter isn't available, and Nick suggested we ask Erin if she could look after our boys that afternoon and evenin'. Would that be all right, do you think? Could she sit for us?"

"Well, I'd have to ask her."

"Of course. If she could maybe give us a call later and let us know?"

Maggie writes down the Wilson's phone number. "I'll give her the message."

The line goes dead.

"Yes, thank you so much," Maggie says, imitating Dr. Dani Wilson's surprisingly tentative Southern drawl. "Pleasure *talkin'* to you." She hangs up the phone, thinking that this was the longest conversation she's had with the woman since they moved in. Seems strange that, after having had little contact with any of her neighbors for months, Maggie would have interactions with two of them in the same day.

"You're being paranoid," she hears Craig say.

"Fuck you," Maggie says as, somewhere

89

outside, she hears the familiar *vroom-vroom* of a motorcycle. The sound vibrates through her body like a drill. Maggie crawls under the covers of her unmade bed and stays there until nightfall.

CHAPTER EIGHT

Erin rings the bell of the Wilson house and stands outside, waiting for someone to answer it. From inside, she thinks she hears voices raised in anger, but the voices fall silent as footsteps approach. *Probably the TV,* Erin thinks as the door opens.

"Erin," a smiling and relaxed-looking Nick Wilson says in greeting. "Thanks so much for doing this. Come on in. My wife's just finishing getting ready. How's everything going?"

She steps inside. "Good."

"Enjoying school?"

"It's okay."

"Well, just a few more weeks till summer break."

Erin nods, glancing toward the interior of the house, surprised by how different it feels from her own, despite having virtually the same layout. *Amazing what a little thought and expensive furniture can do,* she thinks, comparing the Wilson's obvious dedication to detail to her mother's rather slapdash approach to, well, almost everything.

Maybe if her mother had taken greater care to truly make their house a home, her father would still be living there.

"Where are the boys?"

"Ben's in his room, playing video games. Tyler's busy with his pet fish. They shouldn't give you any problems. And we won't be late. It's golf and an early dinner. My guess is we'll be back before nine."

"No rush."

"Assuming we ever get out of here." Dr. Wilson looks toward the stairs. "Dani, sweetheart," he calls. "What's the holdup?"

"Hold your horses. I'm comin'."

"So's Christmas." He shrugs. The shrug says, *What can you do?*

"Be down in two shakes of a stick."

"More like twenty shakes," Nick says. "We might as well go into the den and sit down." He motions toward the back of the house. "You've met Tyler before, haven't you?" he says when they reach the kitchen.

"A while back," Erin says. "Hi, Tyler. Those are beautiful fish you've got there. Do they have names?"

The inquiry is met with a proud smile that stretches from the boy's full lips to his deep blue eyes. "Mine does. Neptune. He's the red one. Want to see him jump through his hoop?"

"Not now, Goldilocks," his father says, ruffling his son's dark blond hair. "You can show her after we leave. He thinks everyone is as captivated by his fish as he is," Nick whispers as he leads her into the den. He motions toward the green leather sofa that sits at right angles to a large oak desk, directly across from a big-screen TV and the cabinet full of guns.

Erin sits down, feeling the leather of the sofa glom onto the backs of her bare thighs. She makes a mental note to wear long pants the next time she babysits instead of the shorts she's wearing. "That's some collection you have," she says.

"Like guns, do you?"

"Not really. They kind of scare me."

"Nothing to be afraid of." Nick retrieves the key from the top desk drawer and unlocks the cabinet. He beckons Erin forward, quickly removing one of the smaller weapons on display. "Come here."

Erin pushes off the seat she's just occupied, hearing the *whoosh* of the leather as it reluctantly releases its grip on her flesh.

"This here's a Springfield Armory nine-millimeter XD," he tells her. "It'd be perfect for you. It's not only a terrific first gun to own, but great fun to shoot with. Here. Hold it."

"Oh, Dr. Wilson, I don't think . . ."

"Take it." He drops the gun into her open palm. "Feels surprisingly comfortable, doesn't it? And please, let's skip the formalities, okay? Call me Nick. How do you like it?"

For a second, Erin isn't sure if he's referring to the gun or his request to call him by his given name. "Feels kind of weird," she says, which is true in both cases. "It's heavier than I thought it would be."

"Well, it's not a toy."

She hands back the gun and motions toward the larger weapons. "These are rifles?"

"Some are rifles. Some are shotguns."

"There's a difference?"

"Mostly in their barrels." Nick removes a rifle from its hooks. "The rifle has a long barrel with thick walls to withstand high pressure, and these ridges here, what they call 'rifling' — no surprise there," he says with a chuckle, clearly relishing his role as educator, "they put a spiral spin on a bullet to increase its accuracy and distance. Rifles are typically used for firing at stationary targets," he explains, returning the weapon to its previous position and removing another, "whereas shotguns, like this guy here, are typically used for shooting at moving targets in the air. They also have long barrels, although they're thinner than a rifle's, and they have a smooth bore that's meant to reduce friction."

"And speakin' of bores," Nick's wife says, entering the den, looking decidedly uncomfortable in her unflattering knee-length shorts and loose-fitting golf shirt, "I'm sure Erin's heard quite enough about barrels and friction and the like for one day."

Nick puts the shotgun back inside the cabinet and locks it, returning the key to the top drawer of the desk. "You're absolutely right. It appears that I'm as bad as Tyler with his damn fish." He smiles. "I've left money by the phone in the kitchen so you can order pizza for dinner, if that works for you."

"Sure does," says Erin.

"Good. Then I believe we're all set. Shall we be on our way?"

"Thank you so much for doin' this for us," Dani tells Erin. "We really appreciate it."

"Anytime." Erin follows the two doctors out of the room.

"Goodbye, sweetie," Dani says to her older son, who is still concentrating on his fish. "You be a good boy and don't give Erin any trouble. You hear?"

"I won't."

"Like I said," Nick tells Erin when they reach the front door, "we shouldn't be late."

"Goodbye, Ben," Dani calls up the stairs.

" 'Bye," Ben yells back as Tyler comes running from the kitchen to give his mother a hug.

"Okay, Goldilocks. Why don't you go upstairs and play video games with your brother for a while?" Nick suggests.

"I don't like video games," Tyler says.

"Well, then, at least try not to bore Erin too much with that damn fish. Apparently, I've already bored her enough." He smiles at his wife. "We want Erin to come back."

"Have a good game," Erin calls, watching the Wilsons climb into Nick's big black Mercedes and back onto the street. She closes the door, surprised to find Tyler still at her side.

"You want to see Neptune jump through his hoop now?" he asks eagerly.

Erin smiles. "Sure." They approach the fishbowl together, and she stares in awe as Tyler guides the small red fish with his index finger around the side of the bowl toward the neon yellow loop, then guides the fish through. "Wow," she says, im-

96

pressed. "Did you teach him that?"

"Yeah. But he's really smart. He learns fast."

"So, smart *and* beautiful."

"He's the best," Tyler says.

"What about the blue one?" Erin asks. "What tricks does he do?"

"He's Ben's fish. He doesn't do anything."

"Why doesn't he have a name?"

"Ben won't give him one." He leans forward, lowering his voice. "He's says there's no point. So I just call him Blue."

"That's a perfect name."

"Wanna see me feed Neptune? He eats right out of my hand." Without waiting for a response, Tyler carefully deposits one small pellet of fish food onto the tip of his index finger and submerges it. Immediately, the fish swims up and grabs the pellet with his mouth, swallowing it. "He gets three a day," Tyler explains, feeding him another. "You have to be careful not to overfeed them because bettas have very delicate stomachs. Are you bored?" he asks in the next breath.

"Not at all," Erin says truthfully. She's finding talk about the fish much more interesting than Nick's lecture on guns. "Why don't you like video games?"

"Too violent," Tyler says. "They're all

about shooting people or chopping off their heads."

"You don't want to chop off anyone's head?"

"I'd rather play with Neptune. Do you want to try feeding him?"

"Would he let me?"

Tyler smiles. "Just don't make any sudden moves." He places a pellet on her fingertip and directs her finger inside the bowl. "Wait for it," he says, as the fish swims up and grabs hold of the pellet with his mouth, then dives to the bottom of the bowl. "You did it!"

Erin feels a surge of unexpected pride.

"He likes you."

"Well, I like *him.*" She glances at the other bowl. "I feel kind of sorry for Blue, though."

"Yeah, I know. Me, too. But Mom feeds him every day, and I play with him a bit when Ben isn't around."

"You're a good kid," Erin tells him.

Tyler looks skeptical. "Dad doesn't think so."

"Sure, he does."

"No. He says I need to toughen up, and calls me Goldilocks. That's a girl's name."

"I think he's just referring to your hair," Erin offers. "It's a . . . what do they call it? A 'term of endearment.' "

"I don't know." Tyler pauses, choosing his words carefully. "Sometimes he says things that *sound* good, but they don't *feel* good."

"Wow," Erin says. "That's pretty deep for a ten-year-old kid." She smiles, fighting the urge to tousle his hair the same way his father had earlier. "I think you might be almost as smart as your fish."

CHAPTER NINE

"You're in my line, sweetheart," Nick Wilson says, glancing over his shoulder at his wife, who is standing approximately twenty feet away at the edge of the putting green.

Dani steps quickly to her right.

"Sorry, hon. I can still see you."

Dani scurries toward the large sand trap on the far side of the green. "Heavens to Betsy. How's this?"

"Perfect. Thanks, hon."

Dani smiles as her husband restarts his routine: lifting his putter into the air to determine the ball's correct trajectory, securing his legs in a parallel position to that line, keeping his head down and his eyes on the ball, followed by a few waggles with the golf club and a couple of practice strikes in the air above the ball, holding his follow-through each time. She takes a deep breath as the ball finally rolls off Nick's putter toward the hole, willing it to go in.

But the ball has been struck too hard, and Nick has failed to read enough of a break, so instead of ending up in or even close to its target, the ball veers a good five feet to its right and rolls down the gentle incline, coming to a stop inches from Dani's feet.

Damn, she thinks, wishing this afternoon was over. They've been on the impeccably maintained private course for more than four hours. Four hours that feel like forty. It's hot. She's tired. She still can't figure out what they're doing here. They barely know Norman Fisher and his trophy wife, a sweet but vacuous young woman with whom she has absolutely nothing in common.

"Looks like you're away again," Norman says, not quite able to disguise the delight in his voice. The two men have a "friendly" competition going, and if Nick misses his next putt, they will be all tied up after seventeen holes.

Only one more hole to go, Dani thinks as, once again, Nick begins his painstakingly slow routine. *Slower than molasses,* she thinks, silently acknowledging that this is probably what makes him such a good doctor, this attention to detail, this thoroughness at every stage of the process, this desire — this *need* — for perfection.

Still, perfection isn't an easy trait to live with, she thinks, watching the ball roll toward the hole. *Go in. Go in.* For almost its entire length, it looks as if Nick's going to sink it. But then the ball hits a slight bump in the grass and ends up doing a three-sixty around the hole to remain stubbornly outside it.

"Oh, so close," Norman says. "Looks like we're all tied up, Doc."

"On to the eighteenth," Poppy Fisher chirps.

Dani watches Poppy drape a congratulatory arm around her husband's shoulders, sees his hand slip casually toward her buttocks. She smiles as they walk toward their cart, trying not to compare herself to the younger woman. Not that there's any comparison. Poppy is six feet of drop-dead gorgeous in her short and flouncy black golf skirt and clinging neon-yellow top, whereas Dani is five feet four inches of average in her plain white polo shirt and long brown shorts that skim the tops of her dimpled knees. The fact that both women are blond only serves to exaggerate the differences between them. While Poppy's hair hangs wondrously straight and shiny beneath her stylish visor, Dani's unruly curls shoot from the bottom of her baseball cap like an explosion. *I look like a circus clown,* she thinks, catching sight of her reflection in the golf cart's rearview mirror as she slides into the passenger side.

Behind her, she hears the angry thrust of Nick's putter as he returns it to his bag.

"You've got to watch where you stand," he says as he takes his position behind the wheel, jaw clenched, eyes refusing to meet hers.

"I'm sorry. I tried . . ."

"Try harder."

"You said where I moved was perfect."

"What else could I say without sounding like some sort of prima donna? I mean, how many times do I have to ask you? Are you deliberately trying to make me look bad?"

"What? No. Of course not."

"I should have had that putt. You cost me a hole."

"I'm sorry," Dani says again, and she is, although she isn't sure why. "Maybe you're taking this competition a bit too seriously?" she ventures.

"Maybe you could learn a little golf etiquette."

"Sorry," she says again. And then, to lighten the mood, "A little golf etiquette comin' right up."

"Com*ing,*" he corrects, refusing to be

103

mollified as he pulls to a stop behind Norman's cart. "Looks like you've got the honors," he tells Norman without a trace of anger or impatience.

Poppy ambles up to the side of Dani's cart as their husbands approach the tee box. "Having a good time?"

"Sure am," Dani lies. "The course is beautiful."

"Yeah, we love living here. The place has everything — golf, tennis, a fabulous gym. The doc would love it."

Dani nods. Her husband *would* absolutely love living here. She, on the other hand, would hate it. Everything about these meticulously maintained gated communities intimidates her. So far she's been able to convince Nick that because the vast majority of these developments are adult-oriented, their boys would have no one to socialize with. But their sons are growing up fast, and Nick is growing bored of the cozy little cul-de-sac that has always made her feel safe. "Yes, he —"

"Ladies, a little quiet, please," Nick calls from the tee box, lifting both arms into the air as if to silence the crowd, the way Dani has seen them do on TV. "The man is about to swing."

"Your husband's so funny," Poppy says as

104

Norman steps up to the ball, gives it a whack, and sends it flying down the center of the fairway. "Woo-hoo!" Poppy shrieks. "Great shot, babe."

Norman acknowledges his wife's enthusiasm with a wink, stepping aside as Nick puts his tee into the ground. Dani looks around, hoping she isn't in his line of sight, as he carefully places the ball on the tee and starts his series of waggles and practice swings.

"The doc's a very good-looking man," Poppy says.

"Yes, he is."

"How'd you ever land him?"

The question hits Dani like a fist to her solar plexus. Not that she hasn't heard it before. She's been hearing variations of it all her married life — *Aren't you the lucky girl! What'd you do to win that? Tell me your secret, girl.* Still, it never fails to shock her. "Excuse me?"

Nick stops, his club dropping to his side. "Everything okay over there?"

"Yes, fine. Sorry."

"Could you watch this for me?"

"I'm watchin'."

"We're all *watchin'*," Poppy repeats with a laugh as Nick restarts his routine from the beginning. "*Watchin'* and *waitin'*," she adds, pointedly.

Dani chuckles in spite of herself.

"Ladies," Norman says. "A little decorum, please."

"Ah, honey," Poppy says. "Your decorum isn't so little."

Norman laughs. "Please excuse my wife," he says, with obvious affection.

"No need," Nick says, smiling. He cuts short his routine, then mishits the ball, sending it into the bushes to his left.

"Take a mulligan," Norman offers. "You were distracted."

Nick nods and tees up another ball, only to repeat the same swing to the same results. "That's it for me," he says with a shrug. "I'm out of this hole."

"Nah," Norman says. "Just drop the ball from where mine landed. We'll call it a draw."

"No way. You won fair and square. I owe you twenty bucks."

"So . . . what would everybody like to drink?" Norman asks, as they enter the wood-paneled bar area of the private club after the completion of the round.

Dani sits down beside her husband at the low round table for four that overlooks the finishing hole of another of the club's three courses. Nick has barely looked at her since they walked off the eighteenth green.

"Gin and tonic," Poppy says.

"Sounds good," Dani agrees.

"Count me in," Nick says.

"Four gin and tonics," Norman instructs the waiter, then checks his watch. "We'll have to drink quickly. Our dinner reservations are in twenty minutes."

"Sorry if I was a little slow," Nick apologizes. " 'Slower than molasses,' as Dani would say." He reaches over to pat her hand. "My fault entirely. Don't get to play nearly as much as I'd like these days."

"I'm sure your practice keeps you very busy," Poppy says. "Must be very gratifying being married to such an important man," she says to Dani.

"Oh, my wife's no slouch," Nick says before Dani can think of a suitable response. "You ever in need of a top-notch dentist, she's the one to call."

"Count me out. I hate going to the dentist," Poppy says.

"Now she tells me," Norman says. "After I paid a small fortune for that mouthful of veneers."

Poppy flashes a brilliant smile of perfect teeth. "Only the best for my guy."

■ ■ ■ ■

"So, did you have a good time?" Dani asks her husband on the drive home after dinner.

Nick keeps his eyes on the road and says nothing.

"They're kind of a strange match," Dani continues. "I mean, they're nice enough, I guess, but . . ."

"I don't recall anybody asking your opinion," her husband says.

Dani's breath catches in her lungs. "You're still mad," she acknowledges.

"Why on earth would I be mad?"

"You tell me."

"Maybe because you deliberately stood in my line of sight?"

"It wasn't deliberate. . . ."

"Because you made fun of my slow play . . ."

"That was Poppy, and she was makin' fun of my accent as much as anythin'. . . ."

"You didn't laugh?"

"Well, it *was* kinda funny."

"I'm glad you thought so."

"Okay, I'm sorry." Dani waits for Nick to accept her apology. "I'm really sorry," she repeats when he doesn't. Then, "Are we good?"

Nick says nothing. They drive the rest of the way home in silence.

Dani goes upstairs to check on the boys while Nick pays Erin for babysitting.

"Oh, that's way too much," she hears Erin say. "Really, you don't have to . . ."

"No. I insist. Please, I'll be insulted if you don't take it."

"That's so nice. Thank you so much."

"My pleasure."

Dani hears the front door close, watching from her bedroom window as Erin disappears inside the house next door. "How much did you give her?" she asks as her husband walks into the room, closing the bedroom door behind him.

But the words are barely out of her mouth before his open hand comes crashing against her cheek.

She collapses to the floor.

"Now we're good," he says.

CHAPTER TEN

"Goodbye, kids. Have a great day," Sean Grant calls from the doorway as Olivia backs her car out of the driveway, then stops, opening her window.

"Good luck today, hon," she says, blowing him a kiss.

"Thanks."

"I have a good feeling about this one."

"Fingers crossed," he says, watching his wife hold up both hands and do just that. "Drive carefully."

"Always."

Sean watches her car disappear down the main road and is about to go inside when the front door of the Wilsons' house opens and out walks the handsome doctor himself.

"Hi, Doc," Sean says, waving.

"Hey, there, Sean," Nick replies. "How's it going?"

"Going great. I have a job interview this morning." He rubs the stubble on his cheeks, forcing a laugh from his throat. "Guess I'll have to shave."

Nick climbs behind the wheel of his black Mercedes. "Looks like you've got a pretty good thing going here. Sure you want to get back into the daily grind?"

Sean shrugs. More than anything, that's what he wants.

"Well, I wish you luck."

"Have a good day," Sean calls after him. He checks his watch. It's a little early for the doctor to be leaving for work. Must have a very busy day ahead of him. *I remember those days,* he thinks. "And you will have them again," he says out loud, seeking reassurance in the sound of his voice.

Seconds later, the Wilsons' garage door opens and Dani Wilson backs her car, also a black Mercedes, but smaller than her husband's, into the driveway. *Here comes another busy day,* Sean thinks, wondering if they purchased their cars through Craig McKay, if he gave them some sort of deal for buying two. He knows Craig moved out about three months ago and is curious why, even more curious about what he was doing back here last week. He certainly looked spooked when he left, Sean recalls, deciding that if he gets this job, the first thing he'll do is give the man a call. No more Hondas for the Grants. No, sir. It'll be matching Mercedes all the way.

He waves as Dani Wilson backs onto the street, but she doesn't wave back. Instead she lowers her head and pretends not to see him. He isn't surprised. She's a cold fish, that one, probably thinks she's too good for the rest of them. Unlike her affable husband, she never stops to chat or inquire about their lives. What's she got to be so snooty about anyway? Sean shakes his head, wondering what the handsome doctor sees in her. She's attractive enough, he supposes, but nothing special. *Must be great in bed,* he thinks, going inside.

He heads to the kitchen and pours himself another cup of coffee.

"I notice we're running low on coffee creamer," Olivia said earlier.

"No," he says now, bypassing the fridge for the freezer at the bottom. "Coffee creamer is not what this needs." He removes the half-empty bottle of vodka, mixing a few ounces in with his coffee, then returns the bottle to its former position. He takes a sip, then heads up the stairs, drink in hand, to shave and dress for his interview. The cup is empty by the time he reaches the bathroom.

"Thank you so much for coming in, Sean,"

112

the officious young woman from HR says, standing up and stretching her arm across her cluttered desk to shake his hand, signaling that their time together is up and the interview is over. "As you know, we're meeting with several candidates, but we'll try to get back to you as soon as possible. It was lovely meeting you."

"You, too. I think we're a good fit."

"Thanks again for coming in."

Sean exits the canary-yellow building at the corner of Royal Palm Way and South County Road, shielding his eyes from the too-bright sun as he steps onto the street. He's not getting this job and he knows it. He could tell the second he entered Carrie Pierce's office that he was doomed. The *Ms.* on her nameplate was the first sign of trouble. Then there was the way she looked at him, that fake smile on her thin lips that didn't quite reach her eyes. What is she — all of twenty-five? And she's the one calling the shots, the one who gets to decide if he advances to the next level, the one he's supposed to impress? The one he *needs* to impress.

She wasn't impressed and he knows it. She paid scant attention to his résumé, seemed bored when he enumerated his list of achievements, gave little value to his years of experience. "We're a young company," she told him several times during the twenty-minute interview. What she was really saying was that he was too old.

"Screw you," he mutters, louder than he'd intended, attracting the attention of two women chatting on the corner. They glance briefly in his direction, then cross to the other side of the street.

He laughs, catching sight of his reflection in a nearby window. Not quite the dashing figure he'd imagined when he left the house. His hair could use a good trim and the extra weight he's put on in the last year makes his once-stylish suit appear ill-fitting and out of date. *Oh well. Too late to do anything about that now.*

He removes his tie and tosses it in a nearby trash can, calculating that he has a few hours before he has to pick up the kids from school. It's almost noon and he's hungry. More important, he's thirsty, and a glass of wine is just what he needs to rid himself of the taste of that demoralizing interview. It isn't often that he's in Palm Beach proper these days, even longer since he strolled the hallowed sidewalks of Worth Avenue, the county's most prestigious address, full of expensive designer shops and pricey restaurants. Might as well enjoy it, since there's no telling when he'll be back.

He's staring at an outrageously priced linen jacket in the window of Ferragamo — *three thousand dollars for a piece of imported fabric that's going to crease like crazy? Are they kidding?* — when he feels his cellphone vibrate in his pocket. Olivia, he knows, even before he checks the caller ID.

"How'd it go?" she asks immediately.

Sean tenses at the hope in his wife's voice. "Great."

"Oh, I'm so glad. Tell me all about it."

"What can I say? It went well. Really well. I think I have a good shot at this."

"That's wonderful. I'm so happy for you."

"Well, it's early days," Sean qualifies, deciding he may have gone too far. "I still have to meet with the head of marketing, and probably the president of the company, and who knows who else. You know how it goes. This could take a while."

"So, when does all this take place?"

"Not sure. Probably next week."

"This is such good news. Are you excited?"

"I am. Just trying not to get too ahead of myself. They still have a few more people to see."

"Oh."

Sean hears a current of doubt resonating

through that tiny word and hates it. "But Carrie Pierce, the woman I spoke to in Human Resources, was extremely positive. She was very encouraging."

"That's wonderful," Olivia says again, although with less enthusiasm than she expressed the first time. "Oh, there goes my other line. I should go."

"Of course. Duty calls."

"Love you."

"Love you, too." He returns the phone to his pocket and stands very still, taking several measured breaths before pushing open the heavy glass door of the designer shop.

A salesman approaches almost immediately. "Can I help you, sir?"

Sean smiles. "I'd like to see the linen jacket in the window."

Sean is sitting at a table by the large open window of the front section of Ta-boo, one of Palm Beach's oldest and best known restaurants. The bag containing his new jacket sits at his feet. He is finishing up his lobster salad, savoring his second glass of Pinot Grigio, and contemplating a third. Outside, a parade of smartly dressed women with unnaturally tight faces saunters by. Snatches of conversation from the next table drift lazily toward his ears.

("Did you hear? Marsha needs to have her implants replaced. Apparently, there's some kind of problem with the manufacturer."
"Her boobs have been recalled?")

He laughs. Booze and boobs. What else matters?

The waitress appears. "All done here?" she asks, and he nods. "Would you like to see a dessert menu?"

Sean checks his watch. It's almost two o'clock and he has to pick the kids up in forty minutes. Luckily, tourist season is over and there shouldn't be too much traffic at this hour, but still, it will be tight. He really should get going. "Just the check, thank you."

A minute later, the check is on the table. He glances toward it, swallowing his shock at the figure he sees. Sixty dollars for two glasses of house wine! Over a hundred dollars in total and he didn't even have dessert! And that's not counting a tip. *Shit.* Olivia will have a fit. *Nah,* he thinks, glancing toward the floor. The fit will happen when she sees what he paid for the jacket!

Unless he gets the job. Then he'll need a new jacket. Maybe more than one.

It's not entirely out of the question, he decides. The interview might not have gone

117

as badly as he thought. He's probably being too hard on himself.

He hands his credit card to the waitress as once again his phone vibrates in his pocket. Caller ID reveals it's the job recruiter he's been working with. "Hey, there, Fiona," he says, adopting Nick Wilson's breezy tone. "How's it going?" Perhaps Fiona has another interview for him. "I think the meeting went well," he continues unprompted. "Of course, they're still interviewing —"

"That's actually why I'm calling," she interrupts. "I was just speaking to Ms. Pierce."

"And?"

"And I'm afraid it's not happening."

"They decided that already?"

"She said that while she was *very* impressed with your credentials, she didn't think you were quite what they had in mind, that they like to think of themselves as cutting edge and you're, well . . . more old school."

Old school meaning old, Sean translates silently.

"Try not to take it personally, Sean. And don't get discouraged. You know how these things work."

"Of course," Sean says.

"We'll keep trying."

"Of course," he says again, pocketing the phone and retrieving his credit card from the waitress, then exiting the restaurant before he can burst into tears.

He's halfway down the street when he hears someone shout his name and turns to see the waitress from Ta-boo running after him.

"Mr. Grant! Mr. Grant!"

Dear God, was there a problem with his credit card?

The waitress's arm extends toward him as she draws closer. "I'm so glad I caught you," she says, handing over the bag from Ferragamo. "I'm sure you don't want to forget this."

CHAPTER ELEVEN

Mark stands in the doorway to his grand-mother's bedroom, watching her sleep. It's after ten in the morning, and this is the first time he's been up before her. For a few seconds, he worries that she may have died in her sleep, and then where would he be? Because then for sure his father would put the house up for sale, and he'd be out on his ear. Unless of course Julia left him the house in her will, in which case they'd probably suspect he had something to do with her death.

Either way, he'd be screwed.

So he hopes she won't go and die on him. Not yet anyway. Not till he has everything figured out.

He feels a jolt of shame, like an electrical charge. What's the matter with him? His grandmother loves him unconditionally. She's been the one constant in his life. Probably his only friend in the world. And he loves her. He would be devastated if anything happened to her.

"Mark?"

The disembodied voice catches him off guard and he jumps.

"What are you doing there?"

"Nana! You scared me."

Julia Fisher sits up in bed, the white bedsheets falling to her waist, revealing the wrinkled skin above the scooped neck of her pink nightgown and a vague outline of the pendulous breasts beneath. "Is everything okay?"

"I was worried about you," he says, entering the room and perching at the foot of her queen-size bed. "You don't usually sleep this late."

Julia glances toward the clock beside the bed. "My goodness. Is it really after ten o'clock?"

"Are you feeling all right?"

"I couldn't sleep, so I took a sleeping pill around two," she says without really answering the question. "Probably not a great idea."

"It seems like you take a lot of pills, Nana," Mark says. "How many do you take, exactly?"

"Well, let's see." Julia raises both hands into the air, counting down the number of pills on misshapen fingers. "There's one for my cholesterol, one for my blood pressure, one for my thyroid, several for my arthritis, one for my bones, half a dozen vitamins, and the occasional Tylenol and sleeping pill as required." She shrugs. "Ah, the joys of aging. It's true what they say, you know — getting old is not for sissies."

"You're no sissy, that's for sure."

"Thank you, sweetie. Is that coffee I smell?"

Mark smiles. "It is. And I was thinking of trying out this recipe I saw on TV for lemon-ricotta pancakes. How does that sound to you?"

"Sounds like heaven. Let me shower and get dressed, and I'll see you downstairs in about fifteen minutes."

Mark moves quickly to her side. "Can I help you?"

"Not on your life," Julia warns. "I'm still quite capable of getting out of bed on my own. Go on now, scoot. Get busy on those pancakes."

Mark leaves his grandmother's side and steps into the hall, where he stands, waiting, until he hears the door to her bathroom close and the shower start. But instead of going downstairs, he returns to the bedroom and tiptoes to the dresser opposite the bed.

Glancing repeatedly over his shoulder, he begins rifling through the bureau's three drawers, hoping to find anything of value, something he can pawn that won't be missed. He's already spent most of the money he stole from Poppy's purse. Luckily, math isn't Poppy's strongest suit or she might have noticed earlier that the forty dollars he recently pilfered was the least of what he's taken over the last six months. But now that bank has closed and he needs money to pay his dealer. What's that old saying — "A day without orange juice is like a day without sunshine"? More like a day without weed.

And his supply is running perilously low.

Too bad opioids aren't part of Julia's daily regimen. Painkillers like Percodan or Oxy would be worth a lot on the black market, whereas he doubts he'd get a whole lot for thyroid medication and pills to lower cholesterol. Still, the sleeping pills might be worth something and something's better than nothing. He should be able to sneak a few out of their bottle without his grandmother being any the wiser. She's probably better off without them anyway.

Except she doesn't keep the pills in her dresser, he discovers, finding nothing but clothing in the top two drawers. "But what have we here?" he mutters, his hand hitting something hard beneath a tangle of undergarments. He pushes the bras and panties aside to reveal a cardboard shoebox.

Inside it, he finds a stack of papers and documents, including his grandfather's death certificate, his driver's license, and Social Security number. He might be able to get something for these. From what he understands, identity theft is a big business these days. Except then someone using his grandfather's identity might just steal the house right out from under him. So, that's not a viable option, Mark decides, returning the papers to the box and closing its lid.

"But what's this?" he whispers, opening the bottom drawer to find another box, this one larger and made of leather. He lowers himself to the well-worn carpet, balancing on the balls of his feet, and opens it, then falls back in horror as the stirring chorus of Beethoven's "Ode to Joy" fills the room. "Shit!" he says, snapping the box shut, silencing it. A goddamn music box! "Fuck!"

His eyes shoot toward the bathroom. The shower is still running, so there's little chance Julia would have heard the unexpected outburst. "Goddamn it!" He needs to be more careful. If Julia catches him going through her things, he'll lose the last ally he has.

Still, he saw something in that split second between opening the box and slamming it shut. What?

Something gold, he's almost sure of that. A bracelet? Maybe a watch? Jewelry of some sort, anyway. He could certainly pawn that. The only jewelry he sees his grandmother wear are small gold hoop earrings and the wide gold wedding band she never takes off, probably because it's buried so deep inside the folds of her flesh, she likely couldn't remove it if she tried. Would she even notice anything was missing?

He stares at the closed bathroom door. The shower is still running. Can he risk opening the damn box again to check things out? How long does the stupid music last?

He balances the box on his knees, cradling it to his chest and surrounding it with his arms to muffle the sound. Then he closes his eyes, says a silent prayer, and lifts the lid, the music vibrating against the cotton of his black T-shirt. *Shit, shit, shit,* he thinks, opening his eyes and staring at the delicate gold-and-diamond bracelet inside a tangle of thin gold chains. He lifts the items into his hands, understanding that it will take hours to separate them. Hours he doesn't have.

Which means it's all or nothing.

Obviously, his grandmother doesn't wear any of these things. But that doesn't mean she doesn't look at them, or that she might not notice them missing. He might get away with taking one gold chain. Maybe even two. But not the whole damn thing. He needs to untangle them, which means he needs time, time when his grandmother is out of the house. Which isn't often. Since he moved in, there have been maybe half a dozen times when she's gone out without him.

"It's so nice having someone to go grocery shopping with," she said to him just yesterday inside Publix. "Your grandfather always refused to go."

To which he'd replied, "It's my pleasure, Nana."

And, to his great surprise, it was.

So, what's he doing squatting on her bedroom floor, going through her belongings, looking for stuff to steal? "Some grandson you are," he says, realizing that not only has the music stopped, but the shower as well.

"Shit!" He shoves the music box back inside the drawer and pushes the drawer shut, clambering to his feet as the bathroom door opens.

"Mark!" his grandmother says, clearly nonplussed by his presence. She is wrapped in a towel and surrounded by steam, giving her a vaguely ghostlike aura. "What's going on? Is something wrong?"

"No. Nothing's wrong. When I got downstairs, I realized I dropped my phone." He pulls it out of the pocket of his skinny jeans and holds it up. "Found it right here on the floor."

"You kids and your phones," Julia says, shaking her head. "Good thing I put on a towel or you would have had a very nasty surprise."

Good thing I'm such a good liar, Mark thinks.

"I saw this birthday card once," she continues in the next breath. "It said 'Happy Birthday! You have the body of a thirty-year-old.' Then you opened it up and it said, 'Give it back. You're getting it all wrinkled!' " She laughs.

"I like your wrinkles," he tells her, one of the few truthful things he's said all morning.

"Thank you, darling."

The phone rings.

Julia walks to the nightstand beside her bed and lifts the phone to her ear. "Hello?" Her expression quickly changes from curiosity to fear. "What? Who is this? What are you saying?"

"Who is it?" Mark asks.

Julia lowers the phone to her chest, her face awash with worry. "Some man. He says he's with the IRS and I owe all sorts of money, and if I don't pay up immediately, I'll be arrested."

"Give me that." Mark grabs the phone. "Listen, you asshole —" He stops abruptly, then slams down the receiver.

"Oh my goodness! Should you have done that?"

"It's a scam, Nana."

"A scam?"

"And it was a recording. Couldn't you tell?"

"A recording? No. I just heard this angry voice and I got so scared. You're sure it's a scam?"

"Positive. The IRS doesn't leave recorded messages."

"Oh my. He gave me such a fright." She glares at the phone. "Asshole!" she shouts toward it.

Mark laughs. "You tell 'em, Nana."

She walks to her grandson's side, burrowing in against him. His arm automatically wraps around her bare shoulders and he feels the dampness of her skin through his

128

thin T-shirt. "What about those pancakes?" she asks.

He hugs her tighter. "Coming right up."

CHAPTER TWELVE

Heidi pulls into her driveway and shuts off the car's engine, a buzz of anticipation building in her chest. What's that old saying — "Today is the first day of the rest of your life"? Well, it's today. And starting today, things in the Young household are going to be very different.

She's been thinking about it all afternoon. The store was exceptionally quiet, which meant she'd spent most of her time straightening the various display tables and standing around, trying to look busy. Which gave her a lot of time to think. Which was when a plan started taking shape in her head.

There were things she could control, she decided, and things she couldn't. And she couldn't just keep complaining about her mother-in-law, hoping that things would change, because they wouldn't. That's not the way things worked. No, if she wanted a different relationship with Lisa, she'd have to be more — what was the word? — *proactive.* You can't change other people, she remembered hearing on *Dr. Phil;* you can only change yourself.

So change she will. Starting today, she will be the daughter-in-law of Lisa's dreams. She will prove to the woman how much she loves her son, that she is all the wife a man — and his mother — could ask for. She will listen when Lisa speaks, she won't argue when she disagrees, she will appreciate and take to heart any help and/or advice that her mother-in-law offers.

Through renewed determination and sheer force of will, she will make Lisa love her.

Even if it kills her.

She's already taken the first step, phoning Lisa from work and inviting her over for dinner tonight, a gourmet feast she intends to prepare all by herself. So what if she isn't much of a cook, and her specialty thus far has been hot dogs and baked beans? How hard can it be?

Aiden's shift doesn't end till seven o'clock, and Lisa, after graciously accepting Heidi's impromptu invitation, has offered to pick her son up from the mall so he won't have to Uber home. "That's so thoughtful of you," Heidi told her, almost giddy with the thought that her plan already seemed to be working.

Heidi climbs out of the car's front seat and opens the rear door, extricating the two bags of groceries she purchased at Whole Foods on her way home from work. Chicken, fruit, lots of healthy fresh vegetables. Surely she'll have no trouble finding an easy recipe online.

"Can I give you a hand?" she hears someone ask.

She pivots around to find a skinny young man walking toward her. A little unkempt, she thinks, but sexy in that *I don't give a shit* kind of way. Early twenties, she thinks. Not that much younger than she is. Jeans very tight and slung a little too low, hair a little too scruffy, a little too long. She's seen him with the old lady who lives next door a few times the last couple of weeks and assumed he's either a relative or someone she hired to give her a hand around the house.

"Hi," he says now, stepping around the Hyundai to introduce himself. "Mark Fisher, Julia's grandson."

"Nice to meet you, Mark. I'm Heidi. Heidi Young."

"The newlywed," he says with a grin. "My grandmother gave me the rundown on all the neighbors."

"Yeah? What'd she say?"

"That's about it." He shrugs, the grin expanding, stretching toward his ears. "She left out how pretty you are."

Heidi laughs, flattered despite the obviousness of the line. "Yeah, well." She laughs again, this time more of a girlish giggle. "Guess I should get these groceries inside."

"Here," he says, lifting the bags from her hands before she has a chance to object. "Let me help you."

Heidi fishes inside her purse for her keys and opens the front door, leading the young man through the hall into the kitchen.

"Wow," Mark says. "Looks just like my nana's house."

"You call your grandmother Nana?"

"Yup. Why? What do you call yours?"

"I don't call them anything. They're both dead."

"That's sad," Mark says, depositing the bags on the kitchen counter.

Heidi shrugs. No point wasting emotions on things she can't change. Concentrate on the things you can. Something else she learned from *Dr. Phil.*

"Looks like someone's planning quite the feast," he remarks, peeking inside the bags.

"I don't know," Heidi admits, feeling less sure of herself now that she's confronted

133

with her purchases. "I invited my mother-in-law for dinner tonight and I may have bitten off more than I can chew. So to speak." She laughs, and is grateful when Mark laughs with her.

"What are you planning on serving?"

"I don't know," Heidi says again, extricating the package of boneless chicken thighs. "Some kind of chicken, I guess."

"Sounds promising."

"Except I have no idea what I'm doing."

"Nonsense. If you can read, you can cook. Where are your recipe books?"

"I don't have any. We usually just pick up something already prepared and throw it in the microwave."

"Then perhaps I can be of help. Let's see what you've got here." Mark lines the groceries up on the counter. "You picked some nice things here. Shouldn't be too hard to pull something together. I assume you have a fry pan and a pot."

"Right here." Heidi quickly opens a nearby cupboard.

"Okay. What do you think of garlic chicken with honey and rosemary over a bed of steamed rice?"

"Seriously?"

"Seriously."

"Sounds complicated."

"It isn't. Come on, I'll talk you through it."

"Seriously?" Heidi asks again.

"I swear, there's nothing to it. You've got all the ingredients right here. And I see you bought blueberries, so how about we finish the meal off with some blueberry bread pudding? You have some day-old bread?"

"Is there any other kind?" Heidi asks, grateful when her question elicits another laugh from Mark.

"Should we get started? And yes," he adds before she can speak, "seriously."

The blueberry bread pudding is in the oven and the garlic chicken has been browned and drizzled with honey and lemon juice, waiting to be put in the oven for a final five minutes before being garnished with rosemary and served.

"I don't know how to thank you," Heidi says for what must be the tenth time in as many minutes. "I can't believe you have all that information at the top of your head."

"Well, there's not a whole lot else in there," Mark demurs. "When does your mother-in-law get here?"

Heidi checks her watch. "She's picking up my husband from work in about an hour."

"Then what do you say we have a little

something to help you unwind?"

"What do you mean?"

Mark opens the palm of his right hand to reveal a fat, hand-rolled cigarette.

"Seriously?"

"Just a little something to take the edge off situations such as this," Mark says.

Heidi glances nervously toward the front door, then down at her watch, then back to the joint in Mark's hands. "You're on," she says, leading him into the den and plopping down on the small navy sectional.

He lights up immediately, taking a deep drag and then passing the joint to her.

Heidi lifts the cigarette to her lips and inhales, feeling the smoke fill her lungs and a welcoming calm almost instantly fill her head. *Just what the doctor ordered,* she thinks, releasing the smoke slowly into the surrounding air.

"Just what the doctor ordered," Mark says out loud.

She smiles and takes another toke before returning the joint to his waiting fingers. "I really can't thank you enough. You saved my life."

"Anytime."

"Where'd you learn all that anyway?"

"TV mostly. The Cooking Channel." He shrugs. "What can I say? It relaxes me."

"Well, you're gonna make some lucky girl a wonderful husband."

"Nah. I'm never getting married."

"Sure, you will."

"No. My dad's been married enough times for both of us."

"Your dad's the one with the Tesla?" Heidi asks.

"The one and only."

"Sounds like the two of you don't get along."

"Let's just say we aren't each other's biggest fans."

"Well, I think it's very nice that you visit your grandmother."

"She's the best. And I'm pretty much living here now," he corrects. "At least for the time being. Till I get my shit together. Which could be a while."

"And speaking of shit, *this* shit is pretty damn amazing."

"That it is."

They continue passing the joint back and forth in silence until it has all but disappeared.

"Oh no. Don't leave us," Heidi says, feeling what's left of the tiny butt burn the tips of her fingers.

"All good things must come to an end," Mark says.

Which is when they hear the front door open.

"Heidi?" a woman's voice calls out.

Heidi is immediately on her feet, spinning around aimlessly, like a top on the verge of toppling over. "Shit, shit, shit, shit!"

"Who is it?"

"It's my mother-in-law. Shit, shit, shit, *shit*!" Heidi checks her watch. Aiden doesn't finish work until seven, and it's just past six-thirty. What is Lisa doing here?

"Heidi? Where are you?"

Heidi swats at the malodorous air, hearing Lisa's footsteps fast approaching. "I'll be right there," she calls out.

But it's too late. Lisa, impeccably dressed in white pants and a floral-print Chanel blouse, every dark hair perfectly in place, is already filling the doorway.

"Good God. What's that awful smell?" she asks, her gaze shifting from Heidi to Mark. "And who are you?"

"This is Mark Fisher," Heidi says. "His grandmother lives next door."

"And you're here because . . . ?"

Heidi, her newfound resolve struggling with the fog in her brain, manages to quell the urge to respond, "And this is your business because . . . ?" Instead she says, "Mark was kind enough to give me a hand with

138

tonight's dinner."

"Really," Lisa states. "And is dinner the cause of this cloying odor?"

"I'm afraid that's on me," Mark interjects. "I had a little puff of something before I stopped by, and I guess my clothes still reek."

"How lovely," Lisa says.

"Is Aiden here?" Heidi asks, trying to see past Lisa's imposing shoulders.

"Your *husband*," Lisa says pointedly, "is still at work. I just stopped by to see if you wanted me to pick up some wine for dinner."

"That's so thoughtful," Heidi says, as she'd said when Lisa offered to pick up Aiden from work. *You could have just called,* she thinks.

"I should go," Mark says.

"Yes, you should," Lisa tells him. "Really, Heidi," her mother-in-law says when he is gone, "do you think it's a good idea to be entertaining young men when your husband isn't here?"

Heidi starts to explain, then stops. "White wine would be lovely," she says instead, refusing to rise to the bait. "We're having garlic chicken with honey and rosemary over a bed of steamed rice."

Silence.

"You know I don't eat garlic," Lisa says finally.

Did I know that? "You don't?" *Since when?*

"It's fine. We can order in."

"But it's already made. And there's not that much garlic. Won't you at least try it?"

"And risk having heartburn all night? I don't think so."

"I'm so sorry. I honestly didn't think . . ."

"Clearly. But it's my fault," Lisa adds, unconvincingly. "I should have reminded you."

"Well, at least there's a delicious blueberry bread pudding for dessert," Heidi offers, feeling the threat of tears building behind her eyes. "No garlic in that."

"No garlic, but hardly worth all the calories! I'll pass, if you don't mind."

Heidi turns away as the tears become a reality. Only after she feels Lisa leave the room and hears the front door open and close does she collapse on the sofa and let them fall.

CHAPTER THIRTEEN

Sean Grant stands at the living room window, staring out at the street. It's almost eleven o'clock and Olivia is already in bed. A large quarter moon sits high and yellow in the sky. Clear, focused, ineffably beautiful. As if it's been photoshopped, he thinks. Picture perfect.

Unlike everything else in his life.

He does a quick scan of the neighboring houses. It's so quiet now. Not that it's ever all that noisy, which is interesting when you count the number of children who live in the small enclave: the two Wilson boys, the two McKay kids, his own three. And now Julia Fisher's grandson, who seems to have taken up permanent residence, although technically he'd qualify as a young adult.

The kid strikes Sean as a troublemaker. What was he doing earlier with that sexy little number from across the street? Sean had been here at the window and he'd witnessed their introductions, then watched the boy take the bags of groceries she was holding and carry them into her house. He'd waited to see him come out again, but after an hour, the kid still hadn't emerged. And then Olivia came home from work, full of questions about his latest round of interviews, and Sean had been forced to abandon his watch.

The kid is definitely playing with fire, Sean decides now, watching hordes of mindless insects buzzing around the lights of the streetlamps. Not the smartest thing in the world to mess around with the wife of an army vet. If the boy isn't careful, he's liable to get himself shot.

A white Lexus is parked in the Youngs' driveway, which means that Lisa — he's pretty sure that's the woman's name — is visiting. Again. She's there so often, she might as well move in. *Nice that she gets on so well with her daughter-in-law,* Sean thinks, wandering into the kitchen and removing the bottle of vodka from the freezer, pouring himself a glass, and downing it in one long, satisfying sip.

He needs to forget all about this miserable day, the string of nonexistent interviews with the company's top honchos he pretended to go on, his subsequent lies to

Olivia, making it sound as if the job at Advert-X was all but in the bag.

Talk about playing with fire! What the hell is he doing?

He's been praying for a miracle, that's what, hoping to have secured another job by now. Or at least a decent prospect. Something tangible. Something real. *Anything.*

"Looks like the job at Advert-X fell through," he could tell his wife then. "But hey, something else has come up. . . ."

At least the lies have forced him to start taking better care of himself, to start shaving every day, to put on some clean clothes. So that's something, he tells himself, trying not to picture that ridiculous linen jacket accumulating wrinkles in the trunk of his car, because there's no way he can risk bringing it inside the house.

"Here's to me," he says, raising his glass in a mock toast. How long does he think he can keep this up? How soon before his lies catch up to him, before Olivia gets wise to his deceit?

What will she do then? Cry? Definitely. Hurl well-deserved obscenities at him? Probably. Pack up the kids and leave? What the hell would he do then?

He pictures the look of disbelief on her

pretty face, watching it morph into anger, and then worse — oh, so much worse — into pity.

I'd rather be dead than see that look, he thinks.

The thought triggers spasms of alarm throughout his body. Although, if he's being honest, Sean has to admit this isn't the first time such thoughts have popped into his head. What good is he after all? What purpose is he serving, now that it doesn't look as if he'll be "bringing home the bacon" anytime soon? Olivia certainly doesn't need him. She's proven that. He can no longer provide for her. And his kids don't need him, other than to pick them up from school. Hell, the insurance money they'd collect from his death would be more than enough to pay for a chauffeur.

Does his insurance policy cover death by suicide? he wonders, warming to the idea of his death as he downs another glass of vodka. If it doesn't, he'd just have to figure out a way to make said suicide look like an accident. He returns the bottle to the freezer before the urge hits to have another. The bottle is edging close to empty. *I notice we're running low on vodka,* he can hear Olivia say, and he laughs, although the laugh is joyless, a hollow bark that scratches at the air like

144

the claws of a cat.

He grabs his laptop from where it's charging on the kitchen counter and opens it, typing in *ways to commit suicide that don't look like suicide.* Immediately, the screen fills with information and suggestions, some straightforward, others pretty far out there. The more practical include drowning, which wouldn't be difficult to accomplish, considering that he lives in Florida and the ocean is only minutes away. The fact that he's an accomplished swimmer means relatively little, given the ocean's strength and unpredictability. Still, he's not sure his survival instinct wouldn't kick in at the last minute. He suspects it's not that easy to purposely drown.

There are also snake and spider bites to consider, along with being eaten by an alligator, although none of these strikes Sean as a particularly pleasant way to go. He's always been terrified of snakes, wouldn't know a poisonous spider from its harmless relation, and short of throwing himself into the Everglades, he imagines that the chances of being eaten by an alligator are slim to none.

Poisonous plants are offered as another option. But Sean knows next to nothing about plants in general, and despite the plethora of recipes he finds for concocting lethal soups and salads, he's come to despise any form of meal preparation in these prolonged months of forced unemployment. Besides, poisoning suggests intense stomach pain, and there's no guarantee that, before dying, he might not spend endless hours throwing up, a thought even worse than death.

There are also recipes for making deadly hydrogen sulfide gas by mixing toilet cleaner with pesticide, recipes for cyanide poisoning, and suggestions for concocting a deadly combination of ricin and castor oil, all of which seem needlessly time-consuming and complicated. But wait — there's a book that makes all this easier to navigate: *Suicide for Dummies.*

Perfect, Sean thinks, laughing and closing the laptop. *Probably easier to just hire a hit man to murder me,* he decides, then laughs again, knowing he has no money to hire a hit man. Maybe his would-be killer would consider a designer jacket instead?

He's suddenly reminded of a wild story he read online a few years back. A man, right here in Palm Beach Gardens, was discovered lying dead by the side of PGA Boulevard at around six o'clock one morning, a bullet in his chest. He'd been on his way to meet friends for their regular morning cup of coffee, and when he didn't show, the police were called and his body was quickly discovered. His wallet was missing, indicating he'd been killed during the commission of a robbery.

But it eventually came to light that the man had, in fact, committed suicide by fastening a gun to a helium-filled balloon, then shooting himself in the heart, the balloon carrying the weapon off into the sky as the man dropped lifeless to the ground. Apparently, he'd gotten the idea from watching an old episode of *CSI: Miami*.

Ingenious, Sean thinks, although it's unlikely the trick would fool anyone twice. Hell, it hadn't even fooled them once!

Besides, he doesn't own a gun.

Not that it would be difficult to buy one. He'd have no trouble passing the background check, having no criminal record and no history of mental illness. And this is Florida, after all, where guns are as accessible as gummy bears. He reopens his computer, types in *guns,* and immediately finds his screen flooded with sites to visit. "Whoa," he says, his mind unable to absorb so many options.

Not that he could afford most of the weapons he sees on display. Shit — he'd had no idea how much some of these things cost.

Although most are considerably cheaper than that stupid jacket he bought, he thinks, and almost laughs.

"Sean," Olivia calls from the top of the stairs. "Aren't you coming to bed?"

Damn it. He hoped she'd be asleep by now. "Be up in a minute," he calls back.

"What are you doing?"

"Just reading up on Advert-X. Be right there."

He takes a deep breath and pushes away from the table, experiencing an overwhelming wave of fatigue as he fishes for a mint in his pocket and pops it into his mouth, hoping to disguise any telltale hint of alcohol on his breath.

He mounts the stairs, each step feeling as if he's walking through freshly poured cement, then peeks in on his three children, Zane and Quentin in their beds, side by side, Katie in her four-poster princess bed in the smaller room next to theirs. Still so sweet, so trusting, so innocent. Is he seriously considering saddling them with the stigma, the guilt, of his suicide? Would they grow up to blame themselves, or worse, to hate his memory?

Maybe it would be better for all concerned

if he took them with him.

"What the hell's the matter with you?" he whispers, genuinely horrified by the thoughts swirling through his addled brain, hoping it's the alcohol that's responsible. *Who knows what evil lurks in the hearts of men?* he hears his father whisper in his ear. "The Shadow . . ." Sean mutters, the word freezing on his lips when he enters his bedroom and sees his wife.

She's standing beside the bed, wearing makeup and a pink satin corset trimmed in black lace, the same black lace as her thong. A garter belt holds up a pair of sheer black stockings, her shapely legs disappearing inside a pair of open-toed silver high heels. Thick brown hair falls around her shoulders and a pair of long rhinestone earrings dangle from her ears.

"What's this?" he asks, although the answer is obvious.

"You like?"

He feels a welcome stirring in his pants. "I do."

"I thought that since your interviews today went so well, you deserved a treat."

His erection immediately disappears.

Not that Olivia doesn't work hard to revive it, doing all the things she knows he likes, the things that always helped before as well as a few new things, things that make him wonder where she picked them up. Is she having an affair? he finds himself thinking, as she continues trying to arouse him. Nothing works. Not her fingers, not her mouth, not her tongue.

"I don't think it's going to happen," he says finally, pulling away. "Sorry, hon."

"You don't have to apologize," she says, her voice quivering. "It happens."

"I'm just so tired. I guess I didn't realize how much those interviews today took out of me."

She smiles through the tears he sees forming. "No problem. I understand."

"We'll try again another time."

"Absolutely."

She retreats to their en suite bathroom, and when she comes out a few minutes later, her face has been freshly scrubbed, and she's wearing a shapeless cotton nightshirt. She climbs into bed beside him, giving him a quick peck on the cheek before turning away from him to lie on her side. He hears her sniffling quietly under the covers, pretending everything is all right, that it's no big deal. Too polite to say what she's really thinking: that he's disappointed her yet again, that she will simply add his shortcomings in bed to his ever-expanding list of failures.

He waits until he knows she's asleep before climbing out of bed, going back downstairs, and pouring himself another drink. He wonders again how long he can keep lying to his wife, and how Olivia will react when she discovers the truth. How understanding will she be then?

Although she bears at least part of the blame for his falsehoods, doesn't she?

Maybe if she'd pushed more, told him to get his head out of his ass and face reality sooner, insisted he take whatever crappy job he could get his hands on, then none of these lies would be necessary. Instead, she encouraged him to take his time, dream big, not settle. And she'd looked so hopeful when he landed that initial interview at Advert-X. So, how could he disappoint her?

Except that's exactly what he's done, he knows, picturing her standing beside their bed in an outfit that, at one time, would have driven him wild.

He grabs his laptop from the kitchen counter and logs in to his favorite porn site, finding a buxom young woman who looks vaguely like his young neighbor, and quickly brings himself to orgasm. Feeling a fresh wave of self-loathing, he closes the computer, returns the bottle of vodka to the freezer, and goes back upstairs to bed.

He climbs in beside Olivia, his arm reaching across her waist to pull her close, his nostrils inhaling a trace of the perfume she was unable to wash away. "Forgive me," he whispers into the nape of her neck. "There is no job. I'm a liar and a fraud."

"Hmm?" Olivia murmurs, her voice coated in sleep. "Did you say something?"

A second of silence follows.

"Just that I love you," he tells her.

He feels her smile. "I love you, too."

CHAPTER FOURTEEN

She's dreaming about being stuck in an elevator with a group of women she doesn't know. They are speaking a language she doesn't recognize or understand, and seem blissfully unaware they're not moving. "Excuse me," she tells them, trying to push her way through the crowd to the doors. One of the women swivels toward her. "You're wearing very strong perfume," she chastises her in perfect English. "I'm afraid you'll have to leave." The doors to the elevator suddenly open and the woman pushes Heidi into the wire-filled black abyss.

Heidi bolts up in bed. "Holy crap," she says when she can find her voice. She takes a series of deep breaths, feeling the nightmare break into pixels around her, until there is nothing left but the dark hole she fell into. "Aiden?" she whispers, peering through the darkness for her husband, seeking the reassurance of his strong arms.

Except he isn't there.

Heidi reaches over to turn on the lamp beside the bed. The lamp looks like a rectangular block of ice topped by an oblong black shade, and Heidi has never liked it. It's too modern for her taste and the black shade guarantees very little light escapes. "It's more than enough light," Lisa had insisted when she selected it over the white-shaded, floral porcelain lamp that Heidi preferred. "It's a bedroom. You don't need it too bright."

"What if I want to read in bed?" Heidi recalls asking.

Lisa hadn't bothered to respond. Her dubiously raised right eyebrow said it all.

"Aiden?" Heidi says again, looking toward the bathroom. But the bathroom door is open and it's obvious Aiden isn't there. Which means he's probably downstairs watching TV, something he often does when his own nightmares keep him from sleeping. But it's almost four A.M. If he doesn't come back to bed soon, he'll have a hard time getting up in the morning, which would make him late for work, putting yet another job at risk.

And what would Lisa, sleeping off too much to drink at dinner in the bedroom down the hall, say about that? Whatever it would be, Heidi was sure she would get the blame.

She lies back down, trying to clear her mind of all things Lisa. But Lisa is as stubborn in the abstract as she is in the flesh, and she isn't about to be so easily dismissed.

They'd ended up ordering ribs for dinner. "Please don't be mad," Aiden whispered to his wife out of his mother's earshot. "We'll have what you made tomorrow. It looks really good."

Heidi watched Lisa devour her entire order of ribs, the fact that they were loaded with garlic not seeming to bother her in the slightest. Then she carried the bottle of wine into the living room and plopped herself down in front of the TV, insisting they watch some boring documentary on the Second World War, before drifting off when it was only halfway through.

Heidi had tried to change the channel, hoping to salvage at least part of the evening by catching the last half of *The Real Housewives,* when Lisa suddenly sprang to life. "What are you doing?" she'd demanded. "I'm watching that."

"You were asleep."

"I was just resting my eyes. One can listen with one's eyes closed, you know."

One can also fuck off, Heidi thought, having to bite her tongue to keep from saying it out loud, remembering her resolve to win Lisa over.

"Is there something you'd rather watch?" Lisa asked her son.

"No," Aiden said, deliberately ignoring the obvious plea in Heidi's eyes. "This is fine."

"It wouldn't hurt you to learn a little history," Lisa said to Heidi. "Wasn't it Winston Churchill who said, 'Those who ignore history are condemned to repeat it'?"

"Yes, I believe he did," Heidi said, although the truth was that she had no idea what he'd said. She wasn't even sure who this Winston Churchill guy was.

Of course, by the time the show ended at eleven o'clock, Lisa announced she was too tired and too drunk to drive home and would be spending the night in one of the spare bedrooms. "I might as well get used to it," she'd said on her way up the stairs.

"What did your mother mean, she might as well get used to it?" Heidi asked as soon as she and Aiden were alone.

"You know," he said, refusing to meet her gaze.

"I don't know."

"She's moving in for a few weeks."

"What?"

"I told you."

"You never did!"

Aiden glanced toward their closed bed-room door, as if afraid his mother might be eavesdropping in the hall. "Don't go getting all upset. It's just for a few weeks, while her kitchen's being renovated."

"Shit!" Heidi exclaimed. "When is this happening?"

"Not for at least another month. Probably July."

"July," Heidi repeated.

"It'll just be for a couple of weeks."

"Renovations always take longer than they say they will. She's liable to be here all summer."

"What do you want me to do?" Aiden asked, helplessly. "She's my mother and she paid for this place. The house is in her name. You want me to tell her she's not welcome?"

That's exactly what I want you to tell her, Heidi thought, knowing her husband could never do this. "Okay," she said. "We'll find a way to make it work."

"You're the best," Aiden said, snuggling up against her in bed.

Heidi immediately flipped over to face him, her hand reaching out to stroke him. There was no reason for the night to be a total waste. And the marijuana had made

157

her horny.

"I don't think it's such a good idea," he said, stilling her hand.

"Why not?"

"You know . . ." Again he looked toward the hall. "She could hear. . . ."

Heidi flipped back onto her other side. *I might as well get used to it,* she thought, Lisa's words echoing in her ears as she drifted off to sleep.

No wonder I had a nightmare, Heidi thinks now, glancing at her bedside clock and noting that another half hour has passed and Aiden still isn't beside her. She gets out of bed, throws a short robe over her naked body, and pads down the hall, stopping at the top of the staircase, listening for the muted sounds of the TV. But she hears nothing. "Aiden?" she whispers as she reaches the bottom of the steps and proceeds into the living room.

But the room is dark and the television is off. "Aiden?" she calls again, approaching the kitchen. But he's not there either. Is it possible he went outside?

She opens the front door and looks around, the warm night air wrapping around her shoulders like a shawl. The moon is a gorgeous yellow crescent in the sky, shining a spotlight on the quiet neighborhood. *Of course it's quiet,* she thinks. *It's four-thirty in the morning. Everyone is asleep.*

Except Aiden.

Where the hell is he?

Lisa's car is in the driveway, which means that their Hyundai is still in the garage. Which means that unless Aiden is out somewhere prowling the streets in his underwear, he's somewhere in the house.

Maybe even back in bed, she decides, ascending the stairs. But a quick peek into their bedroom reveals he isn't there. She moves to the smaller of the two other bedrooms, but the double bed in the center of the room is untouched and empty except for a dozen decorative throw pillows atop its billowy white comforter.

She proceeds slowly to the last bedroom, reluctant to open the door, lest she rouse her mother-in-law. Lisa will no doubt blame her for Aiden's disappearance. Still, what choice does she have?

Slowly, quietly, Heidi opens the bedroom door.

She sees him immediately.

He is standing at the foot of the queen-size bed, staring at the woman sleeping on her side under the covers, unaware of his presence.

"Aiden?" Heidi whispers, tiptoeing toward him.

He doesn't move, his gaze locked on his mother's face.

"Aiden, honey. What are you doing?" She moves to his side, recognizing from the blank look in his eyes that he is in some sort of trance, that he likely has no idea where he is or what is taking place. Probably back in Afghanistan or some other godforsaken place. "Let's get you back to bed," she says, stepping behind him, trying to guide him from the room. Her fingers reach for his.

Which is when she feels the gun in his hand.

Oh God. What's happening?

What the hell is he doing? More important, what the hell is *she* supposed to do now?

She thinks of running, of leaving Aiden to his mother and whatever crazy thoughts are going through his brain. *Is he really thinking of shooting her?* Then, in the next second, she decides that this is all part of her nightmare, that none of it is actually happening.

Except it *is* happening, and she knows it. This might be a nightmare, but it is no dream. The gun in Aiden's hand is real. And as much as the thought of a world without Lisa is very appealing, the thought of her husband spending the rest of his life in prison is not.

"Aiden, honey," she says, her voice as soothing as her panic will allow. "Give me the gun, sweetie. You're safe here. You don't need this."

Several excruciating seconds pass until the grip of his hand on the gun loosens and she is able to pry the weapon from his fingers. He smiles at her as she slips it inside the side pocket of her robe and leads him from the room.

"What's going on?" he asks as she is tucking him under the covers of their bed.

"You had a bad dream," she tells him.

"Did I?"

"You were sleepwalking. You don't remember?"

He shakes his head. "Not a thing."

Heidi removes the gun from her pocket and returns it to the case in the bottom drawer of their dresser. She climbs into bed beside her husband and surrounds him with her arms. "Get some sleep," she says.

CHAPTER FIFTEEN

Nick Wilson pulls his car into the parking lot of Straight Shooters of West Palm Beach, located near the intersection of Dixie Highway and Forty-fifth Street, and shuts off the engine. "Okay. Everybody out."

Ben immediately scrambles out of the backseat, racing toward the front door of the squat ecru-colored building.

"Are you sure this is such a good idea?" Dani asks her husband. Despite his threatening to do this for weeks, she'd kept hoping he'd think better of the idea. She glances back at Tyler. The boy has remained seated, his eyes reflecting a similar concern. In fact, he looks terrified.

"I thought we settled that once and for all this morning," Nick says, his voice weary.

"I know, but . . . I'm thinkin' they're still so young, and Ben's no bigger than a minnow in a fishin' pond. . . ."

"He's as tall as required, and you're never

too young to learn how to defend yourself. What's happening back there, Goldilocks? Why are you still in the car?"

Tyler hesitates. "I can't undo my seatbelt."

"Really?" Nick leans over the top of the seat, reaches behind him, and unsnaps the belt. "Was that so hard?"

"Nick, honey," his wife whispers as Tyler is closing the door behind him, "you know he doesn't like it when you call him Goldilocks."

"You trying to tell me how to talk to my own son?"

"No. I'm just sayin' . . ."

"Well, don't. Just shut up and get out of the car."

Dani's eyes fill with tears. The last thing she wanted to do was upset him all over again. Her cheek is still stinging from the slap he delivered this morning when she'd suggested possibly going to the beach instead, a slap so hard her ears are still ringing.

"What happened to your face?" Tyler asked as she was preparing breakfast.

She tried to shrug it off. "I walked into the side of the bathroom door. You know me, I'm so clumsy."

"You're not clumsy," Tyler said.

"Come on, everybody," Ben calls now

from the front door of the gun shop.

"Don't question my judgment in front of the kids ever again," Nick warns as he comes around the passenger side to grab Dani's elbow and pull her from the car.

What's the matter with me? Why do I deliberately provoke him? Dani wonders as he slams the door after her, then stops suddenly.

"Shit," he says.

"What?"

"Tire's looking a little flat."

"Really? It looks okay to —" She stops when she realizes Nick is already walking away.

The sign on the front door reads, *No loaded firearms please,* an irony that manages to elicit a small smile from Dani despite her discomfort. The smile tugs at her wounded cheek.

The first thing she sees upon entering the enormous square-shaped room is a giant stuffed grizzly bear with an accompanying sign warning visitors not to touch. *Why?* she wonders. *Will it bite?* She quickly discovers that the whole place is filled with the stuffed remains of dead animals: dozens of antelope heads mounted on the walls, entire bobcats, ibexes, and wolves standing guard at multiple intervals along the concrete floor.

And guns. Guns of every shape and size. Guns everywhere: on the walls, on the shelves, in countless display counters throughout the store. The tune to "Old MacDonald Had a Farm" begins wafting through Dani's brain.

Here a gun, there a gun, everywhere a gun, gun.

"Impressive, isn't it?" Nick says, interrupting the silent refrain and approaching the long counter that loops through the middle of the room. Two men stand in the middle of the loop, serving customers on both sides.

Dani marvels that, at just past ten on a hot and humid Saturday morning, the place is already crowded.

"Hi, there, Doc," the older of the two clerks says in greeting. The name tag on his orange vest identifies him as Wes. He's about fifty and sports a barely there brush cut and a tiny diamond stud in his left ear. "I see you brought the whole family with you this morning."

"Been meaning to do it for a long time," Nick tells him, motioning toward Ben. "Just waiting for this one to get tall enough to see over the railing. Ben, get over here. Say hello to Wes."

165

"Hi," Ben says. "This is a really neat place."

"Thank you, son. You gonna learn to shoot like your daddy?"

"Yup," Ben says proudly.

"And this is my wife, Dani, and my older son, Tyler."

"Very pleased to meet you," Wes says. "We all gonna hit the range today?"

"That's the general idea." Nick hands Wes his membership card. "We'll need four guns for one hour. Two stalls should do it."

Wes glances toward the shooting range behind the glass wall opposite the counter. "I think we can manage that."

"How much do I owe you?"

"I'm assuming both kids are under twelve?"

Nick nods.

"Then it's seven-fifty each," Wes says. "Fifteen for the missus. You should come on Mondays," he tells Dani. "Ladies shoot free on Mondays."

"I'll keep that in mind."

"Think these .22 handguns would work best for the wife and kids," Wes says to Nick, laying three such guns on the glass counter-top, along with the appropriate ammunition. "They're lightweight, not a lot of recoil. Should be pretty easy for them to

166

fire. Just got to line your sights up to the target," he says, leaning over the counter to demonstrate to Dani and the boys how it should be done, "and then just let 'em rip. And watch out," he warns, " 'cause the bullet casings go flying all over the place."

Ben laughs. "Let 'em rip," he repeats.

"And I got your favorite .38 right here, Doc."

"Thank you kindly, as my wife would say." Nick puts his arm around Dani's waist, pulls her close. "Right, sweetheart?"

"Right," she echoes.

"You got a real good man here," Wes tells Dani. "Not everyone is as concerned as the doc here about his family's welfare."

Dani nods. He's right after all. Her husband is a real good man. Everybody says so.

"Are these animals real?" Ben asks.

"Well, they *were*," Wes explains. "Till someone shot 'em and stuffed 'em."

"Cool," says Ben. "Hey, I have an idea. We should stuff our fish."

"Shut up, Ben," Tyler says, the first words out of his mouth since they entered the place. "That's not funny."

"Is, too," Ben says, doing a three-sixty surveillance of the premises.

Dani follows her son's eyes with her own. Mixed in with the seemingly endless display

167

of guns and rifles are cabinets filled with knives of every shape and size. *A regular cornucopia of death,* Dani thinks, as Wes lays four sets of headphones on the counter.

"What are these for?" Ben asks.

"They're to protect your ears," Wes states, warming to his role as instructor. "Guns are really loud and we got ten stalls back there, most of them occupied. Wouldn't want you going deaf and suing us. So, you put these on," he says, "and when you get inside the shooting range, you press this button here on the side. You'll hear a beep, and then you'll be able to hear talking but not the gun shots. You got glasses? 'Cause you need to protect your eyes, too. If you don't have any, I got some here."

"We'll need three pairs," Nick says. "I brought my own."

Wes deposits the protective glasses on the counter beside the headphones and guns. "Okay, so I'm assuming none of you smokes, 'cause we got a strict no-smoking policy. Those things'll kill you surer than anything we sell in here. Right, Doc?"

"No arguments from me on that score," Nick concurs.

"Nasty, nasty habit. And no chewing gum once you pass through those doors." He points toward the doors leading to the shooting range. "You want to know why?" he asks, directing his question to Tyler and Ben.

"Why?" Ben obliges him by asking.

"It's because of the lead in the ammunition. You don't want to be opening and closing your mouth too often, letting all that lead poison in. You can talk and stuff. Just try not to open your mouth too wide."

"Won't be a problem," Ben tells him. "We aren't allowed to chew gum."

"My wife's a dentist," Nick explains.

"Is that right? Well, good for you," Wes says, as if Dani has just received an A on a spelling test.

"A damn good one, too," Nick says. "You ever need any work done, she's the one to see. You have a business card you can give the man, honey?"

Seriously? Dani wonders, thinking that this morning is becoming increasingly surreal. "No. I didn't bring any with me."

"Should always carry some with you. Just in case. I've told you that."

"I know. I just keep forgettin'. Forgett*ing*," she corrects.

"I gotta admit, I'm not too fond of dentists," Wes says, winking at Dani. "But it's nice to see a husband so proud of his wife."

Dani forces a smile onto her lips.

"Can we go shoot now?" Ben whines, pulling on Nick's arm.

"Hold your horses," Wes admonishes. "First you gotta pick out what kind of target you're gonna shoot at. You got two choices. This one" — he holds up a shiny laminated square containing a small, bright orange bull's-eye in the center of a series of black concentric circles against a lime-green background — "or this one." He offers up a larger sheet, this one displaying the outline of a man's head and torso against an all-white background.

"I want that one," says Ben.

Nick chuckles. "You heard the man. We'll take two."

"Then you're all set," Wes says, watching as everyone grabs their headphones and protective glasses and Nick retrieves their weapons. "Just remember to wash your hands real good with the special soap in the bathrooms when you're done," he warns, " 'cause you don't want any of that lead sinking into your skin."

Does no one else see the irony here? Dani wonders.

"Stalls seven and eight," Wes says. "Now go in there and . . ."

"Let 'em rip," says Ben, racing for the door to the shooting range.

170

"Do we have to?" Tyler whispers to Dani.

"Is there a problem?" Nick asks.

"No problem." Dani pushes her older son gently forward. "Let's just do this real quick like a bunny," she whispers, as Nick opens the first of two doors leading to the range. They wait in the small glass enclosure for the first door to fully close before the second one opens.

The shooting range itself is mostly concrete and predominantly black and gray in color. A long gray rubber wall at the far end serves as a buffer for the bullets to bounce off. The area is well ventilated, air-conditioned, and soundproofed to the outside world.

A red-and-yellow sign on one wall states: *!!Warning!! Tracer and Incendiary Ammunition Are Not Permitted.* Another advises: *For your safety and the safety of others, No Tracer Ammunition, No Reload Ammunition, No Armor Piercing, No Exceptions.*

Inside, the noise from the weapons being discharged is overwhelming. "Quick, put on your headphones," Dani says, securing her own and remembering to press the button on its side so they can communicate with one another. They dodge an explosion of empty bullet casings as they hurry toward stalls seven and eight, the smell of gunfire reaching so deep into Dani's nostrils that she has to fight the urge to gag.

"You and Goldilocks take stall eight," Nick instructs his wife. "I'll get Ben started, then come back."

Tyler appeals to Dani with his eyes, and Dani replies with a silent plea of her own. *Just go along,* her eyes say. *You know that if I had my druthers, we'd be anyplace but here.*

"I don't need help," Ben announces. "I already know what to do."

"Easy there, cowboy," Nick says, clipping the targets to their respective wires and adjusting their distance. "That should do it. Okay, tough guy," he says to Ben, his voice filled with unmistakable pride. "Show me what you've got."

CHAPTER SIXTEEN

Maggie is walking up and down the aisles at Publix, hoping to see something that will twig her memory, remind her why she is here, what groceries she came in for. Damn it. Why didn't she make a list?

She hates grocery shopping. Always has. Especially since Craig is no longer around to accompany her. "Really, Maggie," he'd said when they first moved to Palm Beach Gardens. "You have to start doing these things on your own again."

Had he been preparing her even then for his departure?

"Milk, yogurt, lettuce, tomatoes, raisin bread, Cap'n Crunch," she says out loud, counting off the items in her cart, knowing she's leaving out a bunch of essentials. "Toilet paper!" she exclaims loudly, attracting the attention of a nearby shopper.

"I believe the toilet paper is two aisles down," the woman volunteers.

Maggie spends the next five minutes trying to decide which brand of toilet paper to buy. Charmin was always Craig's favorite, so she chooses Cottonelle instead, then decides she's being petty and returns the Cottonelle to the shelf, replacing it with a jumbo-size package of Charmin. "You're overcompensating," she mutters, moving on to an aisle stuffed with candies and cookies. "Much better," she says, surveying the mind-boggling selection of sweets.

She's tempted by the variety of M&M's available, and even more intrigued by the many flavors of licorice and jujubes. "What the hell. I could use something sweet about now," she decides. "Something sweet and gooey." She reaches for a box of sticky toffee, opening the package on the spot and popping one of the butterscotch squares into her mouth. It gloms instantly onto one of her back teeth. "Damn it," she says, trying to extricate it with her tongue, wondering if she's going to have to resort to using her fingers, when it finally pops out. "Probably loosened a damn filling," she grouses, mindful of another shopper's stare.

Attention, shoppers. Crazy lady in aisle five.

Maggie completes another tour of the large store until she's satisfied she has everything she needs, plus a lot of stuff she

174

surely doesn't. Still, the more she loads up on now, the fewer trips back here she'll have to make later.

She approaches the busy checkout counters, angling in behind a woman whose groceries have already been bagged. Maggie recognizes the woman as one of her neighbors, Olivia Something-or-other, the one who's married to the man she always sees staring out his front window.

This is the second time she's run into one of her neighbors away from their block, she thinks, wondering at the coincidence.

It's not a coincidence, she hears Craig admonish. *It's Saturday. This is the closest Publix to our house. Of course she shops here.*

You're being paranoid, he adds.

Screw you, Maggie thinks, pretending to study the racks of magazines beside the counter, hoping Olivia is too preoccupied with checking out to notice her.

"Excuse me, but I think there's something wrong with this machine," Olivia is saying to the checkout clerk.

"There is?"

"It keeps declining my card."

The clerk shrugs. "It was working fine a minute ago. Do you have another card?"

Olivia shakes her head and looks helplessly around. "Sorry about this," she says to Maggie. "Oh. I know you. Maggie, right?"

Maggie smiles. "Problems?"

"The machine won't take my credit card."

"Do you have a debit card?" the clerk asks, clearly hoping to speed things along. A line is starting to form behind Maggie.

"I do," Olivia says, inserting it. "I don't normally do the shopping. . . . Declined," she says a moment later. "I told you, there's something wrong with this machine."

"How about cash?" the clerk suggests.

"Over two hundred dollars? Who carries that much cash around these days?"

"Let me take this other customer and see if her card works," the clerk offers.

"It won't," Olivia insists, as the clerk rings in Maggie's purchases. She watches as Maggie inserts her card, waiting for it to be declined, then steps back in dismay when the transaction goes through without a glitch. "I don't understand. I'm nowhere near my limit and I should have more than enough cash in my account."

"I'm sure there's a legitimate explanation," Maggie begins. "Probably some screw-up at the bank."

"I'm so embarrassed."

"Don't be. Here, put her purchases on my card," Maggie directs the clerk.

"What? No," Olivia protests. "I can't let you do that."

"I insist. I know you're good for it." She smiles. "Remember, I know where you live."

Olivia manages a weak smile in return.

The clerk hesitates. "So, I'm putting it through on your card?"

Maggie nods.

"I don't know what to say, except thank you so much," Olivia says as the two women wheel their carts toward the parking lot at the front of the long strip mall. "I'll go to the bank first thing Monday morning and get this straightened out. You'll have your money back by Monday night. I promise."

"I'm not worried," Maggie says honestly.

"At least let me buy you a cup of coffee. I swear I have enough money for that."

"That's quite unnecessary."

"My turn to insist. Please."

"Okay. Sure. Why not?" *Why not, indeed?* Maggie thinks, deciding it would be rude to refuse, and it might even be nice. Olivia is clearly no threat to her. Besides, what does she have to rush home for? Erin and Leo are spending the weekend with their father, and the groceries will keep.

"There's a cute little pastry shop a few doors down."

A few minutes later, they're settled into a

177

table for two in a corner of the small, brightly lit room, steaming cups of coffee in front of them.

"You're sure you don't want one of those delicious-looking tarts?" Olivia asks.

"Quite sure. Thank you."

They sit for several seconds in silence. It's been a long time since Maggie had a real conversation with another woman. She realizes how much she's missed it.

"So," Olivia says, "I understand you're from California originally."

"That's right."

"How do you like Florida?"

"Takes a bit of getting used to," Maggie says. "It's very different from L.A."

"What made you relocate?"

"Long story," Maggie says, deciding it's way too early for such confidences. "You have three kids, right?"

"Twin boys and a girl. Twelve and ten."

"That must keep you hopping."

"It does. Although they'll be spending July with my parents up in Nantucket, so we'll have a bit of a break."

"Sounds great."

"Yeah. I think my husband could really use it. He's been the one at home looking after them most of this past year, and it can get a bit much."

"What do *you* do?"

"I'm in advertising," Olivia says, her face brightening immediately. "I was a stay-at-home mom for years. Then when my husband got laid off, I decided to go back to work. And I have to confess, I'm absolutely loving it. There's something about making your own money . . ." She stops, her mind clearly returning to what happened earlier in Publix. "You?"

"I was a teacher. Now I guess I'm . . . on sabbatical."

"And your husband?"

"He sells luxury cars. But . . . well, I guess it's no secret — we're separated."

"Oh, I'm so sorry. I didn't know."

"Well, nothing's been decided. There's still a chance . . ." Again, too soon for such confidences. "How long have you been married?"

"Going on sixteen years."

"What's your secret?" Maggie says lightly, trying to keep the focus on her neighbor.

"My secret?"

"To a happy marriage."

"Who said I was happy?" Olivia laughs. "No, I'm just kidding. Honestly. We're happy. Mostly," she continues, the words sputtering from her mouth, as if a tap has been turned on and is now stuck. "I mean, some years are better than others. Well, I don't have to tell you that. This last one's been more difficult than most, what with Sean being out of a job and everything."

And everything, Maggie repeats silently. She knows all about *and everything.*

"Not that he hasn't enjoyed being home, being a full-time dad and all. And God knows I've loved having someone do the laundry and make dinner every night. But you and I know it's a pretty thankless job, and I think it's been harder on him than he lets on. His ego's taken a big hit." She sighs. "Anyway, that's all about to change. It's looking as if he may have finally found something. Over at Advert-X in Palm Beach. Do you know Advert-X?"

"No. I'm afraid I don't."

"It's this relatively new agency on South County Road. Very cutting edge." She takes another sip of coffee, continues without prompting. "When Sean first told me he had an interview there, I thought, no way are they going to hire him. Not that he's not capable or anything like that. But Sean's pretty conservative, strictly Brooks Brothers, as he himself admits. And the guys the agencies like Advert-X are hiring these days are young and super hip. You know the type I mean, with their ankle-length, tight pants and thin, monochromatic ties. That's definitely not Sean."

Maggie pictures Sean standing by his living room window, staring out at the street, sometimes for hours on end. *More potted plant than cutting edge,* she finds herself thinking.

"Of course, I would never tell him that," Olivia continues. "And thank God I didn't because, turns out, I was completely wrong. Maybe it's a case of opposites attracting, I don't know, but they seem to really like him. I've lost track of the number of interviews he's had these last few weeks. Wednesday, it was one after another. He met with the head of the creative team, the head of marketing, even the president of the company. Then he had to run to pick up the kids. Poor guy was absolutely exhausted when he got home."

Maggie thinks back to last Wednesday. From her position at the end of the cul-de-sac, she has a clear view of everything that goes on in the street, and she knows that, aside from picking his kids up from school each afternoon, Sean's car rarely leaves his driveway. As far as Maggie can remember, that was true last Wednesday. No way had his car spent most of the day anywhere near South County Road.

Which means, what exactly?

That Sean has been lying to his wife?

That Olivia's year is about to get a whole lot more difficult?

Should she say something?

Don't get involved, she hears Craig warn. *Whatever is going on with them is none of your business.*

"We should know something definite this week," her neighbor is saying, crossing the fingers of both hands and holding them up. "Fingers crossed," she adds for emphasis.

"Fingers crossed," Maggie repeats, finishing what's left of her coffee and standing up, afraid to prolong their visit any further. "I really should get going, get those groceries in the fridge," she says, deciding Craig is right about not getting involved. Have the last eighteen months taught her nothing?

Besides, she likes Olivia. The woman is sweet and open and trusting, and clearly has enough on her plate. Voicing her suspicions would only upset her, probably unnecessarily, end a budding friendship before it has a chance to really develop. And she could be mistaken. There could be a perfectly logical explanation.

Except there isn't, and she isn't.

Still, this isn't her problem to solve. Olivia will undoubtedly discover the truth on her

own, sooner or later. She doesn't need
Maggie's help or advice.

Besides, what is it they say about shooting
the messenger?

CHAPTER SEVENTEEN

Dani's hands are shaking, her fingers still twitching from all the rounds she fired at the range, as they head back home along I-95.

"You okay?" Nick asks.

"I'm fine." *More than fine,* she thinks, her head spinning. In truth, she's exhilarated.

Exhilarated and confused.

"More fun than you thought it would be," her husband says, not bothering to minimize the "I told you so" in his voice.

"It was." Dani had been prepared, indeed had been expecting, to hate everything about this morning's excursion. And she had — right up until the minute she held that damn gun in her hands and squeezed the trigger.

The fact is that Dani is almost embarrassed by how much she enjoyed the experience, especially once she got the hang of lining up the gun's sights to the target and balancing the weapon properly with both hands, remembering to exhale as she pulled the trigger. She'd been initially startled by the force of the bullets as they exited the gun, but what really astonished her was the degree of pleasure she'd felt, the sublime sense of release firing that damn thing had provided.

The first time she actually hit the target sheet, albeit only the edge of its white border, she'd felt an unmistakable surge of pride. The first time she hit inside the outline's torso, she'd felt a rush of adrenaline so strong it almost knocked her off her feet. When subsequent bullets pierced the outline's head and heart, she'd experienced a wave of satisfaction so strong, it was almost sexual.

As if Nick instinctively understands what she's feeling, his hand reaches over to caress her inner thigh, his fingers disappearing between her legs, reaching ever higher. Dani squirms, glancing quickly toward the backseat to make sure her sons aren't watching. But Tyler is busy playing with his Super Mario stuffed figurine and Ben is staring absently out the side window. She opens her legs slightly to accommodate Nick's probing fingers.

What a day this is turning out to be, she

thinks, giving herself over to the surprising gentleness of his touch. *Maybe this morning is the start of a new beginning,* she tells herself. As bizarre as it sounds, as bizarre as it *is,* maybe this activity is something that will bring them closer together. As a couple. As a family.

The family that shoots together . . .

The boys had been less successful in their efforts. Ben, despite his eagerness and bravado, had a tough time balancing the gun and a tougher time lining up his sights to the target. Tyler had better luck lining up the sights but lost his balance each time he pulled the trigger, causing the bullets to fly off in all directions except, of course, the right one.

But perhaps the most surprising thing about the morning was how patient Nick had been with all of them. He never lost his temper, never so much as uttered a disparaging rebuke. It was all "Good effort" and "Don't worry. Keep trying. You'll do better next time."

Next time, Dani finds herself thinking as the car leaves the highway at PGA Boulevard, heading west toward Military Trail. Next time can't come soon enough as far as she's concerned. Firing that gun has given her a sense of power she hasn't felt in years.

She can't wait to do it again.

Ten minutes later they reach Hood Road, and minutes after that, the small cul-de-sac that is Carlyle Terrace. "You boys find something to keep you busy for a bit," Nick instructs, taking Dani's hand and leading her toward the stairs.

"Where are you going?" Tyler asks.

"Your mother and I have some business to take care of," Nick tells him, not breaking stride.

"What kind of business?"

Dani opens her mouth to object, but the sound that emerges is more a groan of anticipation than protest.

"I'm hungry," says Ben.

"Have a glass of milk," Nick calls down from the top of the stairs.

"But —"

"You heard me." Nick guides Dani into the bedroom and locks the door behind them.

Dani can't remember the last time she was so turned on. Her entire body is tingling as Nick pushes her back on the bed, pulling off her shorts and panties in one expert swoop, his head quickly disappearing between her legs, his tongue finishing the job his fingers started in the car. She cries out as she climaxes, a sound so guttural she can hardly believe it's coming from her.

Seconds later, he is on her and inside her, surrounding her with tenderness, and she is almost weeping with pleasure.

And then, suddenly, everything changes.

"My turn," he says, pulling out of her and flipping her over onto her stomach.

"What are you . . . ?"

"Hold still." He parts the cheeks of her buttocks, mounting her from behind.

Nick has mentioned wanting to try anal sex several times over the last few years, but Dani was always able to dissuade him, or at least divert him.

"Wait. I don't know . . ."

But he is already pounding his way into her, her pleasure disappearing into a pain so intense she feels she might split in two.

She tries willing her body to go numb and closes her eyes, picturing herself back at the gun range, the .22 in her hands, pumping bullet after bullet into her target.

Except this time, the target has a face.

She groans as she watches the imaginary bullets shatter Nick's skull, obliterating his once-handsome features, fragments of his flesh and pieces of his bones flying into the air like so many spent casings.

She squeezes the trigger to the rhythm of his thrusts, shooting him again and again, over and over, until there is nothing left of her husband but an empty outline riddled with holes.

The outline crumples to the floor as Nick collapses onto the bed beside her, his body bathed in sweat. "Whew," he mutters, then laughs. "That was intense."

"Mom . . . Dad . . ." Dani hears Ben call from downstairs. "How long are you gonna be? I'm starving."

"Be right there, sport," Nick calls back. "I think you might be bleeding, babe," he says as he pushes off the bed. "Nothing to be concerned about. You'll be fine. I promise it'll be better next time."

Good effort. Don't worry. Keep trying. You'll do better next time.

Dani remains on her stomach, motionless. If she moves, she will fall apart.

"Mom!" Ben calls again.

"Come on, babe," Nick says, giving Dani's backside a playful slap, causing fresh spasms of pain to shoot through her body. "Up and at 'em."

She watches as Nick climbs back into his clothes, then opens the door and disappears down the stairs.

Only then does she find the strength to move, her legs all but giving out when she tries to stand. Her hands, which just a short time ago were shaking with excitement, are now shaking with outrage and shame.

"Did I hear someone say they're hungry?" she hears Nick say.

"I am!" Ben exclaims.

"Where's Mommy?" Tyler asks.

"She'll be down soon," Nick tells him, sounding as sure of himself as he always does.

As sure of *her* as he always is.

Dani pushes one foot gingerly in front of the other, keeping close to the bed so as not to fall over, as she shuffles toward the bathroom. She locks the door behind her and steps into the shower, releasing the hot water and letting it wash over her wounded flesh. She watches the blood drip down her thighs to dance circles around the drain, then disappear, wishing she could follow suit. Grabbing the soap from its dish, she rubs it over her breasts, her belly, her thighs, between her legs, between her buttocks, rubbing even harder than she'd rubbed her hands at the range, trying to obliterate every trace of the poison that is her husband, stopping only when her efforts threaten to draw more blood.

She lifts her head toward the shower's steady spray, opening her mouth and letting the water fill her throat until she gags. Her body doubles over as she empties herself of the taste of Nick's fingers, the smell of his skin, the obscene rhythm of his thrusts. Only then does she shut off the water and step out of the stall. She stands there naked, staring at the steam coating the mirror over the sink, blocking her reflection. "I know you're in there somewhere," she whispers, not moving until she hears a knocking on the bathroom door.

"Dani," Nick calls from the other side. "I'll be out front with the boys."

She nods, says nothing.

"I made you a sandwich," he says.

Is he expecting her to thank him?

"It's on the kitchen counter," he adds when she doesn't.

She waits until she hears the front door close before leaving the bathroom, opening the bedroom window and standing just out of sight while staring at the street below, grateful for the burst of fresh air that fills her lungs. She sees Nick toss a baseball to Ben and watches her son leap up to catch it in midair. Ben immediately throws it to Tyler, who misses, and they both watch helplessly as the ball rolls into the flowering shrubs lining Julia Fisher's front walk.

As if on cue, the old woman and her grandson emerge from the house. The young man quickly retrieves the ball and throws it back to Tyler. "Catch it," Dani whispers, leaning forward to watch, her forehead resting on the glass. "Please catch it." But her sweet son misses it again. "Damn it," Dani mutters as the ball rolls into the McKays' driveway.

"It's Mark, right?" she hears Nick ask the young man. "Feel like joining us?"

Mark smiles. "Sure. That'd be great."

Another door opens and Sean Grant appears, his twins rushing past him to take part in the impromptu game, his daughter choosing to remain at his side. Seconds later, Aiden Young opens his front door. He hangs back, despite calls to join in.

"Hey, you, up there," her husband suddenly calls to Dani, spotting her in the window and waving her down. "Get that gorgeous ass down here."

Heads shoot toward her as Ben bursts into gales of laughter. "You said 'ass'!"

Dani says nothing.

What can she say?

Her husband has robbed her of her voice.

Whatever power she felt earlier is gone.

CHAPTER EIGHTEEN

"What's going on?" Heidi asks, coming up behind her husband, her head sneaking through the crook in his arm. "Oh, fun!" she says, watching her neighbors as they spread out across the road in front of their houses. "Can I play?"

"Everybody's welcome," Nick says. "You, too, Julia." He beckons the older woman forward.

Julia laughs, holding up both hands. "With these fingers? No, thank you. Think you'll have more fun if I just watch."

"Hi, there," Mark calls to Heidi. "How'd dinner go the other night?"

"Who's that?" Aiden asks his wife.

"The kid I was telling you about," Heidi explains, under her breath. "The old lady's grandson. The one who helped me make the dinner your mother didn't eat." The dinner is still a sore spot for Heidi. She'd tried putting it in the microwave the next night, but heating it up had only dried out the chicken, and the blueberry bread pudding, while still tasty, went more than a bit rubbery. "It was great," she lies, watching him effortlessly leap into the air to catch the ball in his right hand.

Which he promptly tosses to her.

Heidi squeals with delight as she catches it and runs into the street to join the others. She throws the ball to one of the twins, who throws it to his sister, who throws it to Nick, who throws it to Ben, who tosses it back to Mark, who throws it back to Heidi.

Heidi turns toward her husband. "Come on, Aiden, honey. Come play with us." She tosses him the ball.

He catches it, allowing himself to be coaxed into the street, and throws the ball to Nick, who passes it, underhand, to Tyler, who misses it again.

"Come on, buddy," Nick says, as the ball rolls into the shadows of a palm tree at the side of Sean's house. "You gotta pay attention. Eye on the ball. Remember?"

"Sorry," Tyler says, running after it.

Maggie's car approaches from Hood Road.

"Okay, guys," Nick instructs. "Everybody off the road."

Everyone gets out of the way to allow

Maggie's car entry.

"What's going on here?" Maggie asks, pulling into her driveway as the game resumes. She exits her car, surveying the scene.

"Neighborhood ball game," Nick explains. "Feel free to join in."

Maggie unlocks the trunk of her car and removes an armload of groceries. "Maybe after I get these put away," she says, deciding that the fates have determined it's high time she got to know her neighbors.

A young man almost crashes into her as he leaps up to catch a ball. "Sorry about that."

Maggie takes a step back. "Who are you?"

"That's my grandson, Mark," Julia calls from the doorway of the house next door.

Maggie nods. "Nice to meet you, Mark," she tells the young man, glad her daughter isn't around. This kid, with his long hair, skinny torso, and bad-boy vibe, is just the sort of young man Erin would probably find attractive. If only to spite her.

"Is Erin home?" she hears a voice ask.

Maggie is startled to hear her daughter's name at almost the exact second she was thinking it. "Excuse me?" She looks down to see Tyler Wilson staring up at her.

"Is Erin home?" he repeats. "Can she

195

come out and play?"

"Oh, no, sweetie. I'm afraid that she and Leo are with their father this weekend."

"Oh."

"But you and Leo should play together when he gets back. Maybe one day this week?" Maggie looks around to see if she can arrange a playdate with Tyler's mother, but unsurprisingly, Dr. Dani Wilson is nowhere to be seen.

"Does Leo like fish?" Tyler asks.

"Well, he's kind of a picky eater. . . ." Maggie watches the boy's face fill with alarm. "Oh, you mean *that* kind of fish! I'm sorry. Yes, Erin told me all about your amazing fish. A betta? Is that right?"

"He can do tricks. . . ."

"Tyler," his father admonishes. "Let Mrs. McKay take her groceries inside."

"Hey, kid, catch," Mark says, gently tossing Tyler the ball.

Tyler catches it and looks toward his father for approval, but Nick is no longer paying attention.

"Here comes another car," someone shouts, as Olivia's car approaches from the main street.

Once again, everyone scurries out of the way, allowing Olivia to pull into the small cul-de-sac. She pulls into her driveway, using her remote to open her garage door and parking beside her husband's car. "The damnedest thing just happened," she whispers to Sean as he's helping her with the groceries. "Both my credit and debit cards were denied in Publix. If it hadn't been for Maggie . . ."

"Maggie?"

"Our neighbor," she says, waving to Maggie as she's about to disappear inside her house. "She happened to be there and offered to put our groceries on her card. You wouldn't happen to have two hundred dollars on you, would you, so I can pay her back?"

"Are you kidding?"

Olivia notes that the color has all but drained from her husband's face. "Don't worry about it. I'm sure it's a mistake. I'll clear it up with the bank on Monday. Hey," she says to the small crowd. "How about I go inside and make us some lemonade?"

The children respond with a chorus of cheers and "all rights."

"Lemonade sounds fabulous," says Heidi.

"And I have some wonderful chocolate chip cookies my grandson made just this morning," Julia tells them. "I'll go get them."

"I believe I may have just died and gone

to heaven," Nick says. "Tyler, go upstairs and see what's keeping your mother. She won't want to miss this."

Tyler immediately starts running toward his house.

"Leave the ball," his father instructs.

"Sorry," Tyler says, dropping it.

Ben runs over to pick it up, then throws it to Mark, who, once again, throws it toward Heidi.

"Looks like someone has a crush," Aiden says to his wife, extending his arms in front of her to catch it.

"What? No. Don't be silly," Heidi says, laughing.

Aiden hurls the ball back at Mark, the ball whizzing by his head to land in Julia's small patch of front lawn. One of Olivia's twins runs to retrieve it.

"Easy there, big guy," Mark says. "Don't want to break a window."

"You okay?" Heidi asks her husband, laying a protective hand across his arm. The air is hot and humid, and Aiden isn't very good with either.

"Yeah, fine."

Behind her, the twins are fighting over the ball, their voices raised.

Heidi watches Aiden wince. He isn't very good with loud voices.

"Sure is getting hot," Mark says, running over to introduce himself. "Mark Fisher, Julia's grandson."

"This is Aiden, my husband," Heidi says.

"I understand you gave my wife weed," Aiden says, his voice flat, expressionless.

"Oh my God!" Heidi exclaims. She had no idea Aiden knew anything about that. What exactly has his mother told him? "Aiden, I . . ."

Aiden turns, about to go back into his house, when the ball comes hurling through the air to hit him squarely in the back. He spins around, fists clenched, eyes filled with fury.

"Sorry," one of the twins yells out as Aiden advances menacingly toward him. "It was an accident. I didn't mean to hit you."

"Aiden," his wife says, running after him.

"Hey, man," Sean says. "My son apologized. It was an accident."

"Easy there," says Nick, edging forward.

"Aiden," Heidi says again, catching up to him and spinning him around. She stares into his eyes, but if he sees her, he gives no sign. "What's happening, babe?"

His eyes suddenly snap back into focus. "Sorry," he whispers. Then more loudly, "Sorry, everyone." He turns and walks briskly back toward his house, pausing for an instant in front of Mark. "Stay away from my wife," he warns quietly.

"I'm really sorry," Heidi apologizes to Mark, then again to everyone, before following her husband inside their house and shutting the door.

"Who's ready for the best chocolate chip cookies you'll ever taste?" Julia calls out, emerging from her front door just as Heidi's door closes, a large platter of cookies in hand.

"Perfect timing," Nick says, relieved the unexpected drama has passed. "Come on, everyone. Dig in." He looks toward his house to see Tyler leading Dani by the hand. "About time you guys got here."

Dani manages a wan smile.

As if on cue, Maggie also steps outside. "Did I hear someone say chocolate chip cookies?"

"Not to mention some delicious homemade lemonade," Olivia says, depositing a large pitcher on her front stoop, along with a tall stack of plastic cups. "Come and get it, everyone."

Maggie sidles up to Dani Wilson as Olivia begins pouring the lemonade. Maybe Dani is just shy. Maybe if Maggie were to make more of an effort to get to know her . . . "I was talking to Tyler before," she begins. "I mentioned that maybe he and my son, Leo, might get together one afternoon this week after school."

"They're in after-school programs till I get home," Dani says, refusing to meet Maggie's gaze.

"Well, there's just one more week of school. Maybe after that . . ."

"Maybe," Dani says. "If you'll excuse me, I'm really not feelin' very well."

"Are you all right, sweetheart?" Nick asks, his voice radiating concern as she hurries away. "I'll be in in a few minutes," he calls after her. "I'll talk to her later," he says to Maggie. "I'm sure we can arrange something."

Maggie smiles, though she doubts anything will come of it. She wonders how such a nice man got saddled with such a cold fish.

"I understand you came to my wife's rescue earlier," Sean is saying, suddenly at Maggie's side.

"Happy to help out," Maggie says.

"Anyone happen to have a tire pump?" Nick asks. "I noticed one of my tires was looking a little flat earlier."

"We do," Olivia says, going back inside her house, then returning seconds later, car keys in hand, heading for the garage. "I'm sure you have one in your car," she says to her husband, opening his trunk and reaching for the tire pump before he realizes what's happening. "What's this?" she asks, holding up the bag from Ferragamo. "Sean," she says, peeking inside it. "What's this?"

CHAPTER NINETEEN

"Okay, calm down," Sean says as Olivia paces angrily back and forth in front of him.

They're in their living room, Sean having ushered his wife inside at the first hint of a raised voice. Outside, the impromptu gathering has dispersed, the adults retreating to their individual domiciles, leaving only the children and Mark to continue playing ball in the street.

"Don't tell me to calm down," Olivia counters over the sound of the children's laughter. "What the hell is this?" She motions toward the bag at her feet. "A jacket from Ferragamo?" she says, answering her own question as she none-too-gently pulls the jacket out of the bag and throws it over the sofa. "For over three thousand fucking dollars?!"

"If you would just give me the chance to explain . . ."

"By all means," Olivia says, plopping

down in the nearest chair, waving the receipt in the air. "Go ahead. Explain."

"Okay," Sean says. "Okay." His mouth is so dry, he can barely put two words together. God, he could use a drink.

"Well?"

He takes a deep breath. "I bought the jacket."

"No shit, Sherlock," Olivia snaps. "Your signature's on the fucking receipt."

"Okay."

"Not okay. What else have you been buying?"

"Nothing. I swear. Look. I get that you're angry, but I had a good reason. . . ."

"Oh, please, do share. I'm dying to hear it."

"Do you think you could drop the sarcasm for a minute?"

"Do you think you could speed this up a bit?"

"Maybe if you'd stop interrupting . . ."

"Maybe if you'd stop stalling."

She's right, Sean acknowledges silently, taking another deep breath, hoping to still the wild beating of his heart. He *has* been stalling, trying to come up with a plausible explanation, a reason that would justify his spending over three thousand dollars on a jacket when he's out of a job and they're barely making ends meet. "You remember the initial interview I had at Advert-X last month?"

"Of course, I remember."

"Well, I got there early," he continues, growing more comfortable with the story he's creating. "And I see all these guys walking around, and they're young and hip and well dressed. I mean, *really* well dressed. European sports jackets over designer jeans. Hell, their jeans are even ironed, for fuck's sake. You can tell just by looking at them that everything they have on cost an arm and a leg. And there I am in my black Dockers pants and jacket from Joseph A. Banks, and I know, I *know*, that there's no way in hell that I'm getting this job. Not looking like that. Not in those clothes." He pauses, trying to determine if she's buying this, seeing a brief flicker of understanding flash across her eyes.

"So, I excused myself," he continues. "Like I said, I was early, and Ms. Pierce in HR was running late, so I had about forty minutes. I headed over to Worth Avenue to see what I could find. First, I went to Brooks Brothers, because you know I've always liked their clothes, but I could see right away that their stuff wasn't going to cut it. And then I saw this jacket in the

205

window at Ferragamo, and it was perfect. I mean, absolutely fucking perfect. So I went in and tried it on, and the damn thing fit like it was made for me — I mean, how often does that happen? — and I said great, I'll take it, not thinking for a second that it was going to cost anything like three thousand dollars. I mean, I thought, eight hundred maybe. A thousand, tops. It wasn't until I'm pocketing the damn bill that I glanced at the price, and by then, of course, it was too late."

"You could have told them . . ."

"It was too late," he repeats. "And to be honest," he says, knowing he's being anything but, "I was too embarrassed. Then I thought, I'll just take the damn thing, hide the tags and wear it to the interview, then return it when I'm done."

"Clearly, you didn't do that."

"I tried. But they only do exchanges. The best they could offer was a store credit. So I was screwed." He pauses, watches her struggling to believe him. "The good news, and I know this doesn't make up for my stupidity, is that the jacket did the trick."

She takes a full thirty seconds to respond. "But why didn't you tell me all this before?"

"Because I knew how angry you'd be, and I felt like such a damn fool."

Olivia lowers her head. When she lifts it again, he can see that he's gotten to her.

"What else?" she asks.

"What do you mean, what else?"

"Not only was my credit card declined, Sean, so was my debit card. Which means that the money I thought was in our checking account — over five hundred dollars — is gone."

"I've paid some bills. There have been other expenses, things you've asked me to pick up during the week."

"That's all?"

"There have been no other purchases, if that's what you're asking."

"So, if I call the credit card company right now to ask about last month's bill," she says, pulling her phone from the side pocket of her skirt, "I'm not going to have any more unpleasant surprises?"

Sean swallows the tiny bit of saliva his mouth has managed to manufacture. "You're accusing me of lying?"

"I'm not accusing you of anything. I'm asking."

"Sounds a lot like the same thing."

"I think you've lost the right to be indignant," Olivia tells him.

"I'm sorry," Sean apologizes immediately. "You're right. It just hurts that you don't trust me."

"Believe me, it hurts me even more."

"You *know* me, Olivia."

"I thought I did."

"You *do*. I promise."

"You promise that there are no other charges on that card?" she asks.

He hesitates, trying to decide which carries the bigger risk, another lie or the truth.

"Sean?"

"There was a lunch at Ta-boo," he says, opting for the truth. He almost laughs. He's been lying for so long, it's the truth that feels wrong.

"A lunch at Ta-boo?" Olivia repeats, her voice flat, void of inflection.

"After the interview. I was starving because I'd been too nervous to eat anything for breakfast, and I was so pleased with the way things had gone, I splurged on a nice lunch. It was selfish and it was a mistake, and I'm more sorry than you know."

Olivia shakes her head. "You're having lunch at Ta-boo and I'm having to borrow money from a woman I barely know to pay for groceries."

He falls to his knees in front of her. "I'm so sorry. Please forgive me. I'll do anything to make this right."

Olivia doesn't answer for what feels like

an eternity. "Is there anything else, *anything else at all,* no matter how small or inconsequential you think it might be, that you're not telling me?"

Sean searches his brain for something he can say that will erase the awful combination of pity and disappointment he sees on his wife's face. It's worse than the anger that was there before, worse than the hate he knows he deserves. It's too much for one man to bear.

"There *is* something," he says, finally.

"Oh God," she says, bracing herself. "What?"

Sean's face suddenly breaks into a wide grin, like a child with a secret too big to contain any longer. "I got the job."

"What?!"

"I got the job."

"The job at Advert-X?"

"Of course, the job at Advert-X," he says with such conviction he almost believes it himself.

"You got the job?"

"I got the job."

"I don't understand. When did you find out?"

"The headhunter called while you were out shopping. She said companies normally wait till Monday to call, but they'd made up their minds and they wanted to let me know right away."

"Honestly?"

"Honestly."

"You swear?"

"I swear."

"I can't believe it. This is so wonderful! But why didn't you tell me? Why did you let me go on and on about that stupid jacket?"

"Because you had every right to be angry. I did a very stupid thing. I deserved to be hauled on the carpet."

"I can't believe it."

"Believe it."

"How much are they paying you?"

"None of that's been finalized. I'll know more next week. But whatever it is, I don't think we'll have to worry about the price of jackets for a while."

"Oh God. I'm so happy for you. For us," Olivia tells him, taking his face in her hands. "When do you start?"

"End of the month," he says. Surely to God, he'll be able to find another position by then. Then he'll explain that he and Advert-X were unable to come to terms on a number of important issues. Whatever. He'll think of something. It isn't important.

What's important is that he's bought

himself some time. What's important is that hope and admiration have replaced the look of pity and disappointment on his wife's face. At least for the time being.

He'd rather be dead than see that look again.

Or she be.

CHAPTER TWENTY

Maggie knows the man is there before she sees him. She feels him walking toward her bed, the air around him parting like a curtain as he approaches. He stands over her for several long seconds, his eyes penetrating the darkness, as if waiting for her to wake up. She won't give him the satisfaction, she decides, keeping her eyes resolutely closed, even as she feels him pulling back the covers and climbing into bed beside her. She feels his warm breath on her neck as his lips tease the side of her mouth and his fingers graze her breasts through the silk of her nightgown.

Her body stirs, although her eyes remain closed, even as the man's hand slips underneath the bottom of the nightgown to caress her, his fingers knowing exactly the right amount of pressure to apply and the exact spot to apply it. "Oh God," she cries, as her body builds steadily toward climax.

Which is when she wakes up, her eyes opening as she rolls onto her stomach, her own fingers replacing those of the faceless man in her dream, her brain making the quick leap from fantasy to reality. *The man of my dreams indeed,* she thinks with a laugh, as her body shudders to orgasm. "Thank you," she whispers into her pillow. "I needed that."

"Needed what?" a voice asks.

Maggie jumps, a scream escaping her lips as she lunges toward the nightstand beside the bed.

"Mom?" her son asks before she can open the top drawer to get at her gun. "What's the matter? What are you doing?"

"Oh my God. Leo! You scared me, sweetheart." Shaking, Maggie holds out her arms for him to come inside. "You can't scare Mommy like that."

"I didn't mean to," he says, fighting back tears.

"I know you didn't. I'm the one who should be sorry." She kisses the top of his head as many times as he will allow before he squirms out of reach. *My God,* she thinks. *Craig was right. If I don't get a grip, I'm liable to shoot my own son.* She shudders again, this time in horror, not pleasure. "What time is it?"

"After eight."

"What?!" *After eight! Day camp starts in less than an hour. And it's the first day. How will it look if they're late?* "Shit. I forgot to set the alarm."

"It's okay," Leo tells her, his voice measured, not fully convinced. "We have time. I already had breakfast. And I'm all dressed."

Maggie sees that her son is wearing his new camp uniform — black shorts and a yellow T-shirt emblazoned with the camp logo, Silver Palm Day Camp — along with white socks and sneakers. The socks are clean and everything seems to be right-side out. Even his shoelaces are tied. "You had breakfast?" she asks, her eyes filling with tears of pride.

"Just some cereal. I spilled some milk on the table."

"Oh God. You're such a sweet thing. I love you so much. You know that, don't you?"

He smiles. "What do you need?"

"What do I need?" Maggie repeats.

"Just before you started yelling, you said you needed something."

Maggie feels a blush building beneath her cheeks when she thinks of her erotic dream and tries to shake both the blush and the memory away with a toss of her head. "I must have been dreaming."

"Was it a nightmare?"

"Can't remember."

Erin is suddenly in the doorway, sleep clinging to her half-closed eyes, a frown dragging her lips toward her chin. "What the hell is going on in here?"

"Hi, sweetheart," Maggie says. "You're up early."

"Like you gave me any choice. What's with all the racket?"

"Mom had a nightmare," Leo explains. "I got dressed myself and made breakfast."

"Well, whoop-dee-doo."

"Erin . . ." Maggie warns, climbing out of bed.

Erin rolls her eyes. "I'm going back to sleep."

"I thought you were going to start looking for a job this morning." Maggie regrets her words even before they're out of her mouth.

"Well, you thought wrong," Erin says. "I told you I was taking some time off."

"School finished over a week ago. Another few weeks and it'll be the end of June. You can't keep sitting around all day, doing nothing."

"Why not? You do."

The words hit Maggie like a slap in the face. "Erin . . ."

"Besides, how am I supposed to look for a

job without a car?"

"Mom," Leo interjects. "We're going to be late."

"You're right. I don't have time for this now. We'll talk later," she says to the now-empty doorway. Down the hall, Erin's bedroom door slams shut.

"I'll wait downstairs," Leo says.

"I won't be long," Maggie assures him.

Why do I keep banging my head against the wall? she wonders as she is washing up and getting dressed. Erin is going to do what Erin is going to do, and that's all there is to it. She has to learn to pick her battles. Isn't that what all the parenting books advise?

But what advice do they offer when *everything* is a battle?

Thank God for Leo, Maggie thinks, heading down the stairs and ushering her son out the door and into the car, making sure his seatbelt is fastened securely around him. Sweet, gentle, kind Leo, still in that happy stage where he loves his mother.

How long is that going to last? she wonders as they turn onto the main street. How long before nature overcomes nurture, before her neediness becomes a burden, and he is embarrassed by the intimacy she still craves? How much time does she have before a sullen silence replaces the unprompted hugs and unexpected confidences? "I don't like it when they kiss in movies," he told her just the other day. "It makes my penis tingle."

"Oh God," she moans, stopping at a red light and laying her head on the steering wheel. "It's happening already."

"What's happening already?" Leo asks from the backseat.

"What?"

"You said something's happening already."

"Did I?" *Shit. What is the matter with me? Can I no longer differentiate between when I'm talking to myself and when I'm talking out loud?* "I meant we're already halfway there." *It's that damn dream. It's affected my whole equilibrium. I'm frustrated, that's all it is. I haven't had sex in . . . what . . . four months? I bet my husband isn't sitting around being celibate. He's out there having a high old time, being an in-demand plus-one at weddings. . . .*

A car honks behind her.

"What's your problem?" Maggie demands, glowering into the rearview mirror.

"It's a green light," Leo says quietly.

"Oh."

"Are you okay, Mom?"

"Sure, I am, sweetie. Just a little distracted this morning."

"Maybe I should stay home today."

"What? No! Why?"

"To keep you company, so you won't be so . . . distracted."

Dear God, what am I doing to my son? she wonders. *First, I scare him half to death, then I worry him with my strange behavior, make him feel responsible for my well-being. He's a child and I'm an adult. How is it that I'm the one who needs to grow up?* "Oh, no, sweetie. I'll be fine. I promise."

Leo nods, although his face looks anything but reassured, and they drive the rest of the way in silence.

She stops in a Starbucks, located in a small strip mall on Military Trail, on the way home. It's crowded and she has to wait in line, a situation she normally avoids like the plague. But this morning has been something of a wake-up call. Her paranoia has already cost her her marriage. Now it's starting to affect her son.

Besides, she's in no hurry to get home. Erin will either be asleep or unpleasant, the only two options she seems to present these days. "A tall, skinny latte," Maggie orders when she reaches the front of the line. "And a muffin."

"What kind?"

"Cranberry walnut?"

"Name?" the barista asks, handing her the

large muffin.

Maggie takes the muffin, gives the girl her name, pays the cashier, then looks around for a seat. But the half-dozen stools by the window are occupied and there are only a few tables, all full. "You're very busy this morning," she remarks idly, stepping aside to let the man behind her place his order. She notes that he's young and very handsome, and tries to imagine what he'd look like minus the shirt and tie. *Where the hell did that thought come from?* she wonders. *What is the matter with me?* "Are you hiring?" she asks the girl behind the counter, in an effort to override such thoughts. "My daughter is looking for a summer job."

The girl behind the counter shrugs, swivels toward her co-workers. "Are we hiring?"

More shrugs.

"She can fill out an application online," one of the employees volunteers.

Fat chance of that, Maggie decides, watching as a table by the door frees up just as her name is called. She hesitates, torn between grabbing her latte or making a beeline for the table.

"You get the table," the man behind her says. "I'll bring the coffee."

"What?"

"You're Maggie, right?"

219

Her body tenses. "How do you know that?"

"The girl just called it out." He smiles. A flash of white teeth. Dimples. "And your name's on the cup."

"Right." *I'm an idiot,* Maggie thinks, heading for the now-empty table along the far wall. She sits down at one of its two chairs, her purse in her lap. The man is right behind her, handing over her latte. "Do you mind if I join you? . . . It's the only available seat," he says when she fails to respond.

"Rick!" a voice calls out.

"Be right back." He's gone before Maggie can object.

Take your coffee and your muffin and run, she thinks. But the man is back before she can muster the necessary resolve to move her legs.

"I'm sorry. I don't mean to make you uncomfortable," he says, sitting down. "I'll just sit here and drink my coffee. We don't have to talk."

"No, that's all right," Maggie says, pretending to sip at her coffee when what she is really doing is studying the man's handsome face. He's younger than she is, although it's impossible to tell how much. Blue eyes, brown hair, deep dimples at the sides of his lips. Well dressed. No visible tattoos. He doesn't look like a hired assassin. "*I'm* sorry. I didn't mean to be rude."

"You weren't. How's the muffin?"

"Not great. It's slightly stale and the walnuts are as hard as stones."

"Good to know."

Maggie sips at her coffee, not sure what else to say. It's been a long time since she's made small talk. And she was never very good at it. She takes another bite of her muffin, feels a sliver of walnut lodge inside the same back filling she loosened a few weeks ago at Publix.

"So, your daughter's looking for a summer job, is she?"

A sharp intake of breath. "How do you know that?"

"You kind of announced it." Another smile. More dimples.

Maggie tries smiling back, but the result is more twitch than smile. "Are you . . . hiring?"

"Me? No. But I know that the hairdressing salon next to my office is looking for a receptionist."

"Where's your office?"

"A few doors down the way."

"What do you do?"

"I'm an accountant." He reaches into his pocket.

Maggie immediately reaches inside her purse for her gun.

"Here we go," he says, withdrawing a handful of small white business cards and handing her the top one. *Richard Atwood, certified public accountant,* the card reads in bold black letters.

So, Maggie thinks, *an accountant, not an assassin.* The tips of her fingers brush against his as she takes the card. The touch sends a barrage of unwelcome tingles up her arm. She drops the card into her purse, gulps at her latte, then jumps to her feet, finally managing to dislodge the stubborn piece of walnut with her tongue. "I really should get going."

He nods. "Well, it was nice meeting you, Maggie."

"You, too."

"Good luck."

"Good luck?"

"Finding your daughter a job."

"Oh, right. I'll need it." Maggie drops the remains of her muffin into a trash bin on her way out. She doesn't look back.

CHAPTER TWENTY-ONE

Nadine's is located four storefronts down from Starbucks, between a RE/MAX office and that of half a dozen certified public accountants, Richard Atwood's name at the top of the alphabetized list etched into the glass. The handwritten sign in the salon's window reads: *Receptionist wanted. Apply within.* "Don't do this. Keep walking," Maggie tells herself, even as she is pulling open the heavy glass door and stepping inside the cool, air-conditioned space. Immediately, the combined smells of fruity shampoo and hair dye reach deep into her nostrils.

It's a pleasant space — wood floor, pale pink walls, white enamel sinks, lots of mirrors, comfortable-looking black leather chairs, six of them along one wall, three on the wall opposite, four of the chairs already occupied. One client is having her hair washed, another is having hers blow-dried, while the third sits, rifling through the latest issue of *Vogue,* waiting her turn. The fourth woman, whose head is covered in strips of tinfoil, is busy scrolling through her phone, a male stylist examining her roots to see how the dye is taking.

"Be right with you," a birdlike, middle-aged woman with skinny legs and asymmetrical red hair chirps in Maggie's direction as the phone at the front counter rings. The woman quickly leaves her client to answer it. "Nadine's," she says into the receiver. "Nadine speaking. What can I do for you?"

Maggie watches the whirlwind that is Nadine check her computer and type in the caller's information. "Certainly, Mrs. Peters. We can do a color and cut at two o'clock Thursday with Jerome. Perfect. We'll see you then." She hangs up the phone, takes a deep breath, and steps around the counter to do a quick appraisal of Maggie's head. "Honey, have you ever come to the right place," she pronounces, pulling at the sides of Maggie's hair. "So many split ends. How long's it been since you had your hair styled? And have you ever thought of going blond? Blond would be perfect with your coloring. Just look at these cheekbones," she says, her hand on Maggie's chin, turning her head from side to side. "You have wonderful bone structure, but trust me, what you've got going on now with your hair isn't doing you any favors."

Holy shit, Maggie thinks, taking a step back. "Actually, I'm here about the receptionist job. . . ."

"You're hired," says Nadine.

"What?"

"My receptionist eloped last week and left me high and dry. I thought I could manage without her over the summer, but you can see how busy we are. When you're good, word gets around. You look smart. Please tell me you've had at least a little experience."

"Yes, but it was a long time ago," Maggie demurs, not quite sure what's happening, "when I was in university, but it was only part-time and —"

"You're familiar with computers?"

"Yes, but —"

"Shouldn't take you long to figure everything out. It's not exactly rocket science. I'll pay you twelve dollars an hour. When can you start?"

"Uh . . . I'll need a day or two to get things organized. . . ."

"Fine. You can start Wednesday. Of course, we'll have to do something about that hair. I can't let this" — she makes vague motions

225

around Maggie's head with her hands — "be the first thing clients see when they walk through the door. Jerome, can you fit in a color and styling for our new receptionist?"

Jerome motions toward an empty chair. "Sit yourself down, sweetheart," he tells Maggie, patting the back of an empty chair. "I'll be with you in a flash."

It's almost three hours later when Maggie turns onto Carlyle Terrace. She's been sneaking peeks at her reflection in the rearview mirror the entire drive home, alternating between terrified and thrilled by what she sees. "Oh my God," Jerome had proclaimed when he was done coloring, snipping, and styling, taking several exaggerated steps back to admire his handiwork. "It's Michelle Pfeiffer's younger sister!" Everyone in the salon had burst into a round of applause.

Maggie is still so preoccupied with the unexpected events of the morning that she doesn't immediately register that the pajama-clad girl talking to the skinny young man on the lawn of the house to the right of hers is, in fact, her daughter. "Shit," she says, pulling into the driveway and turning off the engine, tapping the outline of the gun in her purse as she climbs out of the car. "Erin, what are you doing outside in your pajamas?"

"Holy crap!" Erin exclaims, ignoring her mother's question as she walks toward her. "What happened to *you?*"

Maggie abandons both her outrage and her gun to pat at her hair. "Do you like it?"

Erin makes several complete circles around her mother. "It's amazing. You look, like, ten years younger."

"You really think so? I mean, it's *very* blond."

"It's very . . . everything. Wow."

"Wow?"

"Wow," says the young man ambling toward them. "You look great. Mark Fisher," he reminds her, tucking his own straggly hair behind his ear. "Julia's grandson."

"Yes. I remember. It's so nice that you visit your grandmother so often."

"Actually, Mark's staying with her for a while," Erin explains.

"Oh? Are you from out of town?" Maggie hopes he won't be around for too long.

"No. I'm just hanging out here for a bit."

"Is your grandmother okay?"

"Oh, yeah. She's fine. Great."

Great, Maggie repeats silently, her tongue gravitating toward the tooth at the back of her mouth. The filling definitely feels loose.

"So, what brought this on?" Erin asks, fingers motioning toward Maggie's head.

"I'm not sure," Maggie says, still trying to make sense of it herself. "I went into this hairdressing salon to inquire about a job for you. . . ."

"You asked about a job for *me*?"

"Yes, but —"

"I'm not working in some stupid hair salon!"

"No, you're not," Maggie confirms, exhaling a long, deep breath. "*I* am."

"What?"

"The owner of the salon offered me the job and . . . I think I took it."

"What?" Erin says again.

Maggie isn't sure what else to say. She's been asking herself the same thing for the past three hours. "I know it sounds bizarre."

"No shit!"

"Erin . . ."

"What about Leo? Who's going to drive him to and from camp? Does this mean I get a car?"

"No, it does not. I can still drive him. The hours are pretty flexible."

"I don't understand. You're a *teacher*," Erin says.

"I *was* a teacher."

"And now . . . what? You're a *hairdresser*?"

"I'm a receptionist. For the time being. You were right — I can't just sit around all day, doing nothing. It isn't doing anyone any favors . . ." Maggie says, borrowing Nadine's words.

"Wait," Erin interrupts. "You're saying I was right about something? Who are you, and what have you done with my mother?"

Maggie smiles. She doesn't have an answer for that one either. "It's almost one o'clock," she says instead, checking her watch. "You need to get dressed. You shouldn't be outside in your pajamas."

Erin rolls her eyes. "And she's back."

Maggie turns toward her house. "Nice seeing you again, Mark."

"You, too," he says. "And you really *do* look great."

"Thank you." Maggie begins walking to her front door. "Erin?" she says, stopping when her daughter fails to accompany her.

"I'll be in soon."

"Now," Maggie says.

"Does your grandmother have room for one more?" Erin mutters, just loud enough for Maggie to hear.

Mark laughs. "Catch you later."

"Really, Mom?" Erin demands as they step inside the house. "Do you have to be

229

such a dick?"

"Excuse me?"

"You heard me."

The next thing Maggie hears is the familiar sound of her daughter's bedroom door slamming shut.

CHAPTER TWENTY-TWO

"I'm looking for a birthday gift for my husband," the well-dressed matron announces, stopping in front of Aiden Young, her eyes sweeping across the watches on display inside the glass counter. "Nothing too expensive."

"Well, I'm sure he'd be very happy with any of these," Aiden says, although he's sure of no such thing. In fact, he's sure about absolutely nothing in his life these days. Not his wife, not his marriage, not even his sanity. He shudders, recalling his reaction when the ball slammed into his back during that impromptu game with his neighbors, the near-lethal mix of terror and fury that washed over him.

He'd come so close to losing it.

So how can he say for certain that a man he's never met, husband of a woman he's encountering for the very first time, will like any of the watches he's about to show her?

"Do you see anything that strikes your fancy?" *Strikes your fancy?! Where the hell did that expression come from?*

The woman points to a watch with a heavy silver-links band and a midnight-blue dial. "This one looks interesting."

"Good choice," Aiden agrees, suddenly realizing where he heard that expression last. His mother! She'd used it last night when she dropped over with a selection of fabric samples for the occasional chair she was buying them.

"See anything that strikes your fancy?" his mother had asked, before indicating the fabric that she preferred, and had, in fact, already ordered. "Of course, I can call the store back and change the order, if that's what you want," she'd offered. "I just thought this one would work best. But, of course, it's entirely up to you. What do you think, Aiden?"

Aiden recalls the smile on his mother's face and the frown on his wife's, and knows that he can't win either way. He removes the watch from its perch and holds it out toward the woman. "One of my favorites," he adds, although it isn't. He prefers a more casual watch, one with a wide leather band and an oversized face. This one is much too prissy for his taste. "It's very elegant."

Elegant, but useless. The dial is so crowded with symbols, you can barely make out the numbers.

"Is it waterproof?"

"Water-resistant," Aiden qualifies. "I wouldn't wear it diving or anything like that."

"I don't think that's going to be a problem," the woman says. "My husband is turning seventy-nine. I think his diving days are over. What about that one?" She points to a rose-gold watch with a round brown face and a series of lines instead of numbers to indicate the hours and minutes.

Aiden removes it from the display case, thinking he'd never know what time it was. Which would drive him crazy.

Of course, there's a good chance he's already crazy, he concedes, thinking of the disturbing dream he had last night. In the dream, he was running down a deserted country road, pursued by an angry mob. Hands reached for his back, ripped at his shirt. He twisted around to confront his tormentors, only to discover that the mob had been replaced by a single man, a boy really, no more than ten or twelve.

The boy had no head.

"How much is it?" the woman asks.

"Sorry. What?"

"I was asking . . ."

Aiden's phone vibrates in his pocket. He ignores it. There are only two people who call him at work, his mother and Heidi. And he isn't up to speaking to either of them. He checks the computer as his phone goes mercifully silent. "It's three thousand, four hundred dollars, plus tax."

"Oh my, no. I said nothing too expensive."

"Perhaps you could give me some idea of the price you're considering," Aiden says, trying to be helpful. "A thousand dollars? Five hundred?"

"Five hundred, tops."

Aiden leads her toward the appropriate row of watches.

"I don't like any of these," the woman says, the lines around her mouth growing more pronounced as her lips purse with dismay, reminding Aiden of the look his mother gets whenever she looks at Heidi.

"What about this one?" He bends down to retrieve his favorite watch, the one with a round white face and a brown leather band. "It's nice and sporty, and the big black numbers make it easy to tell time. . . ."

But the woman is no longer there.

Clearly he has lost his touch where women are concerned.

Not that he ever really had one. His good

looks and athletic physique have always been all that were necessary to attract the opposite sex. Good thing, because he's not particularly charming. Nor is he a good conversationalist. He isn't even all that bright. But girls, and later women, have always misread such deficiencies as shyness, assuming hidden depths where none exist.

Of course, he always disappoints them in the end.

He's been disappointing women all his life.

His phone vibrates again. He pretends to be checking something in a lower drawer as he takes it out of his pocket, answering it without bothering to check the caller ID. "Hi," he says, holding it tight against his ear as a knot forms in the pit of his stomach.

"You have to do something," Heidi says instead of hello. "I hate that stupid chair."

He sighs. "I know you do."

"Do *you* like it?"

"Not particularly."

"Okay, great. Tell *her* that." She doesn't have to state who she's referring to.

"What am I supposed to say?"

"How about that while we really appreciate her generosity, we just don't need another chair. Tell her that it's too big for the room. Tell her that it's hideous even without the god-awful fabric she picked out," she continues, warming to the subject.

He laughs. "Come on. It's not *that* bad."

"It *is* that bad."

"It's just a chair. We can get used to it."

"I don't *want* to get used to it. I don't want it in our house."

"Well, technically, it's *her* house."

A moment's silence. "Look. Why don't we just tell her to sell the damn place? We can find an apartment. . . ."

"We can't afford an apartment."

"There must be something."

"What? Where are we going to go?" he asks, hearing the frustration in his voice. He looks around, grateful the store is relatively empty. Heidi doesn't have a shift today, so she's at home. He wonders if she's alone, then shakes away the disquieting thought. "Look. I know it's hard. . . ."

"It's not hard," she counters. "It's *impossible*. And I've tried. I've tried and tried and tried. You know that."

"I know."

"Nothing I do is right. Nothing I do is ever good enough."

"I know it feels that way. . . ."

"It *is* that way. Your mother hates me, Aiden. She hates me."

"She doesn't hate you." He hears her

236

sniffing back tears. "Ah, babe. Please don't cry."

"I just feel so alone."

"You're not alone. You have me."

"Do I? I'm your wife, Aiden. You're supposed to stand up for me. You're supposed to be on my side."

"Why do there have to be sides?"

"Because that's the way your mother operates."

"You don't understand," Aiden says, rising to his mother's defense, as he always does. "She means well."

"She means well? *She means well?*" Heidi repeats, her voice rising. "Is that why she told you that she walked in on me and Julia's grandson, why she made it sound like she might have interrupted something?"

"You weren't smoking weed?"

"Yes, we'd smoked some weed. I told you that."

"Not till after she did."

"Yes, and I've apologized a million times," Heidi says.

"You understand how it must have looked to her," Aiden says. "She walks in, finds you with some strange guy . . ."

"Julia's *grandson.*"

"I don't care who he is. I don't want him in my house anymore."

"You mean *her* house, don't you?" Heidi says, throwing his earlier words back at him. "You know your mother won't be happy until she breaks us up."

"That's crazy. She's just looking out for me. I'm her only child. . . ."

"You're not a child! You're thirty years old."

"It's not about age," he argues. "Don't you understand? I'm all she has. She had to be both a mother and father to me after my father left."

"She didn't have to be anything of the kind," Heidi shoots back, tired of trying to be understanding. "That was her choice. She drove the poor man away, then denied him access and turned you against him —"

"Okay, let's not go there," Aiden interrupts, his head pounding, the knot in his stomach expanding, threatening to explode. "You don't know what it was like. You don't know what she went through when he left."

"I know your mother! I know her need to control everything and everybody."

"It's just hard for her to let go, that's all."

"Are you sure it's your mother who's having trouble letting go?"

Silence.

Aiden pictures himself back on that deserted country road, feels the mob at his back, the hands ripping at his shirt. His breath escapes his lungs in a series of sharp, painful bursts.

"I just don't know how much more of this I can take," Heidi says.

"What does that mean?"

"It means I'm tired of coming in second. It means that, at some point, you're going to have to choose. Your mother or me, Aiden. Who is it going to be?"

Aiden runs an exasperated hand through his hair, glancing from side to side, catching a glimpse of his supervisor watching him from beside another counter. "Look. I have to go. Can you hang in there a little longer? I promise, I'll make this right."

She says nothing.

"Heidi?"

"Sure," she says.

"Sure what?"

"I'll hang in there a little longer."

CHAPTER TWENTY-THREE

Dani is studying her reflection in the small round mirror of her compact, checking on the status of the bruise under her left eye, when her intercom buzzes. "Mrs. McKay is here to see you," the receptionist announces.

"Have her take a seat. I'll be with her in a few minutes." Dani dabs an extra drop of concealer on the bruise, hoping to diminish its mottled mustard-and-purple hue, then pats some powder over it.

She can still see it.

Not that it matters. None of her patients has noticed it so far, closing their eyes almost the second she reclines their chair, too wrapped up in their own issues to worry about hers. It's doubtful that Maggie McKay will be any different.

She should never have agreed to fit her in. But then, what choice had she had? The woman had called her at home first thing this morning, frantic because a filling had fallen out when she was brushing her teeth and she was afraid she might have cracked the tooth. She was starting a new job tomorrow, and she didn't have a dentist, was there any way Dani could see her sometime between when she dropped her son off at camp and picked him up again? She knew it was an imposition but she was desperate and yada, yada, yada.

So how could she say no? Especially if she ever needed Erin to babysit again. She presses the button on her intercom. "Take Mrs. McKay to room 3," she directs the receptionist, taking a final glimpse at her eye before returning her compact to her purse. She closes the door of her small office and heads down the winding hall of the clinic she shares with two other dentists toward examining room 3.

She stops when she sees the beautiful blonde sitting in the chair. Is it possible she has the wrong room? she wonders, checking the number on the door. "Maggie?"

"Thanks so much for seeing me," Maggie tells her. "I didn't know who else to call."

"Happy to help out," Dani lies, approaching the chair where Maggie is reclining, her large purse filling her lap. "You look so different."

"You like it?"

"It's gorgeous. *You're* gorgeous."

"Amazing what a little hair coloring can do," Maggie says.

"Well, it's very lovely."

"Thank you."

"You said somethin' about losin' . . . los-*ing* . . . a filling," Dani says, careful to enunciate the final *g*. She sits on the stool beside Maggie's head and starts adjusting her chair. "Why don't we just put your bag over here, so it's not in our way?"

"No, that's okay," Maggie tells her. "I can hold on to it."

"I'm gonna need a little space. It'll just be on the counter. Right over here. It'll be perfectly safe. I promise," Dani says, lifting the bag from Maggie's lap. "My God, what have you got in this thing? It's as heavy as a possum."

Maggie laughs, although the laugh is more nervous than amused.

Dani continues lowering Maggie's chair until she's satisfied with the angle. "Why don't you open your mouth and let's have a look."

"It's been a while since I've been to the dentist."

"So I see," Dani says, manipulating a small mirror inside Maggie's mouth. "Your teeth could use a good cleanin', that's for sure. Get the receptionist to make an appointment with the hygienist before you leave."

"It's the back tooth. . . ."

"Yes, I see the problem. I'm afraid you're gonna need a crown."

"What? Can't you just refill it?"

"No, I cannot. There's barely enough tooth left to fill. Whole thing would just collapse."

"But how many visits is that going to take? I mean, you have to take a mold and put in a temporary crown and —"

"Oh, my good Lord. It *has* been a while since you've been to the dentist. No, we haven't done that in years. It's all done by computer now."

"By computer?"

"Computer takes a complete picture of your mouth, measures everythin', the space between the teeth, all that stuff, then goes ahead and makes the crown, all by its lonesome. I just fit it in and make a few adjustments, if needed. No big deal. You'll be out of here in a couple of hours."

"You do this sort of thing often?"

"All day, every day," Dani says.

"Wow," Maggie says. "You're so professional."

"Well, it's what I do."

243

"I'm sorry. I didn't mean . . ."

"What exactly were you expectin'?" Dani asks.

"I don't know. You just seem so different than when I've talked to you before."

Dani shrugs, not sure how to respond. "Shall we get started?"

"So, how does it feel?" Dani asks Maggie when she's done.

"Feels good," Maggie tells her. "I can't believe it was so easy."

"The miracle of modern science. You're good to go."

"What happened to your eye?" Maggie asks.

"What?" Dani feels her breath catch in her lungs. Her hand flutters nervously to her face.

"That's quite a bruise you've got."

Dani forces a laugh from her throat. "Would you believe me if I told you I walked into a wall?"

"Is that what happened?"

Dani bites down on her lower lip, fighting the urge to tell Maggie the truth, that the bruise is the result of her face colliding not with a wall, but with her husband's fist. "More or less." Does Maggie believe her? It's hard to tell. "I got up in the middle of the night to go to the bathroom," she continues, "and it was dark and my eyes were pretty much closed, and I misjudged where the door was and walked plumb into it. Poor Nick," she adds for good measure. "I screamed so loud, the man almost had a heart attack."

"And the one on your wrist?" Maggie says, voice quiet, eyes probing.

Dani's head snaps toward her right hand, sees the large purple bruise peeking out from beneath the sleeve of her white lab coat. "My goodness. Didn't even know that one was there." She takes a step back. "You can settle up with the receptionist on your way out, and be sure to make an appointment with the hygienist. You gotta take care of your teeth if you want to keep 'em."

"I will," Maggie says, standing up and walking toward the door. "And thanks again."

"Anytime," Dani says, grabbing Maggie's purse from the counter. "Don't forget your purse."

"Oh my God, no," Maggie says, taking the bag from Dani's hands and clutching it to her chest. "Listen," she says, stopping in the doorway. "I'm around . . . I mean, I live right next door . . . if you ever need to talk . . . about anything."

"Sure thing," Dani says, keeping her voice deliberately light. "Now, if you'll excuse me, I got a patient waitin' for me in the next room." She walks away before Maggie can say another word.

Dani runs into her office and locks the door, collapsing in the chair behind her desk and laying her head in her hands. What is the matter with her? She's such a strong, confident woman at work. Even Maggie, a woman she's talked to only a handful of times in the past, commented on how different she is. So, what happens to her when she leaves the clinic and goes home?

Nick happens, she acknowledges, stifling a cry.

She wonders if she was able to fool Maggie, then wonders how long she'll be able to keep fooling herself. How many times can she tell herself that, despite his bad temper, her husband is a good man?

The first time Nick hit her was right after she announced she was pregnant with Tyler. He'd apologized profusely and begged forgiveness. He was under such enormous pressure, he said, crying copious tears, assuring her it would never happen again. She believed him. Nick loved her; she loved him. He'd never raised his hand to her before.

He never would again.

Except, of course, he did.

At first, she'd tried defending herself, but that only seemed to enrage him more. His open palm became a closed fist, his blows carefully aimed where the bruises wouldn't show. Eventually, he stopped crying, apologizing, promising, and transferred the tears, the apologies, and the promises to do better onto her. He stopped caring where his blows landed. She started rationalizing, deferring, walking on eggshells, afraid to say anything in case what she said might set him off.

Worse, she started accepting the blame. It was her fault that he felt compelled to lash out.

The periods of rage would be followed by weeks, even months, when Nick was the way the rest of the world viewed him: loving, compassionate, kind. During those times, Dani fooled herself into believing that the worst was behind them, that her husband was a changed man, that the beatings would stop. He loved her after all; she loved him. Their love had created two beautiful young boys.

And then the cycle would begin again.

First came the criticism: She could do nothing right. She was either a neglectful mother for going back to work within months of giving birth, or she was smothering her sons with her constant coddling, turning them into sissies; she was either too subservient or too willful; a penny pincher or a spendthrift; too ambitious or too lazy; too smart for her own good or too stupid to live; too friendly or too standoffish. Whatever she was, she was either too much of it or not enough.

Next came the excuses: He was exhausted. Emotionally drained. All he needed when he got home was a little peace and quiet. Was that really too much to ask?

Then came the blame: She was never satisfied. She could never leave things alone. She always had to be right. She was constantly at him about something, contradicting him in front of their sons, questioning his decisions, undermining his authority, pushing his buttons.

Next came the fury.

And finally, the fists.

Too late Dani understands that Nick is never going to change. If anything, the beatings have been occurring more frequently and getting progressively worse. Fear has replaced the love she once felt. She knows she should leave, but she no longer has the strength. She is as useless as he claims.

She knows it's only a matter of time before he kills her.

CHAPTER TWENTY-FOUR

Mark is sitting on the floor of his grandmother's bedroom, her jewelry box open in front of him, his hands dripping with thin gold chains, his fingers working frantically to separate them before Julia comes back inside. She's been tinkering around in her tiny back garden for the better part of half an hour, and he doubts she'll have the stamina to be out there much longer. Gardening is hard work, something he discovered yesterday when she cajoled him into helping her out.

With her unceasing encouragement, he'd mowed the lawn, pulled out a bunch of surprisingly strong and stubborn weeds, then assisted in the planting of several rows of bright coral impatiens along the bottom of the waist-high black iron fences separating his grandmother's property from the backyards of the houses to either side.

"Beautiful," his grandmother had pro-

250

nounced when he was done, her voice brimming with satisfaction. "That looks so much better! Well done, sweetheart."

He'd felt a surge of pride, which was followed immediately by an even bigger surge of shame when she thrust two twenty-dollar bills into his hand as payment for his efforts. "No, Nana," he'd protested, having already removed that same amount from her purse earlier in the day.

"Nonsense," she'd insisted. "You worked hard. You earned it."

Of course, he'd used the money to buy weed.

He shakes his head, recalling the hint of menace in his dealer's voice, the not-so-veiled threat that it was either time to come up with the money he still owed or pay the consequences.

So, what choice does he have? His grandmother isn't going to miss one measly gold chain that she never wears. Hell, she won't even know it's gone. He tugs at the chains, realizing too late that he's only made things worse. "Goddamn it," he whispers.

"What are you doing?" the voice asks from the doorway.

Fuck. Mark feels every muscle in his body tense. He closes his eyes, trying to will himself into invisibility, then considers jumping to his feet and hurling himself out the second-story window. Anything to avoid having to turn around, to confront the mixture of confusion and disappointment he knows he'll find on his nana's face. How could he have been so stupid? More to the point, how could he not have heard her come inside?

"Nana," he says, forcing a smile onto his lips as he swivels toward her, allowing the chains to drop back into the jewelry box. "I swear, this isn't what it looks like." *God, could he sound any lamer?*

"What does it look like?"

"Like I'm trying to steal . . . I'm *not.*" *She's not going to make this easy,* he thinks, hoping desperately to come up with something even vaguely plausible to explain what he's doing in her bedroom, his hand caught in the grown-up equivalent of a cookie jar. "Actually," he says, hitting on something that just might work, "I was hoping to surprise you."

"You succeeded," Julia says, waiting for him to continue.

"It's just that I noticed that these were all tangled up and I thought that, what with your arthritis and everything, you'd never be able to do it, so I thought I'd untangle them for you."

"That's so considerate of you, sweetheart."
She's smiling now.

He smiles in return. "Well, I —"

"When did you notice this?"

Shit. It's not an unreasonable question. *Damn it.* That was the problem with lying. You always had to be ready with a quick follow-up. "The other day. When you couldn't find your glasses," he improvises, gratefully recalling an incident he could exploit, "and I came in here to look for them. I thought maybe you might have left them in a drawer when you were getting dressed, so I started opening them, which is when I saw the music box. And I've always had kind of a thing for music boxes. . . ." *Really? I had to add that? I couldn't stop while I was ahead?* Which was another problem with lying, he understands. The desire to embellish. Not knowing when to stop.

She smiles and Mark feels his body relax with relief. *She's buying it.* "Anyway, I opened it. And I saw all these chains, pretty much glued together. And I thought that if I ever got the chance, I'd surprise you by untangling them."

Julia looks crestfallen. "And I went and ruined the surprise."

God, I'm a shit, Mark thinks. "No, I'm just sorry, the way it must have looked. . . ."

253

The phone rings. Nobody moves.

"Are you going to answer that?" he asks. "It could be the IRS." He tries for a laugh, but the sound scrapes against his throat, then dies in his chest.

Julia walks to the phone by the side of her bed and picks it up. "Hello? Oh, hello, dear. It's your father," she whispers to Mark. "Yes, I'm very well, thank you for asking. You? That's good. And . . . Poopsy?" She smiles, and Mark stifles a laugh. "Yes, sorry, dear. I know. I shouldn't make fun. Yes, Mark's still here. And yes, I know I shouldn't have kept it from you. I've apologized. But he's been a big help to me. No, no trouble at all. Did you know he's a wonderful cook? Well, he is. He's standing right here. Do you want to speak to him? What's that?" she asks, shaking her head in Mark's direction to indicate his father's lack of interest. "Twelve o'clock, Friday? Yes, that should be okay. Shall I invite Mark to join us? Oh. Okay, fine. I guess I'll see you then."

"What's happening at noon on Friday?" Mark asks as Julia replaces the receiver.

"Lunch at The Breakers."

"Wow. Fancy-shmancy. I take it I'm not invited."

"I'm sorry, darling. Your father can be quite the ass sometimes."

"How'd that happen anyway?" Mark asks.

"How did *what* happen?"

"You're just so different from my dad. It's hard to believe he's your son."

"I know." Julia nods in agreement. "I feel that way sometimes, too."

Mark smiles, then stands up, returning the jewelry box to the drawer. "I'll try untangling them again later," he says. "Right now, I think I could use some fresh air."

"Of course, darling."

Mark surrounds his grandmother with his long, skinny arms, kissing the top of her coarse blond hair. She's been so good to him, he thinks as he's running down the stairs — letting him sleep till noon, not pressuring him to get a job, never saying a negative word, trusting him, believing his ridiculous lies. And how does he repay her? By taking money from her purse. By attempting to steal her jewelry. By being an even bigger ass than his father.

He opens the front door and steps outside, feeling for the joints in his pocket. He takes a quick look around, then slips into the shadows.

He floats back inside almost an hour later. "Nana?"

"I'm in the dining room."

He finds her sitting at the table, its glass surface covered with sheets of loose paper. "Hi, sweetheart," she says, smiling up at him. "Come see what I found."

He approaches the table, noticing that most of the pages are covered with a child's drawings, some in brightly colored crayons, some in black magic marker. He lifts up several sheets that have been stapled together.

" 'Mark Goes to the Pool,' " he reads, the words all but leaping off the page and dancing before his eyes. " 'By Mark Fisher.' " He laughs. "You've got to be kidding." The bottom half of the page contains a pen drawing of a boy with a big smile and curly dark hair walking toward a tiny square labeled *Pool*.

Mark turns the page, continues reading the uneven scrawl. " 'One day a boy named Mark was going to the pool and having a great time but . . . he couldn't find the change room.' "

An empty box labeled *Change room* fills the next page, beside another smaller box indicating the time: *1:30.*

" 'But he found it in the end!' " Mark reads, laughing now. " 'So he changed and went into the pool.' " One last drawing, this one of the boy in his bathing suit, splashing in a big pool of blue water. " 'I was happy as a butterfly!' " Mark is surprised to find his eyes welling up with tears.

"What's wrong, sweetheart?"

"Imagine being as happy as a butterfly," he says softly.

Julia smiles and reaches up to touch his arm.

"I can't believe you saved this."

"Of course I saved it. I saved everything you made me. See?" She motions toward the other pages strewn across the table. "You were always such an interesting little boy. So full of contradictions. One minute 'happy as a butterfly,' the next frantic because you 'couldn't find the change room.' Metaphorically speaking, of course," she says with a wink.

"Even if I weren't stoned out of my mind," Mark says slowly, "I don't think I'd have a clue what that means."

Julia laughs. "It means I love you, sweet boy."

"I love you, too." He tosses the story back to the table, then plops down into the seat beside her. "I wasn't trying to untangle those gold chains as a surprise for you," he admits. "I was trying to untangle them so I could steal one."

Julia nods, says nothing.

"And I've been taking money from your purse," he says.

"I know."

A long pause. "If you knew, why didn't you do anything?"

"What should I have done?"

"You could have kicked me out."

"Why would I do that? I like having you around."

"Even though I'm a thief?"

"Small price to pay," she says. "You never took very much. Besides, I'm eating better than I have in years."

"That's not really the point."

"I know." She laughs. "You know I would have given you the money if you'd asked."

"I know. That's what makes it worse. I'm just a worthless piece of shit."

"You are *not* a worthless piece of shit. You're just . . . a little lost, that's all." She motions toward the story. "You just haven't found the change room yet."

He lays his head against her shoulder. "Still have no idea what that means."

"Don't worry, sweetheart," Julia says, kissing his forehead. "I have faith. You'll figure it out."

CHAPTER TWENTY-FIVE

Maggie sits behind the reception desk at Nadine's, watching the three stylists at work and marveling at their different techniques. Nadine is like a brushfire, fast and furious, talking almost as quickly as her hands are moving. Jerome is more of a slow burn, controlled and precise in everything he does, relentless in his pursuit of perfection. Unlike Nadine, he says very little, aside from regularly oohing and aahing over his handiwork. Rita, who works only three days a week, falls somewhere between the two. She's slower than Nadine and more instinctive than Jerome. There's a seeming carelessness about her technique that belies her expertise.

No wonder the small, inauspicious salon is so busy, Maggie thinks. In the short time since she started working here, she has yet to witness a bad haircut or encounter a dissatisfied customer.

"You look lovely," she tells Sandi Marcus truthfully as the woman is settling her bill. Sandi Marcus is nearing ninety years old and looks two decades younger, thanks in large measure to Jerome's expert styling.

"Jerome's a genius," the woman agrees. "I'm going to marry him," she leans in and whispers. "Don't tell him I said that. I want it to be a surprise."

Maggie laughs, something she's been doing a lot lately. She'd almost forgotten how much she enjoys being around people, even if she's making a fraction of the income she made as a teacher. But while the salaries aren't comparable, there's something to be said for a job that ends when she walks out the door. She no longer has lessons to prepare, papers to mark, difficult parents to meet with, disinterested students to discipline. She no longer carries the stress of helping to shape and guide young lives. She no longer has to set a good example. She only has to show up, answer the phone, make appointments and remind clients of future ones, accept payment for services rendered, and smile, something else she's been doing with surprising frequency.

Even Craig has noticed the change. "You're different," he said yesterday when he arrived to take the kids for dinner.

Maggie's hand shot automatically to her newly platinum hair. "I know. It's quite the change."

"It's not just your hair," he said. "You seem . . . I don't know . . ." He let the unfinished sentence hang provocatively in the space between them.

In that moment, Maggie thought he might be about to kiss her, and she leaned forward, her lips parting expectantly, her body tingling with anticipation. Clearly, he'd missed her as much as she missed him.

"I guess the new job agrees with you," he said instead.

Maggie stiffened. "I guess it does." *You're such an idiot,* she thought, not sure if she was referring to her husband or herself. Then, partly to mask her anger and disappointment, and partly because she never could leave well enough alone, she said, "How are things going with the new sales rep?"

Craig frowned. "Maggie . . ." he said, then fell silent, leaving her name dangling, as he had his earlier observation.

Abandoning her yet again.

Damn him anyway.

"Kids," she'd called up the stairs. "Hurry up. Your father's waiting."

"Maggie . . ."

God, she was such a fool.

"Maggie? Hello? Earth to Maggie."

It takes her a few seconds to realize that the person calling her name isn't her estranged husband, but Jerome. "I'm so sorry," she apologizes.

"Where'd you go, sweetheart?" Jerome asks.

Maggie shrugs. "What can I do for you?"

Jerome motions toward his client, a middle-aged woman whose entire head is wrapped in a layer of clear plastic wrap. "I was wondering if you'd mind getting Mrs. Whittaker an egg salad sandwich and a cup of mint tea."

Maggie checks her watch and notes that it's lunchtime. "Not at all." She steps around the counter, grabbing her purse off the floor by her feet.

"Just leave that there," Jerome says, taking the purse from her hand. "My God. You're going to destroy your shoulders lugging this thing around." He returns the bag to its previous position behind the counter.

Maggie feels a moment of panic. She never goes anywhere without her purse. What if someone were to look inside it? Still, she can't risk insulting Jerome or arousing unnecessary suspicion. "I'll need money," she protests.

"Take it from the till," Nadine instructs from her workstation. "We'll settle up later. Who else wants something?"

"I'd love a tall blonde," says Rita's client, referring to Starbucks's special blend.

"Wouldn't we all?" asks Jerome.

Maggie smiles, catching sight of her reflection in the mirror behind Jerome's head and deciding once again that she likes what she sees. She is still smiling as she leaves the salon and heads toward Starbucks, determined to smile more and worry less. It's time to take back control of her life. She's lived in fear long enough.

And speaking of fear, what's going on with Dani Wilson and her husband? Something's not right there, although it's hard to believe that Nick Wilson, a man dedicated to alleviating the pain and suffering of others, could be responsible for Dani's bruises. There must be another explanation. Nick Wilson seems like such a decent man.

Which is more than she can say about Sean Grant. *Something definitely off about that man,* Maggie thinks, although she can't put her finger on it.

Her hand is reaching for the door when she feels someone close behind her and a masculine arm stretch across hers.

Her breath instinctively catches in her

throat, a strangled cry emerging from her mouth. So much for taking back control of her life.

"Sorry, I didn't mean to startle you. I was just trying to be a gentleman and get the door. Sorry," the man says again, his blue eyes narrowing. "My God!" he exclaims. "Maggie?"

"Rick Atwood, certified public accountant," Maggie replies.

"Wow. You look great."

"Excuse me," a woman says from behind them. "Are you going inside or what?"

"Sorry," Maggie and Rick reply, their voices overlapping. They step inside the crowded space and into a long lineup.

"Wow," he says again. "I can't get over how terrific you look. Not that you didn't look nice before," he adds quickly.

"I looked awful before."

"No," he says. "Not awful. Just . . . this is better."

"Thank you." Maggie's smile reappears. "Actually, I've been meaning to stop by your office."

"Really? You need an accountant?"

"No. Well, I don't know. I might," Maggie says, wondering if she and Craig will require separate accountants, if they file for divorce. *When,* she corrects herself silently. *Not if.* "I wanted to thank you for telling me about the job that was available. . . ."

"Oh, right. I remember. Did your daughter get it?"

"No, actually. *I* did."

"*You* did?"

"You're looking at Maggie McKay, Nadine's new receptionist."

"I didn't realize you were looking."

"Neither did I." Maggie laughs, noting the curiosity in his eyes, eyes that are even bluer — and younger — than she first realized. "Very long story."

"I like long stories."

Maggie nods. "Maybe some other time."

"I'd like that, too."

Maggie has no idea what to say to that, so she says nothing. Is he saying he'd like to see her again? She doesn't know, and she's through with jumping to conclusions where men are concerned, trying to second-guess what is really on their minds. If Richard Atwood, certified public accountant, is really interested in seeing her again, as he seems to be implying, if this isn't just her overactive imagination or a case of wishful thinking, if he isn't just being polite, making idle conversation while they wait in line, he'll have to come right out and say so.

"Are you married, Maggie McKay?" he

surprises her by asking.

"Technically, yes. I guess," she hears herself say.

"You guess?"

"We're separated."

He smiles. "In that case, are you free tomorrow night?"

"What?"

"I realize it's a Saturday night and very short notice. . . ."

"I am free, yes," Maggie says quickly.

"Great. Would you like to have dinner with me?"

What's happening? Maggie thinks as they reach the front of the line.

"What'll it be?" asks the girl behind the counter.

Maggie recites her order, then waits as Rick tells the girl he'd like a breakfast sandwich and a large cup of black coffee. They move to the side of the counter to wait. "Well?" he asks.

"Did you just ask me out? Just checking that I'm not hallucinating."

He laughs. "You're not hallucinating. I did just ask you out."

"How old are you?" Maggie asks, the question out of her mouth before she can stop it.

"Twenty-eight," he says easily.

"My God." *He's even younger than I thought.*

"Is that a problem?"

"Well, I'm a bit older than you are. . . ." *More than a bit,* she thinks.

"Is that a problem?" he repeats.

Maggie hesitates. "I don't know."

"It's just dinner, Maggie. We don't have to get married, if you don't want to." He smiles.

"No, of course we don't." She tries to laugh, but coughs instead. "Twenty-eight! Shit! Sure, why not? I'd love to have dinner with you tomorrow night. What the hell!"

"Anywhere special you'd like to go?"

"I've always liked the Palm Beach Grill." She and Craig used to go there whenever they could get reservations. "But it's so hard to get a table."

"It's off-season. Shouldn't be too difficult. Seven o'clock?"

"Seven is good. I'll meet you there."

He regards her quizzically. "You're not going to stand me up, are you?"

Hell, she thinks. *I'm forty-two; you're twenty-eight.* "I won't stand you up," she says.

"Maggie!" a voice behind the counter calls out. "Rick! Your orders are ready."

Maggie smiles. *Ready or not,* she thinks.

CHAPTER TWENTY-SIX

Sean has spent the morning online, researching guns. He's learned that the United States tops the list of countries with the most firearms, with more than one gun per person, and that while Americans make up only four percent of the world's population, they own forty-six percent of the world's firepower. An estimated three hundred and ninety-three million guns belong to three hundred and twenty-six million people, which means sixty-seven million guns left over, if every man, woman, and child owned one.

Twenty-nine percent of gun owners own five or more.

Fully forty-two percent of American households have guns.

There is no federal limit to how many guns a person can own.

One collector compares his gun collecting habit to buying shoes. Another describes guns as "man jewelry." Yet another likens them to tattoos — "You can't have just one."

Sean closes his laptop and finishes the last of the vodka in his glass, laughing at the comparisons. He's never been overly fond of either jewelry or tattoos. He has no interest in accumulating guns.

All he needs is one.

Does he really have the courage to end his life?

Coward, he hears his father scoff, knowing how disapproving his dad would be. He's happy that the man is no longer alive to witness the mess his son has made of his life. He can feel, indeed can almost *taste,* the disappointment in his father's eyes, and knows it will be the same look he'll see in Olivia's when she discovers not only what an abject failure he has proven himself to be, but also the extent of his deception.

He knows she asked her boss for an advance on her paycheck in order to pay back Maggie McKay. He knows how difficult that was for her to do. She has her pride after all.

Sean discards the empty bottle of vodka in the garbage bag under the sink and checks the freezer for another bottle he already knows isn't there. Is Olivia aware of how much his drinking has increased in the past year?

"Add it to my list of failures," he says aloud, stumbling as he pushes himself away from the kitchen table. He checks his wallet as he heads for the front door, counting out forty-three dollars in cash, the last of the money he withdrew from their joint checking account.

He climbs behind the wheel of his car, dismissing the thought that he probably shouldn't be driving. A DUI is the last thing he needs. Although prison might provide a welcome respite, the excuse he needs to do nothing but sit around all day feeling sorry for himself. He chuckles as he backs his car out of the garage, managing an exaggerated wave to Julia Fisher's grandson, who is smoking in the shadows. He saw the old lady the other day bending Dr. Nick's ear and couldn't help admiring the good doctor's patience, the way he leaned in and actually seemed to be listening. "More power to you, Doc," he says now, doffing an invisible hat as he pulls onto the main street on his way to his favorite liquor store.

As he turns onto Donald Ross Road, the impulse strikes him to stop at his former place of work. Maybe showing his face there will remind them how instrumental he was to the company's success, force them to acknowledge how much he's missed, how much he's needed. Maybe they've taken on some new clients and their financial outlook has improved so that now they can afford to have him back. He'd even be willing to take a slight cut in pay, should the talks progress that far.

He pulls into the parking lot of the three-story white stucco building, noting that his former parking spot is now occupied by a charcoal gray Porsche Panamera. "Somebody's moving up in the world," he mutters, wondering which of his colleagues can afford such an expensive automobile. He pulls into the empty space beside it, ignoring the spot's reserved designation. Exiting his car, he's tempted to run his key along the side of the Porsche's shiny new exterior, but is dissuaded by the sight of a man heading his way. Sean quickly pockets his key.

"Beautiful day," the man says as he walks past Sean toward his car at the far side of the lot.

Is it? Sean wonders, breathing a sigh of relief. He hasn't noticed. He glances toward the cloudless sky, the sun so bright it hurts to even look in its direction. *So much for nature echoing the thoughts of man,* he thinks, referencing another of his father's ubiquitous quotes. A quotation for every

271

occasion. The man was a regular Hallmark card, for God's sake.

Sean pulls open the heavy exterior glass door of the building, sauntering through the white marble lobby and stepping into the waiting elevator. When he worked here, he often took the stairs, sometimes two at a time. But that was then, and this is now. Now he has barely enough energy to push the elevator button for the third floor.

Another heavy glass door separates Merit Marketing's reception area from the rest of the workplace. It's one of those open-concept arrangements, with the creative team occupying the large central space and the offices of the president, vice presidents, and various heads of departments running along the outer walls. A large boardroom sits at the far end, beside what used to be his office as one of Merit's five senior vice presidents.

But again, that was then. This is now.

Now he is an unemployed former corporate vice president who is about to lose everything if he can't find a job in the next several weeks. He gave his life's blood to this company, for God's sake, and they tossed him aside as unceremoniously as yesterday's garbage. They owe him.

Sean feels a wave of anger swell inside

him, so strong it almost knocks him over, and he has to lean against the nearby wall to keep from collapsing. He is suddenly dizzy with fury, drowning in defeat. And maybe because his head is still swimming with statistics from this morning's Internet search — shocking fact: Nearly forty thousand people died in gun-related violence in the United States in 2017, the highest annual total in decades — the thought comes to him that it would be ridiculously easy for someone to burst into Merit Marketing with a gun and shoot up the place.

How many articles has he read in the past year alone about disgruntled former employees returning to the places where they used to work and gunning down their erstwhile bosses and co-workers?

He smiles, picturing himself dressed all in black — Keanu Reeves in *The Matrix,* or better yet, as John Wick, avenging the murder of his innocent little puppy — an AK-47 in one hand, another slung across his shoulder.

He shakes the thought aside. Where are all these gruesome fantasies coming from?

The receptionist behind the high black-and-gold marble counter smiles back, although her smile is more practiced than genuine. The woman's name is Kathy Millard and she's been sitting behind that counter for as long as he can remember, flashing that same insincere smile.

"Hello, Kathy," Sean says in greeting, noting that nothing about either the woman or the lobby has changed much since he left. Both are neat and attractive, in flattering shades of black and beige.

"Oh my goodness. Sean!" Kathy says, large brown eyes doing a not-so-subtle sweep of the man standing before her. "I almost didn't recognize you."

Too late Sean realizes how slovenly he must appear. He's dressed in ill-fitting jeans and an old T-shirt that highlights the added weight to his midsection. He's wearing flip-flops.

"I'm so used to seeing you in a suit and tie," Kathy says, clearly flustered.

"One of the benefits of taking extended time off is not having to wear the uniform every day," he says, hating the forced joviality in his voice. *Can she hear it?*

"So, you're not working?"

Sean hears the unvoiced "still" she diplomatically left out of her question. "I'm actually mulling over a few offers. But I want to make sure that where I end up is really where I want to be. I find I'm in no hurry to rejoin the rat race."

274

"Well, wherever you end up, they'll be lucky to have you."

"Thank you. You're very kind." He smiles. *Condescending bitch,* he thinks.

He'll shoot her first.

"Is Harvey in?"

Kathy glances toward the president's office halfway down the north wall. "He is, but I think he's in a meeting."

Sean's smile hardens. "Could you check?"

He waits while Kathy presses the digits of Harvey Shulman's extension. "Mr. Shulman," she says. "Sorry to interrupt, but Sean Grant is here to see you. No, he didn't say." She lowers the phone to her chest. "He's asking if this is in regard to anything in particular?"

Sean shakes his head, determined to keep smiling when what he really wants to do is put a bullet right between the woman's eyes. "No. Just hoping to say a friendly hello."

"He says he's just hoping to say a friendly hello," Kathy parrots into the phone. "Certainly. I'll tell him." She replaces the receiver. "Mr. Shulman is just finishing up with a long-distance call. He shouldn't be much longer. If you'd care to have a seat . . ." She motions toward two black leather chairs tucked into the corner of the reception area.

"No, I'm happy to stand." Sean approaches the door to the inner sanctum and leans against it, watching the imprint of his warm breath stain the cool glass and noting the women in their short skirts and tight pants going about their business on the other side. He zeroes in on Barbara Taylor and Vince McKenzie, two of the senior V.P.s who still have their jobs, conferring over some document. Neither has reached out to him since he was let go.

He'll shoot them next.

Or maybe he'll go right for the big man himself. Hell, might as well start at the top. He imagines himself moving from office to office, spraying bullets in all directions as he goes, every now and then pausing to fire indiscriminately at whoever is foolhardy enough to try to escape.

Someone will undoubtedly call the police, and they'll arrive, order him to stand down, to surrender his weapons. They'll call his wife in hopes of persuading her to talk some sense into him. But she won't answer because she'll already be dead. He'll have shot her before leaving the house.

In the end, of course, they'll kill him, too. And he'll go down in the proverbial blaze of glory. Suicide by cop, he believes is the term they use. The perfect solution.

All's well that ends well. Right, Pop?

He knows they're never going to offer him his old job back. Pride would stop them, no matter how much they wanted him back. Shulman would be far too embarrassed to admit he'd made a mistake. And he certainly isn't going to beg for it, let alone agree to a pay cut. What the hell had he been thinking?

He returns to the reception counter. "I'm gonna go," he tells Kathy Millard. "Tell Harvey I'll catch him another time."

"Are you sure?" she asks, clearly surprised by his abrupt change of mind. "He should be out any minute."

"No, that's okay. I have another appointment, and I didn't realize how late it was." He steps inside the elevator, deciding to head to the nearest gun store, decide on a weapon, then fill out the various forms necessary to get this show on the road. He'll figure out a way to come up with the money later. "Nice to see you again, Kathy," he calls to her as the elevator doors are closing. "Take care of yourself."

CHAPTER TWENTY-SEVEN

Julia Fisher sits in the passenger seat of her son's Tesla, wondering where they're going now. Lunch is finally over, and she's exhausted, having endured almost ninety minutes of mind-numbing small talk with her son and his pea-brained wife. Ninety minutes she'll never get back. Ninety minutes she can't afford to spare. Not at her age. And really, if she has to listen to one more word about Poppy's insane plans for designing a line of high-tech swimwear, despite never having taken a design course or knowing a thing about technology, she just might throw herself out of the moving car. Providing, of course, she can figure out how to open the damn doors.

"Where are we going?" she asks, glancing toward the ocean on her left. She's never been very good with either directions or geography, but she knows they're heading south when they should be heading north.

"Shouldn't we be going the other way?"

"I want you to see something," Norman says.

"What?"

"You'll see."

"Can't you just tell me?"

"I'd rather show you," he says.

"I'm a little tired."

"This won't take long," Poppy says, reaching around from the backseat to pat Julia's arm.

Julia fights the urge to shrug it off.

"Did you enjoy your lunch?" Poppy asks.

"I did."

"You didn't eat very much. Didn't you like it?"

Didn't I just answer that question? Julia wonders. "It was delicious. Thank you again."

"No thanks necessary." Poppy falls back against the buttery leather interior of the backseat. "Would you just look at that ocean. It's so . . . big."

"So big and so . . . wet," Julia says.

"Mother . . ." Norman warns softly.

"My swimsuits are going to be made specifically with the ocean in mind," Poppy says.

Julia reaches for the door handle. If only she could find the damn thing, she'd be mercifully dead in seconds.

"Maybe I should create one line for salt water and another one for pools. Chlorine is just murder on bathing suits, don't you think?"

"Absolutely," Julia says. "But what about fresh water? Shouldn't you have a line for that as well?"

"What do you mean, fresh water?" Poppy says.

Dear God. "*Fresh* water. Like a lake. Or a river. Or a pond."

"Those aren't salt water?" Poppy asks.

"They are not," Julia tells her.

"So, you think I need a third line?"

"You're the expert," Julia says.

"Mother . . ."

"How did you come up with this idea anyway?" Julia asks, curious despite herself. "I mean, you were a personal trainer. I would have thought that, if you were going to design anything, athletic gear would be more up your alley."

"I thought of that, but it's such a crowded field right now. You know my sister Rainbow?"

Julia sighs. The conversation is starting to echo the car ride: She has no idea where either is going. "The one with the long dark hair?"

"No, that's Sunshine."

Rainbow, Sunshine, and Poppy. *That's what happens when your parents grow up in a commune,* Julia thinks. "What about her?"

"Well, I got the idea because of her. She went swimming in the ocean last month, and she was wearing a new bikini. A really nice one. Very expensive. And suddenly, along came this giant wave and knocked her flat on her face, and when she stood up, she discovered that her bikini bottom was around her ankles. Can you imagine?"

"I'm trying not to," Julia says. She glances at her son, noting the big grin on his face.

"So, I decided that someone should design a line of swimsuits that stay up, no matter what. And then I thought, why not me?"

"Why not you indeed?" Julia repeats. Then because she can't help herself, she adds, "But what if you have to go to the bathroom?"

"What?"

"I mean, if they're that hard to get off —"

"Mother, please," Norman interjects. "We'll hire people to figure all that out."

Poppy must be sensational in bed, Julia thinks, nodding and closing her eyes, grateful for the silence that follows.

"Mom . . ." she hears in the next instant. "Mother . . ."

Julia opens her eyes.

"We're here."

"What?"

"You fell asleep," Poppy informs her.

Julia looks around, trying to focus. The car is no longer moving. The ocean is nowhere in sight. They're parked in front of a sprawling white four-story structure in what appears to be the middle of nowhere. The sign on the lush front lawn identifies the building as Manor Born. "What the hell is this?"

"Now, don't go getting all upset," Norman says. "We're just here to have a look."

"I think you're going to be very pleasantly surprised," Poppy says, as the car doors lift into the air.

"I don't like surprises, and I have no intention of setting foot inside that place."

"Come on, Mother. I was talking to Dr. Wilson and he agrees this place would be perfect for you."

"You were talking to Dr. Wilson about me?" So that's what the good doctor was hinting at the other morning when he was ostensibly asking about her health and how she was managing.

"All I'm asking is that you keep an open mind."

"I really think you're going to be very

pleasantly surprised," Poppy says again, as if simply repeating what she said earlier will be enough to change Julia's mind.

"We're not leaving here until we do this." Norman reaches over to unbuckle his mother's seatbelt.

"This is ridiculous." Julia refuses to budge until it becomes obvious that Norman means what he says, that they aren't going anywhere until she complies, and that the sooner she gives in, the sooner she'll be able to leave. "Remind me never to have lunch with you again," she says as she gets out of the car, the outside humidity wrapping around her like a heavy wool sweater.

"Ah, come on, Julia," Poppy says. "You know Norman just wants what's best for you."

"I think *I* know what's best for me," Julia counters, brushing past her daughter-in-law and marching up the front walk, as eager to escape her son and his wife as she is the hot, oppressive air.

The front door opens automatically and Julia steps into the spacious, air-conditioned lobby.

To her great chagrin, she discovers that Poppy is right — she *is* pleasantly surprised. The lobby is bright and beautifully appointed, the art both colorful and tasteful,

283

the well-stuffed sofas and chairs sleek yet comfortable-looking. The air-conditioning is set at just the right temperature, a rarity in South Florida, where indoor thermometers often register only a few degrees above freezing. It even smells good — fresh but not cloying.

"No 'old people' smell," Poppy leans over to whisper, as if reading Julia's mind.

Indeed, from what Julia can see, there are no old people at all. No elderly men shuffling down the corridors in worn-out slippers, no ancient crones milling about aimlessly, no poor souls lining the halls in wheelchairs, staring forlornly toward the front door, vacant eyes praying for visitors.

Or death.

Instead, what she sees is a group of well-dressed seniors, many clearly years younger than she is, talking animatedly by the side of a coffee machine, while others peruse magazines and newspapers in front of a large picture window overlooking acres of well-maintained greenery.

"What do you think?" Norman asks.

"It's a lobby," Julia says, refusing to be charmed so easily. "Are we done? Can we leave now?"

"Not quite yet. I've arranged with Mrs. Reid to give us a tour. That's her now," he says, extending his hand toward the casually dressed middle-aged woman fast approaching.

"Hello, Mr. Fisher," the woman says, green eyes sparkling beneath a fringe of wavy brown hair. "Lovely to see you again. And Mrs. Fisher. How beautiful you are." She directs her attention to Julia. "And so nice to meet you," she says as Norman introduces them, "although you don't look very happy to be here." She smiles. The smile is warm and genuine. "Believe me, I understand. A lot of our residents feel that way the first time they visit."

"Mrs. Reid . . ." Julia says.

"Please, call me Carole."

"Carole, I'm sorry to be wasting your time —"

"Oh, but you aren't! I adore this part of my job. Meeting new people, showing off our beautiful establishment. I feel so honored to work here, to be part of such a vibrant community. Come, let me show you around." She doesn't wait for an answer.

Julia sighs, falling into step with Carole Reid as the woman ushers the small group down the wide hallway to her left. "This is not a nursing home," she stresses along the way. "Nor are you a guest in *our* facility. On the contrary, *we* are guests in *your* home.

While we have doctors and nurses on call, and a staff that includes social workers, personal care workers, cooks, housekeepers, and orderlies, residents must be able to take care of themselves. If the time comes that a resident is no longer able to function independently, we have our sister facility just a few miles away to which he or she can be transferred. And while we have excellent dining facilities, no one is forced to take part. You can choose to have all or none of your meals in the dining room. Rates, of course, vary accordingly."

She opens the door to the large dining room. Julia does a quick count of twenty round tables, each surrounded by eight chairs, the tables covered in white linen tablecloths and already set for dinner. "We have two sittings for each meal, so even if all our residents choose to eat with us, we're able to accommodate them," Carole Reid continues, leading them out of the room and around the corner.

She shows them the well-equipped gym, the indoor and outdoor swimming pools, and the multiple card rooms, all of which are busy, as well as a small theater where movies are shown once a week, and the drama club mounts its yearly productions. "There's also a bridge club, a mahjong club, a book club, and a choir," the woman says proudly. "And we have regular guest speakers and offer frequent and numerous outings. Of course, suggestions of places to go and things to see are always welcome. As well, we offer classes in everything from current affairs to knitting."

Julia can't help being impressed and has to fight to keep her face as impassive as possible.

"I'd like to reiterate that you lose none of your independence when you move to Manor Born. If anything, you *gain:* new friends, a sense of purpose, a real community. Would you like to see our model suite?"

"Lead the way," Norman says before Julia can respond.

They take the elevator to the fourth floor.

Carole Reid opens the door to a spacious one-bedroom apartment as tastefully furnished as the lobby.

"It's beautiful," Norman says. "Lots of space. Plenty of light."

"And no stairs," Poppy adds.

"Very nice," Julia says.

"That's it?" Norman says. "Very nice?"

Julia steps back into the hall, walks briskly toward the elevators.

"It's all right," she hears Mrs. Reid say to

her son. "This isn't for everyone."

They ride the elevator to the main floor in silence.

"I thank you very much for coming," the woman concludes, as they walk toward the front door. "It was a real pleasure meeting you, Mrs. Fisher. If you have any questions —"

"You've been very thorough," Julia says. "Thank you."

"Thank *you*. I hope to see you again."

"We'll be in touch," Norman says. "Could you have been any ruder?" he asks his mother as they step outside.

"Oh, I think so. Yes, quite definitely," Julia says. "Will there be any more surprises?"

"No, Mother," Norman tells her, his voice resonating defeat. "No more surprises."

CHAPTER TWENTY-EIGHT

"Why won't you tell me where you're going?" Erin is asking.

"I told you," Maggie tells her daughter. "I'm going out for dinner."

They're in Maggie's bedroom. Freshly showered, Maggie is wrapped in a large white towel, trying to decide between the blue cotton sundress stretched out on the bed or the pair of white pants and pink silk shirt lying beside it.

"With who?"

"With *whom*," Maggie corrects.

"Really?" Erin says. "We're doing the grammar thing? You're not an English teacher anymore, remember?"

Maggie sighs.

"Fine," Erin says. "With *whom* are you going out for dinner?"

Maggie takes another measured breath and tries to stay calm. Her daughter hasn't shown the slightest interest in her in months. She never asks about her day or if she's enjoying her job, and responds with one-word answers when questioned about her own. So why the sudden interest now? Does the teenager possess some kind of special radar? "Just a friend."

"You don't have any friends."

"Of course I have friends."

"Name them," Erin challenges.

Maggie searches her mind for the names of anyone she could plausibly count as a friend since moving to Florida. "There's Dani Wilson and Olivia Grant," she offers.

"Our neighbors? Are you kidding me? You hardly know them."

"And there's Nadine . . . Jerome . . . Rita . . ."

"Aren't those the people you work with?"

"Yes, but —"

"Are you having dinner with them?"

Maggie hesitates, unable to tell her daughter an outright lie. "No."

"So, I repeat, with *whom* are you having dinner?"

Shit! This is exactly the conversation Maggie was hoping to avoid. "Just somebody I met."

"At the hairdresser's?"

"Close by."

"What does that mean?"

"It means I met him at a Starbucks in the plaza. Okay?" Maggie says quickly. *Too* quickly.

"You met *him?* It's a *man?*"

Shit! Shit! Shit!

"You have a *date?*" Erin looks horrified by the thought.

"Is that so shocking?"

"Yes!"

"Why?"

"Seriously? You've been like one of the walking dead ever since we moved here."

"Yes, thank you for that. But in case you haven't noticed, I've been making a conscious effort to turn things around. I got a job, changed my hair, I'm engaging more with the neighbors . . ."

"Okay, so you're getting out of the house more and you deigned to say hello to the neighbors. . . ."

"I did more than say hello."

"Okay. Fine. You did more than say hello. That's not the point."

"What *is* the point?" Maggie asks.

"The point is that you have a date."

"Okay. I have a date."

"That's it? That's all you're going to say?"

"What do you want me to say?"

"For starters, who is this guy?"

"He's just a guy."

"Some random guy you picked up in Star-bucks," Erin states.

"Well, I wouldn't put it quite like that."

"Really? How would you put it?"

"I've met him several times. He seems nice. His office is a few doors down from the salon."

"What does he do?"

"He's an accountant."

"What's his name?"

Maggie hesitates.

"Please tell me you know his name."

"Of course I know his name."

"What is it?"

"Richard."

"Does Richard have a last name?"

"Atwood," Maggie tells her. "Richard At-wood."

Erin immediately pulls out her phone.

"What are you doing?"

"Checking Facebook."

"What? No. Stop!"

Erin ignores her, scurrying out of Mag-gie's reach, her fingers moving with light-ning speed across the phone's surface. "And here he is! Richard Atwood, certified public accountant. Wow! He's hot. Oh my God!"

"What?"

"It says he was born in . . . Oh my God! Are you kidding me? He's twenty-eight?"

"Is he?" Maggie asks, blushing beet red against the white of the towel.

"That's what it says."

"Must be a mistake."

"Really? You're going with that?"

"He looks older."

"Does he know how old *you* are?"

"Does it matter?"

Erin throws both hands into the air as she paces between the bed and the window. "So, let me get this straight. My middle-aged mother, who has spent the past year and a half jumping at her own shadow, virtually terrified of every strange man she sees, meets this hot, twenty-eight-year-old guy in a Starbucks, and decides to throw caution to the wind and go out with him."

"Well, I'm not exactly throwing caution to the wind," Maggie demurs. "He's an accountant, for God's sake. How dangerous can he be?"

Erin comes to an abrupt stop. "He's twenty-eight!"

"Yes, I think we've established that."

"Okay," Erin says, resuming her pacing, "I can kind of get why *you're* interested. But what about him?"

"What do you mean?"

"Let's get real, Mom. I appreciate that you've been looking really good since you changed your hair and started wearing a bit of makeup and everything, but come on. The guy's gorgeous. He could have anybody he wants. No disrespect, but what's he doing with you?"

"Wow."

"Are you going to have sex with him?"

"What?"

"You heard me. Are you going to have sex with Richard Atwood, certified public accountant?"

"No! For God's sake, I hardly know the man. We're having dinner, period."

"Does he know that?"

"I have no idea."

"Because that would make sense. I mean, he probably thinks you'll be so grateful that someone as young and good-looking as he is has asked you out that you'll just fall into bed with him. . . ."

"Erin . . ."

"Just make sure you use protection 'cause you don't want to pick up any STDs."

"Okay, that's quite enough." Maggie fights the urge to push her daughter out the bedroom window. Instead she pushes her clothes aside and sinks down on the bed. "What's really going on here, sweetie?" she asks when she can find her voice. "Why are you being so mean?"

"I'm not being mean. I'm just trying to understand. . . ."

"You don't have to understand. This isn't about you."

"What *is* it about?"

"It's about me having a life again," Maggie says. "You're right. I've been a zombie the last eighteen months. And I'm not going to lie, I'm still terrified. But I can't let that fear define my life any longer. It's already cost me my career, my marriage, my identity! I can't let it take anything else. I need to take back at least a semblance of control. For *all* our sakes."

"And dating Richard Atwood is going to help you do that?"

"I don't know," Maggie admits. "It's part of it, I guess."

Erin looks toward the floor. When she looks back at her mother, her eyes are filled with tears. "What about Dad?"

"What about him?"

"Does he know?"

Maggie almost laughs. "About my new philosophy on life? How could he? I'm just starting to figure it out for myself."

"Does he know you have a date?"

"Oh." *Back to that.* "No, of course not."

"Are you going to tell him?"

"Why would I? It's none of his business."

"You don't think he deserves to know?"

Maggie buries her head in her hands. "Let's get something straight," she says, slowly lifting her head. "I love your father, Erin. Believe me, his leaving wasn't my choice. I pretty much begged him to stay. He's the one who wanted out."

"Because you were a crazy person."

"Yes. I think we all agree on that."

"So now . . . what? You dye your hair blond and suddenly you're not crazy anymore?"

"I don't know," Maggie admits. "I guess we'll have to wait and see."

Erin sinks down onto the bed beside Maggie. "It's just that I thought . . ."

"You thought what?"

Erin's breath quivers into the space between them. "That you and Dad would get back together."

Maggie nods, her arm reaching around Erin's shoulders, drawing her daughter into an embrace. "So did I," she admits. "But it doesn't look as if that's going to happen. Your father has moved on. And it's time I did the same."

They sit for several minutes in silence before Erin pushes off the bed and walks to the door. She stops, turns back around.

"Wear the white pants and silk shirt," she advises. "You look really pretty in pink."

CHAPTER TWENTY-NINE

Maggie pulls into the parking lot of the
upscale Royal Poinciana Plaza and turns
left, away from the valets lingering in front
of the Palm Beach Grill. She can park her
own car, thank you very much. She has no
intention of handing over her keys to a
stranger. Taking back control of her life
doesn't mean taking unnecessary chances.
Not being a zombie doesn't mean being an
idiot.

She parks under a lamppost close to the
main road. There's little chance of anyone
jumping out at her here. Even so, she does
a careful survey of the area before opening
her car door, her hand around the outline
of the gun inside her beige canvas bag.

"Don't you have another purse you can
wear?" Erin asked her as she was leaving
the house. "That one's kind of . . . ratty."

Maggie smiles. This purse will do just fine.
Maybe one day she'll feel strong enough to

leave her gun behind, but not yet. Despite her fresh resolve, some things are easier said than done. Now is not the time for whole-sale changes. Now is baby steps. Now is one day, one thing, at a time.

She checks her watch as she approaches the small crowd milling outside the restaurant's front door. She's ten minutes early, which means she still has ten minutes to change her mind.

"Have a nice evening," one of the valets says, opening the door for her to go inside.

Baby steps, she thinks, taking a deep breath, straightening her shoulders, and entering the noisy, dimly lit interior.

She approaches the hostess's stand and takes a quick look around. A large, well-stocked bar runs along the wall to her left, followed by a bright, open kitchen. Every barstool is occupied, as are most of the tables in the main body of the restaurant. Lithographs by well-known artists — a swimming pool by David Hockney, a color-ful abstract by Appel, a less colorful one by Jack Bush, among others — line the walls. The place is packed, as it always is. Maggie smiles, wondering how many of the diners are packing as well. More than a few likely have guns secreted somewhere on their per-sons.

The hostess informs her that Richard Atwood hasn't arrived yet, and Maggie wonders if he's changed his mind, which would be a blow to her ego but not the end of the world. More embarrassing would be having to face Erin when she got home, to admit that at least one of them came to their senses and decided to take a pass.

She checks her watch again. She'll give the handsome accountant fifteen minutes and then she'll leave.

Two minutes later, she feels the restaurant door open behind her and a rush of hot, humid air invade the cold, air-conditioned space. She takes a deep breath and turns around. "Oh my God."

"Maggie?"

Maggie finds herself staring into her husband's startled face. "Craig. Hi," she says when no other words are forthcoming. What's he doing here? Did Erin phone him, tell him of her plans?

"What are you doing here?" he asks.

"Same as you, I would imagine. Did Erin call you?"

"Erin? No. Why? Is everything all right?"

"Yes. It's just that . . . nothing." Why is she so surprised to see him? The Palm Beach Grill was always their go-to restaurant of choice. Damn it, of all the places she could have suggested, she had to pick this one.

Unless, of course, subconsciously she'd been hoping to run into him, and that was why she'd picked it.

"You're looking well," he says.

"Thank you. You, too."

"How's the job going?"

"So far, so good."

"Well, it certainly seems to agree with you. You're looking really . . . wonderful."

"Hi," an unfamiliar voice pipes up. Long red fingernails at the end of a delicate bare arm extend toward Maggie. "I'm Selena."

"Sorry," Craig says quickly, then again, "Sorry." He pauses, regroups. "Selena, this is Maggie. Maggie, this is . . ."

"Selena," Maggie acknowledges, shaking the young woman's hand. "Nice to meet you." She takes note of the woman's thick, shoulder-length black hair, and the ample cleavage peeking out from her scoop-necked polka-dot dress. "How do you know Craig?"

"We work together."

"Ah, the new sales rep. Of course."

Selena looks from Maggie to Craig, then back to Maggie, dark eyes blinking confusion. "Yes, that's right. And you know Craig . . . how?"

"He's my husband," Maggie says.

301

Craig stifles a smile. "Well, isn't this fun," he says.

"And speaking of fun," Maggie says, as the door opens again and in walks Richard Atwood, wearing dark pants and a white shirt, looking even better than his picture on Facebook.

"Maggie," he says, edging through the small crowd waiting to be seated. "Sorry if I'm late. I got held up forever at the bridge."

"No worries." Maggie motions toward her husband. "Rick, I'd like you to meet Craig and Selena."

"Nice to meet you both."

"Craig McKay?" the hostess calls out.

Craig raises his hand. "Right here."

"This way, please."

"Excuse us," Craig says. "Good to see you, Maggie. You really do look . . . terrific."

"Thank you."

"Craig *McKay*?" Rick asks, watching him walk away. "Your . . . ?"

"Yes." Maggie lifts her palms into the air, as if to say, *What can you do?* Then says it out loud, "What can you do?"

"Would you prefer to go somewhere else?"

"No. I'm okay. You?"

"I'm happy if you are."

Minutes later, the hostess leads them to a table underneath the Hockney litho. Maggie sits down, quickly locating Craig in a nearby booth. He is leaning forward, supposedly listening to what the lovely Selena is saying, but Maggie notes his eyes drifting repeatedly in her direction, and she can't help smiling.

"What are you smiling about?" Rick asks.

Maggie shrugs. "I wasn't sure you'd show up." Not a lie. Not the truth either.

He laughs. "I was pretty sure *you* wouldn't."

The waitress approaches with their menus, rattling off the night's specials. "I'll give you a few minutes to think it over. Can I get you something to drink in the meantime?"

Rick orders two glasses of expensive chardonnay. "Your husband was right," he says. "You look terrific."

"Thank you. So do you."

He smiles. "Thank you."

"My daughter thinks you're 'hot.' She looked you up on Facebook."

He laughs. "It's a good picture."

"She also wondered what you're doing wasting your time with me."

His eyes narrow. "She sounds like a lot of laughs."

"Yes, she can be quite the comedian," Maggie acknowledges. "Unfortunately, she has a point. What *are* you doing wasting a

303

good Saturday night and an expensive glass of wine on me?"

As if on cue, the waitress arrives with their drinks.

"Why do I think that your daughter had an answer for that?" Rick says.

Maggie ponders her response. *What the hell?* she decides. Might as well come right out with it. "To paraphrase, she thinks *you* think I'll be an easy lay."

"That's some paraphrase." He laughs. "But hell, I'll drink to that." He raises his glass, clicks it against hers. "To easy lays."

"You *do* know that's not going to happen."

"Ever?"

"Well, never say . . . ever."

Now they're both laughing. Maggie sees Craig's eyes shoot toward hers, and the laugh catches in her throat. She picks up her menu, buries her face inside it. "I think I'll have the Dover sole," she tells the waitress moments later.

"Prime rib," Rick says. "Medium rare, with french fries and coleslaw." He hands the menus back to the waitress. "So," he says as the young woman withdraws, "is he still looking?"

"What? Who?"

"Your husband. Is he still looking this way?"

"I haven't noticed," Maggie lies. Then, quickly, "Yes, he is. On and off. I'm sorry."

"Not your fault he's still in love with you."

"Oh, no. You're wrong about that. Believe me."

"I don't think so."

"He's the one who left *me,*" Maggie tells him, as she reminded her daughter earlier.

"Maybe, but he's having second thoughts now."

"He's just surprised to see me with someone, that's all."

"Is he looking right now?"

Maggie pretends to push some hair away from her face as her eyes skirt toward Craig. "Yes."

"Then you know what I think?"

"What?"

"I think we should give him something to look at."

Maggie is about to ask what he means, but before she can get the words out, Rick is leaning across the table and kissing her full on the lips.

"Holy shit," Maggie says as he falls back into his seat. She looks over at Craig, sees his head immediately turn away. "Holy shit," she says again.

CHAPTER THIRTY

One of Aiden's most vivid childhood memories is that of the front door slamming.

He flips over in bed and opens his eyes as the memory expands to include what preceded the slam: his parents' faces contorted with rage, their fists pounding at the air in frustration, their voices spitting fury into the narrow space between them, like venom from a pair of warring cobras.

Damn that new therapist anyway, dredging up all this shit. Like it's going to do any good.

His problems, like his flashbacks, are the result of two tours in Afghanistan — the things he saw in that dusty wasteland, the things he did.

As his previous therapist explained, when faced with danger, your body gets ready to fight, flee, or freeze. Your senses go on high alert, your heart beats faster, and your brain stops normal function to deal with the threat. This is healthy. But with PTSD, your brain doesn't process trauma the right way. It doesn't view the memory of the event as being in the past, and as a result, it switches to danger mode and you feel stressed and frightened, even when you know you're safe. This is called a flashback.

Something Aiden has been experiencing with more and more frequency the past few months. Especially since his old therapist retired and this new one — who insists on bringing up irrelevancies from the past — has taken his place.

How is talking about his childhood going to make anything better? Is it going to make the flashbacks stop or his nightmares go away? Is it going to make the insomnia disappear or improve his self-esteem? Is it going to save his marriage?

He stares at Heidi, asleep beside him, her deep auburn curls stretched across the whiteness of the pillowcase, like a series of incriminating question marks. He knows he's losing her, that it's only a question of time before she leaves him.

Like his father left him.

"Tell me about your father," the therapist says, as Aiden watches this afternoon's session play out in his mind.

"Nothing to tell." Aiden hears the feigned

indifference in his voice. *"I hardly knew the man. He left when I was nine."*

"That's old enough to have some idea what he was like."

"He was a bastard," Aiden says.

"What makes you say that?"

Aiden glares at the man sitting across from him. Dr. Stephen Patchett is close to sixty, but looks easily a decade younger. Probably helps that he has all his hair, Aiden decides, understanding that his father is roughly the same age, and wondering if he, too, has managed to keep from going bald.

Dr. Patchett leans back in his chair and waits, crossing one leg over the other to reveal a pair of yellow-and-black polka-dot socks peeking out the tops of his Air Jordan sneakers.

"Was he abusive?" the therapist asks when Aiden fails to answer.

"How do you mean?"

"Did he ever hit you?"

"No."

"How about emotionally? Was he distant? Withholding?"

Aiden pushes a lock of invisible hair away from his face. *"Not that I remember."*

"What do you remember?"

Aiden pushes aside the unwanted image of his father cradling him in his arms after he'd fallen off his bicycle. *"I remember my parents were always fighting,"* he says instead.

"Was there anything specific they fought about?"

"Not really." Aiden pictures his mother and father sniping at each other from across the room. *"She'd say one thing; he'd say the opposite. Just to be difficult."*

"You understood he was saying things 'just to be difficult' when you were nine years old?"

"I understood my mother was unhappy."

"And it was important to you that she be happy?"

"Of course. Especially after he left."

"It wasn't your job to make her happy, Aiden."

"Yeah? Tell her that," Aiden snaps. *"Sorry,"* he apologizes immediately. *"That was uncalled for."*

"Was it?"

"Yes. Can we talk about something else?"

The therapist nods. *"When was the last time you saw your father?"*

"I can't remember. It's been a long time. To be fair," Aiden continues without prompting, *"my mother didn't make it easy for him. She was furious at him for leaving, and she was the one with the money — her parents*

had left her very well off — and she just inundated him with legal shit. When the courts insisted I had to see him, I made sure things didn't go smoothly. After a while, he got the message and gave up."

"What about now?"

"What about now?"

"Have you tried contacting him?"

"Why would I do that?"

"Curiosity, maybe. You're older now. Circumstances change."

"No, I haven't contacted him."

"Why not?"

"It would be too upsetting for my mother."

"And not upsetting your mother is more important to you than seeing your father?"

Aiden feels his heartbeat quicken. He shrugs, says nothing. He fights the conflicting urges to bolt from the therapist's office or tackle the man to the floor.

"He's never tried contacting you?"

"He tried. Birthday cards, Christmas cards, that sort of thing. I actually got an email from him a few years back."

"And?"

"I didn't open it." Aiden stands up. "Look. I really don't get where you're going with this. I thought the point of Cognitive Processing Therapy was to examine how I feel about the trauma I experienced in Afghanistan so I can figure out ways to live with it."

"*Exactly,*" Dr. Patchett confirms.

"*Well,* my trauma," Aiden insists, "*was watching my friends and fellow soldiers get shot or blown to bits.* My trauma *was blowing the head off a twelve-year-old boy I thought was holding a grenade that turned out to be a rubber ball!*" He swipes at the sudden appearance of unwanted tears. "*It has nothing to do with my parents.*"

Aiden moans and flips onto his other side as Heidi stirs beside him.

"What's up, babe?" she whispers, her voice coated in sleep.

"Nothing."

"You okay?"

"I'm fine. Go back to sleep." Aiden closes his eyes.

The therapist is waiting. "*Look,*" Dr. Patchett begins, uncrossing his legs before recrossing them in the other direction. "*The point is that you've been blaming yourself for a long time about things that were beyond your control.*"

"*Such as?*"

"*Such as your father leaving. Such as not being able to make your mother happy.*"

Aiden sneers. "*That's ridiculous.*"

"*Aiden, you weren't responsible for their*

arguments or the fact your dad left. You weren't responsible for their divorce, or your mother's persistent bitterness, or even your subsequent estrangement from your father."

"I'm the one who threw tantrums every time he showed his face, who told him I thought he was a piece of shit," Aiden argues.

"You were a child."

"And now I'm an adult who sees a shrink every Wednesday afternoon because he can barely make it through the day. Again, how does any of this relate to my PTSD?"

Dr. Patchett uncrosses his legs, plants both feet firmly on the hardwood floor. *"Listen to me, Aiden. This is very important."* He takes a deep breath. *"Just as you aren't responsible for the things that happened when you were a child, you're not responsible for the things that happened in Afghanistan. None of what took place over there was your fault, despite the things you did or didn't do."*

Aiden shakes his head.

"I want you to do something for me. Some homework, if you will."

"More breathing techniques that are supposed to ease my anxiety but just make me dizzy?" He laughs to indicate a joke.

"I want you to make a list of all the things you've been avoiding," the therapist says.

Aiden shrugs. *"I'm not sure I understand."*

What *hasn't* he been avoiding? *"Take your time. Think about it. Make your list."*

"And what good will that do?"

"I don't know. Maybe nothing. I'm not going to insult you by pretending I understand the depth of the trauma you experienced in Afghanistan. I would guess that, at the very least, you felt afraid and helpless pretty much all the time, much like you felt as a child. To say you were stressed would be a gross understatement." He leans forward in his leather chair. *"And I suspect there are things happening in your life right now that are also making you feel stressed and helpless, and those things are contributing to your symptoms. I think you've been avoiding dealing with these issues, and hopefully, making a list of these things will help you learn how to face them."*

Aiden throws off his covers and climbs out of bed, dismissing the therapist with an abrupt wave of his hand. Naked except for a pair of blue boxer shorts, he cuts across the carpeted floor and goes down the stairs to the kitchen.

He opens the drawer directly under the elaborate toaster oven his mother gave them last Christmas, despite the fact they already had a perfectly good toaster, and this one

313

takes up way too much space. Heidi wanted to exchange it for the Dyson hair dryer she'd been lusting after, but he'd convinced her not to. So here the stupid thing sits, eliciting sighs of frustration whenever Heidi deigns to look at it.

Aiden grabs a pencil from the drawer, then searches through the other drawers for a piece of paper he can write on, ultimately settling for a napkin when he can find nothing else. He sits down at the kitchen table, his pencil hovering, his mind an impenetrable jungle of unwelcome thoughts.

He's still sitting there half an hour later when he hears Heidi come down the stairs. She's wearing a short nightgown, the curve of her full breasts clearly visible beneath the white satin.

"Hey, babe," she says softly, pulling up a chair and sitting down beside him. "Whatcha doing down here?"

Aiden maneuvers the napkin underneath his right elbow. "Nothing much."

"You feeling all right?"

"Yup. Just couldn't sleep."

"Poor baby. You want me to make you something to eat?"

He smiles. God, he loves her, has from the moment he laid eyes on her. "It's three o'clock in the morning."

"Perfect time for a donut." She gets up from her seat and grabs two chocolate-covered donuts from the cupboard. "How about some warm milk to go with it?"

Aiden watches as Heidi pours some milk into a pot and turns on the burner, then retrieves two mugs from a nearby cupboard. He doesn't know much, but he knows he can't risk losing her.

"Here we go," she says, returning to the table with their donuts and warm milk.

They eat the donuts and drink their milk in silence. Then she takes him by the hand and leads him back up the stairs to their bedroom, where they make love before drifting back to sleep till morning. The napkin with the list of what he's been avoiding remains on the table. It contains only one word.

Mother.

Chapter Thirty-One

"Nana! Nana, where are you?"

Julia hears her grandson calling her from inside the house. "I'm in the garage," she calls back.

Seconds later, the door separating the garage from the inside of the house opens and Mark appears, fresh out of the shower, his long hair hanging wet to his shoulders. "What are you doing in here?"

"Just going through some of this stuff," she tells him, indicating the stack of old notebooks on the concrete floor beside the stool on which she sits. "Thought it was a good time to clean house."

Mark drops down beside her, crossing one long leg over the other and lifting the top notebook into his lap. "What are these?" He starts flipping through the pages.

"Your grandfather's lesson plans, mostly. From when he was head of the sociology department at the University of Miami."

Mark scans several of the pages. "He must have been very smart."

"He was."

"I didn't really know him that well."

"Well, he wasn't the easiest man to get to know. Not the easiest man, period. Rather like your father, in that respect."

"But you always seemed so happy together."

"Oh, we *were* happy. Not all the time, of course. We certainly had our differences. He could be a bit humorless at times. I could be quite stubborn. But overall we complemented each other nicely."

"Do you miss him?"

"I do. But . . ."

There's a but? Mark thinks, not sure he wants to hear what it is.

"Don't misunderstand me, darling. I loved your grandfather very much. He was a good man. A very good man. Just that, since he died, well . . . how can I say this?" She looks toward the ceiling, as if the answer is floating somewhere above her head. "There's no tension." She smiles. "Do you understand?"

"I understand tension," Mark says, and Julia's smile widens.

"Is that why you smoke so much weed?"

Mark laughs. "What do you know about weed, Nana?"

"Weed's been around a long time, my darling. Yours isn't the first generation to indulge. Of course, in my day, we called it grass or pot."

"And did you . . . *indulge?*"

"I may have allowed myself the occasional puff or two."

"No way."

"Oh, there's lots about me you don't know."

"Tell me," Mark says, laying the notebooks on the floor beside him.

"Tell you what?"

"Everything. Start at the very beginning."

Julia leans back against the concrete of the garage wall, her mind doing a quick scan through her eighty-four years. "Well, my grandparents came from Russia and were either smart or just plain lucky enough to settle in Florida. My grandfather got a job as a traveling salesman; my grandmother stayed home and raised a family, two boys and a girl. The girl was my mother, Emma. She met my father through her older brothers, and they got married and had three daughters. I was the youngest. My father went into business with my grandfather, selling costume jewelry. They'd travel all week together, although they didn't really get along very well, and come home weekends. Heard enough?"

"Not a chance. When did you meet Grandpa?"

"During my last year of university. I was studying psychology. He was a few years older than me, and studying for his PhD. We dated for a few years, then got married. He got a job teaching at the University of Miami. I stayed home to raise what I assumed was going to be a large family. Coming from a family of women, I was positive I was going to have nothing but girls. 'What am I going to do with a boy?' I remember crying to my mother when Norman was born. But she assured me I'd love him just the same, and she was right. And then it turned out I couldn't have any more children, which suited Norman just fine. He always liked being the center of attention."

Mark chuckles. "Not much changed there."

Julia smiles her agreement. "And that's about it. My parents died before you were born, and my two sisters are both gone now, too. I'm the last one standing."

"You have me," Mark says.

Julia smiles. "Yes, I do."

"What's this?" Mark asks, reaching into another box and pulling out a small brass trophy in the shape of a hand holding a bunch of playing cards.

"Oh my God!" Julia exclaims. "I'd forgotten all about that."

"What's it for?"

"I came first in a bridge tournament, God, it must be thirty years ago."

"I didn't know you played bridge."

"Well, I haven't in years. Your grandfather was never terribly good at it, which was surprising, because he was so good at most things. But he never quite got the hang of the bidding, and eventually he lost interest, so we stopped playing. It's too bad. I loved the game."

"You should take it up again."

"No, it's too late now." Julia conjures up the multiple card rooms at Manor Born. *"There's also a bridge club, a mahjong club, a book club, and a choir,"* she hears Carole Reid say.

"Well, a trophy is a trophy! You shouldn't throw it away," Mark says, returning it to the box and exchanging it for a mahogany case that he lays across his lap. The name Smith & Wesson is etched into the dark wood of its lid.

"What's that?"

"Looks like we found Grandpa's gun."

"Careful," Julia warns as Mark opens the case.

Slowly, gingerly, he withdraws the old revolver, holding it by its black textured wood handle. "Oh, wow. It's heavy. Is it loaded?"

"I have no idea. It's been sitting out here for years, and with all this heat and humidity, even if it *is* loaded, I doubt it would work. Plus, I think you're supposed to clean them regularly. But be careful," she warns again. "You never know with guns."

Mark studies the weapon for several seconds before returning it to its wooden case, then depositing the case back inside its cardboard box. "What do you say we go inside and I'll bake you something fabulous?"

"I say, lead the way." Julia is extending her arms for Mark to help her up when they hear a car pull into the driveway.

"Are you expecting company?" Mark asks. Julia shakes her head.

"Mark!" a man calls loudly from outside.

"Shit," Mark says, recognizing the voice.

"Who is it?"

"Just this guy I know."

"What guy?"

"A friend."

"A friend?"

"More like an acquaintance."

"An acquaintance to whom you owe

money?" Julia asks.

Mark sighs.

"How much money?"

"Not much."

"How much?"

"A few hundred dollars."

The knocking grows louder, more insistent. "Hey, man. I know you're there."

"Stay here. I'll get rid of him," Mark says, opening the door to the inside of the house. "And don't worry, Nana. He's harmless."

"If he's so harmless, why do I have to stay here?" Julia asks, but Mark is no longer beside her. Standing by the open door, she hears him moving toward the front of the house. She holds her breath as the front door opens.

"Hey, Gary," she hears him say. "What's with all the racket?"

"Don't play dumb," Gary says. "You know why I'm here."

"I know. It's just —"

"I think I've been pretty patient, letting you pay on the old installment plan, but I'm getting squeezed here myself. I got people to answer to."

"I know, man. I'm sorry. I should have your money by the end of the week. You can wait another few days, right?"

"You gotta give me something now, man.

I'm not leaving here empty-handed."

As if on cue, Julia steps out of the shadows into the hall. She is momentarily surprised by how inconsequential a figure this Gary person is. About the same age as her grandson, but shorter, rounder, and baby-faced. Hardly the intimidating figure she'd been bracing herself for.

"Nana!" Mark says, his eyes moving from her face to the Smith & Wesson in her hands. "Nana, what are you doing?"

Julia raises her arms and points the gun directly at Gary's chest.

"Holy fuck!" Gary immediately falls to his knees.

"How much does my grandson owe you?" Julia asks calmly.

"Five hundred dollars."

"I believe I have about three hundred dollars in my purse. Will that do?"

"Yeah. Yeah, that's plenty. That's good."

"Mark, go get my purse, would you? It's in the kitchen."

"Nana . . ."

"Go."

Mark runs past his grandmother to the kitchen, returning seconds later with her white leather bag.

"Now fish inside my wallet and give your friend his cash."

Mark quickly removes all the cash from Julia's wallet and hands it to Gary.

"Count it," Julia advises. "Make sure you're satisfied."

Gary's hands are shaking as he counts the cash. "It's fine."

"Good. Now, I want you to leave my house and never come back," Julia instructs the young man. "Are we clear on that?"

"No problem." Gary stuffs the money into the pocket of his jeans as he struggles to his feet. "You get your weed from somewhere else from now on," he says to Mark. "Are we clear on *that?*" He backs out the front door, leaping over the row of coral impatiens to his car.

Mark watches the old Mustang disappear down the main road, then shuts the front door and turns back to face his grandmother, who is still clinging tightly to the gun. "Holy fuck, Nana!" he says, borrowing Gary's words.

"Holy fuck," Julia agrees.

"Why don't you let me take that?" he offers, gently prying the weapon from her hands.

"Good idea. Oh dear."

"What is it?"

"My heart is racing."

"Well, no wonder."

"I'm feeling a bit strange."

"You should sit down. I'll get you some water."

"Darling . . ."

"Yes, Nana?"

"I don't want you to be alarmed but . . ."

"What?"

"I think maybe you should call an ambulance."

"Why? What's happening?"

Julia hears the panic in her grandson's voice and watches the color that has only recently returned to his cheeks start to disappear again. It's the last thing she sees before everything goes black.

Chapter Thirty-Two

Dani is sitting behind the wheel of her black Mercedes, its engine running, her windows open, the garage door closed. *In a few minutes,* she thinks, *it could all be over.*

She glances in the rearview mirror, pulling back the hair at the side of her face to reveal the golf ball–sized swelling that is the result of her husband's most recent outburst. Her head is still pounding from when he reached across the kitchen table last night after dinner and grabbed a fistful of her hair, then slammed her head against the table with such force that it cracked the glass. A large jagged line now lies, like a scar, across the table's surface.

"What happened to the table?" Tyler asked this morning when he came down for breakfast.

Dani pretended to notice the crack for the first time. "I don't know," she told him. "That's weird."

In truth, Dani knows exactly what set Nick off. He was annoyed because she'd forgotten to pick up his shirts from the cleaners, and when she casually suggested it might be a good idea for him to pick up his own shirts in the future — the words out of her mouth before she had time to weigh their consequences — he'd exploded.

Luckily, the boys were upstairs getting ready for bed, so they saw and heard nothing.

Nobody ever sees, she thinks. *Nobody ever hears.*

See no evil. Hear no evil.

"Better put some ice on that," Nick told her as they were getting ready for bed. Minutes later, he was tenderly kissing her neck and climbing on top of her.

I'm so tired, Dani thinks now. *Tired of having to weigh my words, of having to consider the consequences of even the most innocent of remarks, tired of walking on eggshells, of being afraid.*

Of being ashamed.

She inhales, wondering how long it would take for the garage to fill with carbon monoxide, then watches the faces of her two sons take shape in the increasingly poisonous air. She pictures the bus bringing them home from camp at the end of the day, sees

327

the looks of confusion on their faces when they get no answer to their repeated knocks on the door, their confusion turning to horror when their father informs them what their mother has done.

Could she really do this to them?

Could she leave them with a monster?

Ben might survive. He's always been the tougher of her two boys. But Tyler . . .

Again, she feels them knocking on the door, the sound growing louder, more insistent. It takes several seconds for Dani to realize that the knocking is coming from outside her garage door and not from inside her head.

"Dani," a voice calls out. "Dani, are you in there?"

Dani quickly shuts off the engine and presses the remote to open the garage door, exiting the car and stumbling into the fresh air.

Maggie stands before her. "My God!" she shouts, pulling Dani into the driveway. "What the hell happened?"

Dani coughs, trying to expel the fog from her brain and come up with a plausible explanation. "I don't know," she says, gasping for air. "I got in the car . . . there was somethin' wrong with the radio . . . I kept tryin' to fix it . . . I guess I forgot the garage door was still closed. And . . ." She realizes that Maggie has stopped listening to her and is staring at the bump on the side of her head. Her hand reaches up to touch it. "I got dizzy and must have banged my head on the steerin' wheel," she improvises. "How did you . . . ?"

"I got home from taking Leo to camp and I heard a car running and thought I smelled gas," Maggie explains. "We should probably get you to a doctor."

"No. No, I'll be fine. I wasn't in there very long."

"Long enough to get dizzy and hit your head."

"I'm fine. I just need to sit down for a few shakes."

Maggie gently lowers Dani to the curb, pulling out her cellphone as she sits down beside her. "At least let me call your husband."

"No!" Dani says, with more force than she'd intended. "Please. I don't want to worry him. He's so busy. Please. Don't call him."

Maggie reluctantly returns the cellphone to her purse. It's several seconds before she speaks. "What's really going on here, Dani?"

"What do you mean?" Tears fill Dani's eyes. "I told you."

"You were trying to fix the radio . . ."

"Yes."

"And you forgot to open the garage door . . ."

"Yes."

"This was really an accident?"

"Of course."

"You got dizzy and banged your head on the steering wheel . . ."

"Yes!" Dani says. *No!* she shouts silently. *Nick did this to me! He did this!* She pushes herself to her feet. "Look. I'm real sorry about all this. I feel like a plumb fool. But I'm fine now and you don't have to fuss about me any longer. Don't you have to be at work?"

"Not till ten. Why don't you come inside and let me make you a cup of coffee? We can talk. . . ."

"No. I appreciate the offer. I really do. But I don't have time." She checks her watch. "I have an office full of patients waitin'. . . ." She walks cautiously toward her garage, Maggie still hovering.

"I'm not sure you should be driving."

"I'm fine. Really. All I needed was a little fresh air. I'm perfectly fine now. I promise. Don't you worry your pretty little blond head about me." She pushes through the lingering miasma and climbs into the front

330

seat of her car. "And thank you," she calls as she backs the Mercedes into the driveway and onto the street, using her remote to close the garage door. "You may have just saved my life."

She doesn't go to work.

Instead she calls her office and tells the receptionist she isn't feeling well and to reschedule her appointments.

What in God's name had she been thinking?

Had she really been giving serious thought to ending her life? To leaving her boys?

She pictures Maggie standing in her driveway, staring after her car as she pulled onto the street, and doubts her neighbor was fooled.

She's seen your earlier bruises.

She suspected then.

She *knows* now.

"What's really going on here?" she'd asked.

Why didn't you tell her?

Dani turns onto the ramp for I-95 and presses down hard on the accelerator, transferring to the passing lane and quickly edging the speedometer toward eighty miles an hour.

She has no idea where she's going until she sees the sign for the Forty-fifth Street exit, and she has to cut across several lanes of traffic in order to get into the proper lane on time. A barrage of angry horns follows her off the exit and into the eastbound lane. Less than ten minutes later, she reaches Dixie Highway. Two minutes after that, she's pulling into the parking lot of Straight Shooters of West Palm Beach.

"Okay," she hears Nick say. *"Everybody out."*

She follows his silent directive, marching purposefully toward the gun shop's front door. The *No loaded firearms please* sign still manages to elicit a wry smile as she pushes open the door. "Well, howdy, partner," she whispers to the giant stuffed grizzly bear that serves as a greeter, then gives a subtle wave to the other dead animals watching through glass eyes as she approaches the counter in the middle of the large room.

Barely nine o'clock in the morning and three of the ten stalls are already occupied, two of the shooters women. "Hi, there," she says to the middle-aged man in the orange vest behind the counter. His brush cut is a tad longer than the last time she saw him, the tiny diamond stud still embedded in his left ear. "Good mornin', Wes."

Wes's brown eyes narrow as his head tilts

to one side. "The doc's wife, right?"

"Dani. Right."

"Well, how you doin'?"

Dani is so grateful for his relaxed pronunciation that she has to fight the urge to reach across the counter to hug him. "Doin' great, thank you. You?"

"Never better." He looks toward the door. "The doc with you?"

Dani's heartbeat quickens as her head shoots toward the door. Is Nick here? Has he followed her? "No," she says, breathing a sigh of relief when the door remains closed. "He's workin'. It's just me."

"Taking advantage of ladies' day, are you?"

"I guess I am," Dani replies. She'd forgotten that ladies shoot for free on Mondays.

"So, what'll it be? Same as last time? A .22?"

"If that's what you recommend."

Wes lays the gun on the counter beside a box of ammunition. "Yeah, I'd suggest getting used to this one before moving on to something a little more powerful."

Dani takes a deep breath and lifts the gun into her hand, a groan of anticipation sliding from her lips.

"Don't you be nervous now," Wes says, mistaking her excitement for jitters. "Just remember to hold the gun steady with both hands, like so," he says, demonstrating, "and line your sights up to the target. Then just . . ."

"Let 'em rip."

"Atta girl." He lays the headphones and the protective glasses on the counter. "Same kind of target as last time?"

"Yes. The male outline."

"Here you go," he says, handing it over. "Why don't you take stall number five, and remember to wash your hands real good when you're done. If I remember correctly, I don't have to worry about you chewing gum. Dentist, right?"

"Good memory."

"Well, the doc's one of my favorite people. I bet he's pleased you're taking this up."

Dani smiles, about to turn away when she stops, turns back.

"We forget something?" Wes asks.

"No, I think I have everythin'." She hesitates. "I was just wonderin' if you would mind not sayin' anythin' to Nick about my bein' here."

Wes's smile stretches across his face. "Hoping to surprise him, are you?"

Dani's finger curls around the gun's trigger. "Yes, sir," she says. "That's what I'm hopin'."

CHAPTER THIRTY-THREE

Maggie watches Dani's car until it is out of sight. There are things she knows, and even more things she doesn't, but one thing she knows for sure is that Dani Wilson didn't get that bump on her temple from accidentally banging her head against her car's steering wheel.

Which leaves only one other possibility, an alternative almost as hard to swallow as the lie Dani told: that Dani's husband is responsible for the bump on her head, as well as the bruises she saw earlier on her face and arm; that the first-class oncologist, Dr. Nick Wilson, is also a first-class wife beater.

"Shit," Maggie says. "What do I do now?"

You *don't do anything,* she hears Craig say. You *stay out of it. This is not your problem.*

I can't just sit by. . . .

You can and you will. Have the past two years taught you nothing?

"Everything okay?" a voice asks, interrupting the argument in her head.

Maggie looks up to see Mark Fisher ambling toward her. "I'm sorry. What?"

"Just wondering if everything is okay," he repeats. "You've been standing in the middle of the road for a while now, and your face has been going, like, a mile a minute."

"What? My face . . . ? *What?*"

"Sorry. I didn't mean to upset you," he says quickly. "I should mind my own business. I'm sorry."

"No, it's fine. I'm fine. Everything's fine." The words sound as false to Maggie's ears as Dani's earlier disclaimers. "How's your grandmother doing?" she asks, changing the subject.

"Much better, thanks." He laughs. "She just overdid it a bit with the gardening."

Maggie nods, recognizing yet another lie in a morning full of them. You don't spend a few days in the hospital because you planted too many impatiens.

"I'm just heading over to Publix to pick up some things for Saturday night's party. Can I get you anything?"

Maggie is about to ask what party, then remembers Olivia Grant mentioning something about getting the neighbors together this weekend to celebrate the Fourth of July.

"And my husband's new job," she'd whispered. "Although we won't tell *him* that."

More secrets, Maggie thinks. *More lies.*

Although she was obviously wrong about Sean, she concedes silently, picturing him leaving for work this morning, clean-shaven and looking quite dapper in his stylish linen jacket.

"You need anything?" Mark asks again.

"What? No. No, nothing. But thank you. It's very sweet of you to ask."

"Anytime." He offers a slight wave as he walks toward his grandmother's garage. "Say hi to Erin for me."

"Will do," Maggie says, although she has no intention of doing so.

Her front door opens as she's reaching inside her purse for her key.

"What were you talking to Mark about?" her daughter asks, waving to Mark as he backs his grandmother's car out of the garage and onto the street. She stands back to let Maggie come inside.

"Coming?" Maggie asks.

"What were you talking to Mark about?" Erin repeats.

"I asked him how his grandmother was doing."

"And?"

"He said she's doing much better."

"That's all?"

"He asked if we needed anything from Publix."

"And?"

"I said we didn't."

"And?"

"And?" Maggie repeats. "Did he say anything about me?"

Maggie sighs. One more battle she has no chance of winning. Might as well give up now. "He said to say hello."

"Thank you." Erin smiles. "Was that really so difficult?"

Maggie walks past her daughter into the kitchen. "He's too old for you."

"Says the woman dating a toddler."

Maggie pours herself a mug of cold leftover coffee, then pops it in the microwave. "It was one dinner over a week ago. We're most definitely *not* dating." While she'd certainly enjoyed her evening with the handsome accountant, the truth was that she still loved her husband, that she wasn't ready to move on.

"Tell your husband I think he's an idiot," Richard Atwood had said after walking her to her car.

"Will do," Maggie agreed, although she hasn't. "So," she says to Erin. "What are your plans for the day?" She removes the

coffee from the microwave and takes a sip, feeling it burn the tip of her tongue.

Erin shrugs and rolls her eyes. "If you're asking if I'm going job hunting, the answer is no. School starts again in, what, six weeks? Who's going to hire me for six weeks? Besides, if you really wanted me to get a summer job, you should have gotten me a car. How am I supposed to get anywhere without a car?"

"There *is* such a thing as public transportation."

Another shrug, a bigger eye roll. "I'm going back to bed," Erin says. "Have fun at work."

"Wow," she says, staring at the sixteen-hundred-foot wooden boardwalk that crosses the clear blue waters of Lake Worth Cove, located in the glorious John D. Mac-Arthur Beach State Park. "This is fantastic. But where's the ocean? I can hear it, but I can't see it."

"It's on the other side of the dunes." He points to the other side of the long wooden bridge.

"I didn't even know this place existed. It's so beautiful."

"Wait. You ain't seen nothing yet," Mark says.

Erin smiles. She takes a quick glance around, half-expecting to see her mother pop out from behind one of the tropical trees that blanket the giant nature preserve. She'd be so pissed if she knew where Erin was. *And with who,* Erin thinks, her smile widening.

"With *whom,*" she hears her mother correct.

Erin's smile twists into a frown.

"Something wrong?" Mark asks.

"No. Why?"

"You made a face." He laughs. "It's the same kind of face your mother makes."

"What?"

"I saw her this morning. . . . She was obviously upset about something. . . ."

"She's always upset. Can we please *not* talk about my mother?"

"Sure. Sorry."

"I'm nothing like her."

"Okay." He shrugs. "You want to walk across the boardwalk or take the tram?"

"Let's walk." As they fall into step beside each other, Erin insists, "I'm really *nothing* like her."

"You're pretty like she is," Mark says.

"Oh. Okay." She feels his bare arm brush against hers, feels her whole body tingle. "What's it like, living with your grandmother?"

"Great," he says easily. "She's sweet and she's funny, and way more interesting than you might think."

"She doesn't get on your case about everything?"

"Nah. She pretty much lets me do my own thing. No judgment."

"Must be nice."

"It is." A sudden breeze blows some hair into his face, and he pushes the hair away. "Although her being so accepting about everything makes it kind of hard."

"What do you mean?"

He shrugs. "I'm afraid I'll screw it up." Another shrug, another push of his hair away from his face. "Look over there." He points over the right side of the wooden railing that encloses the boardwalk on both sides.

"Oh my God!" Erin squeals with delight, watching a bunch of slender silver-colored fish as they leap in and out of the still blue water. "It's like they're jumping for joy," she says, and Mark laughs.

Her mother certainly wouldn't be jumping for joy if she could see her now, Erin acknowledges. Still, this impromptu little trip to the beach hadn't been her idea. She'd merely happened to step outside at the same moment Mark returned from the grocery store and decided it was only polite to inquire after his grandmother. Which was when Mark mentioned that his father had phoned to say he'd be stopping by this afternoon to talk to Julia, and he didn't want to be around when his father got there, so he was going to the beach, and why didn't she grab a bathing suit and a towel and join him?

Why not, indeed?

"This place is North Palm Beach's best kept secret," Mark tells her. "You can go kayaking, canoeing, snorkeling, bird watching, swim in the ocean, whatever your little heart desires."

I already know what my little heart desires, Erin thinks.

"And they have a nature center and walking trails and a gift shop," he continues as they reach the shade of a cluster of giant gumbo-limbo trees at the end of the boardwalk. "Not to mention . . . the main attraction. Are you ready to be blown away?" He takes her hand and leads her up the winding flight of wooden steps.

Erin feels her heartbeat quicken as their fingers intertwine.

"Close your eyes," he instructs as they near the top landing.

She closes her eyes, feeling almost dizzy from the combination of his touch, the ocean air, and the almost deafening noise of the waves crashing against her ears.

"Okay. Now open them."

Erin's eyes open to a stunning two-mile panorama of blue ocean and pristine white sand. "Oh my God. It's gorgeous. I've never seen anything so beautiful."

"Told you."

Mark lets go of her hand to slip off his sandals, then skips down the stairs. "Careful," he warns as she does the same. "The sand's hot."

Erin feels the sand burn the bottoms of her bare feet as she hurries after him. They quickly lay their towels out on the sand and plop down on top of them. "I'm surprised there aren't more people."

"Told you it was North Palm's best-kept secret." He pulls his T-shirt over his head, revealing the pale flesh of his bony torso.

Erin squints into the sun, watching a group of surfers sitting on their boards in the distance, no doubt waiting for the perfect wave, while several teenage girls attempt to bodysurf the small waves closer to the shore.

"You want to go in?" Mark pulls off his

shorts to reveal the lime-green trunks beneath.

Erin stands up and pulls her white lace cover-up over her head, her back to Mark, as she makes sure the pieces of her skimpy black bikini are firmly in place. *Shoulders back, chest out, stomach in,* she reminds herself before slowly spinning around.

"Wow," he says. "You look amazing."

She laughs and runs toward the water, Mark right behind.

The water is warm, the small waves surprisingly powerful. Erin shrieks as the undertow pulls her down and briefly sucks her under. Mark is right beside her, grabbing her upper arm and pulling her back up. She watches him catch an incoming wave and ride it to the shore. Another wave hits him as he struggles to get back on his feet, and Erin laughs with delight.

"Happy?" he asks, once again at her side. He grabs her hand and they ride the next wave together.

"Stupid happy!" she tells him.

They spend the next hour alternately riding the waves and relaxing in the sun.

"I'd really like to kiss you right now," Mark says, his face suddenly looming over hers.

"I'd like that, too."

The kiss is soft and gentle. *Don't stop,* Erin urges silently, never wanting the moment to end. "We should probably head back," she tells him reluctantly, common sense reminding her that it would be wise to get home before her mother returns with Leo. She hasn't decided whether to tell her mother how she spent her afternoon or not. The reckless part of her would like nothing better than to see the look on her mother's face; the saner part thinks this is a look she should probably avoid.

"You want to go for a walk before we leave?" Mark asks, grabbing her hand and pulling her to her feet.

They walk along the water's edge, smiling hello at the people they pass, pointing out the various ships and boats on the horizon, laughing at the assortment of body shapes they see laid out on the sand.

"Hey," Erin says, suddenly tugging on Mark's arm to stop him. "Look." She nods toward a man lying on his back in the sand farther down the way. "Isn't that our neighbor?"

Mark brings his hand up to shield his eyes from the sun and get a better look. "You mean Mr. Grant?" he says, squinting. "Yeah, I think you're right. Should we go say hello?"

"No. He looks like he's asleep. Besides, he kind of creeps me out, the way he's always staring out his window. We need to go back now anyway. Come on, I'll race you."

Erin turns on her heels and starts running.

She doesn't look back.

CHAPTER THIRTY-FOUR

Sean feels the sun warm against his face and fights the urge to give in to sleep. Instead he holds up his left arm and opens one eye to check his watch, gratified to note that it's barely three o'clock. There's still plenty of time for a nap. It wouldn't do to get home too early.

Not on the first day of his new job.

He almost laughs, and might have, had there been anything even remotely funny about the predicament he finds himself in.

It wasn't supposed to be this way. He was supposed to have found something by now. He wasn't supposed to still be lying to his wife, to be getting up early and shaving and putting on a freshly washed shirt and silk tie and that goddamn linen jacket — *"You've got it; you might as well wear it,"* Olivia had volunteered cheerily, looking as happy as he'd seen her in months — and pretending to go off to work.

How long can he keep this up?

As long as I have to, he decides as he flips onto his stomach, allowing the soothing sun to settle on his bare back. He already has a deep tan. A little more sun won't make a noticeable difference. Although he has to be careful not to burn. Good thing he thought to pack sunscreen along with the bathing suit in his briefcase, not to mention the beach towels in the trunk of his car, towels he'd put there after he and Olivia came back from driving the kids to the airport on Saturday. Thankfully, his offspring would be spending the next month with Olivia's parents up in Nantucket, so that was one good thing.

Three fewer people to lie to.

He should have asked for help from Olivia's parents when he had the chance. They'd offered to loan them money until he was back on his feet, but his pride — and his father's voice in his ear reciting Shakespeare's famous advice from *Hamlet: Neither a borrower nor a lender be* — had prevented him from accepting.

Now it was too late.

Too late to ask for help.

Too late to stop the lies.

"Good luck, sweetheart," Olivia said this morning as they were climbing into their respective cars. "Knock 'em dead."

"Will do."

"Call me as soon as you get the chance. Let me know how it's going."

"Will do," he'd said again.

Except he hadn't.

And he wouldn't.

Sorry, hon. I was just so busy. First day back. You know how it is.

His cellphone rings.

Sean pushes himself into a sitting position and extricates his phone from the pocket of his old, ill-fitting blue bathing suit, praying it's the headhunter he hasn't heard from in weeks, calling with news of a job interview.

But no, caller ID reveals it's Olivia. "Goddamn it," he says, debating whether to answer it. Except that if he doesn't, she's liable to call the main switchboard and ask to be put through to Sean Grant, and then where would he be? Up the proverbial shit creek without the proverbial paddle, that's where. He holds the phone close to his ear and swipes right.

"Sean?" Olivia says immediately.

"Hi, sweetheart."

"I've been waiting for you to call me all day."

"Sorry. I meant to. Things just got away from me, I guess."

"Does that mean it's going well?"

"Going great."

"Tell me."

"Tell you what?"

"Everything. I want to know every last detail."

"Can it wait? I promise I'll tell you everything when I get home." That should give him time to get his story straight, Sean thinks.

"Oh," Olivia squeals. "Can't you give me a little something to tide me over in the meantime?"

Something to tide her over. How about a kick in the head? "Well, I've just been settling in, meeting everyone . . ."

"What's Tom Gerrity like?"

"Who?"

"Tom Gerrity? The founder and CEO of Advert-X! Hello?!"

"Of course. Sorry." Sean watches a young girl darting in and out of the ocean, each dart accompanied by a loud shriek of delight.

"Where are you?" Olivia asks, the question catching him by surprise.

"What do you mean, where am I? I'm at work."

"It sounded as if somebody screamed."

Shit! Sean presses the phone tighter

against his ear and cups his free hand over the speaker, angling his body away from the ocean. "Looks like one of the secretaries just got some good news," he offers, the first thing that pops into his mind.

"Careful, sweetheart," Olivia warns.

"What do you mean?" he asks again, holding his breath.

She laughs. "Nobody calls them secretaries anymore. They're assistants or aides. You don't want to sound like a dinosaur."

He breathes a sigh of relief. "Guess I'll have to watch that."

"I've been reading all about your new boss online. Did you know he made his first billion before the age of forty?"

"I didn't know that," Sean concedes.

"So, what's he like?"

"What can I say? He seems like a nice enough guy."

"That's it? A nice enough guy?"

"Well, I only spent a few minutes with him when he came into my office to welcome me on board."

"That was nice. Is it a big office?"

"Of course. As befits a man of my stature," he embellishes. *What the hell?* he thinks, chuckling. *Why not?*

"I can't wait to see it."

Shit. "Well, maybe when things settle

down a bit."

"Of course. Maybe this weekend."

"This weekend?"

"Oh, no, not this weekend," she corrects. "It's the Fourth of July. I forgot. We're having a party."

"A party?"

"With the neighbors? Outside on the street? We'll barbecue some hot dogs and hamburgers?" she asks, as if she isn't sure. "I told you."

"Oh. Right. Guess I forgot." Sean has no memory of being told any such thing. But the truth is that he barely listens to his wife these days.

"So, do you know who you'll be working with? Have they assigned you to a particular client?"

"Nothing definite yet."

"Really? You'd think they'd be more organized than that. I mean, they must have had someone in mind when they hired you."

Shit. Shit. Shit. "Well, there *is* talk of putting me on the Burger King account."

"Burger King?" Olivia asks. "Aren't they with one of the big New York firms?"

"They are. But apparently they've been very impressed with the work Advert-X has been doing, and they're thinking of shaking things up. . . . Look. It's all very preliminary, and I probably shouldn't be talking about it. It's highly confidential."

"Oh my God. Burger King! That would be so fabulous!"

"It would," he agrees. "But even if it's a go, it's going to take a while for all the details to get worked out, and you have to promise me that you won't say anything to anyone."

"My lips are sealed."

"Good. Look. This isn't a great connection . . ." Sean begins, desperate to get off the line.

"I know. You sound like you're in the middle of a washing machine."

More like the Atlantic Ocean, Sean thinks. "It's my phone. It's been giving me problems lately."

"Do you have a private line? I should get the number."

"Yeah, I'll give it to you later. Look, honey, I'm afraid I'm going to have to cut this short. Someone's here to see me."

"Of course. I'm sorry. I'm just so excited. We'll talk when we get home. And remember — I want to know everything."

"You got it." He clicks off the phone before she can say another word. "Shit!" he yells, throwing his phone into the sand, then immediately scooping it up again and shaking the sand from its face. "Goddamn, son of a bitch, *fuck*!"

"Excuse me!" a woman on a nearby towel proclaims, her face twisted in anger, her hands over the ears of her wide-eyed toddler. "In case you hadn't noticed, there are children present."

"I'm sorry."

"You should be."

"Yeah, well, fuck you," Sean says, gathering up his towel as he scrambles to his feet.

He plods through the sand with as much speed as he can manage toward the wooden steps, his bare feet burning. He has to wait on the landing for a couple of teenagers to finish using the foot showers before he can wash the sand from his feet, then waits another five minutes for the tram to chauffeur him across the one-third mile of boardwalk to where his car is parked in the first of a series of small, adjoining lots.

He reaches inside the trunk of his car for his clothes, putting on his shirt and socks, pulling his pants up over his bathing suit, and finally, pushing his feet into his tan-colored loafers. The goddamn jacket can stay in the trunk, at least till he gets home, he thinks, then thinks better of it and throws it into the front seat. Just his luck, Olivia will have left work early and be waiting in the driveway when he pulls up. He has enough to worry about without having to come up with a plausible explanation for what his three-thousand-dollar jacket is doing in the trunk of his car next to a beach towel spotted with sand and smelling of the ocean.

He checks his watch again, noting that it's still too early to go home. He can't risk one of his neighbors spotting him and unintentionally giving him away to Olivia. That's the main reason he chose this place. Not too many people come here, at least in comparison to the public beaches of Riviera Beach and Juno. Probably because they're too damn cheap to pay the five-dollar entrance fee.

Which means he can't afford to come here more than a few times a week himself.

Sean climbs into his car, musing about how much friendlier his neighbors have become since that impromptu little game of catch a few weeks back. Hell, they're even planning a neighborhood barbecue to celebrate the Fourth of July!

Which means that everyone will be congratulating him and asking about his new job.

Which means he better have something to tell them.

He exits the sprawling park grounds and drives west along PGA Boulevard till he spots a seedy-looking bar at the end of a strip mall at the corner of A1A. *Perfect,* he thinks, pulling into the parking lot. No chance of running into anyone he knows here. He'll sit in a darkened corner and nurse a beer, maybe two, while he combs the Internet for any fun information he can glean about Advert-X and its founder.

No one will be interested in the actual details of his job.

No one, of course, except Olivia.

"Shit," he mutters as he pulls open the bar's heavy front door. He could really use a drink.

CHAPTER THIRTY-FIVE

Julia hears her son's car pull into her driveway and sighs, wondering when it became such an ordeal to see her only son. She fills a kettle with water and carries a tray of freshly baked cherry scones to the coffee table in front of the living room sofa. Seconds later, the doorbell rings.

She takes a quick look in the mirror beside the front door before opening it, pinching her cheeks to make sure they have enough color, fluffing out her hair, then smoothing the skirt of her floral-print dress. It's important she look, if not her best, then at least well enough to assure Norman that she isn't about to keel over dead in front of him.

"Hello, darling," she says, ushering her son inside. He looks as put together and confident as he always does. Light blue sports jacket, open-necked white shirt, trim navy slacks, Gucci loafers, no socks. The picture of success. She glances toward his car. "Poopy isn't with you?"

"It's *Poppy*, Mom."

She smiles. "I know. I'm just teasing you."

"Joke's wearing a little thin." He gives his mother an obligatory peck on the cheek. "And no, she isn't with me. I came right from work." He brushes past her into the living room. "Sorry if I'm a bit late. I thought I'd be able to get away earlier, but well, you know . . ."

"I don't know, actually."

Her son looks puzzled. "You don't know what?"

Julia shrugs. "Many things, I suppose. For starters, what exactly it is you do."

Norman's eyebrows crease toward the bridge of his nose. "Are you feeling all right?"

"I'm fine."

"Are you sure? You fainted. You spent two days in the hospital."

"Yes, and they gave me a clean bill of health and sent me home."

"But now you're confused."

"I'm not confused. Who said I was confused?"

"You just said you don't know what I do."

"I know you run a hedge fund. I just don't know what that entails." She lowers herself to the sofa. "Perhaps you could enlighten me."

"Now *I'm* confused."

"About what?"

"About the sudden interest in what I do. You've never been interested before."

"Of course I have."

"No," Norman counters. "You haven't."

Oh dear, Julia thinks. Her son has been in the house less than two minutes and already they're at odds.

"It's fine, Mom. It really doesn't matter."

"Of course it matters." She pats the seat cushion beside her. "Why don't you have a seat, I'll make us some tea, and you can tell me all about running a hedge fund?"

"No tea for me, thank you." Norman sits down in one of the chairs across from the sofa.

"How about a scone? Mark made a fresh batch this morning, and they're delicious."

"My son made scones?"

"He's very talented."

"A regular Duncan Hines." Norman looks around. "Where is he? Is he here?"

"No. I think he went to the beach."

"Nice life," Norman sneers.

Julia folds her hands in her lap. "You're too hard on the boy."

"And you're too soft. But I didn't come

here to talk about Mark."

"Why *did* you come?"

"Because you're my mother and I'm worried about you."

"Well, as you can see, there's nothing to worry about."

"You collapsed. You were in the hospital."

"I stood up too quickly and I fainted. That's all. I have low blood pressure. I used to faint all the time when I was younger."

"Well, you're not young anymore. And you're damn lucky you didn't hit your head when you fell."

"I'm damn lucky Mark was here," Julia corrects. She and her grandson have decided not to tell Norman the real reason she passed out. No point in upsetting him more than she already has. "Now tell me," she continues, "what exactly *is* a hedge fund?"

Norman shakes his head. "Seriously?"

"Indulge me."

Another shake of his head. A long, deep exhale. A nod of defeat. "A hedge fund is a pool of money put together by a group of investors and run by a fund manager — me — whose job it is to maximize returns while eliminating risks."

"That's quite a mouthful," Julia says. "And how exactly does one eliminate risks while maximizing returns?"

"By investing in different assets, call them alternative investments, if you will," Norman elaborates, warming to his subject, "with the hope of either beating the market or providing a *hedge* in the event of unforeseen market change. We'll buy or short any asset."

"What do you mean, 'short'?" Julia asks, more interested than she thought she'd be.

Norman takes a deep breath. "Shorting a stock is when an investor sells shares that he doesn't own at the time, and then buys the equivalent amount of those shares at a later date when, hopefully, the price of those shares has gone down. This way the investor makes a profit even though the market price has fallen."

"So, what you're really saying is that you're a gambler."

"I prefer the word 'speculator.' "

"Fascinating. Really. Quite fascinating. Tell me, does your wife understand any of this?"

"Not a word," he concedes. "And she doesn't try. One of the many things I love about her."

"What are the others?" Julia asks.

"Excuse me?"

"What are the other things you love about Poopsy . . . Poopy . . . Sorry . . . Poppy."

"You're serious?"

"I am."

"Well, for starters, she's obviously very beautiful."

"She is."

"And she has a killer body."

"She does. And I'm assuming she's great in bed, so we don't have to go there."

"Thank you for that."

"What else?"

"She makes me laugh."

"Deliberately?"

"What's that supposed to mean?"

Julia's turn to take a deep breath. "Well, I grant you that she's a beautiful girl and she has a killer body, but face it, sweetheart, she's not exactly — what is it they say? — a rocket scientist. I mean, that swimsuit idea . . ."

"Not the worst idea in the world," Norman says. "Besides, I don't *want* a rocket scientist. I just want someone who looks good and smells good and makes *me* feel good. And I finally found someone who does just that. *You* may not like me very much, Mother, but Poppy looks at me like I'm the greatest thing since sliced bread."

"Who said I don't like you very much?"

"You don't have to say it," Norman tells her.

Julia lowers her head, guilt surrounding her like a poisonous halo. "You're my son. I love you very much."

"Love more or less goes with the territory," he says. "Liking's another story altogether. And it's okay," he adds quickly. "We're just two very different people. We don't have to like each other."

Julia's eyes shoot to Norman's. "You don't like me?"

"You're my mother," he says with mock solemnity, throwing her words back at her. "I love you very much."

Tears fill Julia's eyes. It appears her son might have a sense of humor after all. "What an awful thing to say," she says.

And suddenly they're both laughing. Julia laughs until her sides ache and she's gasping for air.

"Are you okay?" Norman asks as the laughter subsides.

"I'm fine, darling."

"I'm sorry if I've disappointed you," he says.

"I'm sorry if I've disappointed *you,*" Julia says in return.

"I could really use that cup of tea now."

Julia jumps to her feet. "Follow me. And bring the scones."

"Slow down," Norman cautions, trailing

her into the kitchen and laying the plate of scones on the kitchen table. "Remember your blood pressure. You don't want to faint again."

"I'm not going to faint." She turns on the burner under the kettle. "Have a scone."

Norman dutifully picks one up and takes a bite. "These are really good," he admits before his mother can ask.

"Your son has a real gift. I'm eating better than I have in my entire life."

"Much as I hate bringing this up," Norman says as his mother is pouring the tea, "I don't suppose you've given any more thought to selling the house."

"I haven't, no," Julia lies. In fact, she's been thinking about it quite a bit the last few days.

"Look. It's not that I'm insensitive to your feelings or trying to minimize what your independence means to you," Norman tells her. "I understand. Believe me, I'm not trying to take that away from you. It's just that this is a lot of house for someone your age, and face it, Mom, Mark isn't going to hang around here forever. Even if he sticks around another year or two, there's no guarantee he'll be here the next time you faint or, God forbid, fall down the stairs or . . . whatever. I'm not some heartless bastard who's out to steal your house and pocket the cash. You can give it all to charity if that's what you want. I don't need the money. I happen to be a very good . . ."

"Gambler," she says.

"Speculator," he corrects.

They smile.

"And it doesn't have to be Manor Born," he says. "We can look around, find a place you like better. . . ."

"Drink your tea," Julia says, depositing two china cups on the table and sitting down across from him.

"Yes, ma'am." He finishes one scone and reaches for another. "These really are very good."

"Take some home for . . . Poppy."

"Thank you," her son says.

"No problem. Mark can always make more."

"That's not what I meant."

"I know."

They drink the rest of their tea in silence.

CHAPTER THIRTY-SIX

The middle-aged woman marches into Lola's Lingerie as if on a mission.

"I need a new bra," she tells Heidi.

Heidi takes a glance at the literally hundreds of bras on display throughout the store. "Well, you've certainly come to the right place. Any particular style in mind?"

"Not really, no."

"Well, why don't you have a look around and see if anything appeals to you?" Heidi glances surreptitiously at her watch, noting that her shift is up in less than ten minutes. And while she's normally very patient with customers who have no idea what they want, she's been feeling tired and a little nauseous the last few days, and she's been looking forward to going home and putting her feet up.

Especially since Aiden's mother has announced she'll be moving in over the weekend, and this is probably one of the few evenings she'll have to relax over the next few weeks.

Dear God, please don't let Lisa's renovations drag on any longer than that.

"What size are you?" Heidi asks.

"That's part of the problem," the woman answers. She has long flaming-red hair and is what might euphemistically be described as full-figured. "I don't know anymore. I used to be a 38D, but everything's so damn tight, I can hardly breathe anymore. God, I hate these things." She motions toward her ample bosom. "What men see in them, I'll never know."

Heidi nods sympathetically. The cancer that killed her mother had started in her breasts, and Heidi has always had something of a love-hate relationship with her own as a result. While they've always been enviably round and full, lately they've been looking swollen and feeling heavy. As if they belong to someone else.

Something is wrong.

Her mother wasn't much older than Heidi when she succumbed to the disease — the cancer having metastasized from her breasts to her lungs, spine, and brain — and Heidi knows there's a possibility that she inherited the deadly genetic strain.

How else to explain the fatigue, the nausea, the swelling of her breasts despite her recent loss of appetite?

She has cancer. She knows it.

Heidi reaches into a drawer containing a colorful selection of size forty DD bras. "Suppose we go up a size. How about something like one of these?"

"I guess I could try one on." The woman reluctantly takes the lined sepia-toned bra from Heidi's hands.

"The fitting rooms are over there." Heidi swivels to her right. A wave of dizziness sweeps over her, and she grabs the woman's arm to keep from falling.

"Are you all right?" the woman asks.

"I have cancer," Heidi whispers.

"Oh my God. I'm so sorry." She thrusts the bra back into Heidi's hands. "I'll come back another time." She runs from the store as if Heidi's cancer might be contagious.

Heidi watches her bright orange head of hair disappear into the steady flow of people walking the mall's main thoroughfare.

"What the hell did you say to her?" her co-worker, Shawna, asks, appearing at Heidi's side.

"I told her I have cancer."

Shawna takes a step back, her brown eyes opening in shock. "Why on earth would you tell her something like that?"

"Because it's true."

"You have cancer?"

Heidi nods.

"What kind?" Shawna asks.

"Breast."

"You've been to the doctor?"

"No."

"You found a lump?"

"No."

"Then what makes you think you have cancer, for God's sake?"

"Because I'm nauseous and I'm tired and my breasts are sore and heavy, and my mother got it when she was my age. . . . What the hell are you smiling about?"

"You don't have cancer, dude," Shawna says gleefully. "You're pregnant!"

"What? No. That's not possible. I have an IUD."

Shawna shrugs. "My mother had an IUD when she got pregnant with me. Apparently I came out holding the damn thing in my fist."

"Are you kidding me?"

"Don't look so upset. Wouldn't you rather have a baby than cancer?"

"You really think I could be pregnant?"

"Well, I'm no doctor, but unless you've been celibate this past month, which would be a real waste considering how hot your husband is, I think I'd rule that out before I start writing my will. Anyway, it's easy enough to find out. Get one of those pregnancy kits. That way you'll know for sure."

"Oh my God," Heidi says, her hands reaching down to cradle her flat stomach. She'll stop at a CVS on the way home.

If it's true, how will Aiden take the news? she wonders, trembling with a combination of joy and terror.

More to the point, what will Lisa say?

Heidi sits on the tile floor in her bathroom, staring at the thermometer-like device in her hands. *Pregnant,* it reads. *1–2 weeks.*

"Oh my God," she whispers, staring at the two other discarded pregnancy kits on the floor, both of which have revealed the same thing: She's going to have a baby.

But while a baby might be what she's always wanted, she knows Aiden is ambivalent about fatherhood, his own father having deserted the family when he was a child. There's also his PTSD to consider. So, if she's being practical, this is probably not the best time to be adding to their family.

Then there's Lisa.

She has no doubt that Lisa will be apoplectic when she finds out. When Heidi first mentioned her dream of starting a family,

Lisa had pretty much demanded they postpone any such talk for at least a few years. *"Babies are expensive. You can't afford one,"* she'd said. *"Besides, you need to give yourselves some time alone together. To make sure your marriage is on solid ground. For Aiden's nightmares to fade,"* she'd continued, unprompted, couching her directive in a veneer of concern for their welfare.

"You're the nightmare," Heidi says to the image of Lisa in her mind's eye. She pushes herself to her feet. "I'm having this baby, and there's not a damn thing you can do about it."

We'll see about that, she hears Lisa say, as downstairs, the front door opens and closes.

"Babe?" Aiden calls out. "You home?"

"Be right down." Heidi gathers up the pregnancy kits and tosses them into the wastepaper basket, then heads down the stairs, deciding to tell Aiden the news straightaway. They can figure out together the best way to tell his mother.

He's watching her from the bottom of the stairs. "Hi, you," he says as she reaches his side.

"Hi, you," she says in return, standing on her tiptoes to plant a tender kiss on his lips. "How'd it go with the therapist?"

He shrugs. "Okay, I guess." He walks into

371

the living room and plops down on the sofa.

Heidi sits down beside him. "I have some pretty exciting news."

"You got a raise?"

"No. It has nothing to do with work."

"Then, what?"

"You know how I haven't been feeling so hot the last couple of days . . . ?"

"Yeah."

"Well, I got myself all worked up this afternoon, convinced myself I had cancer . . ."

"Cancer?"

"I don't."

He laughs nervously. "Well, thank God for that."

"And Shawna said . . ." She stops, sniffing at the air. "What's that smell?"

"We picked up some KFC on the way home. It's in the kitchen."

Heidi's stomach turns over at the thought of a bucket of greasy fried chicken and then turns over again when she realizes exactly what Aiden just said. " 'We'?"

"My mother."

"She's here?"

"In the bathroom, washing her hands. She picked me up at the therapist's, said she was really in the mood for some Southern fried chicken, so . . ."

"She's staying for dinner?"

"Is that a problem?" Lisa asks from the hall. She's dressed in white capris and a clinging navy jersey. Her makeup is impeccable and matching red polish adorns her fingers and toes.

"No, of course not," Heidi says, trying to remember the last time she could afford a mani-pedi. "I just didn't realize . . ."

"Are you all right? You're looking a little green around the gills."

"Heidi hasn't been feeling great," Aiden begins, chuckling. "She thought she had cancer."

"Oh my God," says Lisa.

"I don't," Heidi assures her quickly.

"No, of course you don't," Lisa says. "You're pregnant, aren't you?"

"What?" Aiden says. "No, she isn't. . . . Heidi?"

"That's what I was trying to tell you. My exciting news. I just took a test. Three of them, actually. They were all positive. It's still very early. Just one or two weeks."

"Well, thank goodness for that," Lisa says. "We have lots of time to make arrangements. I'll call my gynecologist in the morning, find out who to contact, whether a hospital or clinic would be best. . . ."

"What are you talking about?"

"What do you *think* I'm talking about?"

"I'm *having* this baby." Heidi turns toward Aiden, willing him to say something. But he remains silent.

In the next instant, Heidi is racing for the front door. A second after that, she's doubled over, emptying the meager contents of her stomach on the front lawn.

"Oh my God! Heidi?" she hears a woman say, as footsteps approach and solicitous arms surround her. "Are you all right?"

Heidi looks up to see the kind face of Maggie McKay. "I'm pregnant," she hears herself say.

"Well, isn't that wonderful!" Maggie exclaims. "Congratulations. That's terrific." She gives Heidi a gentle hug. "Except for the throwing-up part, of course."

"Thank you," Heidi says through tears of gratitude. "I really needed that."

"Heidi?" Lisa calls from the doorway. "What are you doing out here?"

"I should go back inside."

"Congratulations," Maggie calls to Lisa. "You're going to be a grandmother. How exciting is that?!"

Lisa manages a tight smile. "Stupid girl," she whispers as Heidi brushes past her into the house.

CHAPTER THIRTY-SEVEN

Well, she certainly looked less than thrilled with the news, Maggie thinks, as Lisa closes the front door. *Wonder what the story is there?*

None of your business, she hears Craig admonish.

"Screw you," she mutters, looking toward Hood Road for his car. There are a couple of things she wants to talk to her husband about, and she'd come outside hoping for a few minutes alone with him before he took the kids out for their weekly Wednesday night dinner. She checks her watch. She'd also been hoping to make an exercise class at a nearby gym at seven, and it's already closing in on six-thirty.

But instead of Craig's car, she sees the Grants' front door open and Olivia step outside. "Hey," Olivia calls, crossing the street to the Youngs' front lawn. "What was that all about?"

"Not sure," Maggie says truthfully. It's up to Heidi to decide if and when to share the news of her pregnancy. "So, how's it going?"

"Good. Great, actually. Sean started his new job Monday and he really seems to be enjoying it."

"I'm sure that's a big relief."

"Yeah. No more credit cards being declined. Thanks again for coming to my rescue."

"Please. Don't mention it."

"Mom!" Erin calls from their front door. "Do you have my phone?"

"Why would I have your phone?" Maggie calls back. "Why would I have her phone?" she repeats to Olivia.

"I can't find it," Erin whines. "I've looked everywhere."

"Look again."

Even from two houses away, Maggie can see Erin's eyes roll toward the sky. "I'm not leaving here without it."

"Then I better get moving," Maggie says. She can't afford to waste time searching for Erin's phone after Craig arrives, not if she wants to make that seven o'clock class.

"See you Saturday," Olivia says.

Maggie takes another glance down Hood Road before heading back to her house at the rounded end of the cul-de-sac. "Where did you see your phone last?" she asks as she steps inside the front hall.

"She found it," Leo says, walking toward her from the kitchen.

"You found it?"

Erin's response is a barely perceptible nod as she walks past her mother into the living room and flounces down on the sofa.

"Where was it?" Maggie asks, following after her.

"Does it matter?"

"It was in her jacket pocket," Leo says, joining them. "When is Dad getting here?"

Maggie fights the urge to check her watch again. "Soon, I hope."

"I'm hungry."

"He's late," Erin says, as if Craig's tardiness is somehow her mother's fault.

"I'm sure he'll be here any second. Traffic's probably bad." Maggie gives in and glances at her watch.

"You're getting awfully chummy with the neighbors," Erin remarks. "What were you talking to Mrs. Grant about?"

"Not much."

"Her husband's creepy, always spying on everyone."

"Well, he won't be doing that so much now that he's got a new job."

"He got a job?"

"Started Monday."

"That's quite the job," Erin says, scrolling through her messages. "Is he some kind of sand tester or something?"

"Sand tester? What are you talking about?"

"I'm talking about the fact I saw him sunning himself on the beach Monday afternoon."

"No. It must have been somebody else."

"It was him. You can ask Mark."

"Why would I ask Mark?"

"Because he saw him, too."

"You were at the beach with Mark?" Maggie watches the color drain from her daughter's face. "You told me you went with a bunch of kids from school."

"Shit," Erin mutters.

"Erin . . ."

"It's no big deal."

"If it's no big deal, why did you lie to me?"

"Because I knew how you'd react, that's why. You blow everything way out of proportion."

"No, she doesn't," Leo interjects.

"Shut up, Leo."

"Don't tell your brother to shut up."

"If you weren't so paranoid about everything, I wouldn't have to lie."

"Stop trying to turn this around. This is

not about me."

The doorbell rings.

"Finally!" Erin says, jumping off the sofa. "Sanity has arrived."

"This is not over," Maggie says to her daughter's back.

"Oh, it's over."

"What's over?" Leo asks.

"You're late," she hears her daughter say as she opens the front door.

"There was an accident on 95," Craig is explaining as Maggie and Leo step into the hall. "Everything okay here?"

"Just Mom having her daily meltdown," Erin says.

"And I suppose you had absolutely nothing to do with that?" Craig says.

"I'll be in the car," Erin tells them. "And you guys are separated, which means you don't have to stick up for her all the time anymore," she says to her father on her way out.

Maggie exhales, watching Craig do the same. *Thank you,* she says with her eyes, and Craig smiles, *You're welcome.*

We're still in sync, she finds herself thinking, dismissing the unwelcome thought with a shake of her head.

"Anything I should know?" Craig asks.

Just that I want you to come home, that I

need you, that I still love you.

"I'm hungry," Leo says.

"Why don't we talk later?" Maggie tells her husband. She needs time to calm down and regroup, to rid her mind of these troubling thoughts. And if she really hurries, she might still be able to make that exercise class by seven o'clock.

"You're sure?"

A car horn blasts its impatience from the driveway.

"I'm sure. Have a nice dinner."

"Erin lied to Mom about Mark," Maggie hears Leo tell his father as they walk toward the car.

"Who's Mark?" Craig asks.

Maggie barely has time to close the front door before she bursts into tears.

It's five minutes to seven and Maggie is sitting, naked except for her sports bra and bikini briefs, on her bed, unable to move. She's been sitting here for the past half hour, her exercise clothes spread out beside her — the shiny new black tights, the bright yellow T-shirt and matching ankle-length yellow socks. A pair of recently purchased charcoal-gray sneakers rest on the floor by her bare feet. All she has to do is put the damn stuff on.

What's the point? she wonders with her next exhale. The class will have started even before she leaves the house, and there are *No Latecomers Allowed,* as she recalls reading online.

So much for her resolve to use this time every week to get back into a regular exercise routine. So much for her determination to stop pining for a man who has clearly moved on, despite what Richard Atwood, certified public accountant, might think.

"Not your fault he's still in love with you," he'd said.

"Yeah, right." Maggie forces herself to her feet. "Enough!" she says, stepping into the tights and sliding them up over her legs and hips, then pulling the T-shirt down over her head and pushing her arms through its sleeves. "Enough!" she repeats, donning her socks and shoes. "It's time to get your act together. Time to get on with your life."

She may have missed the scheduled exercise class, but there's nothing preventing her from working out on her own. Half an hour on a treadmill should be enough to clear her head, sift through the fog of emotions clouding her brain, help her separate fact from wishful thinking.

She reaches into the nightstand by her bed for her gun, holding it securely with both hands, her arms stretched out in front of her, as she carries it down the stairs. "Clear!" she shouts as she reaches the bottom. *Just like they do on TV,* she thinks, marching into the living room. "Clear," she says again, laughing as she goes from room to room. Would she have the guts to use it? she wonders as she drops the gun inside her canvas bag. Could she really kill another human being?

And does she really want to go to the gym when she could just crawl into a nice hot bath, grab a box of chocolates, and climb into bed? "Yes. Yes, you do!" she tells herself as she gets into her car and backs out of the garage into the driveway.

She's almost at the road when she stops suddenly, looking toward the Wilson house next door. On impulse, she leaves her car running and hurries up the Wilsons' front walk to ring the doorbell. Seconds later, the door opens and Nick Wilson stands before her. He's wearing jeans and an open-necked, button-down blue shirt, and he leans into the doorway, the fingers of his right hand wrapped around the side of the door.

"Hi," he says, clearly surprised to see her. "Everything okay?"

"Everything's fine. I was just wondering . . . is Dani here?"

Nick Wilson looks toward the interior of the house. "She is. But she's a little busy right now. Anything I can help you with?"

"Not really. I was just heading out to the gym, and I thought she might like to join me."

"The gym's not exactly Dani's thing," Nick says with a laugh. "And like I said, she's a little busy at the moment. But hey, it sounds like a great idea. I'll certainly mention it to her. Maybe next time."

Maggie is about to respond, but the door is already closing. She returns to her car, trying to banish the image of the handsome Dr. Wilson slouched in his doorway, one hand on his hip, the other wrapped around the side of the door, the knuckles of that hand bruised and red.

"It's none of your business," she tells herself as she climbs back inside her car and slams the door shut. "It's none of your damn business."

CHAPTER THIRTY-EIGHT

"It's none of your business," she is still repeating as she pulls into a parking space in front of the boutique gym located at the intersection of Military Trail and Donald Ross Road. "Stay out of it. It is none of your business." Her new mantra.

Besides, what can she do? Call the police and report her suspicions? She can just imagine how that little scene would play out. *Yes, I realize that Nick Wilson is a highly respected oncologist, that his job is saving lives, and that the affable doctor hardly seems like someone who regularly beats his wife. . . . No, I've never personally witnessed any abuse, although I've seen evidence of it on his wife's face and arms. And I'm aware that the bruises I saw on the good doctor's knuckles could be the result of any number of things. . . . Yes, I understand that his wife has never filed a complaint, and that she flatly denies her handsome husband is abusing her.*

But my instincts all tell me . . .

At this point, the police would undoubtedly interrupt to point out that instincts aren't evidence. They would remind her that Dani Wilson doesn't fit the popular image of an abused wife any more than her husband fits the popular image of an abuser, that Dani is a successful professional in her own right, and that she has both the means and the wherewithal to leave her husband should she desire to do so.

I'm afraid that until such time as Dani Wilson files a complaint, the police would surely inform her, *our hands are tied.*

And if Maggie decides to report her suspicions anyway? If the police decide to investigate and show up at the Wilsons' front door? What then?

Furious denials all around? Dani Wilson stops talking to her? A promising friendship is nipped in the bud? Maggie makes enemies of her next-door neighbors? She is forced to move yet again?

Where can she run this time?

Especially now, when she's only just beginning to stand on her feet again.

Maggie lowers her head to the steering wheel and groans.

And what of the Grants?

If Erin isn't mistaken, and it really was

Sean Grant she saw at the beach on Monday afternoon, that means Sean is still lying to his wife. Should she say something to Olivia?

You should most definitely not, she hears Craig say.

And that little scene that just played out on the Youngs' front lawn? Clearly, there's trouble brewing there.

"Also none of your business," Maggie whispers as she climbs out of her car and approaches the gym's front door. "No one has asked for your help. No one is interested in your instincts."

"Hi," chirps the perky young brunette behind the reception counter. The name tag on her bright orange T-shirt reads *Paula.* Paula's smile is wide and toothy. "Can I help you?"

"How much to join?"

"Depends on what you want." Paula hands Maggie a price list. "Basic membership is twenty dollars a month. Classes and personal trainers are extra, and you have to be a member to make use of either."

Maggie takes out a basic membership and adds her name to the sign-in sheet.

"Changing rooms and the main gym are through the door behind me on my left. Exercise classes are through the door to my right." Paula checks her watch. "The last class is almost over, but you're free to have a look-see."

"Thank you. I think I'll just hop on the treadmill."

Paula swivels toward the door on her left. "Have fun."

The gym is bright and spacious, full of the usual assortment of treadmills, rowing machines, recumbent bicycles, and free weights. Plus a bunch of scary-looking machines whose use Maggie can only guess at. "Stick to the treadmill," she says, acknowledging with a small wave a young woman jogging on a treadmill two machines down.

Maggie steps onto the closest treadmill, gently dropping her canvas bag to the floor beside her and taking note of two teenage boys laughing and lifting weights at the far end of the long room. Nearby, a red-faced, middle-aged man is grunting his way through a series of pull-ups on one of two Gravitron machines. He looks as if he's one pull-up away from a major coronary.

"Not my concern," Maggie mutters, selecting a program and instantly feeling the machine start moving beneath her feet. She turns on the small attached television, giving herself over to the soothing confidence of the Property Brothers, as the machine finishes its two-minute warm-up and starts picking up speed. Soon, Maggie is alternating between a comfortable three-mile-an-hour walk and two-minute sprints of double that.

She's halfway through the thirty minutes when she realizes that the woman on the other treadmill and the heart-attack-waiting-to-happen have both left the room. The teenagers at the far end of the gym have stopped lifting weights and are sweating their way through a series of squats and push-ups.

Maggie returns her attention to the TV — a man is demolishing a wall with a hammer while his tiny but surprisingly strong wife is pulling out kitchen cabinets with her bare hands. *Looks like fun,* Maggie thinks as she begins another two-minute sprint. A minute in, she hears the door to the reception area open and turns, beads of perspiration dripping into her eyes as she watches two men enter the gym.

The men are white, muscular, bearded, and heavily tattooed. The shorter of the two men wears a black T-shirt with a Harley-Davidson logo. The taller one sports a sneer and a handlebar mustache.

"Oh God," Maggie whispers as the taller man mounts the treadmill next to hers and his companion in the black T-shirt selects a machine closer to the door, trapping her in between.

"You must be Maggie," the taller man says.

Maggie understands in that instant that there is no escape.

The men are here to kill her.

She hears laughter and turns to see the teenage boys wrapping towels around their necks and heading for the door. Which means that, in a matter of seconds, she'll be alone with these men.

And seconds after that, she'll almost certainly be dead.

"Wait!" she calls, breathlessly, to the teenagers as they walk toward the door. But they don't hear her over the whir of the treadmill, and in the next instant, they're out the door. Immediately, Maggie presses the red emergency Stop button on the treadmill, bringing it to an instant halt and throwing her backward off the machine. She scrambles to stay upright as both men move toward her.

Maggie feels one hand on her back and another on her arm. She sees a snake tattoo wrap around her wrist. "Please," she cries.

"You all right?" the taller man asks, the natural sneer of his lips at odds with the seemingly genuine concern in his eyes.

"Please just let me go."

"Sure thing, Maggie," he says, releasing her arm. "Just making sure you're okay."

"I'm fine. Please, I have to go."

The man steps out of her way.

"Maggie," the other man calls.

Maggie freezes, bracing for the impact of a bullet to her back.

"I think you're forgetting something."

Maggie turns toward the man in the Harley-Davidson T-shirt. He smiles and lifts one muscular tattooed arm toward her. In his fingers is the canvas bag with her gun.

She gasps and grabs the bag, clutching it to her chest, the Glock 19 snapping against her sternum. "How do you know my name?"

He offers a sheepish smile. "It was on the sign-in sheet. You were the only woman here, so I figured . . . Sorry if that freaked you out."

Maggie nods, unable to move.

"You're sure you're all right?"

"Yes. Yes, I . . . I'm fine. Thank you." She walks quickly to the door, then stops, turns back around. "Enjoy your workout," she offers weakly.

"Have a nice night."

She's in her living room, still in her sweat-stained exercise gear, and nursing her third glass of red wine when Craig returns with Erin and Leo.

"Everything okay?" he asks, after both kids have retreated to their respective rooms.

Maggie takes a deep breath. "I think we should get Erin a car."

He looks surprised. "I thought you were opposed to the idea."

"I was," Maggie admits. "But I've been thinking about it. Palm Beach Gardens isn't the easiest place in the world to get around without one. I'm working now, and once school starts again, it'll be difficult to keep chauffeuring the kids everywhere. This way, Erin can drive Leo to and from school, and, I don't know, it just seems like it's the right time. . . ."

"I agree."

"So, can you look into it, see if you can get a deal on something?"

"That depends."

"On what?"

"Can I have a glass of that wine?"

Maggie shrugs. "Help yourself."

Craig walks to the cabinet in the dining area and comes back with the appropriate wineglass. "This particular Shiraz has always been my favorite." He empties what's left of the bottle into his glass, regarding

Maggie quizzically, his eyes asking, *You drank the rest of this bottle all by yourself?*

"It's been an interesting night," she says in response.

He lowers himself to the olive-green velvet sofa across from the white-and-green-striped wing chair where Maggie sits and takes a sip of his wine. "How so?"

"Well, for starters, I'm pretty sure that Nick Wilson is beating his wife and that Sean Grant is lying to his. Plus, something's definitely not right with the Youngs. I know you're going to tell me I should mind my own business. . . ."

"Since when have you ever listened to me?" Craig asks with a grin.

A small smile wobbles across Maggie's lips. "And then tonight at the gym," she continues, "I was positive these two guys were there to kill me, and of course they weren't, I was just being paranoid, as you would say. . . ."

"I say a lot of stupid things."

"Well, yes . . . you do. But you were right about that."

He laughs. "Please tell me you didn't shoot them."

"I didn't."

"Well, that's a step in the right direction."

He takes another sip of his wine. "Anything else?"

"It's just all got me thinking."

"About . . . ?"

"I recognize there will probably always be moments like tonight at the gym, moments where I let my anxiety get the better of me. But I can't let those moments turn into days, weeks, *years* of my life," she says slowly, carefully measuring out each word. "I've been in limbo for so long. Afraid of my own shadow, afraid to move forward, to trust my instincts, to be . . . who I am."

"What are you saying, Maggie?"

"That it has to change. I can't keep waiting, hoping, for things to be different. I want my spark back. I . . ." Maggie downs what's left of the wine in her glass and stands up. "I want a divorce."

CHAPTER THIRTY-NINE

It's almost seven o'clock on Saturday night and most of the residents of Carlyle Terrace are gathered outside to celebrate the Fourth of July. Sean Grant, beer in one hand, cooking utensils in the other, stands sweating over his barbecue, which he's moved from his backyard to the middle of the street. His wife, Olivia, waits behind the rickety old bridge table provided by Julia Fisher, where stacks of hot dogs and hamburgers, courtesy of the Wilsons, are piled high on a platter. A small wooden table belonging to Maggie McKay holds buns, potato salad, and a variety of condiments. Next to it is a large cooler of beer and soda pop, contributed by Aiden and Heidi Young. An impressive collection of communal fireworks lies off to one side in a cardboard box, awaiting the first hint of darkness to be sent soaring skyward in loud, colorful bursts.

The adults chat amiably to one another as

brothers Tyler and Ben Wilson engage in a rowdy game of tag, weaving in and out of their elders and into the middle of the road without fear of traffic or reprisals.

Their mother has yet to put in an appearance.

"Typical," Sean grouses to his wife. "Thinks she's too good for the rest of us."

"Hey," Tyler calls to Leo, who's been standing on the sidelines, watching. "You want to play?"

"Can I, Mom?"

"Of course," Maggie tells her son. "Just be care — Have fun," she says, looking around for Erin, who seems to have vanished.

As, Maggie notices, has Mark Fisher.

Ben Wilson immediately swoops in and slaps Leo's arm. "You're it!" he shouts.

"How was your workout?" a voice asks as the boys take off running.

Maggie recognizes the seductively smooth tones of Nick Wilson without having to turn around. "It was good," she tells him, swiveling toward him. "Hopefully next time, I can convince your wife to join me." Once again, her eyes search the small gathering. "I don't see her. Isn't she coming?"

Nick looks toward his house. "Still getting ready. She should be out soon."

Maggie nods. "How'd you hurt your hand?"

If he's surprised by the question, he doesn't show it. "Oh, that. So stupid," he says, barely glancing at his bruised knuckles. "I was upset about a patient's diagnosis and I took it out on a wall in my office. Really dumb thing to do. Could have broken my wrist. Think I'd know by now that you can't save everyone." He smiles sheepishly.

Maggie finds it interesting that in proclaiming his stupidity, he's still managed to pat himself on the back.

"If you'll excuse me," he says, still smiling, "I'll go see what's keeping Dani."

"Of course." Maggie watches him walk away.

"Hey," Heidi Young says, quickly taking his place.

"How are you feeling?" Maggie asks, noting Aiden and his mother standing off by themselves at the curb in front of their house.

"Not great. I'm pretty much nauseous all the time. Sorry about the other evening."

"No need to apologize. It was *your* lawn."

Heidi manages a small chuckle. "In case you couldn't tell, my mother-in-law isn't exactly thrilled with the news."

"Yeah. I kind of got that."

Heidi takes a deep breath and lowers her voice to a whisper. "She wants me to have an abortion."

"Oh? What do *you* want?"

"I want this baby."

"Then that's that. It's settled."

"Not really. She's pretty much convinced Aiden that this isn't the right time. . . ."

"Nobody can force you to do anything you don't want to do," Maggie assures her. "Stick to your guns. Your husband loves you, Heidi. He'll come around."

"You promise?"

Maggie smiles and takes her hand. "Have faith," she says. "It'll all work out." She takes a quick look around. "Have you seen Erin?"

"She was with Mark a few minutes ago. I think they went into Julia's house."

Great, Maggie thinks.

"Hey, everybody," Sean calls. "I've got a bunch of hot dogs and burgers ready here. Who's hungry?"

"Me!" yells Ben, making a beeline for the barbecue.

"Me, too," echoes Leo, chasing after him.

"Me, three," Julia says, grabbing a paper plate and holding it toward Sean.

"How are you feeling?" Olivia asks as the older woman is applying mustard and relish to her burger. "I understand you were in the hospital last week."

"It was nothing," Julia tells her. "I stood up too fast, got dizzy, and fainted. My grandson, bless him, overreacted and called 911."

"Where *is* Mark anyway?" Maggie asks, joining them. "I haven't seen him."

"I believe he went inside to check on his apple pie."

"Your grandson made an apple pie?"

"Only the best apple pie you've ever tasted," Julia says proudly.

"Sounds heavenly. Do you mind if I go have a look?" Maggie asks.

"Be my guest. Door's unlocked. Just follow your nose."

Maggie walks up the pathway to Julia's front door.

"Where are you going?" Leo yells after her.

"Be right back, sweetie." Maggie pulls open the door and steps inside Julia's sweet-smelling house. "Erin?" she calls, walking toward the kitchen. "Erin, are you in here?"

"Shit," Erin mutters, pulling out of Mark's embrace. "It's my mother."

"What's she doing here?"

"Snooping. What else? Do I look okay?"

"You look great," he says with a grin.

"Your hair's a little messy."

"Shit." She tries smoothing it down. "Now?"

"Better."

"What's going on in here?" Maggie asks from the doorway.

"Just checking on my apple pie," Mark says, refusing to meet her gaze.

"It smells wonderful."

"Something you want?" Erin asks.

"Sean's starting to serve the food," Maggie tells her. "I thought you might be hungry."

"How considerate," Erin says, although her tone and the look in her eyes say otherwise.

Maggie pretends not to notice either. "Shall we go get something to eat?"

"I'll just take the pies out of the oven," Mark says, "let them cool down."

"Erin?" Maggie says, motioning toward the hall. "Are you coming?"

"I'll wait for Mark."

"I'm sure he can manage on his own. Can't you, Mark?"

"Sure thing," Mark answers. "You go. I'll see you outside."

"Honestly," Erin snaps as she stomps past her mother. "You are *such* a pill."

"Does he know you're only sixteen?" Maggie asks in return.

"Wait. What?" Maggie hears Mark exclaim from the kitchen as she's closing the front door.

"So, what'll it be, ladies?" Sean asks as Maggie and Erin approach.

"Hamburger for me," Maggie says. "Erin?"

"I'm not really hungry."

"You gotta eat something," Sean urges. "Come on. It's a celebration."

"Fine," Erin says grudgingly. "I'll have a hot dog."

"Speaking of celebrations," Maggie says as Sean lifts a hamburger off the grill, places it inside a bun, and deposits it on her plate, "I understand congratulations are in order."

Sean looks confused.

"Your new job," Maggie says.

Sean glances sideways at his wife. "Of course. I didn't realize Olivia had told anyone."

"Well, it's not exactly a secret, is it?" Olivia leans over to ask. "I'm just so proud of you. I want to shout it to the world."

"Yeah. Let's hold off on that awhile, shall we?" Sean reaches over to grab another beer from the cooler. "Give it a few months, let the dust settle, see how everything goes. Assuming all is going well, then we can let the whole world know. Hey, there, you guys," he calls to Aiden and his mother. "Come and get it."

"You know you have a clone," Erin tells Sean as he's lifting her hot dog off the grill with his tongs.

"A clone?"

"A double," Erin explains. "I could have sworn I saw you at the beach on Monday afternoon."

"What? No! No way!" Sean's grip on the tongs loosens and Erin's hot dog drops to the pavement, bouncing toward Olivia's feet. "Whoever you saw, it definitely wasn't me. Shit! Where'd that damn thing go?"

Erin laughs as Olivia stops the errant hot dog with the toe of her sandal.

She isn't laughing.

CHAPTER FORTY

Dani is sitting on her bed, staring at the far wall, when she hears the front door open and her husband's footsteps on the stairs. *Get up,* she tells herself. *Get up and get moving. At least change your shirt.* She can't very well go downstairs wearing the one she has on, not with the blood covering it still so fresh.

But when Dani tries to move her feet, they collapse under her, and she's forced back into her previous position. She knows Nick will be angry when he sees her. He gave her explicit instructions to get herself cleaned up, apply ice to her injury, and put on a happy face for their neighbors. He'll accuse her of deliberately trying to make him look bad. Just as he accused her earlier of trying to undermine his authority with the boys over . . . God only knows what.

"Dani?" she hears him call. "Dan . . ."

She feels him staring at her from the

doorway.

"Dani?" he says again. "Sweetheart, are you all right?"

Dani can scarcely believe her ears, let alone respond. Can he have forgotten what transpired barely an hour ago? Forgotten that he struck her with his fist over some perceived minor transgression, catching the side of her nose, and unleashing a torrent of blood down the front of her white blouse? Is such a thing possible?

Slowly, gingerly, Dani turns her head toward him, careful not to move too fast lest the sudden motion cause the bleeding to start up again.

"Oh, sweetheart," Nick says, walking into the room and kneeling at her feet. "Have you been sitting here all this time?" He reaches up to touch her cheek. His fingers move cautiously to the side of her nose.

Dani instantly recoils.

"Hold still," he tells her, pressing down gently. "The good news is that it's not broken. Just a little swollen. You obviously didn't apply ice, as I suggested. . . ." He withdraws his hand. "When will you learn to trust me? I'm a doctor, remember?" he says, with a smile.

"I'm sorry," she mumbles, fresh tears filling her eyes and dripping down her cheeks to mingle with the dried blood at her chin.

"Yes, well, it's too late now. You'll probably end up with a black eye." He pushes himself to his feet. "Which could have been avoided if you'd only listen to your husband once in a while. Come on," he says. "Let's get you out of this shirt." He undoes the blouse's delicate white buttons and slips it off her shoulders, trapping her arms at her sides as his fingers trace the lace outline of her bra, also stained with her blood. "Better get this off, too," he says, undoing the clasp at the back of the bra and sliding it down over her breasts.

His hand moves to her neck, and Dani finds herself holding her breath, not sure if he means to caress her or choke the life out of her.

Given the choice, she'd choose the latter.

The front door opens. "Mom? Dad?" a small voice calls up the stairs.

Nick's hand moves to cover Dani's lips. His index finger wiggles into her mouth. "What is it, Ben?"

"Mr. Grant said to tell you the food's ready, and you want to get it while it's hot."

"Be right there, buddy."

"Mom, too."

"We're coming." Nick slowly withdraws his finger from Dani's mouth as the front door closes. He walks to the dresser and tosses Dani a lime-green T-shirt and a change of bra. "Get yourself washed up," he instructs. "Put these on, apply some concealer under that eye, and get your ass downstairs. Wear sunglasses. If anyone asks, tell them the truth — you had a nosebleed." He walks to the bedroom door and stops. "And hurry up. Don't make me have to come back again."

"Well, there you are," Sean calls as Nick rejoins the party. "What'll it be, Doc? Hamburger or hot dog?"

"Hamburger with the works."

"Here's your burger." Sean drops a hamburger onto a paper plate and hands it to Nick, then points to the condiments on the next table. "Help yourself to the works." He looks toward the Wilson house. "Will the Mrs. be joining us?"

"Should be down momentarily."

"Hey, Dad," Tyler calls. "Can I show Leo my fish?"

"Later, Goldilocks."

"How come he calls you Goldilocks?" Leo asks. "That's a girl's name."

"Your sister says it's a . . . a term of endearment."

"What's that?"

"It's supposed to be a good thing." Tyler shrugs. The shrug says he isn't so sure. "Race you to the end of the street."

Maggie watches them run, grateful that her son seems to have found a friend, only moderately surprised it's turned out to be Tyler and not Ben. *"Tyler's the sensitive one,"* she remembers Erin telling her.

She looks around for her daughter, dismayed that once again, she is nowhere to be seen.

She hears footsteps approaching from behind and turns to see Aiden's mother. "Lisa Young," the woman says, extending her hand. "I don't believe we've been formally introduced."

"Maggie McKay."

"I'm staying with my son for a few weeks while my kitchen is being renovated."

Maggie notes Lisa's deliberate exclusion of Aiden's wife. "Kitchen renovations are a big job."

"Yes, but some things can only be put off for so long. I like what you've done with your hair," Lisa adds, as if one thought naturally follows the other. "The blond suits you."

"Thank you. I love your blouse," Maggie feels compelled to add. Although the long-sleeved violet silk shirt doesn't strike her as the most appropriate of choices for what is, after all, a simple neighborhood barbecue, especially in this heat. "And your shoes," she says of Lisa's equally inappropriate four-inch heels.

"You can't go wrong with Louboutins," Lisa says.

Maggie nods, feeling suddenly dowdy in her no-name sandals, beige capris, and plain white T. She spots Aiden and Heidi at the barbecue, loading up their plates. "You're not eating anything?"

"Hamburgers aren't really my thing."

"You're sure? Everything's delicious."

"I may treat myself to a piece of the apple pie I understand is coming."

Maggie looks toward Julia Fisher's house. Is it possible that Erin has gone back inside?

"I've been wanting to talk to you," Lisa says.

"Oh?"

"Yes. It's about the other evening."

"Oh?" Maggie says again.

"I'd appreciate it if you wouldn't say anything to anyone else about . . . the situation."

The situation, Maggie repeats silently. "If you're referring to Heidi's pregnancy," she says pointedly, "I wouldn't dream of it. I understand it's very early days, and that they would probably prefer to wait a few months before telling people —"

"That's not the point," Lisa interrupts.

"I'm sorry. What exactly *is* the point?"

"The point is that we're not altogether sure that a baby at this particular time is a good idea."

"Really? Heidi seems quite excited about it."

"Yes. The poor girl is quite delusional about the joys of motherhood, I'm afraid. I was hoping you would talk to her."

"Me?"

"Well, she obviously feels comfortable enough to confide in you. So maybe she'll listen to you. She certainly won't listen to me."

"Just what is it you want me to say to her?" Maggie asks.

"That she should terminate this pregnancy."

Maggie takes a step back. "I can't do that," she says. "I *won't.*"

"Look. We all know this marriage was a mistake, and the last thing my son needs is to be saddled with a child. If I'm being honest, we're not even sure the child is *his.* . . ."

A loud gasp fills the surrounding air.

Maggie turns to see Heidi, her skin ashen, her mouth open in disbelief. Aiden stands a few steps behind her, a similar expression on his face.

"Please don't make a scene," Lisa says, her voice icily calm.

"How could you say such a terrible thing?" Heidi demands.

"Oh, please. Don't play innocent with me. You forget I walked in on you getting very cozy with one of the neighbors."

"What are you talking about? You mean Mark? I told you, he'd been helping me make dinner."

"In the den? On the sofa? The whole house stinking of marijuana?" Lisa scoffs. "God only knows what happened before I got there."

"Nothing happened!" Heidi swivels toward Aiden. "I swear, nothing happened."

"You have to admit that the timing of this pregnancy is very suspect," Lisa says.

"You miserable bitch," Heidi whispers.

"Well, I certainly don't have to stand here and be abused." Lisa straightens her shoulders and turns toward Maggie. "If you'll excuse me . . . ." She starts walking away, then stops, turns back toward her son. "Aiden? Are you coming?"

Maggie finds herself holding her breath. Hadn't she used that exact tone with Erin earlier? She makes a silent vow never to do

409

it again.

Aiden's eyes dart between his mother and his wife.

"Please don't go," Heidi says.

Don't go, Maggie repeats with her eyes.

"Can't catch me!" Ben suddenly hollers, cutting between them, Leo and Tyler on his heels.

"Aiden . . ." his mother beckons.

Aiden sways toward her.

"Don't go," Heidi says again. "What your mother said about the baby . . . it's not true. You know it's not true."

Aiden watches Leo, Ben, and Tyler running increasingly noisy and narrow circles inside the small cul-de-sac and feels the pavement beneath his feet crumble and turn to sand. His eyes scan the shadows of the nearby palm trees for signs of insurgents. He sees an enemy soldier emerge from Julia's house, carrying what appears to be a bomb. . . .

In the next second, he is flinging himself at Mark and wrestling him to the ground. The apple pie Mark was so proudly holding goes flying into the air, then crashes to the ground, chunks of crust and apple exploding like shrapnel. All around people are screaming.

"Aiden! What are you doing?"

410

"For God's sake, Aiden, stop!"

"Help! Somebody, stop him!"

Aiden feels hands at his back, on his shoulders, on his arms, pulling him off the young man he now recognizes as Julia's grandson. He looks around helplessly as Nick and Sean release him to go help Mark.

"This is *your* fault," Lisa says to Heidi. She surrounds Aiden with her arms and leads him back toward his house.

"What the hell just happened?" Olivia asks her husband.

Sean does a quick scan of the small dead-end street, its residents seemingly frozen in place. "Looks like the fireworks have already started."

CHAPTER FORTY-ONE

Heidi stands in the middle of the street, crying and issuing apologies to all within earshot. "I'm so sorry," she mutters repeatedly.

"This wasn't your fault," Maggie assures her.

Heidi looks toward where Mark stands on the grass in front of his grandmother's house, Julia's protective arms around him. "I don't know what to say," she tells him, "except I'm so, so sorry. I don't know what got into Aiden."

Mark nods. "Not your fault," he mutters, echoing Maggie's sentiments.

"Are you sure you're all right?" Julia asks her grandson, caressing his long hair.

"Yeah. Just a little shook up. How about you? You look kind of pale. You're not going to pass out, are you?"

"No, darling." Julia takes a deep breath to still the rapid beating of her heart. "At least,

I hope not."

"Give me your wrist," Nick Wilson says, kneeling beside her. "Let me check your pulse."

"Okay, kids," Olivia says to the three young boys giggling nervously on the sidelines. "Five dollars to whoever picks up the most pieces of pie. And no putting any of it in your mouths," she calls as they rush off before she can finish the sentence.

"Five dollars?" Sean asks. "Isn't that a little extravagant?"

"We're a two-income family again, remember?" Olivia says.

Is she being sarcastic? Sean wonders, watching Maggie's daughter, Erin, as she hovers by Mark's side. Stupid girl almost ruined everything. Just his luck she was at MacArthur Beach on Monday afternoon, a beach he'd specifically selected because no one he knew ever went there. And that's the beach she had to pick! He shakes his head, knowing that he'll have to be more careful in the future. He can't risk any more sightings of his "clone."

"Your beautiful pie," he hears Erin moan.

"It's okay," Mark tells her. "I made two."

Erin smiles, laying a gentle hand on his arm.

"Are you really only sixteen?" he whispers

out of the side of his mouth.

"Does it matter?"

He grimaces. "Yeah. It kind of does."

Erin withdraws her hand, glares at her mother.

"Heartbeat's a little elevated," Nick says to Julia. "Which under the circumstances, I'd consider perfectly normal. Maybe someone could get Mrs. Fisher some water?"

"I'll go," Olivia volunteers, disappearing inside her house and returning with a full glass.

"What about you?" Maggie asks Heidi. "How are you doing?"

"It's Aiden's baby," Heidi says. "I swear it is."

"Of course it is. I know that." Maggie spins Heidi around to face her. "Listen to me, sweetheart. Your mother-in-law is an evil witch. She got Aiden all riled up. What happened here is not your fault."

"I can't go back to that house. Not with her there."

"You don't have to go back."

Tears fill Heidi's eyes and spill down her cheeks. "I have nowhere else to go."

"What about your parents?"

"There's no one."

"No brothers or sisters?"

"No one."

x

414

Maggie nods. "Okay. Fine. You'll stay at my place."

"What? No. . . . I can't impose on you like that."

"It's not an imposition. You'll take Erin's room. She can sleep with me."

"Oh God. I don't know what to do."

"Then for the time being, you'll do what I tell you," Maggie says.

Heidi nods, relieved that someone else is making the decisions. "Okay, but it'll just be for a day or two. Till I figure out what to do."

"Take as long as you need. Just know that whatever you decide, you and your baby are going to be fine."

"You promise?"

Maggie takes a deep breath. "I promise."

"I win!" Ben shouts, his hands overflowing with errant pieces of apple pie, as the three boys rush to Olivia's side.

"So, you did." Olivia watches them toss the pieces of pie into the garbage bin. "Sean, do you have any loose bills on you?"

Sean is reaching into pockets he knows are empty when Nick stops his hand. "Allow me," he says, giving his younger son a five-dollar bill. "And one dollar for the runner-up." He lays a dollar bill in the palm of Leo's hand.

"Cool," Ben says.

"Cool," Leo echoes.

"Don't I get anything?" Tyler asks.

Nick laughs. "You get the incentive to try harder next time. You can't keep letting your little brother get the best of you."

"That's not fair," Tyler grouses.

"Life's not fair," his father says.

Ain't that the truth, Sean thinks as the front door to the Wilson house opens and Dani steps outside.

"Mom," Tyler calls, running to her and burying his head in her side.

"What's the matter, sweet pea?"

"He's upset 'cause he didn't get any money," Ben yells from the middle of the road.

"Am not."

"Are, too. I got five dollars 'cause I picked up the most pieces of pie. And Leo was second, so he got a dollar."

"I'm not sure I understand," Dani says. "What pie were you pickin' up?"

"The pie that got ruined when Aiden and Mark were fighting," Tyler explains quietly.

"Aiden and Mark were fightin'?"

"Let's not get into that now," Nick says, walking over and guiding Dani toward the barbecue. "Nice of you to finally join us." He gives Dani's elbow a painful squeeze.

"She'll have a hamburger," he tells Sean. "This man makes the best hamburgers in town. Bar none."

Sean feels a surge of pride as he flips over the patty already cooking on the grill. Maybe instead of having Burger King for a client, he can get a job behind the counter, he thinks, and almost laughs. "Don't think you're going to need those much longer," he says, indicating Dani's oversized sunglasses. "Should be getting dark pretty soon."

"Almost time to get this show on the road." Nick walks over to the box of fireworks and starts rifling through its contents.

"Have some potato salad," Olivia says as Dani is smoothing mustard on her burger. "I bought it myself." She waits for a laugh that doesn't come. *Guess Sean is right about you,* she thinks, wishing Dani would remove those big ugly glasses. She's never liked talking to someone when she can't see their eyes. "You missed quite the scene," she confides, waiting for Dani to ask what happened, then continues when she doesn't. "One minute, everything was fine. The next, total chaos. Julia's grandson comes walking out of the house carrying this apple pie he made, and suddenly Aiden goes flying through the air, like some crazed aerialist, and tackles him to the ground. Honestly, you had to see it to believe it!" She leans across the table. "I think it has something to do with Heidi. Looks like she and Mark might be —"

"Hey, hey," Nick interrupts, returning to his wife's side, his left arm falling heavily across her shoulders. "No gossip allowed."

"Oh, you're no fun," Oliva says.

Dani feels the full weight of her husband's arm on her shoulders as she does a slow survey of the cul-de-sac, the focus of her gaze obscured by her dark glasses. She watches Ben, Tyler, and Leo as they dart in and out of the street's growing shadows, notes Mark, his grandmother, and Erin standing silently by the curb, sees Maggie comforting Heidi in the middle of the road. "Where *is* Aiden?"

"His mommy took him home," Olivia says.

"So, how's the burger?" Sean asks.

"Good," Dani says, although the truth is that she can barely taste it over the lingering taste of dried blood in her mouth.

"Just good?"

"Sorry," Dani corrects. "It's wonderful. Best burger in town."

"Eat up," Nick tells her.

Dani takes another bite of the burger, willing herself not to gag. All she wants is to go back to her house and crawl into bed, pull the blankets up over her head, and disappear. She doesn't want to be here, to make mind-numbing small talk with people she barely knows, to watch a bunch of celebratory fireworks light up the night sky.

It might be the Fourth of July, but she has nothing to celebrate.

"Hey, Dad," Ben calls. "When are we gonna start?"

Nick glances at the others. "What do you say, everybody? We can light a few of the smaller ones now, save the more extravagant ones till it gets darker?"

"Fine by me," Olivia says.

"Light 'em up," Sean agrees.

"Yay!" the boys yell, their voices overlapping.

Dani watches Heidi lower herself to the curb in front of Maggie's house. Even from this distance and through her dark glasses, she has no trouble making out the distraught look on the young woman's face.

"Hey, there," a voice says, and Dani turns to see Maggie. "I was wondering where you were."

Dani tries for a smile, manages only a brief twitch. She glances over her shoulder to where Nick is kneeling over the box of fireworks. "Just couldn't seem to get

419

movin'."

"Yeah. Some days are like that."

"They tell me I missed quite the scene."
Dani looks toward Heidi. "Is she okay?"

"She will be. What about you?"

"Me? I'm fine."

"Are you?"

Dani's gaze drops to her feet. " 'Course I
am. Right as rain."

There is a loud *whoosh* as a series of Ro-
man candles suddenly explode above their
heads.

"Whee!" the boys yell. "Woo-hoo!"

"Did Nick tell you I stopped by the other
night?" Maggie asks, noting the look of
surprise on Dani's face, even with her dark
glasses. "I was going to the gym, thought
you might like to join me."

"I'm not really big on gyms."

"So your husband informed me."

Another burst of fireworks. "That was
really pretty," Dani remarks.

"You'd see better without the dark
glasses," Maggie says.

"It's okay. I'm good."

"Are you?"

"Dani," Nick calls. "Come give me a
hand."

"Talk to me, Dani," Maggie says quickly.
"I can't help you if you won't talk to me."

"Dani," Nick calls again, rising to his feet. Dani takes a last look at Maggie. "No one can help me," she says.

Chapter Forty-Two

"No way," Erin is saying, hands on her hips in front of her mother. "I am not giving her my room."

"Erin, please. Lower your voice. She'll hear you."

"She's downstairs. She can't hear anything." Erin looks toward her mother's closed bedroom door. "There is no way I'm sleeping in the same bed as you."

"It's a king-size bed. There's plenty of room."

"I don't care how big the damn bed is," Erin retorts. "I'm not sharing it with you."

"It's only for one night. Maybe two," Maggie amends, over the sound of fireworks exploding in the distance.

"No. No way. I'm not doing it."

"Why are you being so stubborn?"

"Why did you have to tell Mark I'm only sixteen?" Erin counters.

"What has that got to do with anything?"

Erin shrugs.

"You're saying this is . . . what? Payback?"

"Call it whatever you want."

"Well, first of all," Maggie says, trying to remain calm, "I didn't tell him."

"A technicality. You made sure he heard."

"Yes, I did," Maggie admits. "I thought he should know. He's twenty, Erin. You're only sixteen. He could get in a lot of trouble. . . ."

"Like you care."

"I care about *you.*"

"Yeah, well, thanks a lot. Now he says we have to cool it."

"Which speaks well of him," Maggie says, trying not to imagine how hot it had been getting.

"He's a nice boy, Mom."

"He's a *man,* Erin."

Mother and daughter release simultaneous sighs.

"Okay," Maggie says. "Can we please get back to the matter at hand? Heidi needs a place to stay for a couple of nights. . . ."

"You had no right to offer her my room," Erin says as the bedroom door opens and Leo walks in.

"I honestly didn't think you'd object."

"You didn't *think,* period."

"Okay. You're right. I'm sorry. Next time —"

"*Next time?* You do this *every* time! You butt your nose into everyone else's business and the rest of us have to live with the consequences."

"Stop yelling at Mommy," Leo says.

"I'm not yelling," Erin snaps. "And I am not sleeping in this bed with you," she tells her mother.

"I'll sleep with you," Leo offers.

"What?"

"Heidi can have my room."

"There," Erin says. "It's settled. Problem solved." She marches from the room.

"Are you sure, sweetheart?" Maggie asks her son.

"Yeah. I like this bed."

Maggie smiles. "Okay. Thank you. That's great. Go get your pajamas."

"Can I bring Mario?" he asks, referring to the plush toy he sleeps with every night.

"Absolutely."

Leo turns and runs from the room, colliding with Heidi in the upstairs hall.

"You're sleeping in my room," Maggie hears her son say.

Seconds later, Heidi appears in the doorway. "I'm so sorry. . . ."

"Please stop apologizing."

"I didn't mean to cause you problems."

"You didn't."

"I can sleep on the couch."

"I am not letting a pregnant woman sleep on my couch, and that's final. Leo has very graciously offered up his room. End of discussion." Maggie goes to her closet and brings out a white cotton nightshirt, then guides Heidi into the hall. "This should fit. And there are some extra toothbrushes in the drawer to the left of the sink," she adds as they pass the bathroom, stopping in front of Leo's room.

"I don't know what to say," Heidi says.

"How about 'good night'?"

"It hardly seems enough."

"It's all that's necessary."

Heidi collapses into Maggie's embrace. "Good night. And thank you."

"I left you Toad and Squirrel Luigi," Leo announces, joining them in the hall and pointing to the two stuffed toys lying on his pillow. "So you'll have company."

"That's so sweet of you," Heidi says through her tears.

"If you don't like them," Leo says quickly, "I can leave Mario, too." He offers up his favorite plush toy.

Maggie is so proud of her son that it's all she can do to keep from bursting into tears of her own.

"No," Heidi says. "I love Toad and Squirrel . . ."

". . . Luigi," Leo says. "He's in disguise."

"Thank you for letting me stay in your room," Heidi tells him.

"I'll be setting the burglar alarm," Maggie tells her, "so don't open any windows."

Heidi nods.

"Sleep well," Maggie says. "We'll see you in the morning."

She's dreaming of squirrels.

"Rats with good PR," Craig says.

"There's a real fat one," Erin says, pointing to the squirrel's stomach.

"She's not fat," Maggie announces. *"She's pregnant."*

"Who's the father?" Erin asks.

"Tom Cruise," Maggie says.

Which is when she knows she's dreaming. In the distance, a barrage of fireworks explodes, lighting up the dark sky with showers of neon pink and green. The sound of the explosion bangs against the side of Maggie's head.

She stirs as another round of fireworks shake up the sky, this salvo even louder than the ones that preceded it. Maggie opens her eyes, stares through the darkness at her son, asleep beside her. She lifts herself up on

426

one elbow to see the clock.

Two thirty-eight.

Surely too late for anyone to still be playing with firecrackers.

Which is when she hears another loud bang and realizes someone is at her front door.

Maggie climbs out of bed and goes to the window, staring through the darkness at the street below.

More banging.

"Mommy?" Leo asks, sleepily. "What's that noise?"

Maggie hurries to the nightstand by her side of the bed. "It's okay, sweetheart. Close your eyes. Go back to sleep."

Leo promptly lies back down, burying his nose in his stuffed Mario.

Maggie opens the drawer of the nightstand and removes her gun, carrying it back with her to the window. She stands there, waiting. But aside from the distant drone of traffic, all she hears is the silence of the night.

And then, another sound. Something guttural and all too familiar.

It takes Maggie a few seconds to recognize what it is.

Someone is crying.

Maggie returns the gun to her nightstand,

throws a robe over her pajamas, then tiptoes down the stairs. She peeks through the keyhole, then turns off the alarm and opens the front door.

Aiden is sitting on the front step, wearing the same clothes he had on earlier, hugging his knees to his chest. His feet are bare, his shoulders shaking.

"Aiden," Maggie says gently, sitting down beside him. One arm reaches up to stroke his back. "What are you doing here?"

He lifts his head. "I need to see Heidi. I know she's here."

"She's asleep."

"I need to see her."

"It's the middle of the night. You need to go home."

"I have to talk to her."

"You can talk to her in the morning."

"Is she all right?"

"She will be."

"She hates me."

"She doesn't hate you."

"I love her so much."

"I know you do."

"I've made such a mess."

"Nothing that can't be undone."

He shakes his head. "Except I don't know what to do."

"You'll figure it out."

His eyes plead with hers. "Can't you just tell me?"

Maggie almost smiles. "I think you already know." She stands up. "Now go home. Get some sleep."

He wipes his eyes, swallows one last sob, then pushes himself to his feet. "Okay. Sorry that I woke you up."

"Get some sleep," Maggie says again, watching him walk away, grateful that Heidi seems to have slept through this latest disturbance. Only after she sees Aiden disappear inside his house and close the door behind him does she follow suit.

Erin is standing at the top of the stairs. "What are you doing?" she asks as Maggie is resetting the alarm.

"I thought I heard something, so I . . ."

Erin shakes her head, rolls her eyes, and returns to her room before Maggie can finish.

"That's my girl," Maggie says, proceeding up the stairs and down the hall, fatigue clinging to her every step like a dead weight. What a night! All she wants now is to crawl beneath her covers and sleep till morning.

"Don't move!" a voice orders as she reaches her bedroom. "Hands in the air."

"Oh my God!"

Maggie slowly reaches behind her to flip

429

on the overhead light. What she sees sends shivers from the top of her head to the bottoms of her feet, as if she has just stepped on a live wire.

Leo is sitting in the middle of the bed, giggling, the drawer to the nightstand open, his stuffed Mario in one hand, his mother's Glock 19 in the other.

Chapter Forty-Three

Sean is standing at his bedroom window, staring at the street below.

What the hell was that all about? he wonders, as Aiden and Maggie retreat to their respective houses.

He'd been lying in bed, unable to sleep, when he became aware of something happening outside. He'd climbed out of bed and gone to the window, witnessed Aiden at Maggie's door, then watched him collapse on the step and bury his head in his hands. Maggie had appeared seconds later to sit down beside him, her hand on his back.

How he would have loved to have been able to listen in on that little tête-à-tête! Except that he couldn't chance opening the window and having them notice him. As it was, he'd been forced to hide behind the curtains, sneaking only sporadic peeks at the scene below, in case one of them should glance his way.

Not that he doesn't have his suspicions as to what Aiden was doing there. He'd had a front-row seat for the man's unprovoked attack on Mark and watched Maggie comforting his distraught wife. He'd seen Heidi leave with Maggie and assumed she was spending the night at her place. Aiden had likely come to the same conclusion when Heidi failed to come home at the end of the night's festivities.

Hence his middle-of-the-night foray.

Fortunately, whatever Maggie said to Aiden had been enough to calm him down.

For now.

But Aiden strikes Sean as a hothead, and he suspects it's only a matter of time before he erupts again.

Some celebration tonight turned out to be! he thinks, and might have laughed out loud, had Olivia not been sleeping only a few feet away.

The last thing he wants to do is wake Olivia.

"So, it appears you have a clone," she'd said as they were getting ready for bed.

"They say everyone has a double," Sean had replied casually, silently cursing both Erin and her mother: Erin for almost giving him away and Maggie for butting her head in where it didn't belong. He liked her bet-

432

ter when she was a timid little mouse who kept to herself and rarely said a word to anybody. Suddenly, she's everyone's best friend, coming to his wife's rescue at the grocery store and now to Heidi's. Hell, she's even managed to befriend that snooty bitch, Dani Wilson.

How the good doc ever got himself saddled with that one is something he'll never understand.

He looks toward the Wilson house next door and thinks he sees Nick in his bedroom window. The commotion likely woke him up, Sean decides, lifting his hand to wave. But the doctor, if he was there at all, disappears before Sean can complete the gesture.

Sean climbs back into bed, careful not to disturb Olivia. He knows he can't fool her forever, that by continuing to lie to her he's digging his own grave.

What he doesn't know is how to stop.

Olivia feels the weight of her husband's body as he sinks into bed beside her. She fights the urge to ask him what was going on outside, feigning sleep so as not to risk a conversation that would inevitably end with her confronting him with her suspicions.

Suspicions that his drinking has gotten out of hand.

That he's been lying to her about Advert-X.

Lying about everything.

She buries her head in her pillow to stifle a groan. How else to explain his persistent vagueness when questioned about his job, how evasive and general his answers always are, how fidgety he gets when she presses for details, how she rarely sees him without a drink in his hand?

Take tonight. He must have consumed at least half a dozen beers, which might be acceptable if he were Mark's age, but even Mark had stopped at three. And Mark had every reason to indulge. He'd been assaulted, for God's sake!

What the hell was that about?

Was Julia's grandson really having an affair with Aiden's wife?

Olivia opens her eyes, stares into the darkness. She has a much more important question to consider than whether two of her neighbors are sleeping together. Namely, who was the man Erin saw on the beach last Monday afternoon?

Was it Sean's clone?

Or was it Sean himself?

She sighs as she closes her eyes.

There's only one way to find out.

Nick comes out of his bathroom and returns to the window, relieved to find the street empty again. As it should be at this hour of the morning. He looks over at his wife, wondering if she's asleep or just pretending to be. Normally, she's an extremely light sleeper, so attuned to the kids' needs that she wakes up at the slightest disturbance. But she didn't so much as stir when Aiden started banging on Maggie's door.

"What were you talking to Maggie about earlier?" he'd asked Dani as they were getting ready for bed.

"Nothin'," she'd insisted.

"You were talking for quite a while. It had to be about something."

"Just the usual small talk. 'How are you? What's been doin'?' That sort of thing. Nothin' important."

"You're sure?"

" 'Course I'm sure."

"I don't like her."

"What? Why?"

"I don't trust her. She's a troublemaker."

"She's not . . ."

"Don't be naïve. Some women, when their husbands leave them, they can't resist making trouble for other people under the guise of friendship."

"Maggie's not like that."

"How do you know what she's like?"

"Well, I don't. . . ."

"No, you don't. But *I* do. And I don't think you should be talking to her anymore."

"What?"

"You heard me."

"But that's crazy. We live right next door."

"Are we going to have a problem here, Dani?"

"What? No. No problem."

"Good."

Luckily, that ended the discussion. Now there was only one more thing that needed to be dealt with. Nick takes a last look out the window, then walks to the bed. He gives Dani's raised thigh a not-too-gentle slap. "Wake up."

Dani bolts up in bed. "What's happenin'? Are the boys . . . ?"

"The boys are fine."

She struggles to get her breathing under control. "Is somethin' wrong? Are you okay?"

"I'm fine."

"I don't understand. Why'd you wake me up?"

"Because I've made a decision, and I

didn't want to get into an argument with you about it in front of the boys."

"A decision about what?"

"We're moving."

"What?"

"First thing tomorrow, I'm calling a real estate agent and putting this house on the market."

"What?" Dani says again.

"It's high time we moved to a better neighborhood, preferably a gated community with a golf course, somewhere like where Julia's son lives."

Dani struggles to make sense of what her husband is saying. "Can we please talk about this in the mornin'?"

Nick climbs back into bed. "There's nothing to talk about."

Mark stands in the doorway to his grandmother's bedroom, watching her sleep, the gentle rise and fall of her shoulders reassuring him that she's alive and sleeping peacefully.

Which is a miracle, considering what he's put her through lately.

He shakes his head, trying to erase the image of her confronting his dealer, his grandfather's Smith & Wesson in her frail hands, the way the color drained from her face when it was over and she collapsed to the floor, and how for a minute, he thought she was dead. She'd spent two days in the hospital, for God's sake.

All because of him.

And now, tonight. Her complexion and blood pressure were just starting to return to normal when Aiden had come flying out of nowhere to wrestle him to the ground.

"I don't understand," Julia had cried. "Why would he do such a thing? What's the matter with him?"

Mark pushes his shoulders back, reliving the impact of Aiden's body crashing into his. *The lunatic could have killed me,* he thinks, walking to the window and looking toward the house next door.

I'm *the matter with him,* he acknowledges. *I'm the matter with everything.*

Maggie knows that. That's why she doesn't want him anywhere near her daughter.

To be sure, Erin's age may have something to do with it — *shit, is she really only sixteen?* — but that's not the only reason. It's not even the main one.

The real reason Maggie doesn't want him anywhere near her daughter is that she knows instinctively that he's a loser, that despite his grandmother's unwavering faith in him, he's never going to be anything but

438

bad news.

Mark tiptoes to the dresser and slowly opens the drawer containing Julia's jewelry box. It's too risky to open it here, so he carries it into his bedroom and closes the door. Beethoven's "Ode to Joy" assaults his ears as he opens the box and grabs a handful of gold chains, stuffing them inside the pockets of his jeans.

He returns the box to Julia's dresser drawer, then crosses to her bedside and gently pulls the covers she's dislodged in her sleep over her shoulders. "I'm sorry, Nana," he whispers, kissing her dry cheek. "I love you." Then he hurries down the stairs and disappears into the night.

Chapter Forty-Four

"I said, don't move. Put both hands in the air."

Maggie struggles to remain calm as she raises both arms above her head, her eyes riveted to the gun in her son's unsteady hands. "Leo, honey. Listen to me very carefully. I need you to put the gun down on the bed."

Leo giggles, causing the Glock in his hands to shake. "But Mario wants to play."

"It's not a toy, sweetheart."

"You were playing with it before. I saw you." Leo twists the gun over in his hands, so that the barrel is now pointing directly at his head.

"Oh God," Maggie gasps as she watches him examining it. "No, honey. It's a real gun. Please, put it down."

"It's real?"

"Yes."

"Is it loaded?"

"Yes."

"With real bullets?"

"With real bullets," she repeats. "Which means it's very dangerous. You don't want Mario to get hurt. Please put it down."

Leo lowers the gun to his lap.

His finger remains on the trigger.

"Okay. That's good. Now, slowly and carefully, take your hands away."

"I can't."

"Yes, you can."

"Mario's scared," he says, starting to cry.

"It's okay, honey. Listen to Mommy, and everything will be fine. Just lift your finger off the trigger and let go of the gun."

"I can't. I'm afraid."

"Okay. It's okay. Can Mommy help you?"

He nods.

"Okay. Don't you move. Mommy's coming." Maggie slowly lowers her hands as she takes baby steps toward the bed. "Okay," she says when she reaches his side. "Now you sit very still, and Mommy's going to help you lift your finger. So, watch that you don't press down. Okay?"

"Okay."

"All right. Here we go." Maggie holds her breath as she reaches over to gingerly pry her son's finger from the trigger. "Thatta boy. You're doing great. Almost off." Slowly,

441

carefully, as if she is dismantling a bomb, she removes Leo's finger from the trigger and his hand from the gun's handle. She lays the weapon beside the alarm clock on the nightstand, then bursts into tears.

She pulls Leo to her chest, aware it could have just as easily been his dead body she was clinging to. "Oh God. Oh God. Oh God," she cries, imagining what could have been.

"You're squeezing too tight," Leo says. "Mario can't breathe."

Maggie immediately loosens her grip, although she doesn't let go.

"Am I in trouble?" he asks.

"No, sweetheart. You're not in trouble. This was my fault, not yours."

"How come you have a gun?"

"Because I was scared."

"Because Daddy isn't here?"

Maggie shrugs. She's been scared for so long it's hard to know what she's scared of anymore. "First thing tomorrow, I'm going to get rid of that stupid gun," she tells him. "And then you know what?"

"What?"

Maggie smiles through her tears. "Then I'm not going to be scared anymore."

Aiden sits at the kitchen table in the dark,

the only light coming from the iPad open in front of him. He clicks onto Facebook and types in the name Gordon Young, then stops, erases it, types it in again, then erases it again.

What the hell is he doing?

How much more of a mess can he make of this night?

He's hated Fourth of July celebrations ever since he came back from Afghanistan, the intermittent, bomb-like explosions of the colorful displays, the rifle-like *rat-a-tat-tat* of the firecrackers, the easy patriotism that knows nothing of death and destruction.

He knows that he made a complete ass of himself by tackling Julia Fisher's grandson in front of all the neighbors, that he embarrassed Heidi and scared the poor old lady half to death. He's lucky Mark wasn't seriously injured.

And for what? Had he really thought the kid was an enemy combatant? Did he honestly believe his mother's accusations had any merit?

He bites down on his bottom lip till he tastes blood. What is the matter with him? He knows that Heidi would never cheat on him. He knows the baby is his. Why does he let his mother put such stupid ideas into his head? Why does he continue to let her manipulate and control him?

"She's just using this baby to try and trap you," Lisa said even before they were fully through their front door. "You know that."

"I don't think . . ." he started to reply.

"That's the problem. You aren't thinking clearly. Not where she's concerned. You never have. Darling, don't you see? She's just using you. This baby is her meal ticket. You deserve so much better."

Heidi's the one who deserves better, Aiden thinks now.

He'd waited for her to come home when the night's celebration was over and the last of the fireworks had been sent soaring into the sky. From his living room window, he'd watched the neighbors packing up and putting everything away and waited for Heidi to break from Maggie's side and come back home to him.

But she didn't come home.

Instead, he watched her go home with Maggie.

"It's better this way," his mother said.

Was it?

"I don't know what to do," he'd said to Maggie.

"You'll figure it out."

Would he?

"I think you already know," she'd said.

Once again, Aiden enters the name Gordon Young into his iPad. The screen is suddenly awash with images. There are literally dozens of Gordon Youngs on Facebook. Gordon Youngs of all shapes and sizes, all ages. White, black, and brown Gordon Youngs. Aiden scrolls through the photos until he finds the one he's looking for.

Even though the man is decades older and twenty pounds heavier than he was the last time Aiden saw him, he instantly recognizes the man who is his father. According to his profile, Gordon Young works as a building contractor and lives in San Francisco with his wife of twelve years and their three dogs. If the photos posted are an accurate reflection, they look happy. Hell, even the dogs seem to be smiling.

What has he missed out on all these years by stubbornly refusing all contact with the man?

Now he's about to become a father himself. Is that why he's feeling this sudden overwhelming compulsion to reach out?

Aiden presses the blue button marked Message. *Hi,* he types. *It's Aiden.* He counts to ten, his fingers hovering over Delete, then sends the message before he can change his mind.

It's three hours earlier in California. There's a chance his father is still up.

Within seconds, he receives a response.

My God, Aiden. Is that really you, son?

"Aiden?" his mother calls from the top of the stairs as if she senses something is amiss. "What are you doing? Where are you?"

Aiden promptly closes his iPad.

"Aiden?" Lisa appears in the doorway seconds later. "What are you doing down here? Do you know what time it is?"

"Couldn't sleep. Thought I'd play some video games. I didn't want the noise to disturb you."

"That's very sweet, but you need your rest." She guides him toward the stairs. "Tomorrow's going to be a very busy day. We have a lot of decisions to make."

CHAPTER FORTY-FIVE

It's seven o'clock in the morning, and everyone in the McKay household is sleeping, except Maggie.

In fact, she hasn't slept at all.

How could she sleep when every time she closed her eyes, she saw her son with the gun in his small, trembling hands? Followed by an image that was even worse: her beautiful little boy with half his head blown off, his sweet face obliterated by the force of a heartless bullet, his own kind heart forever stilled.

"Oh God," Maggie moans, trying to wipe the disturbing picture from her brain.

But, like a stubborn stain, it keeps coming back.

She is sitting at her kitchen table, her gun, now emptied of bullets, resting on the table beside her laptop, her laptop open to a list of the best ways to dispose of an unwanted firearm. Much as she would like to, she understands she just can't throw the damn thing in the garbage.

She has learned there are five reasons to get rid of a gun legally: that the gun is unsafe or incapable of being fired, that it's not worth fixing, that there is a court order, that the owner wishes to create a gun-free household, or that the owner has inherited the gun and doesn't want it. She has also discovered that there is an organization that will have the gun appraised for her, as well as cover all shipping and transaction costs.

Maggie isn't interested in recouping her investment. She just wants the gun out of her house.

Which, she discovers, leaves her with four options.

The first is to contact the federal Bureau of Alcohol, Tobacco, Firearms and Explosives and explain her situation.

But it's seven o'clock on a Sunday morning, and it's unlikely anyone will be around to answer her call. Plus, it seems a bit extreme to bring the federal government into what is, after all, a relatively minor personal matter.

The second option is to surrender the gun to local law enforcement, either the sheriff or a police station. It is highly recommended that one call the nonemergency line and declare one has an unwanted gun before simply showing up at the station with it and risking getting shot or placed under arrest.

"Sounds reasonable," Maggie says, finishing what's left of the coffee in her mug.

The third alternative is to surrender the weapon to a Federal Firearms License holder, also known as FFL. All legally operating gun shops and gun dealers possess an FFL. Maggie knows she wouldn't have any trouble finding either.

The final option is to donate the gun to a gun safety training program or museum.

Maggie decides on option number two. She'll call the police, tell them she owns a firearm and wants to surrender her weapon. *Sounds easy enough,* she thinks. Almost as easy as buying the damn thing had been.

She's reaching for her phone when she hears a noise behind her and turns to see Heidi. The young woman has changed out of Maggie's nightshirt back into the shorts and T-shirt she wore to last night's barbecue. Her auburn curls have been pulled into a ponytail, and she looks surprisingly fresh and serene for someone in the middle of a marital crisis. *Oh, to be young,* Maggie thinks. "You're up early," she says.

"I smelled coffee."

Maggie is instantly on her feet. "Would you like some?"

Heidi nods, approaches the table. "Oh," she says, stopping when she sees the gun next to Maggie's laptop. "Your son's toy?" she asks, not bothering to disguise her obvious skepticism.

Maggie returns to the table and picks up the gun as Heidi takes an automatic step back. "Don't worry. I took the bullets out last night. I'm turning it in to the police station later. Going to create a 'gun-free household.' In the meantime," she says, her eyes scouting the room for a place to put it, "I'll just put it . . . here." She opens the freezer and deposits the gun behind a package of frozen peas. Then she returns to the counter and pours Heidi a full mug of coffee. "Cream? Sugar?"

"A bit of both would be great."

Maggie adds a small amount of cream and a teaspoon of sugar to the mug and places it on the table. "Why don't you have a seat?"

"Thank you. For everything."

"How'd you sleep?" Maggie asks as Heidi sinks into the chair across from hers.

"I was out the minute my head hit the pillow. Toad and Squirrel Luigi obviously did the trick. You'll have to thank Leo for me."

"You can thank him yourself when he gets up."

"No," Heidi says, taking a long sip of her coffee. "I'll be out of your hair as soon as I finish this."

"There's no rush."

"I know. And I really appreciate your generosity. But I can't stay here forever. I have to go home sometime."

"Aiden was here last night," Maggie tells her.

"What?"

Maggie relates the scene that unfolded on her front stoop.

"Oh my God. I can't believe I slept through that."

"You were exhausted."

"Still . . . I'm so sorry."

"Do you have any idea what you're going to do?"

"I know what I'd *like* to do." Heidi looks toward the freezer.

Maggie smiles.

"What do *you* think I should do?" Heidi asks her, the same question Aiden asked last night.

"I can't answer that."

"What would *you* do?" Heidi immediately amends.

"I don't know," Maggie says honestly.

451

"I'm hardly an expert on marital bliss. But I remember that there was this advice columnist when I was a kid, and she always used to say that, in the end, what it all boiled down to was: Will you be happier with him or without him?"

Heidi nods. "I guess that's what I have to figure out."

It's just after eight o'clock when Heidi leaves Maggie's house for her own. The door opens as she's heading up her front walk. Aiden fills the doorway.

"I'm glad you're back," he whispers, stepping aside to let her enter.

"I'm not staying."

"What do you mean?"

"I just came back to get a few things."

"I don't understand."

"I think you do." Heidi walks up the stairs. Aiden is right behind her. "Look. I'm sorry about last night," he says, following her into the bedroom.

Heidi grabs a small suitcase from the closet and starts throwing handfuls of clothes inside it.

"I promise it won't ever happen again."

Heidi spins toward him. "What won't happen again, Aiden? You won't get jealous over nothing? You won't attack some poor kid

452

whose only crime was helping me make a nice dinner for your mother? You won't question who's the father of this baby? You won't believe your mother's ridiculous insinuations and outright lies? What *exactly* won't happen again?"

"All of it."

Heidi looks toward the window, then back at her husband. "Prove it."

"How?"

"A while back, I told you that, sooner or later, you were gonna have to choose between your mother and me, and you asked me to hang in there a little longer, that you'd make things right, and I said I would, and I have. But now I'm gonna have a baby — *your* baby, in case there's any doubt — and I can't hold on anymore."

"What is it you want me to do?"

"Tell your mother to get out of our house."

"I think you mean *my* house, don't you?" Lisa says from the doorway.

Heidi's head snaps toward her chest at the sound of Lisa's voice. Of course, she'd been listening. "*Your* house," Heidi agrees. "*My* mistake."

"You've made a fair number of those, haven't you?" Lisa glances pointedly at Heidi's stomach.

"Look. She'll only be here a few more

weeks," Aiden tells Heidi. "Till her renovations are finished. Then —"

"Then what?" Heidi asks. "You're missing the point here, Aiden."

"Just what *is* the point?" Lisa interjects.

"You heard her, Aiden," Heidi says. "Her money, her house, her rules. I've had enough, Aiden. Haven't you?"

Outside, a car honks.

"That'll be Shawna. From work." Heidi grabs a handful of underwear from the top drawer of the dresser and stuffs it inside the suitcase before closing it. "I'll be staying with her for the time being."

"Please don't go."

Heidi takes a long, deep breath, deciding to give it one more try. "Come with me."

Aiden sways toward her, then stops.

"I didn't think so." Heidi grabs her bag and walks into the hall. "Congratulations," she says to Lisa. "You win again."

Lisa smiles. The smile says, *I always do.*

Maggie returns from the police station at just after noon. She laughs, recalling the surprised look on the officer's face when she'd surrendered her gun.

"How'd it get so cold?" he'd asked.

She notices an unfamiliar car in the Wilsons' driveway and automatically checks

454

the license plate.

REL8TOR.

What's going on there? she wonders, exiting her car at the same time as Julia Fisher steps outside. The old woman stands on her front stoop, staring up and down the street.

"Hi!" Maggie waves. "How's Mark doing?"

Julia turns around and reenters her house without answering.

"Okay. That was weird," Maggie says as she opens her front door.

"What's weird?" Leo asks, rushing to her side.

My beautiful boy, Maggie thinks, kissing the top of his head and hugging him tight, shuddering at the thought of what might have been. "I said hello to Mrs. Fisher and she just ignored me."

"She's like a hundred years old, Mom," Erin says, skipping down the stairs. "She probably didn't see you."

"She was looking right at me."

"Okay, so maybe she doesn't like you."

"Why wouldn't she like Mommy?" Leo asks.

Erin rolls her eyes, heads for the door. "I have to go."

"Where are you going?"

"Dr. Wilson called while you were out and

455

asked me to babysit this afternoon while he and the Mrs. go house hunting."

"They're moving?"

Erin shrugs. "I guess they're thinking about it."

"Seems kind of sudden," Maggie says. "I wonder why."

Erin smiles as she opens the front door. "Maybe they don't like you either."

CHAPTER FORTY-SIX

Olivia sits in her car, its engine running, near the corner of Royal Palm Way and South County Road, taking deep breaths and trying to convince herself that she's doing the right thing.

It's not that she doesn't believe her husband, or that she's checking up on him. Although, of course, that's exactly what she's doing. It's just that she has to make sure. She has to still the nagging voices in her head telling her that Sean is being, at best, less than honest about his new position. There are simply too many inconsistencies, coupled with too many excuses. Too much vagueness. Not enough concrete details.

"No, it's not a good idea to phone me at the office. I'm so busy learning the ropes, and the company discourages personal calls during the workday." "No, I can't show you my new office. Maybe in a month or two. When things

settle down. When I'm not so new." "No, I really can't discuss the projects I'm working on or the clients I'm working with. Everything is highly confidential."

"I don't understand," Olivia has said on more than one occasion. "It's not like you're working for the CIA."

"Feels like it sometimes," came Sean's instant rejoinder. "Honestly, hon. There's really nothing to tell."

Okay, Olivia thinks. She kind of understands his reticence when it comes to talking strategy or discussing clients. But Sean has been equally vague about the people he works with. True, he's only been at Advert-X just over a week, so it's a little early to be passing judgment on his co-workers, but come on. Not even a "This one is a real gem" or "That one is a royal pain in the ass." No recounting a funny story, no venting of minor frustrations. Not even any real excitement about being back in the saddle after such a long layoff, no understandable worries about his performance or how he's being perceived.

She remembers how excited she'd been when she went back to work, how nervous she'd been about whether she was doing a good job, and how she couldn't wait to get home to share the details of her day with

Sean. Nothing was too small or unimportant to leave out. No tidbit too inconsequential. No anecdote too dull.

Sean had been the same way at his old job. He'd come home every day full of stories and office gossip. He'd never been shy about voicing an opinion, no matter how premature, or offering up his two cents when he disagreed. He'd never given two hoots about being discreet.

Which was maybe why he'd been let go, Olivia thinks now, deciding she's being ridiculous, that this little detour into Palm Beach is both unfair to her husband and a waste of her time.

She checks her watch. Almost four o'clock. She was on her way home from a meeting with clients in Fort Lauderdale when the impulse hit to surprise Sean with a visit. Olivia shakes her head, knowing she's not being truthful. It's one thing to lie to others, another thing entirely to lie to yourself.

And the truth is that this idea has been germinating in her brain ever since Saturday night, when Erin dropped that bombshell about seeing Sean's clone at the beach.

God, the look on Sean's face!

Olivia might not have given the matter much thought had it not been for his over-the-top reaction, the unexpected flash of

459

anger in his eyes, his overly vehement denial. *"What? No! Whoever you saw, it definitely wasn't me."* And then losing his grip on the tongs, dropping the hot dog . . .

Combined with his reluctance to share his good news with the neighbors, his drinking, the lies he's already told . . .

So here she sits, near the corner of Royal Palm Way and South County Road, two buildings — one white and one bubble-gum pink — away from the bright yellow, six-story structure that is home to Advert-X. All she has to do is get out of the car and go inside. *Hi, honey. I just happened to be in the neighborhood. . . .*

"Screw it." She turns off the engine and climbs out of the car. *What's the worst that can happen?* she wonders, marching toward the entrance without considering the answer.

The small lobby is all large white marble tile and sleek black leather furniture. Olivia approaches the directory beside the elevator, noting that Advert-X occupies the building's top two floors. She presses the button and waits while the elevator descends, then steps back to let its two occupants — one male, one female, both young and the epitome of cool — exit. She nods hello, feeling slightly dowdy in her navy cotton dress and matching cardigan. No wonder Sean felt the need to buy that crazily overpriced jacket.

She presses the button for the fifth floor and watches the small TV in the upper right corner of the elevator flashing the latest in headlines, weather, and stock market returns. In the few seconds it takes to reach the fifth floor, she learns that Bank of America stock is up, today's temperature hit a high of ninety-three sweltering degrees, and there was a mass shooting in Iowa that left fourteen people dead and another sixteen injured.

The elevator doors open to reveal a picture straight out of a design magazine: floor-to-ceiling windows overlooking a magnificent vista of palm trees and purple bougainvillea, slate-gray marble floors, exposed steel girders, and a stunning, giant knotted-pine staircase suspended from the floor above. Six legless armchairs in a variety of DayGlo colors are grouped haphazardly around a large wooden coffee table in the middle of a royal blue area rug across from a reception desk made from the same huge wooden planks as the staircase behind it. "This is spectacular," Olivia says to the young male receptionist, whose chin-length blue-black hair is cut on the diagonal.

"Isn't it fabulous? We just love it," he enthuses. "How can I help you?"

"I'm here to see Sean Grant."

"Sean Grant," the young man repeats, turning the name over on his tongue. "Don't recognize the name. Do you happen to know what department he's in?"

"He's in Strategy."

The receptionist scrolls through his computer. "I'm not seeing him."

"He's new. Just started last week."

"You're sure he's in Strategy?"

"I thought so, but I could be mistaken. Maybe they call it something else."

"No, they call it Strategy." The receptionist smiles. "And he's with this office?"

"You have other offices?" Olivia asks hopefully.

"Oh, yes. One in New York and one in Miami."

"Oh, no. It was definitely in Palm Beach."

"Well, then you've come to the right place. But I'm not seeing his name anywhere, which is very strange. You have an appointment?"

"Actually, no. I was hoping to surprise him."

"And you're sure he's with Advert-X? Not another company in the building?"

"I . . . I . . ." Olivia begins, panic building

in her chest as she absorbs the now undeniable fact that Sean has been lying to her for weeks, possibly even months, that he doesn't work here, and that he has been getting up early every morning for the past week and a half to shower, shave, and dress before heading off to a job that doesn't exist. She stumbles back toward the seating area, her heel catching on the area rug, sending her tumbling into a bright orange chair.

The receptionist is instantly on his feet. "Oh my God. Are you all right? Can somebody please get this lady some water?"

A small bottle of water suddenly materializes at Olivia's lips.

"Take small sips," the receptionist advises.

"I'm so sorry," Olivia says, fighting the urge to throw up. "There's obviously been a misunderstanding. . . ."

"Is there a problem?" a voice asks from somewhere beside her.

Olivia lifts her head, absorbing the young woman now standing before her from the floor up, first the open-toed espadrilles, followed by the bare legs, the hot pink sundress, and finally, the bright red lips and high blond ponytail.

"Exactly the person who can help us," the receptionist says.

No one can help, Olivia thinks.

463

"This is Carrie Pierce. She's with HR. If there's a Sean Grant anywhere at Advert-X, she'll find him for you." The young man returns to his desk.

"Sean Grant?" Carrie Pierce repeats, as Olivia pushes herself to her feet. "You're looking for Sean Grant?"

"He's here?" Olivia asks hopefully.

"The name is very familiar."

"I believe you interviewed him for a position . . . ?"

The young woman's blue eyes look toward the partially exposed floor above, then back at Olivia. "Yes. That's right. Now I remember."

"So, he *does* work here," Olivia states.

"No," Carrie says, apologetically. "He didn't get the job. No reflection on his ability. He just wasn't a good fit. I'm sorry. You are . . . ?"

"Not important," Olivia says. "We obviously got our wires crossed." She lowers the bottle of water to the table. "Sorry to have bothered you."

"No problem."

Olivia walks quickly toward the elevator.

"I hope you find him," Carrie calls after her.

Oh, I'll find him, Olivia thinks as she steps inside the elevator. *Don't worry about that.*

CHAPTER FORTY-SEVEN

Julia Fisher leans forward in the straight-backed, but surprisingly comfortable, wooden chair and crosses her hands in her lap. She glances at the plaque on the far wall — *You are not a guest in our facility; we are guests in your home* — and then at the pleasant-faced middle-aged woman on the other side of the large paper-strewn desk. The woman had said much the same thing to her the last time she was here. "It was very nice of you to agree to see me again on such short notice," Julia says, "especially after I was so rude the last time we met."

"I don't remember you being rude," Carole Reid says, and seems to mean it.

"She was definitely rude," Norman interjects from the chair beside his mother.

Julia smiles. "My son is right. I was angry at being blindsided, and I took it out on you."

Carole shrugs. "Don't give it another

465

thought. Your son tells me you've reconsidered."

"Let's just say I'm . . . reconsidering," Julia corrects.

"I thought we decided," Norman says.

"We decided to reconsider."

"Well, what can I do to help you make up your mind?" Carole asks. "Would you like another tour of the premises?"

"No," Julia says. "That won't be necessary. As I recall, everything was first-rate."

"Well, then, do you have any questions?"

"I can come and go as I please?" Julia asks.

"Absolutely. You're not a prisoner."

"I'm allowed as many visitors as I want?"

"Of course." Carole smiles. "We would ask that you refrain from any wild parties. . . ."

"Yes, well, that could be a sticking point," Julia says, accompanied by a smile of her own. "What if I don't like it here?"

"I can't imagine that being the case."

"But if it is?"

"Then you're free to leave. Although, of course, you would be responsible for the remaining months on your contract."

"Of course."

"Anything else?"

"Is the apartment furnished?"

"No. You can either choose to bring in

your own furniture, or we can put you in touch with the company we used for our model suite. Would you like to have another look at it?"

"Yes, I think I would."

Carole Reid pushes off her chair and comes around to the front of her desk. She's casually dressed in black slacks and a loose-fitting turquoise blouse that accentuates the green in her eyes. "After you." She motions toward the open door of her office. "Your lovely wife couldn't join us today?" she asks Norman as they proceed through the spacious lobby.

"No old people smell," Julia hears Poppy say.

"I came right from work."

"I didn't give him a lot of notice," Julia says. In fact, her exact words to her son this morning had been, "If you still want me to move to Manor Born, you'd better get your ass over here as quickly as possible."

"What's Mark done this time?" came Norman's immediate response.

"This isn't about Mark," Julia told him, choosing not to elaborate. "I repeat, do you still want me to move to Manor Born?"

Her son hadn't asked any more questions. "I'll call Carole Reid and set up an appointment for this afternoon."

And so, here they are, in the elevator on their way to view the model suite. Is she seriously considering moving?

Why now?

Is Mark the reason for her sudden change of heart?

The truth is that it's not so sudden. She's been thinking about the move ever since her last visit. She'd been far more impressed with Manor Born than she'd let on. It had everything: a gym, multiple pools, a small theater, a drama club, regular guest speakers.

And, of course, there's Mark.

The fact that her grandson took off during the night without so much as a word of goodbye, that he made off with a handful of her jewelry and most of the cash in her wallet, that he hasn't so much as phoned in the four days since he left, that he betrayed the trust she had in him, caused her to doubt every instinct she's ever had, and made her feel every one of her eighty-four years, yes, that's certainly part of it.

But the larger part, the main reason that Julia is considering the move, is that having her grandson around all the time has reminded her how lonely she'd been without him. The fact that he's run off has only served to underline how lonely she'd be again.

And, much as she hates to admit it, her son is right about the house being too much for her to care for on her own. All those damn stairs. Her knees are always aching; her hips constantly sore. What if she were to fall? Or faint? She's already spent two days in the hospital. She has no desire to spend any more.

"Would I have this view?" Julia asks, as they enter the one-bedroom suite.

"Identical," Carole Reid says. "Just one floor down. But not all the apartments overlook this part of the grounds, so it would be a question of whether that particular unit is still available when you come to a decision."

"We'll take it," Julia says.

"Well, that's wonderful," Carole says. "I'm delighted."

"You're sure?" Norman asks his mother.

"Absolutely."

"Well, then. If you'll just come back to my office, we can get started on the paperwork."

"Wow," Norman says, clearly relieved. "You're just full of surprises today."

"I *do* have some conditions," Julia says.

"Conditions?"

Julia pats his hand. "We'll talk about it on the drive home."

She sees him even before they turn onto the small cul-de-sac.

He's sitting on her front stoop, his straggly hair pulled into a neat ponytail, his long legs stretched out in front of him, a white plastic bag at his side.

"Well, what do you know," Norman says, pulling his Tesla into the driveway as Mark jumps to his feet. "Looks like you were right."

Julia is smiling too hard to reply.

"You still have to keep your end of the bargain," Norman says. "We signed a lease. . . ."

Julia nods. "If you could just open the goddamn doors . . ."

Norman presses a button and the doors lift up and out.

"Nana!" Mark says, rushing to her side and sweeping her into an almost suffocating embrace.

Julia reaches up to stroke her grandson's cheek. "How are you, sweetheart? Are you all right?"

"I'm fine. I'm just so sorry."

"Sorry about what exactly?" his father asks, joining them.

"There's no need to get into that now," Julia says. "Let's just go inside. . . ."

"For taking off in the middle of the night," Mark tells his father. "For stealing a bunch of Nana's gold chains and about a hundred dollars from her purse."

"You stole from your grandmother," Norman repeats, as if he's known all along.

Mark retrieves the white plastic bag from the front stoop. He reaches inside it and pulls out several smaller clear baggies, each containing a single gold chain.

"You separated them?" Julia asks.

"Took about three hours!" Mark returns the baggies to the larger white one, then hands the bag to Julia. "Don't get me wrong. When I left, I had every intention of pawning the damn things. But I kept seeing your face and . . . I just couldn't let you down. I couldn't let *me* down."

"And the hundred dollars?" Norman asks, not about to be so easily mollified.

"Gone," Mark admits. "But I'll pay it back. I promise. I'll get a job, do whatever I have to. . . ."

"I have a better idea," Julia says. "Come inside. There are some things we have to tell you."

"I don't understand," Mark is saying, his

471

face awash in confusion. "Why would you do something like this?"

"Because your grandmother is either a very foolish woman or a very wise one," Norman says, smiling across the table at his mother. "She wouldn't tell me why you left, but she kept insisting you'd be back."

"But how could you know that?" Mark asks.

"Because I know you," Julia tells him. "And I knew that, sooner or later, you'd find the change room."

"What change room?" Norman asks. "What are you talking about?"

Mark smiles. "Long story."

Norman sighs, accepting there are some things about both his mother and his son that he'll never understand. "As to why your grandmother is doing this, it appears I'm not the only speculator in the family. Turns out your grandmother is an even bigger gambler than her son. I gamble on stocks. She's gambling on you. And apparently, she's done a significant amount of research these last few days, and this is the solution she feels works best for everyone."

"Look. I get why Nana is selling the house and moving to Manor Born," Mark says, repeating what has been explained to him, tears filling his eyes.

"But?"

Mark shakes his head in continuing disbelief. "But sending me to the Florida College of Culinary Arts in Miami, covering my tuition and living expenses . . ."

"As long as you stay in school and get your degree," Norman stresses. "You drop out, you're on your own."

"I would never drop out."

"Well, then, I guess it's settled." Norman pushes away from the table and stands up. "I'll call Rainbow, get the ball rolling."

"Rainbow?" Julia asks.

"Poppy's sister. She's a real estate agent."

"Rainbow the Realtor?"

"Don't start," Norman says, trying — and failing — to hide a smile. "I'll phone you tomorrow."

"I'll look forward to your call," Julia says, realizing she means it.

"Are you sure about this, Nana?" Mark asks, after his father has gone.

"About as sure as I've ever been about anything." Julia hugs her grandson to her side.

"Wow. I can't believe it."

"Are you happy, sweetheart?"

Mark smiles. "As a butterfly," he says.

CHAPTER FORTY-EIGHT

Sean sits on a long leather bench at the rear of the narrow, dimly lit bar, his back against the cheap wood paneling of the wall behind him, a tiny round table in front of him, nursing a glass of vodka and trying to decide if it's time to go home. He's been here for the better part of an hour, holding this same drink, and the bartender has been throwing suspicious glances his way for the last twenty minutes. Any second, the guy is going to walk over to ask if he wants another drink. And then what? Twenty dollars is all the cash he has left, and he can't very well charge it to his card. Not with Olivia going over their every expense with a fine-tooth comb. But he knows he can't keep sitting here if he doesn't keep buying drinks. He knows the rules. You sit; you drink. *This isn't a park bench, fella,* he can almost hear the bartender sneer.

Except even park benches are off-limits to

him now. Nowhere is safe. Not the beaches, not the parks, not the malls. There's simply no telling who could show up where, who he might run into. He thought he was safe at the MacArthur State Park, and who should show up but one of his goddamn neighbors! A neighbor, for shit's sake!

So, dimly lit, verging-on-seedy bars are about the only places left to him. His safe houses, he thinks, and almost laughs.

He checks his watch. Closing in on five o'clock. Another ten minutes and he should be good to go. Olivia has a meeting this afternoon in Fort Lauderdale, and with any luck, she'll be late getting home. She's picking up dinner again, which is great. Now that he's supposedly working again, he's no longer expected to prepare meals. One of the perks of the job!

But what will happen when his expected paycheck fails to materialize at the end of the week? What excuse will he give to Olivia then? He's fresh out of options. He's running out of time.

Maybe he should disappear, he thinks, swallowing what's left of the vodka in his glass. Get in his car and just drive away. Where? And with what? The clothes on his back? Twenty dollars in his pocket? No, not even that, not once he pays his tab.

So running away isn't the answer. And at almost fifty years of age, it's a little late to turn to a life of crime. Not that he'd have any idea which way to turn. Some criminal he'd be! What's he going to do? Hold up a 7-Eleven? A gas station? A grocery store? With what? His finger?

So, it appears he's screwed, whichever way you look at it.

"Hey, there," a voice — soft, husky, inviting — says from somewhere beside him.

He looks up to see a woman with long dark hair and a crooked smile staring down at him. She's wearing a white T-shirt that's at least two sizes too small and a tight black skirt that's a good six inches too short. He marvels that he didn't hear her approach.

"Penny for your thoughts?" she says.

He almost laughs. "Make that a twenty and you have yourself a deal."

"Those thoughts must be pretty deep."

"They aren't."

She smiles and wiggles in beside him. "Tough day?"

"Aren't they all?"

She shrugs. "Some days are diamonds . . ."

He recognizes the start of the old John Denver song. "Some days are stones," he says, completing the lyric.

"I take it this one's a stone," she says.

476

"Maybe I can make it better. My name's Brandi."

Of course it is, he thinks, estimating her age as late thirties, maybe early forties. Attractive in a slightly sullied kind of way, sexy the way a cheap perfume can sometimes be. You don't always want champagne, he acknowledges, as Brandi signals for the bartender. Sometimes you just want a beer.

"Gin and tonic," she says.

The bartender's glance shifts from Brandi to Sean.

What the hell, Sean thinks, tapping his empty glass. "Guess I'll have another one of these."

"You haven't told me *your* name," Brandi says as the bartender departs.

"Sean."

"Sean," she repeats. "That's such a nice name."

"Is it?"

"What — you don't even like your name? You *really* had a shitty day."

He laughs.

"That's better. So, Sean, what about your day was so miserable? You get fired or something?"

"Or something."

"Tell me about it."

"Trust me. You don't want to know."

477

"Sure, I do," she says, as the bartender returns with their drinks.

"You a therapist or something?"

"Or something," she says, and they both chuckle. "That's better," she says again. "So, Sean, tell me all about your miserable day. I guarantee I can make you feel better." Her hand falls to his thigh.

What the hell? he thinks. *Why not?* Sometimes you want a therapist. Sometimes a cheap hooker will do. "Well, let's see. Where to start? I'm unemployed, broke, been lying to my wife about a job I don't have, and she'll probably leave me when she finds out. I'll be lucky if I ever see my kids again. I have violent fantasies that scare the crap out of me. My drinking's gotten way out of hand, I'm angry all the goddamn time, and when I'm not angry, I'm so depressed I want to shoot myself. But I can't even do that because I can't afford a goddamn gun!"

"You're broke?" Brandi says, her hand quickly returning to her side.

Sean laughs out loud. "That's what you took from that?"

"Hey," Brandi says. "I'm a working girl. I can't afford to waste my time. Seriously — you're broke?"

"I am so seriously broke that I can't even afford to pay for your drink."

"Shit," Brandi says, sliding off the bench, guarding the drink in her hand, as if she's afraid he's going to snatch it from her.

"Wait — what about your guarantee?" Sean calls after her.

The response he gets is a raised middle finger.

"Thank you. Feeling much better now."

Brandi approaches the long mirrored bar and whispers something to the bartender. The young man, whose man-bun is at odds with his impressive biceps, leaves his post to approach Sean. "Are we going to have a problem here?"

"I don't know. What kind of problem were you thinking?"

"Suppose you just pay up and go home."

"Sure thing." Sean downs his drink in one long gulp. "How much do I owe you?"

"Let's see. Two vodka rocks and one gin and tonic . . ."

Sean is about to object, then thinks better of it.

"Thirty bucks," the bartender says.

Sean fishes inside his pocket, pulls out two ten-dollar bills. "Take it or leave it."

The bartender snatches the bills from Sean's fingers. "Get the fuck out of my bar, and don't come back."

Sean scrambles to his feet. One more place he can't come back to.

Sean pulls into the cul-de-sac just as Julia's son is pulling out. He rolls down his window. "Nice-looking car," Sean tells him. "I've been thinking of getting one myself."

"Can't recommend it highly enough," Norman says.

Sean ignores the skeptical look on the other man's face, the look that tells Sean he couldn't possibly afford one of these babies, so who's he trying to kid? "What kind of mileage do you get?"

"Couldn't say. Haven't really kept track."

Of course you haven't, Sean thinks. *Pompous ass.* "How's your mom? Everything all right?"

"She's fine. Thanks for asking." Norman pauses. "We're actually planning on putting the house up for sale, so if you should hear of anyone who's looking . . ."

"I'll be sure to tell them." *Like I don't have anything better to do with my time,* Sean thinks, then laughs, because he doesn't.

He waits till the Tesla has disappeared down the main road, then parks his car in the garage, happy to see that Olivia isn't home yet. He has time for another drink, time to conjure up one of those stupid little

480

vignettes about his job that Olivia loves to hear.

So, he thinks, it looks as if two houses on their small cul-de-sac will soon be on the market. Not that Sean knows for sure that the Wilsons will be moving, but he couldn't help noticing the real estate agent's car that was parked in their driveway the other day. He wonders idly whose house will sell first and how much they'll get.

Maybe he and Olivia should consider selling. That way, at least, he could get his hands on some much-needed cash. He's pretty sure he could talk Olivia into renting an apartment and investing whatever profit remained after the mortgage is paid off. By that time, surely to God, he'll have a job.

"Yeah, right," he says, extricating his phone from his back pocket as he enters the kitchen. He presses in the number he still knows by heart, even though it's been a while since he used it.

"Fiona Geller," the woman answers.

"Fiona," Sean says, grabbing a beer left over from Saturday night's festivities, and carrying it into the living room, plopping down on the brown corduroy couch. "It's Sean Grant," he says when the woman fails to recognize his voice.

"Sean. How are you?"

"Still unemployed," he tells her.

"I know. And what can I say? I've been talking to firms from Orlando to Miami. What can I say?" she says again. "There's just not much out there right now, especially for a man with your qualifications and experience."

"Look. Just get me an interview. Anywhere. At this point, I'll take anything."

"I know that. But you know what it's like in the summer, especially in Florida. Nobody does much hiring. They all wait till the fall. I'm certain something will come up in September."

"That's what you said last summer," Sean reminds the headhunter.

"What can I say?" she says yet again. "I know it's hard, but try to be patient. We'll find you something. It's important to stay positive."

"Right you are," Sean says, hearing Olivia's car pull into the garage.

"I promise I'll call you as soon as I hear of anything. Hang in there."

"Hanging by a thread," Sean whispers as the call disconnects.

"Sean?" Olivia calls as she enters the house. "Sean, where are you?"

"In the living room." He's returning the phone to his pocket when she reaches the doorway. "How was your day?" he asks, trying to sound interested. Much as it pains him to admit, it hurts that his wife is succeeding in an industry that no longer wants him.

She stares at him, an inscrutable look on her face. "Interesting. How was yours?"

Sean does a quick mental run-through of the stories he's spent hours dreaming up, the charming anecdotes he's memorized, the fresh lies hovering on the tip of his tongue.

Except he has no more strength for lies, no stamina for further deceit.

"The truth will out," he hears his father say.

Slowly, Sean lowers his bottle of beer to the floor and looks his wife straight in the eye. "I need help," he says.

CHAPTER FORTY-NINE

It's closing in on six o'clock and Maggie is doing a final check of the day's receipts when she hears footsteps behind her and feels Nadine at her back. "Busy day," Nadine remarks. "I'm pooped."

"When you're good, word gets around," Maggie says with a smile, recalling one of the first things Nadine ever said to her.

They watch Jerome cleaning up his station and preparing to leave. "You like working here?" Nadine asks Maggie.

"I do."

"But you're not going to stay." Nadine says this without anger or recrimination. "At least not for long."

Maggie is about to protest when Nadine stops her.

"It's okay. I knew when I hired you that you wouldn't be here more than six months, tops. That's the problem with hiring smart people. They catch on quick, do a great job, get bored, then leave. And you are by far the smartest receptionist I've ever had, so I knew from the start that it was only a matter of time."

"Well, I'm not leaving yet," Maggie says.

"Thank God for that. But when you do, I just ask that you give me a little notice. Don't you go eloping on me."

Maggie laughs. "I don't think there's any chance of that."

"You never know. You're smart *and* you're beautiful. And not all men are as stupid as your husband."

"Craig's not stupid."

"He is if he lets you get away."

"Okay, I'm out of here," Jerome says. "See you tomorrow. Have a good night, everyone."

"You, too," Maggie says as Nadine waves him out the door.

"So, what are your plans for the evening?" Nadine asks.

"Well, it's Wednesday, so Craig's taking the kids for dinner, and I signed up for this stupid gym membership, so maybe I'll take a class. . . ."

"Ooh. Be still, my heart."

Maggie grabs her purse from behind the reception counter and slings it across her shoulder, something that's much easier to do now that it's no longer weighted down by her gun. "See you tomorrow."

"Don't strain anything."

"I'll try not to," Maggie says, deciding to stop at Starbucks for something sweet before heading home.

She sees Richard Atwood even before she reaches the door. He's sitting at a table near the window talking to a young woman with waist-length brown hair. She watches as the woman throws her head back to laugh at something the handsome accountant has said and sees her hand reach across the table to cover his.

"You go, girl," Maggie says, doing a quick turnaround and heading directly to her car. She pulls out her phone and punches in Dani Wilson's number.

Dani answers on the second ring. "Maggie?" she whispers, having obviously glanced at her caller ID. "Is there a problem?"

"No problem. Why are you whispering?"

"Didn't realize I was," Dani says, although her voice remains barely audible.

"I was thinking of going to the gym, and I know you said it wasn't exactly your thing, but I thought I'd ask anyway. . . ."

"Well, bless your heart. That's real sweet of you, but . . ."

"Is that call for me?" Maggie hears Nick ask.

"No. It's for me."

"Who is it?"

"Just a patient with a problem."

"Why'd you tell him that?" Maggie asks.

Dani's voice descends even lower. "Look. I don't mean to be rude, but I'm just fixin' to get dinner on the table."

"Dani, for God's sake," she hears Nick say. "Tell them to call you at the office."

"I gotta go."

"We have to talk," Maggie tells her. But the line is already dead.

Maggie gets back from the gym at just before eight-thirty. She's tired and sweaty and common sense tells her that she should probably use this time before the kids come home to relax her sore muscles in a nice, hot bath. She laughs. When has she ever listened to her common sense?

So instead of stripping off her exercise clothes and submerging her stiff joints in a combination of steaming water and Epsom salt, she finds herself walking up the Wilsons' front path. "What's Nick going to do?" she asks the star-filled sky. "Shoot me?"

The front door opens before she's halfway up the walk. Dani Wilson, wearing jeans and a long-sleeved blouse, takes a quick glance over her shoulder and then steps outside, closing the door quietly behind her and plastering a big grin on her face. "Hi," she says. "I saw you comin' from the window. How was the gym?"

"Good. Exhausting, but good. I haven't worked out like that in a long time. And I was definitely the oldest person in the class."

"I'm sure you did just fine."

"Well, I tried. That's all you can do, right?"

"Right." Dani takes another glance over her shoulder. "Was there somethin' you needed?"

"Erin tells me you're thinking of moving."

"Oh. Yes, that's right."

"Seems kind of sudden," Maggie says. "Mind my asking why?"

Dani's smile disappears. "It's not really sudden. Nick's been thinkin' about it for a long time. He wants a bigger house, a gated community. You know, somewhere with tennis courts and a golf course, that sort of thing."

"What do *you* want?"

A brief pause. "I want my husband to be happy."

"What about you?"

"What *about* me?"

"Dani," Maggie says. "I know what's go-

488

ing on. You don't have to keep pretending."

"What are you talkin' about? I'm not pretendin' anythin'. There's nothin' goin' on."

"I've seen the bruises."

"I told you . . ."

"I know what you told me, and I know it's not true. I know that Nick is responsible, that he's been beating you."

"That's plumb crazy."

"Is it?"

A laugh scrapes at Dani's throat. "You are madder than a wet hen."

"Am I? All the makeup in the world can't hide that bruise under your eye, Dani."

Dani's hand moves automatically to her face.

"Show me your arms."

"What?"

"Roll up your sleeves and show me your arms."

"I'll do no such thing. I really think you should go now. All that exercise has clearly done a number on your head." She turns to go back inside, then stops, turns back again. "You don't understand."

"What don't I understand?"

"It's not always like this," Dani says, her voice a plea. "Most of the time, Nick's good and he's gentle and he's kind. Just when I get him riled up, when I go shootin' my mouth off about stuff I know nothin' about, when I —"

"Listen to me, Dani," Maggie interrupts. "You are not to blame for your husband's bad behavior. Nothing you say or do can ever justify his hitting you. And I don't care if, nine days out of ten, Nick is a fucking saint. The only day that means anything, the day that tells you who he really is, is the day he hits you. You're fooling yourself if you think otherwise. And you're fooling yourself if you think anything's going to change."

Dani shakes her head, dislodging the tears that have been clinging to her lashes. "Just what are you proposin' that I do?"

"Call the police, file a formal complaint."

"And what good will that do?"

"They'll arrest Nick, charge him with domestic abuse. . . ."

"He'll deny it."

"They'll believe *you.*"

"You sure about that?"

Maggie runs a frustrated hand through her hair. Her own experience with the legal system has taught her that you can't be sure of anything. "You can leave him," she offers instead.

"Where will I go?" Dani asks. "To a

shelter? I can't go draggin' my boys to a shelter. And there's no way I'm leavin' them with Nick."

"You have a busy practice, a good income, you can find another place to stay. I'll help you look. . . ."

"He'll come after me."

"He might not," Maggie says, again thinking of her own experience.

"Now who's fooling herself? Nick's never gonna let me leave."

"What if *I* call the police?" Maggie asks. "Report my suspicions . . ."

"Oh, God, no. Please don't do that. He'll kill me for sure."

"He'll kill you anyway!"

The front door to the Wilson house opens. Nick fills the doorway. "Maggie," he says, pleasantly. "I didn't hear you ring the bell."

"I saw her comin' up the walk," Dani says, quickly wiping away her tears. "I came outside before she had the chance."

"Something on your mind?" Nick asks.

"Not really. I just heard you were thinking of moving. . . ."

"Yeah. It's time."

"Just when we were all starting to get to know each other."

"Yeah, well." He shrugs. "They *do* say it's never a good idea to get too chummy with the neighbors." He looks back inside the house. "The boys are fighting over the damn fish again. I think they could use your help," he says to his wife.

" 'Course," Dani says. "Nice talkin' to you, Maggie." She disappears inside the house.

Maggie nods, about to turn around when Nick's voice stops her.

"Stay away from my wife," he says, all traces of cordiality gone.

"Excuse me?"

"You heard me. Dani's too much of a polite Southern belle to say anything, but talking to you upsets her."

"Talking to me upsets her," Maggie repeats, her voice a monotone.

"It does. So how about you keep to your house and we'll keep to ours."

Maggie takes a deep breath. "How about you stop using your wife as a punching bag."

The silence that follows is so intense, it all but shouts.

"I'm sorry. What did you say?"

"You really want me to say it again?"

Nick takes a menacing step toward her. "No. I think you've said more than enough. I'd get the hell off my property, if I were you."

"What are you going to do, Nick?" Maggie asks, holding her ground. "Hit me? Show me what a big man you are?"

"You're crazy," he says, as out of the corner of her eye Maggie sees an unfamiliar car pull into her driveway.

"Mom," Erin says, exiting the driver's seat. "Come see my new car!"

Maggie glances toward her daughter, then back to Nick. "Dani might be afraid of you," she says, her voice rising, "but I'm not." It takes a second for Maggie to realize this is true, that she doesn't need a gun to feel safe, that she has finally emerged from the long shadow of her own fear. "And I'm warning you that if I see so much as one more bruise on your wife's body," she continues, "not only am I calling the cops, I'm calling everyone I've ever met and telling everyone I see that the revered Dr. Nick Wilson is a goddamn wife beater. I'll stop total strangers on the street. I'll picket your office. Hell, I'll post the news on fucking Facebook!"

"Maggie?" Craig cuts across the lawn to the Wilsons' front walk. "What's going on here?"

"Your wife's a goddamn lunatic," Nick tells him. "No wonder you left."

"Wait just a minute . . ."

"I'm warning you," Nick says to Maggie.

"Stay away from us." He goes back inside his house, slamming the front door behind him.

Craig looks at Maggie. "Looks like you got your spark back."

CHAPTER FIFTY

"You want to tell us what that was all about?" Craig says after they return home.

"Can't wait to hear this," Erin says, as they walk into the kitchen and Maggie collapses into the nearest chair, shaking.

"Suppose you make your mother a cup of tea," Craig suggests. "Unless you'd prefer something stronger," he says to Maggie.

"No. Tea would be great."

"Why was Dr. Wilson so mad?" Leo asks.

"I guess I said something he didn't much like."

"That's a shock," Erin says. "So unlike you."

"Erin," her father warns. "The tea . . ."

"Leo, honey," Maggie tells her son, "why don't you go upstairs and get ready for bed."

"I want to hear."

"There's nothing to hear. Dr. Wilson and I just had a disagreement. . . ."

"About what?"

"Nothing. Stupid stuff. I told him his generator is too loud," she continues when the look on her son's face tells her he isn't satisfied with her answer. "It's at the side of his house, and he's supposed to have a cover around it so it doesn't make so much noise, but he doesn't. So, I told him I was going to complain to the city council if he didn't do something about it."

"And he got mad?"

"He got very mad."

"He yelled at you."

"Yes, he did."

"That wasn't nice."

"No, it wasn't."

"Are you going to shoot him?"

"What?" Maggie.

"What?" Craig.

"What?" Erin.

"No!" Maggie sputters. "Of course not."

"Where would you get an idea like that?" Erin asks her brother.

"Mom has a gun," Leo says matter-of-factly.

Erin's head snaps toward her mother. "You have a gun?"

"I *had* a gun," Maggie explains quickly. "I turned it in to the police on Sunday."

"Well, thank God for that," Craig says.

"Are you kidding?" Erin says. "The timing kind of sucks. Considering that Dr. Wilson has a cabinet full of them."

"He has a cabinet full of guns?"

"Guns, rifles, shotguns."

"Oh my God. Why didn't you tell me?"

"Because I knew you'd freak and wouldn't let me babysit there anymore. I didn't know you were Annie fucking Oakley."

"Erin, please. Your language!"

"You said 'fucking Facebook'!"

"Who's Annie Oakley?" Leo asks.

"I'll tell you all about her while you're getting into your pajamas," Craig says, leading Leo from the room. "I'll be back in two minutes. Looks like we have a lot to talk about."

"Water will be boiled in a minute," Erin says. "You want regular tea or herbal?"

"Regular. A drop of milk. No sugar."

"So," Erin says, putting a tea bag into an empty mug and retrieving a carton of milk from the fridge, "do we have to move again?"

Maggie sighs and shakes her head. "We're not going anywhere."

"Good. 'Cause I kind of like it here."

"Me, too."

Erin pours the boiling water into Maggie's mug and watches as the tea bag turns the liquid a golden brown. Then she removes the bag and adds a drop of milk before placing the steaming mug on the table in front of Maggie. "Careful. It's hot."

"Thank you, sweetheart."

"The argument wasn't really about Dr. Wilson's generator, was it?"

"No, it was not. How was your dinner?" Maggie asks before Erin can ask a follow-up.

"Great. We went to the Pelican Cafe. Then we went and picked up my new car." She grins. "Dad tells me I have you to thank for that."

"It was a joint decision." Maggie reaches over to touch her daughter's hand. "What kind is it? I'm afraid that, in all the excitement, I didn't get a very good look at it." In fact, all she remembers as Craig hustled her back inside the house is a sleek black blur in her driveway.

"It's a Toyota Corolla. Just a couple of years old, and only fifteen thousand miles on it. Dad said he got a great deal on it."

"Well, congratulations, and drive carefully."

"I will. How's the tea?"

"Perfect."

"It's my specialty," Erin says as Craig reenters the kitchen. "Would you like a cup of tea?"

498

"It's her specialty," Maggie says.

"Sure. A drop of milk. No sugar."

Both Maggie and Erin smile.

"I told Leo he could watch cartoons for half an hour," Craig says, sitting down across from Maggie. "So, what's the story?"

Maggie fills her husband and daughter in on her conversation with Dani and her subsequent altercation with Nick.

"Dr. Wilson has been beating his wife?!" Erin exclaims.

"I know. It's hard to believe."

"It is," Erin states. "But, at the same time, it kinda isn't."

"What do you mean?" Maggie asks. "Did you see something?"

"No, but . . . I don't know. I mean, Dr. Wilson was always super nice to me and everything. But there was just something a little . . . I don't know . . . off. Are you really going to tell everyone?"

Maggie shrugs. What mess has she gotten them into now?

"Erin, sweetheart," Craig says, "why don't you give your mother and me a few minutes."

Erin groans her displeasure as she gets up from her chair and walks toward the hall. "You don't think he'd do anything crazy, do you? I mean, he has all those guns and he was pretty pissed. . . ."

"He won't do anything," Craig says. "Men like him are essentially cowards. But, if it'll make you feel better, I'll stay the night."

"Thanks, Dad."

"That's really not necessary," Maggie says. "I can handle this."

"I know you can," he tells her. "I'd like to stay. It would make *me* feel better."

Maggie says nothing, deciding to wait until Erin is out of the room.

"Thanks for the tea," Craig tells his daughter.

"Thanks for the car," Erin counters. She returns to the table to give first her father, then mother, a lingering hug. "Love you guys."

"Love you, too," Maggie and Craig say together.

"Do you really think that staying the night is a good idea?" Maggie asks as Erin's footsteps retreat down the hall.

"Best idea I've had in months."

What does that mean? Maggie thinks, but is too tired to ask.

There are several seconds of awkward silence.

"So, what's happened to our quiet little cul-de-sac?" Craig asks. "The kids told me all about Aiden attacking Julia's grandson

500

on Saturday night, and now it turns out that the well-respected oncologist next door is a wife beater with an arsenal of guns. Anything else I should know about?"

"I think that's probably enough information to absorb for one night," Maggie says, deciding to spare him her suspicions regarding Sean Grant. "How are things in your neck of the woods?"

"Uneventful. A little boring."

"*She* didn't look boring," Maggie remarks.

Craig smiles. "If you're referring to Selena . . ."

"I was."

"That was never anything serious. And nothing ever happened. I swear. Selena is a lovely woman, an excellent sales rep, and yes, since you asked, a little on the boring side. Especially compared to you."

"You didn't want me," Maggie reminds him.

"I've never wanted anyone else."

Maggie fights to make sense of her husband's last remark. "I don't understand."

"I don't want a divorce."

"What?"

"I don't want a divorce," he repeats. "I love you, Maggie. I've always loved you. I've never stopped loving you."

"You left me."

"I know. And it was the stupidest thing I've ever done in my life."

Maggie lowers her head into her hands. "Maybe it wasn't so stupid."

"Now I'm the one who doesn't understand."

"I'd *already* left me," she says. "Every day, another little piece of me disappeared, till all that was left was this frightened little shadow of who I used to be. A shadow afraid of her shadow." She looks into her husband's eyes. "You can't leave someone who isn't there."

"What are you saying?"

"That your leaving was a wake-up call. You said I lost my spark. I did. But I lost way more than that. I lost me. In a way, your leaving forced me to find myself again."

"So where does that leave me? Where does it leave *us*?"

"I love you, Craig," she says, repeating his words. "I've always loved you. I've never stopped loving you." She takes a deep breath. "But I'm too exhausted — physically, emotionally — to think straight right now." She pushes back her chair and stands up. "I'm going to bed." She walks to the door. "Can we talk about this in the morning?"

He smiles. "I'll be here."

CHAPTER FIFTY-ONE

Dani hears the front door slam and holds her breath, bracing herself for her husband's rage. She doesn't know what Nick and Maggie said to each other, but she knows it wasn't good. "Boys, go on upstairs," she says to her sons, trying to usher them from the kitchen before Nick appears.

"I want to play with Neptune," Tyler says.

"Not now, honey. Please, boys, go upstairs." Her arms reach for their shoulders, trying to steer them away from the island counter. "Tyler, Ben. Go on now."

"You heard your mother," Nick says from the doorway, his voice calm, his face void of expression. "Get moving."

Tyler glances warily from his father to his mother. "You come, too," he tells her.

"It's okay, possum," Dani assures her son. "You go get yourselves ready for bed and I'll be up real soon to tuck y'all in."

"Race you," Ben says, pushing past his

brother into the hall.

Dani hears her sons' footsteps on the stairs, followed by Ben's cry of "I win!" and Tyler's "No fair. You cheated!"

"So," Nick says. "You going to tell me what that was all about?"

Dani shrugs. "Just what Maggie said. You know, she heard we were thinkin' of movin'."

"Think*ing*," Nick corrects. "Mov*ing*."

Dani nods.

"Say it."

"Nick . . ."

"Say it!"

Dani feels her throat go dry. "Think*ing*. Mov*ing*."

"There. That wasn't so hard, was it?"

"No."

"Just takes a little effort. Right?"

"Right."

"So, I'm going to ask you again, and this time you're going to make a real *effort* to tell me the truth. What was that all about?"

"I already told you. She heard we were movin' . . . mov*ing*."

"Nothing else?"

"No, nothin' . . . noth*ing*."

"You didn't tell her that I hit you?"

"What? No!"

"Then where did she get that idea, I wonder?"

"She saw my bruises and she was concerned. . . ."

"You told her I was responsible?"

"No! I told her that my bruises had nothin' to do with you."

"So . . . you *did* talk about your bruises," he says with a smile, as if she's fallen into some sort of trap.

"No. *She* talked about them. She was concerned 'cause she's seen them other times as well. . . ."

"What other times?"

Dani hesitates. "At the barbecue."

"You said other *times*. Plural."

"Well . . . when she came to my office . . ."

"When did she come to your office?"

"It was a bit ago. She needed a crown. I told you."

"No. You didn't."

"Well, then, I guess it slipped my mind. It wasn't that important."

"Our neighbor accuses me of beating my wife and you don't think it's important?"

"That's not what I said."

"What *did* you say?"

"I don't know. You're gettin' me all confused."

"People don't get confused if they're tell-

506

ing the truth."

"I *am* tellin' the truth."

"Tell me exactly what you said to her when she accused me of beating you."

"I told her she was crazy, that you had nothin' to do with my bruises, that I was just plain old clumsy, and that you were good and kind and gentle. But she just kept at me."

"Really? How so?" He takes a step forward.

Dani takes a step back. "She said that she knew what was goin' on, that she knew you were beatin' me, that I wasn't responsible for your bad behavior, that you were never gonna change. . . ."

"What else?" He takes another step forward.

Dani backs up until she feels the island at her back. "She said I should call the police, file a complaint . . ."

"You going to do that, Dani? You going to call the police? You going to file a complaint?"

"No, of course not. I would never . . ."

"Go ahead," he says, grabbing the landline from the counter and waving the receiver in front of her face. "Call the police, Dani. Call them now."

"I don't want to."

"I said call them!" He swings the receiver at her head.

Dani feels a flash of intense pain as the receiver connects with the side of her head, and she stumbles, her knees buckling, one hand grabbing at the island to stop her fall, the other shooting behind her, slapping against the glass of the fishbowls. She brings her hand to her face, swipes at the blood seeping from the gash on her cheek.

"You dumb bitch!" he yells. "Now look what you made me fucking do!"

"I'm sorry, Nick. I won't do it again. I promise. Please don't hit me again." She struggles to stand up straight.

Which is when his fist comes crashing against her jaw. The blow sends Dani sprawling across the island.

"Mom!" Tyler cries, running into the room and rushing to his mother's side. "Stop!" he yells at his father. "What are you doing? Stop!"

"It's okay, possum," Dani says. "Go back to your room. It's okay."

"Stop hitting Mommy!" Tyler screams at his father. "Get away from her!"

"Go back upstairs, Goldilocks," Nick orders, as Ben enters the kitchen. "Both of you."

"Look at the fish!" Ben shouts.

Instinctively, all eyes turn toward the fishbowls, the glass of one having been pushed up against the glass of the other during the fracas. The two fish are now fully engorged and flailing against the glass at each other.

"Neptune!" Tyler cries, flinging himself toward the bowl.

"Leave the goddamn fish alone!" Nick shouts, grabbing his son by the collar of his pajama top to stop him as Tyler kicks at his father's legs.

"It's okay, sweetie," Dani tells her son. "I'll move the bowls."

"I said, leave the goddamn fish alone!" Gripping his son's collar in one hand, Nick moves to the island and sends the fishbowl flying to the floor with the back of the other. Glass shards shoot in all directions as water gushes from the bowl and the fish flops between jagged pieces of glass along the tile floor.

"Neptune!" Tyler breaks free of his father and scoops his fish into the palms of his hands as Ben stands there, wide-eyed. "Help me. He needs water."

"I'll get it," Dani says.

"Goddamn, son of a bitch," Nick mutters, marching from the room.

Her hands shaking, Dani fills a glass bowl

with warm water and Tyler gingerly drops the fish inside.

"Is he gonna be all right?" Tyler asks. "Is he bleeding?"

"He's not bleedin'. He'll be fine. See? He's swimmin' around, all happy." Dani looks toward her younger son, seemingly frozen to the spot. "Oh, honey-pie. Are you okay?" She kneels down and takes him in her arms.

"Your face is bleeding."

"It's nothin'. Just a little scratch."

"What did you do to make Daddy so mad?" Ben asks.

Dani collapses on the floor. "Oh God," she says, the force of her son's words stronger than any blow to the head. "I didn't do nothin', darlin'. Your daddy was just a little upset. . . ."

"Trying to turn my sons against me now, are you?" Nick says, reentering the room.

Dani gasps when she sees the .22 in his right hand. "Nick . . ."

"It wasn't enough you poisoned the neighbors against me. Now you're trying to do the same thing with our boys."

Dani scrambles to her feet. "Please put the gun away, Nick. You're scarin' them."

Nick's gaze vacillates between Ben and Tyler. "I'm not scaring them. Well, maybe

Goldilocks here a little bit. But not Ben. You're not scared, are you, Benny-boy?"

Ben shakes his head, although his eyes remain frozen wide with terror.

"You go back upstairs now," Nick tells his sons. "Mommy and I have some unfinished business to take care of."

"I'm not leaving Mommy," Tyler says.

"You will, if you know what's good for you."

"Mom?" Tyler cries, his eyes darting between his mother and the gun in his father's hand.

"What are you asking *her* for?" Nick demands. "I just told you to do something. Now do it."

"Go on, possum. Take Neptune with you. I'll be up soon."

"You heard your mother. Now, unless you want me to flush that goddamn fish down the toilet, I suggest you get your ass out of here."

"Go on, boys," Dani urges.

"And don't worry about your mom," Nick says. "I'm not going to shoot her." He laughs. "Gun's not even loaded."

The boys take a final look at their mother, then leave the room, Ben running, Tyler more slowly, carefully cradling the bowl with Neptune against his chest.

"Well, what do you know?" Nick says, examining the gun in his hand. "I lied. It *is* loaded."

"Oh God. Nick, please . . ."

"Oh, don't go getting your panties all in a knot. I meant what I said. I'm not going to shoot you. Not till I figure out a way to dispose of your body without getting caught, that is." He laughs. "I'm joking," he says, although his eyes say otherwise. "Besides, right now, I'm kind of turned on. It seems I've got all this excess energy you're going to help me take care of. Aren't you, *darlin'*?"

"Sure, Nick. Whatever you want."

"That's my girl." He walks toward the den, the gun dangling carelessly from his fingers. "I'll just put this baby away and be right with you. Now get upstairs and make yourself pretty for your husband."

CHAPTER FIFTY-TWO

Aiden sits in front of the TV in his living room, watching his mother sleep on the couch beside him. The television is on, tuned to some awful British series about the lives of a bunch of boring people speaking in posh accents he can't understand, talking about things he couldn't care less about.

And neither, it would appear, can his mother, since she fell asleep half an hour ago.

Still, he can't risk waking her up by trying to change the channel. If she wakes up, she'll want to talk, and he doesn't want to talk. Not to her. Not anymore. God knows they've talked enough. He doesn't want to hear any more of her negative thoughts about Heidi.

So instead, he watches his mother sleep and wishes she were dead.

That would solve all his problems. His

money worries would be over. He would no longer care about disappointing her. He wouldn't give a good goddamn whether she was happy or not.

Heidi would come home.

He leans forward, checking on the gentle rise and fall of his mother's breathing. Her head is back, her mouth is open, a strange whirring sound, like a tiny motor, emanates from somewhere deep in her throat. For a second, he wonders if she's his mother at all, if it's possible she's been replaced by some sort of unfeeling alien being, like what happened in that old black-and-white movie he and Heidi watched on TV a few months back.

Or maybe she's a robot, he thinks, and laughs softly. Maybe she was never human at all.

That certainly wouldn't surprise Heidi, Aiden thinks, extricating his phone from his pocket and clicking onto his wife's Instagram, flipping from image to image: Heidi inhaling a colorful bouquet of spring flowers, Heidi walking along the beach, she and Aiden wrapped in each other's arms in front of a spectacular sunset, Heidi proudly displaying the chicken dinner she'd prepared for his mother.

God, he misses her!

He wonders what she's doing, if she's happily ensconced in front of Shawna's TV, enjoying her *Real Housewives*. Or maybe she and Shawna are out at a bar or a club; maybe she's letting some guy buy her a drink or lead her onto the dance floor; maybe she's relishing her life without him.

Without Lisa.

Maybe she doesn't miss him at all.

He tried speaking to her at work, going around to Lola's Lingerie yesterday morning, but Shawna informed him that Heidi would be in the storeroom all week doing inventory and was unavailable. When he'd gone around again after he finished work, he was told she'd already left, even though she was staying with Shawna and Shawna was still there. "It's probably better if you don't keep coming by," she'd advised him. "Give Heidi some space. She needs time to think."

Except, how much space? How much time?

What exactly is she thinking about?

People don't separate to get back together, his therapist told him this afternoon. They separate to get divorced.

Is that what Heidi is thinking about? Asking for a divorce?

There were always three people in your

marriage, the therapist had elaborated. And that was one person more than Heidi had signed up for.

Clearly, Dr. Patchett said, the time had come for Aiden to make a choice: his mother or his wife?

Except it wasn't quite as easy as the good doctor made it sound.

His mother had made it clear that if he got back together with Heidi, she'd be forced to take drastic measures, if only to save him from himself. She would cut him off financially. She'd write him out of her will. She'd put the house up for sale and stop the monthly payments on his car. She'd even stop funding his weekly visits to the therapist.

"Do you really think that girl is going to stick around once she finds out you're broke?" his mother had asked. *"Trust me, darling. She'll be gone in two seconds flat. And don't come crying to me then, because it'll be too late. You'll be on your own."*

Aiden understands that his mother isn't bluffing. Indeed, the more he thinks about it, the more certain he is that she means every word she says. And he realizes that the best solution for all concerned would be for his mother to die.

Although his mother might disagree.

He laughs and jumps to his feet, as if trying to distance himself from such thoughts. Lisa stirs, her mouth opening and closing, like a fish. But her eyes remain shut and the strange little whirring sound from deep in her throat soon resumes. Aiden goes upstairs to his room and sits on the edge of his unmade bed, staring at his phone and willing Heidi to call.

Miraculously, she does. Aiden answers immediately. "Heidi?"

"Hi," she says.

"I'm so glad you called. I think about you every minute of every day —"

"Can you talk?" she interrupts.

He knows what she's really asking is whether his mother is within earshot. "Yes."

"Let me guess. Lisa fell asleep in front of the TV."

"Out like a light."

"And you're . . . ?"

"In the bedroom."

"How are you?" she asks.

"Miserable."

"Me, too."

"Come home," he says.

"I want to."

"Then, come."

"I can't. Not while she's there."

"I know."

"So, what do we do?"

"I don't know."

"I think you do."

He smiles. "That's what Maggie said."

"What do *you* say?"

Aiden rubs the space between his eyes. "That my mother isn't the problem," he acknowledges. "*I* am."

"What do you want, Aiden?"

"I want *you.*"

"It's not just me anymore," Heidi reminds him.

"I want you *and* the baby."

"*Our* baby."

"*Our* baby," he repeats. "That's what I want. That's *all* I want."

"That's all *I* want," Heidi echoes.

There is a moment of silence. "You have to understand that she'll take back everything — the house, the car . . ."

"Let her. I don't care. We'll figure it out."

Another silence, this one longer than the first. Aiden pictures himself sneaking along the dusty, bombed-out streets of Kabul, no clear idea where he's going or what he's supposed to do. He jumps to his feet, sweeps the image aside with a wave of his hand.

He's not in Kabul anymore.

And he knows exactly where he has to go.

What he has to do.

"I love you," he tells Heidi.

"I love you, too."

Yet another silence, this one longer than the first two combined. Aiden fights to keep his resolve strong.

"I'll call you later," he tells her.

"I'll be here."

The line disconnects. Aiden sits on the side of his bed, staring at the phone in his hands, his breath stabbing at his chest like a knife. Does he have the courage to do what needs to be done?

Another unbidden image floats across his mind's eye: his father on the day that he left. Aiden watches him come into his room and close the door, his head down, his broad shoulders hunched forward in defeat. Lisa is screaming obscenities from the hall. He's there to break the news he's leaving. *"I'm so sorry, Aiden,"* he says, his voice as clear now as it was then. *"Please understand. I've tried everything."*

"Can't you try harder?" the child Aiden pleads.

"Sorry, buddy. I got no 'try' left," his father says. *"It'll be better this way. You'll see. For everybody."*

"Please don't go."

"Hey. It's not like we won't see each other

anymore. I'm still your father. I'll see you every week."

"Can I come with you?"

"I wish you could. But we both know that your mother would never allow that. You're the one thing in her life that makes her happy. And you want your mother to be happy, don't you, Aiden?"

You want your mother to be happy.

Aiden closes his eyes and the image disappears. His father responded to his recent overture on Facebook, although Aiden has yet to reply.

Why not? What is he so afraid of?

"It would be too upsetting for my mother," he remembers telling his therapist.

"And not upsetting your mother is more important to you than seeing your father?"

Than *being* a father?

"What are you doing, sitting there?" Lisa asks from the doorway.

Aiden jumps at the sound of her voice.

Lisa laughs. "Somebody was very deep in thought."

"You have to leave," he says, his words sliding out between barely parted lips, his voice so soft he's not even sure he spoke the words out loud.

"What did you say?"

Aiden straightens his shoulders, stares

directly into his mother's eyes. "I said you have to leave."

"Don't be ridiculous," Lisa tells him. "I'm not going anywhere but to bed."

"I choose Heidi," he says as his mother swivels toward the hall.

She stops, turns back. "Then you know the consequences."

CHAPTER FIFTY-THREE

It's almost three o'clock in the morning and Dani is still awake. She props herself up on one elbow to stare at her sleeping husband through eyes swollen almost shut from the steady flow of her tears.

She's been crying for hours. Sometimes it feels as if she's been crying all her life.

"What are you crying about now?" Nick had demanded earlier, climbing off her back and wiping himself off with a tissue. *"You want the boys to hear you? Is that what you're trying to do?"*

"No, Nick."

"Good. Then get cleaned up and come back to bed. Tomorrow's a busy day. First thing in the morning, you're going to go next door and tell your new best friend that if she so much as breathes a word of her unfounded accusations to anyone, we will sue her ass from here to eternity. You understand?"

"I understand."

"I have half a mind to just go over there right now and shoot the bitch."

Dani had said nothing, overwhelmed by a combination of relief and guilt. Relief because, for once, Nick's anger was directed at someone else, guilt for the relief.

Now she peers through the darkness to study her husband's face in repose. He looks so peaceful. So calm. There's no tension in his jaw, no snarl in his lips, no trace of fury in the set of his shoulders. Maybe the latest cycle is complete and the worst is over. Maybe once they find a new house, a new environment . . .

"You're fooling yourself if you think anything's going to change," she hears Maggie say.

She's right, Dani acknowledges, slipping out of bed and tiptoeing down the hall. She checks on the boys, first Ben, then Tyler. Both are asleep, Tyler curled into a fetal position, Ben on his back, his arms shooting out from his torso like limbs from a tree.

What would happen if she were to rouse them, tell them they were leaving, warn them not to make a sound? Would they ask questions? Would they protest? How far would they get before Nick got wind of what they were doing and came after them?

"Nick's never gonna let me leave," she'd

told Maggie. *"He'll kill me for sure."*

"He'll kill you anyway."

Not if I kill him first, she thinks.

The first time Dani remembers consciously considering killing her husband was at the shooting range. She'd thought of it again after the first time he sodomized her, and every time he'd struck her after that. Still, it was one thing to fantasize about something, another thing entirely to make that fantasy a reality.

Could she do it? Could she kill another human being, especially someone she once loved, the father of her children, for God's sake, even in self-defense?

Does she really have a choice?

Dani hurries down the stairs, through the kitchen, and into the den. She can't afford the luxury of thought. If she thinks about it, she'll lose her nerve. *Just do it,* she thinks, recalling Nike's famous motto and stifling a laugh. Not exactly what the company had in mind. She walks directly to the cabinet filled with her husband's impressive collection of weapons.

It's locked.

She pulls on its glass door, but it doesn't budge. "Damn it," she whispers, crossing quickly to the desk, her shaking hands locating the key in the top drawer, then promptly dropping it, watching helplessly as it bounces along the carpet and disappears under the leather couch. "Damn it," she says again, louder this time, as she falls to her knees and stretches out prone on the floor, her right arm reaching out in front of her, the palm of that hand searching blindly for the key beneath the sofa.

It feels like forever until she finds it, although it is likely that only a few seconds have elapsed. Her fingers wrap around the jagged piece of metal as she pushes herself back to her feet. In the next instant, she is fitting the key into the lock and opening the cabinet. Seconds later, she is holding the .22 her husband was brandishing earlier.

"I lied," she hears him say. *"It is loaded."*

She checks to make sure the bullets are still in place. Can she do it? she wonders again. Can she really march back up the stairs, put the gun to her husband's head, and end this misery once and for all?

"Oh God," she moans, as she approaches the bottom of the stairs. She stops, her tears resuming their seemingly endless flow. She might be fooling herself if she thinks Nick is ever going to change, but she's fooling herself even more if she thinks she's capable of killing him.

Dani stands at the bottom of the stairs for

several long seconds before lowering the gun to her side and walking back to the den, returning the gun to the cabinet and locking the cabinet door. She's returning the key to the top drawer of the desk when she hears footsteps behind her.

"Oh God," she mutters, closing her eyes and bracing her body for the blow she knows will follow.

"Mom?"

Dani spins around. "Oh my God. Tyler! What are you doin' up?"

"I had a bad dream. I went into your room, but you weren't there. I was afraid Daddy hurt you again."

"No, sweet pea. I just couldn't sleep, so I came downstairs," she improvises. How much has he seen? "How long have you been standin' there?"

"Just a couple seconds."

Dani walks to her son's side and takes his hand. "Well, what do you say we go back upstairs and get back into bed, try to get some sleep?"

"I'm scared."

"I know, sweetie. I'm so sorry about everythin'."

"I don't want him to hurt you anymore."

"He won't." Dani sees the fear in her son's eyes. "I promise you, I'm not gonna let him hurt any of us ever again."

"Will you stay with me?" Tyler asks when they reach his room. "Until I fall asleep?"

"Sure thing, possum."

The bed is narrow, but Tyler doesn't take up a lot of space. Dani curls her body around her son's, the heat of his body as soothing as a hot-water bottle. Within minutes, she's asleep.

Sean wakes up from a dream in which he is trying to climb his way out of a deep, dark pit. But every time he's only feet away from reaching the top, he loses his footing and slips back down to the bottom, dragging ever more dirt on top of him until he risks being buried alive.

"No!" he cries, jolting up in bed, his body bathed in sweat.

"Sean?" Olivia says, sitting up beside him. "Are you all right?"

"Sorry," he says, wondering if he'll ever stop apologizing. "Bad dream."

"Try to sleep," she says, laying a gentle hand on his arm to guide him back down, then smoothing the covers over his shoulders, and laying her head back on her pillow, smiling at him through the darkness. "It's going to be all right," she tells him. "Everything is going to be all right."

Sean marvels at his wife's support, recalling the changing expression on her face as he unveiled the depth of his deception, the full extent of his lies. They'd talked for hours. During that time, he'd watched her eyes alternately widen and narrow in disbelief and outrage, her expression careening between loathing and concern. Amazingly, the outrage and loathing had faded, replaced by compassion, acceptance, and most amazing of all, love.

He's promised to see a therapist, to join AA, to accept help from her parents until he's truly back on his feet. Hopefully he can eventually regain her trust.

Regain himself.

Only time will tell, he hears his father say.

Sean closes his eyes and slowly drifts off to sleep.

Julia is returning from her fourth trip to the bathroom in as many hours. *Too much excitement for too small a bladder,* she thinks as she climbs back into bed.

It's been quite the day: agreeing to sell the house she's lived in for much of her adult life, deciding to move to a senior living community, actually signing the lease on a new apartment. Not to mention the rapprochement with her son, the return of her grandson, the knowledge that come the fall he'll be back in school, that he's turned a corner, is on the right path.

Maybe.

Hopefully.

Of course, there's always the chance that things will fall apart, that she'll hate Manor Born, that her newfound admiration for her son will prove temporary, as will his patience with her, that Mark will drop out of college, lose his way again.

There's also the chance that she might not wake up tomorrow, she acknowledges, accepting that there are some things she can control, and many more things she can't.

She hopes that everything will work out. She hopes that she'll wake up in the morning to face another day.

In the end, she decides as she closes her eyes in sleep, hope is all we have.

Lisa turns over in bed and opens her eyes, not sure what she's doing up. She squints at the clock radio on the bedside table. Not quite three in the morning. "Are you kidding me?" she mutters, flipping onto her other side, trying to will herself back to sleep. But after twenty minutes, she's more awake than ever, unable to rid her mind of her son's strangely obstreperous behavior. *"I choose Heidi,"* he'd told her.

Fat chance of that, Lisa scoffs. She knows her son. He's just lonely, and likely more than a little horny. He doesn't miss having Heidi in his life so much as he misses having her in his bed. Come morning, he'll have come to his senses. He'll realize that girls like Heidi are a dime a dozen and that he deserves better. He'll apologize for ordering her out of the house she paid for, tell her he understands that, by making those threats to cut him off financially, she was merely forcing him to acknowledge his reality.

And then they'll move on.

Without Heidi.

It's taken Lisa longer than she thought it would to get rid of the girl — she'd proved surprisingly tenacious — but now that it was done once and for all, they could get on with their lives. She'd arrange for Aiden to see a good divorce attorney, maybe even offer Heidi a small settlement in order to get rid of her as quickly and painlessly as possible. She has no doubt that once Heidi realizes Aiden is serious about ending the marriage, she'll opt out of motherhood as well. A pretty girl like her will have much less trouble finding another sucker to marry if she comes without a screaming infant attached.

After another ten minutes of lying in bed wide awake, Lisa decides she might as well go downstairs and watch TV. That always seems to put her right to sleep. She gets out of bed, throws on a robe over her nightgown, and walks toward the stairs.

The light is on in Aiden's bedroom.

So he's having trouble sleeping as well, she thinks, so upset is he at the shabby way he treated her earlier. Might as well go in there and comfort him, assure him that all is forgiven. "Aiden," she says, stopping in the doorway.

Except he isn't there.

"Aiden?"

She knows he's gone even before she checks the closet and finds all his clothes missing. She opens the dresser drawers. But the only things she finds are the guns he's left behind.

Craig opens his eyes to find Maggie, her bare feet protruding from the bottoms of her cotton pajamas, standing in the doorway. "What?" he says, his breath catching in his lungs as he swings his legs off the family room sofa and sits up. "Has something happened? Is anything wrong?"

"I can't sleep," Maggie says.

Craig exhales with relief and pats the cushion beside him. "Come sit."

Maggie walks slowly to the couch and drops down beside him. "Did I wake you?"

He shakes his head. "Not really. I've kind of been drifting in and out. What's up?"

"Nothing."

"Do you want to talk?"

"Not really."

"Do you want to watch TV?"

"No."

"You just want to sit here for a while?"

"That sounds nice."

Craig smiles. "Sounds nice to me, too."

Dani feels his presence looming over her even before she opens her eyes.

"What the hell is going on here?" Nick demands from the side of Tyler's bed.

Dani looks nervously from her husband to her sleeping son. "Shh. You'll wake him up."

"Don't tell me to shh!" Nick grabs Dani by the hair, pulling her from the bed and dragging her back into their bedroom as she struggles to stand up straight. "What are you trying to do? Turn our son into a sissy, a goddamn mama's boy?"

"No, Nick. I was just tryin' to comfort him. . . ."

"He doesn't need comforting. He needs a good kick in the ass. Like his mother," Nick says, the toes of one bare foot piercing the thin cotton of her nightgown, his fists pummeling her head. The blows crash against the side of her temple, her cheeks, her jaw. He continues his assault as her body sinks toward the floor, blood dripping from her split lip, the room spinning around her.

"Stop!" she hears a small voice shout as she struggles to stay conscious. "Get away from her!"

Through her tears, Dani sees Tyler in the doorway, his face ashen, his arms stretched out in front of him, the gun in his shaking hands aimed squarely at his father's chest.

"Well, would you get a look at Goldilocks! Give me that thing." Nick steps toward Tyler.

Which is when Tyler closes his eyes and pulls the trigger.

Maggie and Craig are still sitting silently side by side when they hear what sounds like a car backfiring down the street.

"Oh God," Maggie cries instantly, jumping to her feet. "He did it! The bastard shot her!"

Craig hesitates only a fraction of a second. "I'll call the police," he says.

■ ■ ■ ■

Dani screams as the gun goes off, the bullet missing Nick by a good foot and tearing a hole in the white shade of the bedside lamp.

"You stupid kid," Nick says, advancing menacingly toward his son. "If you're going to shoot at someone, you damn sure better not miss."

The gun in Tyler's hand falls to the floor as his father grabs him by the neck of his pajamas, Nick's free hand raised and poised to strike.

Dani throws herself at the gun, scooping it up off the floor and aiming it at her husband's head.

"You dumb bitch," Nick starts, the last words out of his mouth before Dani pulls the trigger.

She doesn't miss.

EPILOGUE

It's a year later.

To an outsider, the street looks essentially the same as it always has: a tree-filled horseshoe-shaped cul-de-sac containing five identical two-story homes in a variety of pastel shades, each with an attached double-car garage to the left of its front door.

But, of course, it's not the same.

Death changes everything.

Only two of the houses are occupied by the same families as were living here on that hot July night. The other residents have moved away, some to neighboring communities, some clear across the country.

Lisa was the first to sell. The same morning that most of the residents were gathering outside, trying to make sense of what had happened, she was on the phone with a real estate agent, arranging to make good on the threat she'd delivered to her son. She'd been awake when the police cars and ambulance arrived, observing the scene from her window as the officers and paramedics rushed into the Wilson house. She saw the body bag being carried out on a stretcher, watched as a blank-faced Dani Wilson and her two sons, one of them carrying what appeared to be a bowl of some sort, were led down the walkway into a waiting patrol car.

As for Lisa's son, Aiden, he was nowhere near the so-called scene of the crime, having left hours earlier to be with Heidi. Shawna subsequently helped them find a tiny apartment close to hers, which they rented for several months before relocating to San Francisco. Aiden now works for his father and continues to see a therapist weekly. Heidi is a stay-at-home mother to a beautiful baby girl they named Annie, after Heidi's mom. She sends regular updates and pictures of her daughter to Maggie.

Lisa hasn't talked to her son since the night he left, has never met her granddaughter. When asked, she tells people that her son reenlisted and was killed in Afghanistan.

The house sold quickly and for a good price. A new family moved in last October: a limousine driver, his artist wife, and their two daughters, ages thirteen and eleven.

Which is good news for the couple who bought Julia Fisher's home the following month, since they also have two daughters, roughly the same ages.

As for Julia Fisher, she's alive and well, and totally enjoying life at Manor Born. Her son visits weekly, sometimes with Poppy, more often without. Amazingly, Poppy's swimsuit designs have proved to be very popular, and the online company Norman helped her found is an unqualified success. So she's very busy designing and running the company, which may or may not bode well for the continuing success of her marriage to Norman.

As for Mark, he's also a frequent visitor to Julia's new residence, driving up from Miami whenever time allows. In another month, he'll be starting year two of his three-year degree program at the Florida College of Culinary Arts, and he remains as happy as a butterfly.

Things haven't been quite so rosy for Sean and Olivia Grant, one of the two families still living on the tiny cul-de-sac. They've had their share of ups and downs this past year. Sean did indeed follow through on his promises to see a therapist and join AA, and has remained clean and sober ever since. And three months ago, he was offered a job in the marketing department of a small but prestigious agency in nearby Stuart. But recapturing Olivia's trust has proved harder than either of them anticipated. They're now in couples' counseling, and as Sean's father would undoubtedly say, *Only time will tell.*

Ironically, for someone who spent as much time as Sean did staring out his window, he was sound asleep at the time Tyler Wilson awoke to the sound of his father beating his mother and tiptoed down the stairs to the den. He found the key he'd seen his mother drop in the desk drawer, opened the cabinet, retrieved his father's loaded gun, then entered his parents' bedroom to confront his father. Olivia heard what she assumed was either a car backfiring or some kid setting off firecrackers, but she, too, was asleep by the time the police arrived.

In the end, no charges were filed. The district attorney's office decided that Dani had acted in defense of both herself and her son, and that no jury in the world would convict her. It was agreed that Dani and her sons would receive ongoing counseling, and the family, unable to face returning to the house, rented a small bungalow a mile down the road.

Dani put the house on Carlyle Terrace on

the market and it sold to a middle-aged couple for well below market value because of the grisly shooting. Nick's gun collection, on the other hand, was appraised for a small fortune, and the proceeds from its sale helped support Dani and her sons during Dani's extended leave of absence from her practice.

She'll be starting work again when the boys go back to school next month. Last year, she transferred them out of their expensive private school and enrolled them in the same public school as Leo McKay. All three boys have since become good friends, almost as close as their mothers.

Erin is as popular as ever. She has a new age-appropriate boyfriend and is looking forward to going off to college in another year, although she has no idea where she wants to go or what she wants to study.

Tyler Wilson, on the other hand, has confided in his therapist exactly what he wants to be when he grows up: an oceanographer. He's getting taller, filling out more; his hair is getting darker.

Nobody calls him Goldilocks anymore.

Maggie and Craig reconciled. He remains his dealership's top salesman. She'll be returning to teaching high school English at the start of this semester, having given

Nadine more than enough time to find her replacement. They still reside in the house at the rounded end of the cul-de-sac.

"How do you like our little enclave?" Maggie recently asked the couple who bought Julia Fisher's home.

"We love it," the husband responded.

"Hard to believe what happened here," his wife added, taking a long, satisfied look around. "It's such a peaceful neighborhood. Such a quiet street."

ACKNOWLEDGMENTS

Amazingly, *Cul-de-sac* is my twenty-ninth novel! — I had to count to make sure — and, shockingly, the list of people I have to thank has remained startlingly consistent. Regular readers of my novels will no doubt recognize many of the names. While there are some new additions, many of those mentioned have been with me a very long time.

First, of course, is Warren, my husband of forty-seven years! I can't believe the man has stuck it out so long, since I am often crabby and not always the easiest person to live with. I truly lucked out as far as he is concerned.

Next in line are my two gorgeous and talented daughters, Shannon and Annie, who have been a constant source of pride and joy, as well as providing me with enough material to write another twenty-nine books. Additional thanks to Shannon for doing

541

such a good job managing my Twitter (@joyfielding) and Instagram accounts (@fieldingjoy).

By now, readers will surely recognize the names Larry Mirkin and Beverley Slopen, two close friends who also serve as early readers of my manuscripts. As always, your advice and encouragement are both needed and appreciated, as is your friendship. Thank you also to a newer member of my team of literary first responders, Robin Stone, a gifted writer in her own right, whom I met when I was teaching a course in creative writing at the University of Toronto some years back and who has since become a close friend as well as professional sounding board.

Another familiar name is Tracy Fisher, my terrific agent at WME, who works tirelessly on my behalf. We've been together a long time, and I hope our association continues for many more years to come. Thanks also to her former assistant, Alyssa Eatherly, for all her help and kind words, and to her new assistant, Oma Naraine.

Special thanks to Anne Speyer, my wonderful editor at Ballantine. *Cul-de-sac* marks our third collaboration, and my writing is all the better for her input.

Thanks also to the entire team at Ballantine — Jennifer Hershey, Kim Hovey, Kara Welsh, Cindy Murray, Allison Schuster, Justine Magowan, Steve Messina, and Scott Biel.

Thank you to everyone at Doubleday, a division of Penguin Random House Canada. I am, more than ever, grateful to be a Canadian, and so pleased to be part of this amazing team. In particular, I would like to thank Kristin Cochrane, Amy Black, Val Gow, Kaitlin Smith, Robin Thomas, Susan Burns, Emma Ingram, and Martha Leonard, whom I inexplicably left out of my acknowledgments for my last novel, *All the Wrong Places,* and who has been gracious enough to never mention it.

Thank you to my various publishers and translators all over the world, whose support has meant so much to me. While I rarely understand the finished results, you're clearly doing something very right. I would like to give a special shout-out to Milena Havlová, my Czech translator, with whom I exchange regular emails. We have developed a special bond over the years and I love hearing about and seeing photos of your beautiful twin grandsons. Thank you for keeping in touch all these years. Hopefully we'll get to see each other again soon in person.

Thanks also to Corinne Assayag, who designed and runs my website — joyfielding.com — for her hard work, suggestions, and occasional reminders to update my monthly letters.

Virtual hugs to my son-in-law, Courtney, my sister, Renee, and my housekeeper, Mary. I hope that by the time you're reading this, COVID will be a distant memory and we can hug in the flesh.

I would also like to thank my good friend Vic Senese, one of the nicest and most decent men I know, despite our being on opposite poles, politically speaking. Vic graciously volunteered to accompany me to a gun range in Florida and even let me fire off a few rounds from his gun. (I actually managed to hit the target several times!) If we can come through these last divisive years with our friendship intact, there's hope for everyone.

I would also like to thank and apologize to Veronika Sorek, my hairdresser of many years, who provided me with all the information on dating sites that I used in *All the Wrong Places,* and whom I forgot to thank in that book's acknowledgments. So, thank you, Veronika, for showing me how these sites work, and for the wonderful scalp massages and haircuts. They are much appreciated.

A final thank-you to my grandson, Hayden, whose story "Hayden Goes to the Pool," which he wrote when he was seven years old, is the story I incorporated into *Cul-de-sac.* I owe you, sweet boy.

Again, my thanks to all of you who buy and read my books. Stay safe and healthy. My love to you all.

Warmly,
Joy

ABOUT THE AUTHOR

Joy Fielding is the *New York Times* bestselling author of *All the Wrong Places, The Bad Daughter, She's Not There, Someone Is Watching, Charley's Web, Heartstopper, Mad River Road, See Jane Run,* and other acclaimed novels. She divides her time between Toronto and Palm Beach, Florida.

joyfielding.com
Twitter: @joyfielding
Instagram: @fieldingjoy
Find Joy Fielding on Facebook